MW01284800

# Jenny
# Plague-Bringer
## (The Paranormals, Book Four)

by J.L. Bryan

Published October 2012

www.jlbryanbooks.com

Jenny Plague-Bringer by J.L. Bryan
Copyright 2012 Jeffrey L. Bryan. All rights reserved.

ISBN-10: 148012561X
ISBN-13: 978-1480125612

# ACKNOWLEDGMENTS

In July 2009, when I first began to write a story about an unfortunate, lonely girl with a deadly touch, I certainly never imagined that this book would connect so strongly with so many readers, or that it would lead to a full-time career as an independent author. Jenny's story has grown and deepened over the years, and I think this book takes that to another level. I'm already starting to miss Jenny, Seth, and all the others as I wrap up this book in September 2012.

The *Jenny Pox* books have freed me from the need to work a day job so that I can stay home with my son Johnny, who is now almost sixteen months old. This time in my life has been more precious than I can say, and so I want to start by thanking every single reader who has bought my books and made this possible. Double thanks to those of you who've taken the time to recommend my books to other people, to post a positive review on major retailers, or otherwise helped to get the word out. As an indie author, I depend almost entirely on word of mouth from readers. Thank you so much for all you've done! I'm amazed every time I hear from a new fan.

Next, I want to thank my lovely wife Christina, who has helped out in every way, from believing in me more than I did, to giving honest feedback on drafts of my books, to spending plenty of time with the baby so that I can write each day. You are a true companion and best friend! (Also, thanks to Johnny for being a happy, good-natured sort of baby!)

I have to thank those who helped me create this book. Vicki Keire did the editing, full of her usual love of and insight into Jenny's world, while Claudia from Phatpuppy Art again provided the beautiful cover art. My beta readers, including the fabulous authors Rhiannon Frater, Samantha Young, Courtney Cole, and Heather Hildenbrand, helped get the story into shape. Also, Amy Leigh Strickland, who I forgot to ask to look over it.

I also want to thank the people who helped the *Jenny Pox* books reach their audience. First is Amanda Hocking, who first put *Jenny Pox* in front of huge numbers of people when she offered to excerpt it in her bestselling book *Ascend*, the third book of the Trylle series, which has since been reissued by St. Martin's Press. Without Amanda, Jenny might have had a much shorter life.

Many people in the indie author community have been supportive fans of my books. I want to thank some of my indie friends like Stacey Wallace Benefiel and LK Rigel, people with whom I can talk about anything. There are people like epic fantasy author David Dalglish, who will probably never read books as girly as these, but his constant support, advice, and help to fellow authors is amazing. Hanging out with writers like Daniel Arenson, Michael Crane, and Daniel Pyle helps keep life entertaining.

Lots of thanks to Rosie Jane Shepherd, who made the Jenny Pox book trailer as a project for film school, so it has actual actors and amazing special effects. You can view it at my website: http://jlbryanbooks.com/books/jennypox.html.

Then, the book bloggers! I know I won't be able to come up with all the book bloggers who've supported, promoted, and reviewed the Jenny Pox books, but I will try to name all those who've been particularly supportive, in more or less chronological order!

So, here's a HUGE thanks to: Heather, Heather and Danny from Bewitched Bookworms, Jenny from Supernatural Snark, Kim the Caffeinated Diva, Karen from the Slowest Bookworm, Tori at Smexy Books, Emma at Belle Books, Kelly at Reading the Paranormal, Ashley from Bookish Brunette and Loretta from Between the Pages (both of whom repeatedly harassed me to write a fourth Jenny Pox book, so you can thank them...), Giselle from Xpresso Reads, Shawna LeAnn from Dreaming in the Pages, Sabrina from About Happy Books, Ash from Smash Attack Reads!, Jennifer from Tale of Many Reviews, Jordan from Ink Puddle, Heather from Buried in Books, Isalys at Book Soulmates, Jennie from My Cute Bookshelf, Kristen from Wholly Books, MoonStar from MoonStar's Fantasy World, Jessi from Reading in the Corner, the mystery girl who runs Unabridged Bookshelf, Shirley from Creative Deeds, Aimee from Coffee Table Reviews, Savannah from Books with Bite, Jennifer from Feminist Fairy Tale Reviews, Kristina from Ladybug Storytime, Kristin from Blood, Sweat & Books, Misty at Kindle Obsessed, Kat from the Aussie Zombie,

AimeeKay from Reviews from My First Reads Shelf (who also reviews at Books and Things), Brie from Confessions of the Reading Housewife, Elizabeth from Fishmuffins of Doom, Angie at Books 4 Tomorrow, Diayll at Mother/Gamer/Writer, Tara from Basically Books, Katie and Krisha at Inkk Reviews, Laura at Roses and Vellum, Shelleyrae at Book'd Out, Liliana at Lili Lost in a Book, Mary Grace from The Solitary Bookworm, Jennifer from Book Den, Lauren from Lose Time Reading, Kelsey from Kelsey's Cluttered Bookshelf, Kristilyn from Reading in Winter, and Heidi from Rainy Day Ramblings, and to all the other book bloggers who have taken time to read and let people know about these books!

*For Christina*

# Prologue

Ward Kilpatrick and his friends stalked the prissy glam boy as he left the broken sidewalk to squeeze through a ruptured chain-link fence into the abandoned railyard. The boy's name was Joey Barrons, but Ward and his friends called him "JoJo" because he looked so girly. It bothered Ward just how girly JoJo sometimes looked. It made him want to grab the kid and just pound him. They'd been messing with him since sixth grade, and nothing had changed now that they'd started high school.

Ward watched through the rupture in the fence as JoJo cut across the abandoned rail yard, stepping around and through rusty old boxcars parked on the ruins of old tracks. It was a shortcut for JoJo to get home fast from the high school and off the garbage-filled streets of East St. Louis...but it wasn't the safest path, as the glittery little hairsprayed freak was about to learn.

Ward nodded at his friend Lars, who was fifteen, Ward's own age. Lars scurried to peel up the broken chain-link as if he were Ward's personal butler. Ward walked under, followed by his other friend, Carl. Carl was a second-year freshman, sixteen years old.

JoJo was fourteen but looked twelve, what Ward's father would have called a "faggy little pinko." A huge fan of the newly elected President Reagan, Ward's father, who had repeatedly referred to the recently ousted Jimmy Carter as a "lily-wristed pinko Commie."

Ward and his friends were not faggy or pink. When the kids at school were listening to Roxy Music and David Bowie, Ward and pals slammed to hardcore bands that played parties in the city's countless empty factories and warehouses. You didn't need an ID to get in, because the shows weren't legal in the first place. If there wasn't a party, they usually played bootleg Black Flag cassettes on Carl's ghetto blaster

The glam boy looked back over his shoulder, and his mouth popped open in an "O" shape that was almost cartoony. He wore glitter on his face—*glitter*, for God's sake—trying to look like one of those weird English rock stars.

JoJo turned to run, but he had to cross a lot of gravel slag and two more dead rail lines littered with boxcar corpses before he could reach the fence on the far side of the yard.

"Don't run!" Ward shouted, as he and his friends took off after JoJo. "Don't run, little JoJo! You run like a girl!"

JoJo picked up speed, but his dark purple platform boots failed him. He staggered and fell, his wavy blond hair flaring out into a fluffy mane as his face hit the gravel. Ward and his two friends burst into laughter as they caught up with him.

"What do you want?" JoJo looked up at Ward. His lower lip was split open and bleeding, and it trembled. He was almost pouting like a baby.

"Why are you crying already?" Ward asked, folding his arms. "You don't cry until I tell you to."

"Yeah, nobody told you to cry yet," Lars quickly agreed.

JoJo looked too scared to even try standing up. Ward's heart pulsed a little faster. He was eager to get working on the kid.

JoJo was in their class at school. They were all freshmen, though Ward's friend JoJo was.

Ward and his friends had a certain look, keeping their hair shaved close, with black denim jackets adorned with patches—skulls, flags, guns. Nobody fucked with his crew, not for long.

"Okay, cough it up." Ward kicked JoJo in the ribs. "Cash."

"I don't have any," JoJo said. It was believable enough, considering the shitty half-boarded-up house where JoJo lived with his grandmother. It was just beyond the fence, in a neighborhood where half the houses were empty and collapsing, like all the neighborhoods in this part of East St. Louis.

"No money?" Ward smiled and dropped to a knee beside JoJo. "Then what are you going to give us, JoJo?"

"What do you want?" JoJo asked in a low whisper.

"I don't know. You could suck Lars' cock, couldn't you? You'd like that, wouldn't you?" Ward asked him, trying to sound cold and tough.

"What?" JoJo gasped.

"Lars, get over here and let him suck your cock," Ward commanded. Lars stepped forward, grinning, pretending to unzip his fly. He stood there for a minute, smirking down at JoJo, and finally gave Ward an uncertain look, not sure how far he was supposed to carry the gag. Ward was amused watching both of them squirm, waiting for Ward's next words.

"Well?" Ward said to JoJo. "Are you going to pay us in cash or suckage?"

"Do I have to?" JoJo squeaked, looking up at Lars' husky, shaven-head form leering down at him.

"Do I have to?" Carl imitated, and Ward and Lars laughed. JoJo tried, pathetically, to laugh along as if he were in on the joke.

Ward seized JoJo's face in both hands and glared into JoJo's frightened, wet blue eyes (which were trimmed in eyeliner, for God's sake!) Ward gave him a sly smile, and then he reached into JoJo's brain.

He dug through a bunch of crap—shopping for records, helping his stupid female friends pick out make-up and hair products. Then he found useful tidbits—JoJo socking away spare coins, scrounged from lunches he'd chosen not to eat and the occasional gift of a dollar from his grandmother. He kept it all hidden in the box of an old watercolor set from childhood, which he stashed under his bed.

"Eighteen dollars and seventy-three cents," Ward said. "You've got it hidden under your bed. You want to buy a ticket for Iggy Pop." This set Ward's two friends laughing.

"How did you know?" JoJo asked. Ward's knowledge of his secrets seemed to scare him even more than the threat of getting his face bloodied, or sucking off Lars. "How can you know that?"

"Go fetch it for us, you little mutt," Ward said. "All of it."

"No!" JoJo's face broke down, and he really did start to cry. "I've been saving it forever."

"What did you say?" Ward grabbed JoJo's blousy shirt and lifted him to his feet, and JoJo goggled up at him, shocked. "Did you say *no?*"

"That's what he said!" Lars told him.

"I can't, I need it," JoJo whined.

"I can't, I need it," Carl imitated, which made Lars laugh.

Ward didn't laugh, but instead drew back his fist and popped the little silky runt in the face. JoJo cried out as blood flung from his nose and splattered across a graffiti-covered train car. Ward let him stagger away a few steps, and then he pounced.

He punched JoJo in the stomach, doubling him over, then shoved him down to the gravel again. He kicked at JoJo's ribs while the kid squirmed on the rocks. Lars and Carl joined in, slamming their heavy black boots into JoJo's face and arms.

Ward dropped to his knees, straddling the bleeding, mewling little glam brat. He turned JoJo onto his stomach and laid his face across the nearest rotten chunk of old railroad track. JoJo struggled and squirmed, but Ward held him in place.

"I could have Carl bring his boot down, smash out all your teeth," Ward whispered into JoJo's ear, where a shiny blob of gold dangled from his pierced lobe. "Ever seen that happen before? They spray out like popcorn, pieces of tongue, blood all over. Is that what you want, kid?"

JoJo whimpered a "no."

"So, tomorrow, you bring the cash to school. Eighteen dollars, seventy-three cents." He petted JoJo's pretty blond head. "And if you whine about it, we'll break your fingers, one by one." Ward had heard these threats in cheap gangster movies. "Do you understand me, JoJo?"

JoJo nodded, his eyes regarding Ward with naked fear. Ward winked at him and stood up. Carl and Lars both had fear in their eyes, too, after his calm, matter-of-fact threats to JoJo. Good. Let everyone fear him. Fear meant respect.

Ward turned and walked away without another word.

"See ya, glitter girl!" Lars shouted. He gave JoJo an extra kick in the stomach before following Ward and Carl out of the train yard.

Ward smiled to himself. Tomorrow, he and his buddies would

each be six dollars richer. Ward believed in dividing the spoils evenly, because he wasn't interested in spoils. He was interested in respect, loyalty, and fear. Even in this dirt-poor, rat-infested hell of a city, money was nothing compared to such things.

# Chapter One

Esmeralda Medina Rios rode the bus home to their studio apartment on South Boyle Avenue, where they could hear traffic from Interstate 5 all night long. Their building was old, with some exposed wiring and gaping holes in the plaster walls. Esmeralda stepped over an unconscious, tequila-drenched heap of an old man on the stairs and continued up to their second floor apartment.

She was exhausted. Ashleigh's spirit had possessed her only for a matter of weeks, but in that time, Ashleigh had managed to wreck Esmeralda's life.

First, her mother had kicked her out, or rather not allowed her to move back in, when Esmeralda had returned home to Los Angeles on the back of Tommy's bike. Ashleigh had been a terror who never showed Esmeralda's mother the least amount of respect, and of course Esmeralda's mother had always hated Tommy, the dirty blond gringo she'd brought home. Her mother had much preferred her previous boyfriend, Pedro, who worked construction while studying law at night. Esmeralda hadn't spoken to Pedro in over a year.

Esmeralda had also lost her mortuary cosmetics job at Garcia y Garcia Funeral Home. The only job she could find was part-time at the much larger and cheaper Hernandez place, where the pay was poor and the jobs were all rushed. She'd been spoiled by the quiet, leisurely speed of work at Garcia y Garcia. Hernandez was more like a factory, a fast-paced corpse processing plant.

She had finally saved up enough for tuition, though, and she was about to start her final classes toward her Associate of Applied Science in Funeral Service degree. Then she would find better work while continuing her education, and in time, all would be well.

That was what she told herself as she walked down the crumbling second-floor hallway, sore and miserable, worrying about which utility she would have to pay next, and whether it would be easier to live without water or power.

She slid the key into the rusty lock and opened the door.

Tommy sat on the bed, smoking a Basic cigarette and watching their small TV set. The ashtray on the windowsill was overflowing with cigarette butts, and the entire place reeked of cheap tobacco. The only light came from the open window behind him, sunlight that turned fuzzy and nicotine-yellow inside the cramped one-room apartment.

"I told you to stop smoking in here," Esmeralda said. She closed the door behind her and hung her purse on a nail in the wall. "It's so bad for our health."

"Well, hey, nice to see you, too," Tommy replied.

"I mean it." Esmeralda sank to the bed next to him. Tommy was watching a rerun of an old Christopher Reeve *Superman* movie. He smelled like cheap whiskey, probably Ten High. "Are you working tonight?"

"It's Thursday, right?"

"Thursday."

"Then I'm working." He glanced at the rumpled blanket heaped beside him, then gave a little shrug, reached under it, and slid out a bottle of Ten High. He gave her a little defiant look as he lifted it to his lips. It was a fight waiting to happen, and he knew it.

Tommy had trouble getting good work because he couldn't even use his real name or identification. Esmeralda had a cousin who was good at finding jobs for illegals, so he'd set Tommy up on a job unloading produce trucks. He'd gotten fired for being late and missing work, so her cousin then found him a job washing dishes in a Taiwanese restaurant in Monterey Park. He'd gotten fired for the same reasons.

Now, he worked a few nights a week as a bouncer at a seedy
North Hollywood bar. Tommy wasn't an especially big and muscular
guy, but his touch spread fear into anyone. He could seize a
troublemaker, fill him with his own worse nightmares, and then shove
him out the door as easily as a crying child.

"I still don't like you at this job," Esmeralda said. "Using the fear.
It troubles you so much."

"It doesn't trouble me." Tommy snorted at her and swigged his
whiskey.

"The more you use it, the worst your own nightmares become.
You're screaming and crying in your sleep."

"Who wouldn't, living in a shithole like this?" Tommy waved his
bottle at the small, rank room around them.

"I understand about all your bad dreams from childhood,"
Esmeralda said. "That's why you must let the fear rest. It stirs up
these things."

"You don't understand anything. What else can I do? Your
cousin won't even talk to me anymore. He calls me an embarrassment
to his reputation, whatever that means."

"It means he can't vouch for you as a good worker. You're
always late and hung over."

"Nobody at the bar cares if I'm hung over," Tommy said. "It's a
good job for me."

"It's too dangerous. And it doesn't pay enough..." Esmeralda bit
her lip.

"You want more money, is that it?" Tommy snarled, leaning
towards her. His breath was full of smoke and bad whiskey. "I can
get more money. Anyone out there on the street, I can walk right up,
grab them—" Tommy seized her arm, and shivers of fear shot through
her body, terrifying and deliciously exciting at the same time. "They'll
give me anything I want. That's how I always made my living before.
Now I have to stick with your stupid rules."

"They're not stupid," Esmeralda said, her voice shivering with the
intense feelings he stirred up inside her. "I just don't want to see you
burn in Hell."

"Come on, you don't believe in that." His face loomed closer
through the shadowy smoke.

"I believe we can burn in Hell while we are still alive. We build
the fire around ourselves, and we damn ourselves. If we are not

careful."

"You won't see me in Hell unless you're there with me." He seized her other arm and pulled her closer. Esmeralda trembled. His paranormal touch filled her with conflicting desires to run away screaming and to wrap her legs around him and fuck him until dawn. He drove her crazy, and she hated him for it. Deep down, she knew her mother was right about this boy.

"I'm already there with you," Esmeralda whispered, and he kissed her. It felt like an electrical jolt, filling her body with dark energy. Her fingers clawed into his back, nails digging into his muscles through his stained, flimsy t-shirt.

Tommy reached for his bottle again, but she caught his hand and stopped him. He snarled again, threw her back on the bed and climbed on top of her.

Esmeralda couldn't get her blouse off fast enough. Tommy ripped open her bra and sank his teeth into her left breast, and she cried out in pain and pleasure. She couldn't get enough of him, and he couldn't move fast enough to satisfy her. She shoved down her slacks and her panties together.

When he was inside her, the fear and the pleasure swept her away on the most powerful wave of feelings she'd ever known. His long, unwashed hair hung in her face, and she couldn't get enough of his foul reek. Nothing else in the world mattered, just the glorious sweaty, heat igniting her body.

Later, he slept beside her, and she watched the smog-tinted orange sunlight burn away out the window. The boy was pure poison, she knew. Addictive poison.

She entertained her daily urge to leave the apartment and never look back, never tell Tommy where to come and find her, but that was a useless fantasy.

She closed her eyes.

# Chapter Two

Jenny and Seth drank coffee in a small indoor garden on the *Rue de l'Hôtel de ville*, on the Right Bank of the Seine. It was a short walk from Notre Dame cathedral, but hidden enough that tourists were rare. Currently, the only other customers were a few elderly pensioners. The place had gourmet fair-trade coffee from all over Africa, and the price of one cup would have given Jenny's father sticker shock. Even after a year of living in Paris, with a plentiful stash of money from Seth's family, Jenny hadn't fully adjusted to her new life. Happily, the city was so full of eccentrics and artists that the sight of Jenny wearing gloves and scarves in the summertime attracted no particular attention.

Now it was fall, and she had plenty of coats and hats. The colder the weather, the more fully she could wrap herself against the constant danger of touching others.

"What are we in for today?" Seth asked. "Another art gallery? Another play? Touring another old palace?"

"You sound burned out, Seth." Jenny sipped her organic coffee from Sierra Leone. It was so delicious she couldn't help sighing.

"Maybe if I had a better idea of what was happening at those things." Seth said. His French was still shaky...and that was a generous description. Jenny was fluent, owing more to her past lives than her high school French lessons, though sometimes people would give her an odd look if she used an archaic word or expression.

"You should listen harder when I try to teach you," she told him.

"I do try. But you're so sexy when you speak French, how am I supposed to learn anything? My teacher's too hot, that's the problem."

Jenny blushed slightly. Their French lessons did have a way of straying to other activities that, while still quite French in nature, weren't entirely focused on building vocabulary.

"Only you could get tired of French wine, truffles, and palaces," Jenny said.

"And the electro-techno-whatever music," Seth added. "Please, God, make it stop."

"Come on, we've seen some great shows. We just saw Pink at the Bercy."

"Want to get cheesecake?" Seth glanced over the dessert menu.

"For breakfast?"

"How many times are we going to have this conversation?"

Jenny had a second coffee while Seth ordered his cake. He had a great system for burning off calories. He could eat cake for breakfast, then find an excuse to brush past an elderly or handicapped person on the crowded sidewalk, offloading the extra energy as a touch of healing. Jenny couldn't touch anyone, but her appetite was usually small and her metabolism left her scrawny, as if she suffered from a deadly wasting disease.

They stepped out into the mid-morning sun and strolled along the Seine. The trees had turned their autumn colors, tender reds and golds softening the regal but austere Second Empire architecture. Jenny had mixed feelings about the magnificent and symmetrical look of the city. On the one hand, it was breathtaking to see an entire city remade as a single work of art. On the other, she missed the chaotic, twisting streets of the Paris she'd known centuries earlier. There was something disturbing about the idea of smashing and rebuilding a city where people lived, of a single vision imposed on so many individuals, thousands of whom had their homes razed to make way for Napoleon III's dream city.

Jenny slowed as they entered the *Musée de la Sculpture en Plein Air*, a vast outdoor sculpture garden tucked alongside the river. She loved this park. Jenny had plenty of time to work on her pottery and clay sculpting, and even intended to take some informal classes, but she was rethinking her ideas about what sculpture could be.

Here, many of the large sculptures were abstract, depicting ideas and emotions rather than trying to look like copies of objects in the real world. Some of them were low, dark masses of granite, reminding her of the enormous graveyard behind Seth's house in Fallen Oak. Others looked like colorful totem poles or twisted metals reaching toward the sky. In the galleries of Paris, Jenny had seen sculptures that included all kinds of materials and found objects, and sometimes unusual lighting arrangements or glowing images and words cast from a projector or television screen, multidimensional art.

Jenny was getting ideas for new kinds of sculptures, things that would express the love, guilt, and horror inside her.

Seth sidled up next to Jenny and took her silk-gloved hand nervously. It was an odd move for him. They'd been intimate too long for him to be so uncomfortable approaching her.

"Look," he whispered.

Jenny followed his eyes to a tiered, sunken semicircle of concrete right on the river, which offered three levels of seating. Teenagers were using it to practice leaps with their skateboards. Two of them, a boy and girl, sat apart from the others, much more interested in kissing than in streets sports.

"How old do you bet they are?" Seth whispered.

"Sixteen, seventeen." Jenny shrugged. "Just kids."

"We were kids like that, a long time ago."

"Now we've reached the ancient age of twenty," Jenny said. "Better make our reservations at the nursing home."

"I was thinking..." He squeezed her hand tight, which worried her a little. "Maybe we should get married, Jenny."

His unexpected words were like an electric shock to her heart. She looked at him in surprise, but finally she laughed. "Seth! We can't get married."

"Why not?"

"For one, people who are officially dead don't usually have weddings," Jenny pointed out.

"That could be our theme. A zombie wedding, Day of the Dead stuff everywhere..."

"Now you sound like Alexander." Jenny heard herself say it, but immediately regretted it. Seth's face hardened.

"Don't ever say that."

"I just meant, that was his decorating scheme..."

"Don't ever say 'Alexander' to me."

"What if I'm talking about Alexander the Great? Or Alexandre Dumas?" Jenny tried a smile to lighten things up.

"I ask you to marry me and you immediately mention him? You don't want to get married?"

"We can't, Seth. I mean, if we did that, we might as well send an invitation to the Department of Homeland Security."

"I'm not stupid, I know we couldn't tell anyone. It wouldn't be that kind of wedding."

"What kind would it be? Our fake identities getting married?" Jenny's passport claimed she was from Alsace. Since nobody believed Seth could pass as French, he carried a Canadian passport instead.

"I just think we should," Seth said. "I wasn't thinking about paperwork or anything."

"It's sweet of you, Seth. The bond we have is so much more than marriage, though, isn't it? Lifetime after lifetime, we can be together. Even death won't do us part. We don't need some piece of paper from other people acknowledging that."

"I'm not thinking about 'lifetime after lifetime,'" Seth replied. "I don't have all these tons of crazy past-life memories like you. For me, it's just this life and who we are today."

"That's all that matters, Seth." She embraced him, resting her cheek against his warm chest and looking up at him. "But we can't have that normal life, with marriage. Or children."

"Children? Why not?"

Jenny felt like she'd been slapped. She couldn't believe he was even asking. He didn't have all the past-life memories she did, but this one should have been obvious. She felt herself crumple as she answered the question.

"Because I can't. The pox. The baby will miscarry, or it will die on the way out...just like I killed my own mother, on the way out. The babies are never immune." In her mind, a collection of extremely painful past-life memories sprung up, and she shoved them back. She felt heartsick. "Seth, you're lucky you don't remember much before this lifetime."

"I'm sorry, Jenny," he said, looking into her eyes. "I should have known. I really haven't thought about kids one way or the other, so—"

"There's only one way to think about them. We can't, ever."

Seth took this in, looking out at the river again. Jenny could see a mix of disappointment and confusion on his face.

"That's cool," he finally said. "Who wants a bunch of kids, anyway? I'd hate to bring some poor little Jonathan Seth Barrett the Fifth into the world. Screw my great-grandfather and his overused name. Screw Alexander. I mean, you did, right? You totally screwed my great-grandfather."

"It's so gross when you put it that way. He was reincarnated."

"It's gross any way you put it. Or any*where* you put it," Seth added, raising his eyebrows a couple of times.

Jenny elbowed him in the stomach, and he countered by tickling her ribs until she stood up and escaped, squealing. He ran to catch her, spun her back, kissed her under a tall old linden tree, its heart-shaped leaves blazing with the fiery colors of their slow autumn death.

Things would settle now, Jenny knew. They would drop any talk of marriage and children, continue on into *le Jardin des Plantes*, a sprawling 28-acre botanical garden that had been carefully developed over the past four centuries. Jenny particularly loved the old labyrinth maze and the garden with hundreds of different breeds of roses. She liked to pass close to the garden of bees and birds, but she never walked through it out of fear that some friendly feathered creature would land on her and die.

As they walked through the rich colors of the park, Jenny felt unsettled and a little sick. No bacteria or virus could survive the pox long enough to make her ill, but the pox did nothing to protect her against worry, fear, and guilt. She could feel her stomach clenching.

The past year had been too good to believe, aside from the lack of any contact with her father. After she'd unleashed the pox on the mob in Fallen Oak, leaving hundreds dead, her father didn't seem to want much contact with her, anyway.

She and Seth were young, flush with money and living in one of the most beautiful cities in the world, drinking in art and culture every day. They had an apartment only blocks from the Seine, in a district full of theaters and nightclubs. They ate masterfully prepared French meals and drank the best wines.

Life in Paris hadn't exactly turned Seth into a poet, but he had his hobbies. One of them was volunteering at hospitals around the city, particularly children's hospitals, where he would spread his healing touch. He didn't do any dramatic mass healing that would risk attention, but he helped them quietly. He'd touched thousands by now, making his anonymous, angelic way around Paris while she stayed in their apartment, played records, and tried to create art.

"Our life here is too good," Jenny said. "It's like riding a magic carpet."

"What's wrong with magic carpets?"

"There's nothing holding them up. The magic could stop anytime...and then you fall."

# Chapter Three

Senator Junius Mayfield, of the great state of Tennessee, great-uncle of one officially dead boy named Jonathan Seth Barrett IV, smoked a cigar as he reclined in an antique Federal-style divan embellished with hand-tooled scrollwork and curving arms. The divan was from an age when Americans made things, Junius thought. The timber had probably been cut in Virginia and carved by a master craftsman, an American with the skill and industry to do more than drool in front of some computer screen all day.

The divan was like the senator: old, creaky, so far out of fashion as to be comical. Just waiting for the inevitable crack, the day it transformed from a valuable antique into scrap wood.

Junius smoked his cigar and sipped a glass of fifty-year-old Scotch in the candle-lit suite of a very exclusive hotel. "Hotel" wasn't the proper word for this establishment, located in an old Greek Revival mansion just outside the District of Columbia, but that was the polite word for it.

A well-endowed young lady with blond hair, pretty as a fashion model, was handcuffed to one of the four high posters of the antique bed. She wore bits of white ribbon and lace in her hair, like a bride, and she had recently become topless. She knelt on the bed, still dressed in her lacy white panties and silk stockings. The straps of a leather scourge lashed across her backside, and she bounced forward against the poster and cried out.

The scourge was wielded by a dark-haired woman in a black mask that hid her eyes, black leather lingerie, and high stiletto heels. Their costumes clearly divided into them into good girl and bad girl, angel and devil.

"Please," the blond girl in white lace begged. "Please, stop!"

The girl in the black mask gave her a cruel smile and lashed her again.

Junius himself would watch from the divan, too old to indulge himself like he used to. He was more of a watcher now. Junius would take in this little tableau, then straighten his tie and attend yet another fundraiser dinner, eating gray chicken while pumping defense contractors for extra campaign cash. From one whorehouse to another, but Junius would be switching roles.

Same old, same old.

Junius watched quietly as the masked girl spanked the blond girl, against the blond's pretended struggles and protests. The blond girl wriggled and screeched as her cheeks were smacked red, and then the masked girl reached between her legs and stroked her. The blond girl's head turned toward Junius as she cried out in pleasure, real or pretended.

The blow came from nowhere, striking Junius just behind his left eye. He'd been kicked by a horse once, as a boy on his father's farm, and the feeling was similar. This kick might have been from an invisible ghost horse, something from an old Indian tale.

After it hit him, the world dimmed and half his body turned numb. For a moment, all Junius could see was the preacher at the scrapwood mountain church he'd attended with his grandparents, a sweaty, bug-eyed man slapping the pulpit and shouting about fornication and hellfire. Then that faded, too, gone like a flash of lightning.

A thin, dark drop of blood crept out from his left nostril, making its gradual way toward his dry, wrinkled lips.

The esteemed gentleman from Tennessee slumped down in the divan, inch by inch. The candle-lit room grew darker and darker around him.

The two girls on the bed, caught up in their performance, didn't notice anything strange until he toppled out of the divan and crumpled to the floor. The whiskey glass dropped from his hand, sloshing aged Scotch onto the 19th-century Khotan rug, followed by his burning cigar. He was vaguely aware of the sound of two shouting girls, and he wasn't aware of much after that.

# Chapter Four

Jenny was pregnant.

The little plastic stick from the home pregnancy test insisted it was true. Since this was the third kit she'd bought today, she was starting to believe them. They all came back the same: *oui*. Pregnant.

She looked at herself in the mirror. Pale little Jenny Mittens, murderer of hundreds. Thousands, if you counted past lives, and maybe it was more like tens of thousands. There was no way to know. She had slain an army or two, brought down cities, wiped out tribes to make way for empires. Her kind had always seen the human world as a kind of board game, like chess or Risk. Most humans were pawns, dumb as animals, to be conquered, killed, or ruled according to the turns of the game.

Jenny didn't see things that way anymore, and neither did Seth. They'd learned from life after life of being human, feeling love and pain. They'd let the fleshly experience change their dark and ancient souls, something most of their kind chose to resist. For good reason, Jenny thought. Love and compassion opened entire new avenues of potential suffering.

She washed her hands in the big marble bowl sink, rubbing them again and again with a jasmine-scented ball of soap. She kept washing them long after any pee from the pregnancy test was obviously rinsed away. The steaming hot water provided a sensation strong enough to distract her from the thoughts spinning inside her mind.

"I can't be pregnant," Jenny said to her reflection. "Right?"

Her blue eyes stared back at her.

"We know we can't do this," Jenny said. She imagined herself speaking to that strange primordial part of herself, her own soul, that had incarnated as human again and again. "It won't survive. There's nothing we can do. So...no reason to tell Seth about it, right? This will just take care of itself, whether I want it to or not. Right?"

Her reflection offered no wisdom. It was just the image of a girl with a frightened face.

The sound of bells chimed through the apartment, announcing someone at the front door.

Jenny absolutely didn't feel like speaking to anyone at this moment—she was in a state of shock, and she could feel the confused flood of emotions waiting to crash in on her.

Still, she left the bathroom, walked out through their sumptuous bedroom and expansive, sunlit living room with a picture window and a balcony overlooking the boulevard below. Her bare feet sounded oddly loud in her ears, slapping against the dark oak floor.

The doorbell rang again. Jenny looked through the peephole lens, but she didn't recognize the girl outside. The apartment building had a full-time security staff, so the only way the girl could be inside the building was if she was a resident or an approved visitor. Jenny guessed the girl was visiting someone else, but had accidentally approached the wrong door.

Jenny stepped back. The girl would surely double-check the apartment number and realize her mistake. There were three other apartments on the same floor.

Jenny decided to return to the small extra bedroom she used as a studio, play a record, and resume her latest attempt at making art. Then she decided to wait until the strange girl left, since playing the record would make it obvious that she was home.

The doorbell rang a third time. Jenny looked out again, feeling suspicious—though officially dead, she and Seth were actually on the run from the United States government. It was always possible someone had discovered they were alive and living in Paris.

The girl didn't look like any kind of police or law enforcement, though. She looked no older than Jenny, with dark Mediterranean skin, deep auburn hair and sea-green eyes. Unlike most law enforcement officers, she wore a short choker dress with vivid purple designs. The bright dress was damped down by the long black coat she wore over it.

Despite her revealing dress, the girl also wore purple lace gloves that reached well up her forearms.

She rang the doorbell a fourth time, still not figuring out she was at the wrong apartment. She was probably just some random pretty airhead, Jenny decided, who couldn't be bothered to read the door number.

Jenny pulled on her own gloves and opened the door, but not too far. The girl was in heels, too. She probably wasn't here to capture Jenny. Jenny looked out at her, but didn't say anything.

A bright smile had bloomed on the girl's face as the door opened, but now it died. The girl's mouth dropped open in confusion. *That's right, genius,* Jenny thought. *You've been annoying the wrong apartment.*

"*Bon jour,*" the girl said, uncertainly.

"*Bon jour,*" Jenny replied.

The girl looked at her for a moment, then continued, hesitantly, speaking in French, but not with a native accent. "I am sorry. I am looking for a young man."

A second possibility flared into Jenny's mind, hot and angry. Maybe the girl didn't have the wrong apartment. Maybe she did know Seth, and she was the kind of friend that Seth chose to keep secret from Jenny...

"What sort of young man?" Jenny asked.

"He is this tall or so." The girl held a hand above her head. Jenny looked again at the lacy purple glove clinging to her fingers. "Blond, handsome, shoulders like this, a muscular build. Eyes are blue, like..." The girl gazed at Jenny's eyes. "You must know him."

Jenny shook her head. "You have the wrong address."

"No, I am certain..." The girl pushed Jenny's door open—quite rudely, Jenny thought—and took in their apartment with her strange, intense green eyes. "Yes. This is just as I have seen it."

"Seen it when?" Jenny asked.

"It would make no sense to explain." The girl shook her head. "I do not understand. Perhaps I am too early."

"Too early for what?"

The girl studied Jenny again. "Do you have any plans to move out? Is someone else moving here in the future?"

"I have no real plans either way," Jenny said. "When have you seen my apartment before?"

"You live here alone? There is no boy as I described?"

"If there were a boy like that here, I would be too busy to answer the door," Jenny told her, and the girl laughed.

Then the girl looked off into the distance, down the short hall to the elevator. Her eyes seemed to cloud over.

"I don't understand," she said quietly. "Everything keeps changing."

"Maybe you should visit a doctor," Jenny suggested.

The young woman's eyes cleared, and she made an effort to smile. "I think I may be too early. Should you see someone as I described, perhaps sometime in the future, will you tell him to contact me?"

"I suppose," Jenny said. "What's his name?"

"I have only seen his face. I do not know his name."

*Okay, it's a creepy stalker lady*, Jenny thought. "How did you get into my building?"

The girl's smile seemed more genuine now. "That is easy. Watch for an older man, chat with him as he walks inside, as if you are his guest."

"That's it?"

"You can add the trick to your repertoire, if you like."

"What makes you think I have a repertoire of tricks?" Jenny asked.

"Every woman should have one." From her purse, she brought out a pen and a paperback by someone called Giuseppe di Lampedusa. She wrote on a mostly-blank page of the book, then ripped it out and passed it to Jenny. They gave each other a look as the torn page passed from one gloved hand to another, but neither commented on the fact that they'd both chosen to wear long gloves on a warm day.

"There is my mobile number and my home address. I'm at school most days, so evenings are better," the girl said.

"School?"

"Art history. The Pantheon-Sorbonne. Do you attend

university?"

"Not at the moment," Jenny said. On the scrap of paper, the girl's handwriting looked like some kind of advanced calligraphy, which was a little odd. Her name was Mariella Visconti, so Jenny supposed her accent was Italian. Jenny folded the page. "I'll keep it just in case, but I don't believe anybody like that lives here. You must have the wrong apartment building."

"You never know what the future may bring." Mariella winked at her. "Thank you." She took a long, unsettling look at Jenny's gloves.

"Good luck to you." Jenny was eager to close the door. The longer Mariella stood there, the more uncomfortable Jenny felt. Jenny worried Seth would show up at any moment, blowing Jenny's lie.

"Perhaps we will meet again," Mariella said. "Until then..." She gave a small wave as she walked toward the stairwell and elevator.

Jenny closed the door and locked it, her heart racing. The girl talking about how she'd "seen" Seth, but didn't know his name, made her think of how she'd dreamed of Alexander for weeks before meeting him in the flesh. Of course, Mariella could have just been some psycho who'd followed Seth to see where he lived, but there was also the weird matter of the gloves, plus the intense uneasy feeling the girl had stirred in Jenny's gut. Though it might be normal to feel concerned when a gorgeous and expensively dressed Italian girl showed up at her door, eager to find her boyfriend, this went a little deeper than that.

She didn't think the girl was any kind of government agent, but she might be something worse...one of their kind, like Jenny and Seth, or like Ashleigh and Tommy. This was very bad. Besides Seth, Jenny had never met another one who didn't bring her grief. Even Alexander had only pretended to love her in order to use her to enhance his own powers. Or maybe he really had felt whatever twisted thing passed for love inside him, but he'd tricked her and betrayed her. The last thing Jenny wanted was to meet another of their kind.

Mariella apparently lived in Paris, too, so this problem wasn't going to disappear anytime soon.

Jenny hurried to hide the girl's information, as well as the pregnancy tests, before Seth returned home.

* * *

"You okay? You look like you saw a ghost," Seth said as he closed the front door behind him. "Not like a Casper-type ghost, either. More of a Headless Horseman kind."

Jenny sat on the sofa in the living room, rereading a vampire book by Anne Rice that she'd loved as a kid. She'd always identified with Louis, the moody vampire who didn't really want to kill anyone. Now she was staying in Paris, as Louis had for a while.

"I'm fine." Jenny followed Seth into the kitchen, where he set his cloth grocery bag on the marble counter. He unloaded tomatoes, three kinds of cheese, and a long, crusty baguette, which had been baked very recently, judging by the delicious aroma that filled the apartment.

"You're sure?" he asked. "Nothing happened today?"

"Sometimes you just have a bad day."

"I'll cook dinner, then. That'll make you feel better."

"Um...I doubt it. You should let me do it." Jenny approached the stove.

"Are you questioning my cooking skills?" Seth asked. "Who poured you that awesome bowl of Chocos cereal yesterday? Tell me that."

"You're a master at adding milk."

"As long you acknowledge that, I'll let you cook. There's pasta, there's organic chicken..."

Jenny reached for the bottle of wine Seth had brought home, then hesitated. She could really use a glass just now, but the idea of drinking while pregnant bothered her. It was ridiculous. One night, she knew, she would wake up to find her thighs painted with blood and gore, and that would be the end of that. There was no reason to worry about the well-being of a fetus destined to die from the pox. Still, she resisted her desire for a drink.

"There's really nothing wrong?" Seth twisted the corkscrew. "Something feels different today, doesn't it?"

Jenny worried what he meant by that. Those of her kind who had powerful emotional bonds with each other, positive or negative, could sometimes sense and be drawn to each other. Alexander had become aware of Jenny's location the night she flared up and killed the mob in Fallen Oak.

Now, this strange girl had found her way to Seth...and Seth might be feeling her energy, too.

"Just a regular, boring day," Jenny said.

"Then tell me what's on your mind." He started to pour her a glass of wine, then gave her a puzzled look when she shook her head.

"I was just thinking about past lives," Jenny told him. That was one topic guaranteed to lose Seth's interest right away. He only had random fragments of past-life memories, and they were wicked enough that he didn't want to learn more. He would usually change the subject immediately.

"What were you thinking about?" Seth asked. "Were we raping and pillaging our way across the ancient world or something?"

"No...we weren't really together until our last couple of lives, actually. We were enemies before that."

"So tell me." He leaned against the counter, sipping wine. "Tell me about our last life."

"Seriously?" Jenny hadn't expected that. Again, she worried he could sense the girl who'd been searching for him...and maybe his sudden interest in the past had more to do with her than with Jenny, even if he didn't consciously realize any of it.

"Why not?" Seth asked. "We never talk about it. I think I'm ready to learn about our past."

"You're sure?"

"You keep thinking about it, I want to hear about it. I bet I was a cowboy, right?"

Jenny took a deep breath. "It was the Great Depression."

"That figures. We wouldn't want to miss a time of worldwide misery, would we?" Seth said. He refreshed his wine glass.

Jenny placed a ripe tomato on the wooden cutting board. As she sliced it, she began to tell him.

"I was in the carnival," she said. "I had a stage name, in the carnival. Juliana Blight."

Seth spat wine as he laughed. "Were you a stripper?"

"Do you want to hear the story or not?"

"Oh, I'm listening. This already sounds good."

# Chapter Five

Juliana waited on the low, narrow wooden stage, separated from the small dirt-floor audience pit by a wooden rail and a ragged curtain, which hadn't yet opened for the evening. Out in the tent, customers who'd paid a few pennies could see Alejandro the sword-swallower, Zsoka the tattooed lady, some creepy marionette puppets, a knife-throwing act, and Punchy Pete, the dancing, juggling dwarf. For a few pennies more, they could step past the back curtain to view the star attraction of the freak show: Juliana Blight, The World's Most Diseased Woman.

She only thought of herself as "Juliana" now. Her given name was Greek, and she'd been born in a squalid, crowded tenement in New York. Because of her diseased nature, she was rejected by everyone except a crazed aunt, who repeatedly bathed her with lye and called her "daughter of Hell." She'd run away when she was seven years old and spent much of her life scrounging and stealing, protected from everyone by the demon plague within her. Here and there, she'd left men dead in the gutter when they'd tried assaulting her.

She was nineteen now, and she'd been with the carnival five years.

"Right this way, right this way, come see the most jaw-dropping female on Earth, the most diseased woman in the world! Don't worry, ladies and gentlemen, she's not contagious...unless you touch her! You, sir, would you care to see this princess of pestilence unveiled, laid bare for your education? I thought so, sir, I can see you are man with a healthy interest in science!"

The curtain opened. Radu, the sideshow talker responsible for herding the customers, led in the first group of nine or ten gawkers, the usual mix of red-faced farmers and drooling, wide-eyed children. Men and kids seemed most attracted to her show. Missouri was no different from anywhere else.

Juliana stood, still wrapped in the quilt she wore between shows, and approached the wooden rail at the front of her stage. Dirty upturned faces blinked at her in the low light.

"Juliana Blight," Radu continued. "Bitten by a swarm of rare giant African mosquitoes, Juliana carries all forms of disease within her flesh...from Egyptian mummy pox to Arabian leprosy, and the mysterious Chinese worm virus...stay back from the railing, sir, or you risk infection!"

"She don't look too sick to me," one man said, leaning on the railing.

"Prepare to be dazzled and horrified, sir!" the barker replied. "By the wonders of medical science."

Juliana shrugged off the quilt and let it fall to the stage. Underneath, she wore only white cotton underpants and a silk scarf, which hung loose around her neck to conceal her breasts. The crowd was free to inspect the rest of her body.

She held out her arms. Dark, bloody sores ripped open along them, from her shoulders all the way to her fingertips. The crowd gasped and drew back—the man who'd leaned on the rail nearly tripped over his shoes in his hurry to get away from her. A small, freckled boy screamed until his slightly older sister slapped and hushed him.

Juliana turned slowly, letting the crowd gasp and whisper at the sight of boils erupting up her back, blisters blooming along her thighs and calves. When she faced them again, a rash of bloody abscesses, cysts, and tumors broke open in a wave from her ankles to her hips, then across her stomach and chest. Her face became a horror-show mask, and her eyes darkened with diseased blood the color of bile.

As usual, the little crowd screamed and ran away through the curtain. Radu winked at her—he loved that "first scare" of the night, the one that was sure to draw plenty of curious lookers with coins to spend.

She wrapped herself in the quilt and sat down in the plain wooden chair at the back of her stage, reading a dime novel about pirates, and Radu left to round up the next audience.

She usually held back, but tonight she was really letting the plague out, giving them an extra-gory display. The others at the carnival didn't know it yet, but this would be her last night as the World's Most Diseased Woman, if things turned out as she hoped.

The next little group was ushered in, much quieter than the first, eager to see whatever had sent the first group running in terror.

She gave them a good show.

* * *

The next day was a Sunday, and local officials had made it clear that the carnival had to stay closed, lest it distract people from church. Many of the carnies had prepared for the day off with heavy drinking the night before, so the dusty midway was cold and silent in the morning as she left her tent and walked the dirt avenue between the booths. The smell of traveling carnival still hung in the air: popcorn, fried chicken, cotton candy, horse shit from the Wild West show.

The midway looked sad by day. No colored lights, no steam-powered calliope music from the carousel. The morning sun washed out the giant paintings of clowns, gorillas, and dragons—instead of weaving a fantasy world, they simply looked like drab, flat cartoons, painted onto wooden booths with all the games, toys, and other flash packed away inside. Without the mystery of the night beyond the lights of the midway, even the Ferris wheel looked small and pathetic. Spooky Manor, the haunted house, just looked silly, with its yarn spiderwebs and the skeleton peeping out the front window, though it could look convincingly scary at night with the proper lighting and sound effects.

Most of the carnival was devoted to crafting illusion, making a pretend world of color and magic to open up wallets and purses. Even the rides were meant to inspire a false feeling of danger, the games rigged to conjure a false sense that the mark might win big.

Juliana wasn't a trick or a scam. Everyone in the carnival assumed she was, of course, that she'd mastered a kind of theatrical illusion using some combination of makeup and lighting. Probably most or all of the customers believed that, too, once they had time to think it over and wrap the memory into a familiar packaging. They might even tell each other how obvious the fakery had been, later, when they were well away from the sideshow tent.

Juliana walked off the fairgrounds and followed the dirt road into town, which wasn't much more than two strips of brick and wood buildings, a well, and a corral. The largest building was the train depot.

She drew odd looks and whispers from the crowd of townspeople gathered in the street. She'd dressed as plainly as she could, in her brown dress with a few flower designs sewn here and there, a scarf to help shield her head from human contact, a white straw hat for the hot sunlight. Of course, she had to wear the black gloves unrolled all the way along her forearms, something very out of place in the Missouri summer. Everyone knew she wasn't local, and so they would correctly assume she was with the carnival camped outside town.

Along the street were multiple wagons with people piling in, ready to ride to the next town, just as she'd hoped. A man in a tie, possibly the town preacher, was yelling at them not to go, telling them they'd be damned, that they should instead attend a proper church, such as his own, for example.

Juliana approached a woman sitting in the back of the wagon with three small children, one of whom was a boy, five or six years old, with a badly shriveled leg. It looked like polio.

"Excuse me, ma'am," Juliana whispered to the woman, who wore a dress that had once been fine but was now patched many times over. "Is this wagon going to the revival?"

"We are," the woman said. "You must be from the circus."

"Yes ma'am," Juliana said, trying to sound a little Southern. "Might I ride with you? I could pay you a penny or two for it."

"Not on the Lord's day, you don't!" the woman snapped. She might have been in her late twenties or early thirties, but her sun-wrinkled skin made it hard to tell. She turned toward the bearded man in the big brown hat who sat on the driver's bench, holding the reins of the two horses. "Henry, we can take this circus girl to see the preachers, can't we?"

"Don't see why not." Henry puffed his pipe, not even looking back at his new passenger.

"Let me help you up." The woman reached down a hand.

"No!" Juliana jumped back, not wanting to infect her with the demon plague. "I can manage, thank you."

She climbed up into the straw-littered wagon and sank into a back corner, as far from the family as possible. She drew up her knees and wrapped her arms around them.

The three children stared at her. The crippled boy seemed the youngest, but his brother and sister couldn't have been older than nine or ten years.

"Are you in the circus?" asked the boy with the bad leg.

"Yes," she told him.

"Are you a clown?" the older boy asked.

"Or an acrobat?" the girl asked, hopping to her filthy bare feet. "I can do flips. Want to see?"

"I'll burn your hide if you step down from this wagon, Izzy May!" the woman snapped. "Sit back like you were."

Izzy May quickly sat down beside her brothers, next to a trunk roped into place. The mother sat on another large trunk. It looked like they planned to be away from home overnight.

"I'm nothing special," Juliana said. "I work a sugar shack."

"What does that mean?" the girl asked.

"I make cotton candy," she told them, and the kids looked very impressed.

"Do you have some?" asked the boy with the bad leg.

"Sorry, I don't," she said, and the kids immediately lost interest. Juliana turned to their mother. "The next town isn't a very long way, is it? You're returning tonight, aren't you?"

"These can last for days," the woman replied. "We won't be back until the Lord sends us."

"I have to be back for my show tomorrow."

"Oh, honey," the woman replied. "If the Lord wants you back here, He will find a way."

Juliana couldn't argue with that.

The wagon finally started to move. A train of half a dozen crowded wagons rolled out of town, kicking up a cloud of brown dust from the dry dirt road. Juliana tilted her hat forward to keep it out of her eyes, but the rest of her was soon covered in earth. Her sweat under the hot sun slowly converted it to a thin sheen of mud.

During the long, slow ride, the children peppered Juliana with endless questions about the carnival. She described how cakes were fried and cotton candy was spun, detailed each of the games on the midway from the ring-toss to the rifle-shoot to the test-your-strength. She explained that she did not have her own elephant or giraffe. She told them about each of the characters in the sideshow, except for the attraction behind the final curtain, Juliana Blight. She explained how they jumped from town to town by rail.

In time, they reached the tent of the revival, almost as big as a circus tent, pitched on a grassy pasture by the wide, slow Mississippi River.

People had flocked in from all around, judging by the wagons and tents jammed in on either side of the road. There were even a few automobiles and trucks. The center of the action was the single large tent, from which she could hear pained shouting, music, and stomping. It sounded louder than a tavern on a Saturday night.

Juliana thanked the family for the ride and quickly scurried out of the wagon. She didn't want the kids following her around, asking more questions about candy, magic tricks, and carnival games, because then she would have to make an effort not to kill them.

She drew her arms in tight around her as she walked toward the revival tent, trying to avoid any contact with the ever-thicker crowd, where people didn't mind doing a little elbowing and jostling. She hoped her gloves, dress, and headwear were enough to protect them from her.

The revival traveled the same general railroad circuit as the carnival, so they often saw each other's posters in the towns they visited, though they'd never pitched tent in the same town at the same time. There wouldn't have been enough money for either group.

Juliana had heard of miraculous healings at this particular revival. Naturally, she'd first assumed that the performances were trickery, either making people feel momentarily better using dramatic stage techniques, or else the healed people were just shills in cahoots with the preacher.

However, she'd heard repeated stories from town to town. An old blind man who could now see, a World War I veteran who'd regrown an ear he'd lost in combat. A woman who'd been coughing up blood, dying of consumption and too weak to walk, who was now well and could take care of her children and work around the farm.

After hearing one miraculous story after another about locals in one town after another, Juliana had begun to believe something magical might actually be happening at that revival. She'd become determined to visit it the next time it passed close to the carnival. With the carnival shut down by local authorities for Sunday worship, it was the perfect time for Juliana to sneak off and see the revival for herself.

The front flaps of the tent wall were tied open, and nobody collected an admission fee. People were free to walk in and out of the tent, if the thick crowd allowed it.

She eased her way inside. The tent was packed full, everybody cramming in to stand under the shade and listen to a preacher on the stage at the far end of the tent from the entrance. He was a white-haired, pudgy man in a gray suit, dabbing his sweaty double chin with a handkerchief, his eyes bugging as he shouted at the audience, who responded with shouts and cries of their own.

"The devil is not some character in a radio program or a child's picture book!" the preacher shouted, and a number of audience members shouted back, agreeing. "The devil is real, brothers and sisters. The devil walks among us, wearing masks! He can come in any form at all! But when he does, you'll know him! You'll know him because he tempts you with gold! With fornication! With sin and worldly pleasures...but those pleasures are false! Yes, they are! And those tempting, earthly pleasures will fall away, and you'll see they come drawing hellfire behind them! Yes, sir! The Lord is great...abh ah loch tay moota howklo tarris be hock bot a mok nay hapa tah..." His eyes closed and he raised one shaking arm, clutching the handkerchief in his fist.

Juliana didn't understand what the preacher was saying, but lots of people in the crowd started making similar nonsense words. Some waved their hands high and closed their eyes, while others went into convulsions, crashing into those around them and finally flopping on the dirt like dying fish. Many of them simply screamed or howled. She didn't know what to think as the crowd seemed to turn rabid.

"Isn't this wonderful?" A hand seized Juliana's arm, and she gasped. It was the woman from the wagon, with kids and husband in tow. The husband carried the boy with the crippled leg. With the heavy crowd, Juliana hadn't penetrated far into the tent, and now the family had caught up with her.

Juliana looked down at where the woman clutched her—fortunately, her sleeve protected the woman from a rapid, painful death, but Juliana didn't feel comfortable about it.

"Is this the preacher does the healing?" the husband asked. He bounced the little boy in his arms, and the boy cried out in glee.

"Is he?" the woman asked Juliana.

"I don't know," Juliana answered. "I hope so."

The preacher went on and on, getting louder, stomping the stage, sending the crowd into hysterics. The kids from the wagon joined the rest of the audience in screaming, howling, and flopping around, except for the smallest boy, who just watched from his father's shoulder, unable to join the fun.

Juliana couldn't believe how long the preacher continued. The sound of rain battered the tent top, and people drenched from the downpour pushed their way into the packed tent. Soon the crowd was twice as large, and the air in the tent turned steamy and foul with the odor of so many bodies.

After a long, long time, and much more speaking in tongues, the first preacher finally staggered offstage, exhausted, while the audience cried and clapped.

A tall, gaunt man carried a woven basket onstage, followed by three other men. From their look and their ragged clothes, Juliana thought they might be mountain people. The gaunt man addressed the audience while the other three lingered behind him.

"The Lord says, if we have faith, we may take up serpents without fear," the man told the crowd. "For even the sting of the serpent is nothing next to the power of God."

The audience chattered excitedly.

"We have come to show the power of faith as a testimony." He lifted the lid from the woven basket, and the crowd pushed forward to see. "For the tempter comes in the form of a serpent, hissing lies into our ears...But we show him that only the Lord is our master!"

From the basket, he lifted out a pair of thick, long rattlesnakes, one in each hand, both of them shaking out a warning with their tails. Screams erupted from the audience, and a number of people near the front tried to push their way back, by they were trapped in place by the rest of the crowd.

The gaunt man stalked slowly across the front lip of the stage, holding out his arms while the deadly rattlers coiled around him. The crowd gasped and shrieked.

Behind him, his three cohorts approached the basket one by one, each taking one or two rattlesnakes and letting them wrap around their arms and necks.

Juliana's heartbeat raced as she watched, waiting for one of them to suffer a fatal bite. In the carnival, the show would have been a fraud—the snakes would be a harmless species that only looked dangerous, most likely, or their venom would have been removed—but she'd heard that the snake-handling preachers used fully lethal wild snakes.

The children stopped playing at flopping and fainting, and they watched quietly, eyes wide open. The whole tent had gone from boisterous to silent. In the silence, the gaunt preacher's voice seemed to echo back from the canvas walls.

"Faith is not some small thing we do once a week," he said. "We must hold faith inside of us all times. With faith, there is no danger, for there is no door through which Satan can enter. Close your hearts against evil, and open them to the Lord!"

Voices whispered throughout the crowd as the largest rattlesnake nosed its way up the preacher's neck and cheek, its forked tongue tasting his ear.

"We have no need to fear," he continued. "God has already vanquished the devil, and He will do it again, and there will be a final Judgment. If the Lord chooses to take us today, or ten years from now, or a hundred years from now, it's all the same...we're all going to face Him, we're all going to answer for our sins...and there will be a reckoning!" He thrust a fist into the air to make his point, startling the rattlesnake, which drew back and opened its jaw, poised to bite his face.

The preacher fell still and quiet, looking right back into the snake's eyes.

"Go ahead," he said in a loud stage whisper. "Go ahead and try, Satan. God is with me. I'm filled with the Spirit and the light."

The entire audience stayed silent. After a minute, the rattlesnake relaxed and turned away, crawling back down his arm. The preacher resumed his sermon, while his three acolytes walked to different areas of the stage, letting the audience see the snakes in their hands.

He spoke on and on, like the previous preacher. As he wrapped up, the three men returned their snakes to the basket and picked up buckets on long rods. They held these out to the audience, collecting coins and cash from the stunned crowd.

The next preacher was a different sort. He wore an odd pastel-colored suit, and his dark, curly head of hair looked like a wig to Juliana, because it didn't quite match his handlebar mustache. He was followed by a chorus of three young women wearing high-neck dresses and no makeup, who stood together at one corner of the stage. Behind him, a black man in a green snap-brim hat and matching suit took over the piano.

The preacher walked to stage center, looking around, apprising the crowd, with the automatic bright smile of an experienced showman.

"I hope this is him," the woman from the wagon said. "I'm exhausted." Night had fallen, and the rain hadn't let up, so the tent remained crowded and humid. Everyone was sweating. Juliana worried that her sweat might fall on somebody, like one of the two children who insisted on staying close to their pet carnival girl. She didn't know whether her sweat could harm anyone, and she certainly didn't want to find out the hard way.

"He don't look no healer to me," commented the woman's husband, Henry.

"I'm sleepy," their little girl complained.

"I want to play with snakes!" the older boy announced.

"Ladies and gentlemen, brothers and sisters, let us pray," the preacher finally said. Nobody was going to argue with that, so everyone lowered their heads and closed their eyes, and many grasped the hands of the people around them. The little girl, Izzy May, grasped Juliana's gloved hand and wouldn't let go, which made Juliana edgy and nervous.

"...as Your wonders are limitless, oh Lord, we beseech you to bless this humble house of worship with Your grace today. As Your Son healed the blind and the sick, we ask that You pour Your love upon our brothers and sisters here, those who are in need, those are ill, those who live in pain..."

Juliana opened her eyes and looked up. Maybe this was the healing preacher, after all. If so, he didn't inspire much confidence.

"Amen," the preacher eventually said, and many people echoed him. "Children of the Lord, we have been called together for a great purpose today," he began. "And that purpose is to recognize the Lord's place in our lives..." As he spoke, the piano player went to work, providing a backdrop of fast, punchy notes that helped rouse the crowd as the preacher continued. Soon the preacher was keyed up, racing around the stage. "...and when trouble arrives, what do we say? We say oh, precious Lord, take my hand!"

This was the cue for the three women to sing the hymn 'Oh, Precious Lord, Take My Hand,' a hymn which a lot of the crowd seemed to know, because they sang along. The piano player immediately switched from his jazzy melody to a deeper gospel sound.

When the song ended, the preacher resumed strutting up and down the stage, talking up the healing powers of God and recalling the stories about Jesus and the lepers. He grew more and more animated, slapping his hands together and stomping his foot for emphasis.

"Hallelujah! I feel the Spirit!" cried out one of his chorus girls. She closed her eyes as if in ecstasy and brushed her hands from her bosom down to her hips. "It's in me!" She moaned and toppled backwards. The audience gasped as the two other girls scrambled to catch her. It looked like a rehearsed move to Juliana, but she supposed most of the crowd hadn't seen five years' worth of midway tricks.

This inspired people in the crowd to scream and squirm in response. The punchy piano music accelerated, and the writhing and screaming spread through the tent.

Juliana frowned. She doubted this man was anything but a big talker who knew how to sway a crowd. She was beginning to feel stupid for coming to the revival, like just another mark who couldn't see the game.

"I know why many of you are here tonight," the preacher said. "Word gets around, don't it, about the wonders of the Lord that unfold right here, in this very tent? I've heard people say I can cure the blind, heal the sick, chase out the demons of illness." Many of the crowd shouted excitedly. "They say I can take a crippled man and make him walk, that I can cast out all manner of pox and measles." The crowd grew more excited, and many began trying to push their way to the front.

Juliana tensed. This was it, the alleged healing part of the show.

"Those folks are plain wrong!" the preacher shouted. "I'm just a simple country preacher. It's the Lord that heals! It's the Spirit that heals the sick and the suffering little children, and the lepers and all of 'em! I am just a humble vessel of the Lord, that's all!"

The crowd roared their enthusiastic response.

The preacher's assistant brought up a man with his arm in a sling. The preacher prayed, danced around, and laid his hands on the broken arm. The man took off the sling and waved the bandaged arm at the crowd, grinning, and the crowd shouted things like "Hallelujah!" and "Praise the Lord!" There was no way to tell whether he was a shill or not.

The family with the polio-stricken boy was trying to push their way to the stage, but the thick crowd wasn't budging. Juliana decided to let the little boy's leg be her test of whether the healing was real. She jumped in front of the family.

"Crippled boy, coming through!" she shouted. "Let us through, he's crippled! Please!" She did her best to look sad, pulling out every carnival trick she knew. A few people eased aside, but they didn't get far, so she raised the stakes. "Dying boy! Look out, this boy's going to die right now! Help this dying boy reach the stage!"

More people took an interest now, and some even helped out, passing the word along and urging others to step aside. She kept repeating her plea as she advanced, opening a narrow path for the family, who followed right behind her.

She kept up her patter until they reached the very edge of the stage, where the father was able to pass the little boy to the preacher's assistant, who carried him over to the preacher. His parents watched, the father hard-eyed and skeptical, the mother full of hope.

Juliana crossed her arms and waited to see whether a miracle would happen.

"Oh, yes, this boy's been stricken, all right," the preacher said. "Sick leg, does everyone see that? The boy cannot walk!" The preacher's assistant held the boy out for the crowd to see, then turned him toward the preacher, who said, "But the Lord is merciful, and offers us hope. Tell me, boy, do you love the Lord?"

"Yes," the boy answered, in a small voice.

"And the Lord loves you, too. And we can ask Him for the great gift of healing, we can ask for His blessing..." The preacher danced around the stage a little, then shouted, "Demon of affliction, I cast thee out! Go back to the fires of damnation from which you rose!" He slapped the boy's leg, hard enough that Juliana jumped in surprise and the boy's mother cried out.

The assistant turned the boy to face the audience again and held him up high. Beneath his overalls, which were cut off at the knees, everyone could see that both his legs appeared perfectly healthy. The crowd gasped.

The assistant lowered the boy to his feet. He looked off-balance for a moment, then finally took a chance and put his weight on his newly healed leg. A smile burst across his face, and his mother cried out again.

"Healed, praise the Lord!" the preacher said. "God is in this tent with us today, ain't He?"

The crowd roared that yes, He was, while the assistant carried the boy back to the side of the stage and handed him back to his shocked father and weeping mother. Juliana immediately stepped forward and grabbed the assistant's sleeve.

"Me next," Juliana told him.

The assistant looked at her. She hadn't paid much attention to him before, focusing on the preacher like everyone else. The assistant wasn't much older than her, and he was handsome despite his scratchy, fuzzy attempt at growing a beard. His intense blue eyes took her in, and something fluttered in her stomach.

"Do I need to carry you, too?" he asked, with an amused smile.

"I can manage on my own, thanks."

"I don't think you'll make it to the stairs." He tilted his head to the far end of the stage. Dozens of people, crammed tightly together, blocked her path. "It's my way or no way."

"Then be a gentleman about it." She held up her arms and let him grab her around the waist and lift her to the stage. For a moment, her body was pressed against his, and the sensation of his strong, firm chest through her clothes made her flush red. He set her on her feet.

They waited while the preacher finished healing a man who'd lost a finger harvesting grain—it grew back, to the great delight of the crowd, who shouted lots of "Hallelujah!" So did the chorus of three women. The piano player kept the tempo moving fast.

"Who else comes for the Lord's healing?" the preacher asked, scratching his head through his odd-colored curly hair.

"You're on," the assistant whispered in Juliana's ear. He steered her toward the smiling preacher. As he did it, he pushed back her sleeve and laid his fingers on her bare arm, before she realized what he was doing.

She gasped and tried to pull away, but he held tight. Incredibly, his fingers did not boil and blister where they touched her, and he did not cry out and leap back in pain. The boy's touch was warm and gentle, and caused no unpleasantness for either of them.

Her eyes widened in awe. This was truly a place of miracles, because no one had ever been able to touch her without suffering infection. She understood now that God truly was in this tent, and now He could cast the demon plague out of her forever. She would no longer be a freak, and she would be free to touch anyone she liked. She was more than happy to start with the preacher's young assistant, whose hand lingered on her arm even as she faced the preacher.

"Ladies and gentlemen, the Lord has brought us another sweet lamb," the preacher said, eying her up and down. He smelled like sweaty armpits and chemical hair dye. "And what is your name, little angel?"

"Petra," she said, giving her old, long-abandoned birth name.

"Petra, Petra. Will you let me lay my hands upon you, Petra? Will you open yourself to receiving the Lord's blessing?"

"Yes..." she replied uncertainly.

"And what is your affliction, dear lamb?"

"I have...all kinds of diseases and plagues," she told him.

"Afflicted!" the preacher shouted to the audience. "Afflicted by many diseases, many plagues, ladies and gentlemen? And do you know who afflicts with many diseases at once...a legion of plagues?"

Some in the audience shouted back their opinion that "Satan" or "the Devil" might be responsible.

"I said, do you know who causes such affliction?" he shouted, his face turning red.

"Satan!" more of the audience shouted back.

"Satan, Satan, Satan!" the preacher howled. "That's right! And do you know who drives out Satan? Can you say His name? Can you, say, Oh, Lord, cast out these demons?"

The crowd shouted it back. The preacher and crowd shouted back and forth several times, the preacher giving them an "Oh, Lord, cast out these demons!" The crowd repeated it back to him each time: "Oh, Lord, cast out these demons!"

Emboldened by the power and energy of the crowd, and the little boy's healed leg, Juliana slipped off both her gloves and held her bare hands high.

When the crowd was at a fever pitch, the preacher turned, seized both of her hands, then closed his eyes and shouted one final "Oh, Lord, cast out these demons!"

Juliana clutched his hands, closed her eyes, and threw back her head, waiting for God to finally break her evil curse.

A wave of quiet rolled over the room, displacing the shouting, singing, and loud praying that had accompanied all the other healings. She didn't feel any different. She opened her eyes.

The preacher stood in front of her, squeezing her hands, his jaw hanging open. Diseased sores had opened all over his face, and dark blood drooled from his lips. His face and jaw swelled and change shape, as if tumors were sprouting all over his skull. His hands, still gripping tight to hers, had turned rotten and leprous.

Juliana gasped and released him, realizing too late that the preacher didn't have any power over the demon plague, after all. It was eating him up. The preacher staggered toward the front of the stage, groaning and raising his decayed hands. He fell to his knees, and the audience screamed and drew back. The chorus girls grabbed each other and screamed.

The piano player took one look at what was happening and wisely grabbed his hat and darted out through the canvas flaps at the back of the stage.

The crowd continued shrieking, panicked but not sure whether to run or pray or just shout. Many pointed at Juliana. She felt glued to the spot where she stood, though she knew she ought to leave the stage. There was nothing she could do. The preacher would die, and it would be her fault.

The preacher's assistant hurried over to the horribly infected preacher and knelt beside him. He took the man's contorted, blistered face in both hands, showing no fear at all. He spoke quietly to the preacher, and though Juliana couldn't hear his words over the frightened crowd, she could hear his tone—calm, measured, focused.

Then, incredibly, the demon plague was reversed. The preacher's face and neck healed, and his hands returned to normal. In less than a minute, it looked like he'd never been infected at all, except for the splotches of blood and pus on his suit and tie.

The assistant helped the preacher stand. The preacher looked down at his hands, turning them back and forth, then held them up for the audience to see. "Healed! Healed, by the grace of God!" he shouted. The crowd shouted back with hallelujahs and amens.

Then the preacher turned to Juliana and scowled as he pointed one trembling finger at her.

"The devil is here today!" the preacher announced. "This is no girl. She's a demoness, sent from Hell!"

The crowd roared and surged toward the stage, shouting all kinds of filthy names and curses at Juliana.

"I'm not!" Juliana said, though she doubted anyone could hear her over the din. "I can't help it! I don't want to hurt anyone, I came to be healed..." She realized she was crying. Why not? She'd been foolish, letting herself hope for too much. She turned toward the preacher's assistant, giving him a desperate look. He was the one with the miraculous power, she now understood, and not the preacher. Maybe he could still help her.

"Devil!" someone shouted from below.

"Witch!" screamed someone else.

Men and women from the crowd clambered up onto the stage with fear glowing in their eyes.

"Destroy her!" the preacher shouted. "Drown the demon in the river! We'll baptize it back to Hell!"

The crowd swarmed the stage, all of them closing in on Juliana, and she realized they would kill her, unless she killed them first.

"Stop! Get back!" she shouted. She raised her bare hands and let the demon plague appear all over her skin, even her face, mutating her appearance into something infernal.

The crowd slowed. Suddenly, nobody wanted to be the first to grab her.

"I don't want to hurt anyone," Juliana said. "I'm here for healing...but I can kill you if I want. Please don't make me."

One person advanced toward her, the preacher's assistant. He grabbed her hand and pulled her toward the back of the stage. She noticed that her boils and blisters vanished where he touched her, and she felt a warm glow there instead.

"I have the touch of God, as you have just seen," the young man told the confused, edgy mob. "I will take care of the girl." He tugged Juliana toward the canvas flaps that served as the backdrop of the stage.

"Don't you take that witch out of this tent!" the preacher shouted. "She'll use her devilry on you!"

The assistant gave Juliana a long look. The crowd, emboldened by the preacher's words, advanced on her again.

"We ought to run," the assistant whispered to her.

They dashed away through the canvas curtain into the dim area behind the stage, where a number of preachers and their supporting performers had crowded to escape the rain. The snake handlers were still there, kneeling on the dirt floor and praying, their snakes rattling and hissing inside the basket. They looked up as Juliana and the preacher's assistant leaped over the stage's back steps, landed in the muddy dirt, and ran out of the tent into the rainy night.

A few trucks and automobiles were parked behind the tent, as well as a number of wagons, their horses hitched under tent tops to keep them out of the rain.

He led her into the horse tent and drew a knife from his boot. He cut free one horse after another as they moved down the temporary hitching rail. The crowd burst out through the back flaps of the tent, shouting and looking for them.

"What are you doing?" Juliana asked, as he cut free yet another horse. "We have to run!"

"Then let's run." He climbed up onto a tall brown horse, then held out his hands. "Hurry!"

She hesitated. She couldn't risk her legs touching the horse, or she would poison the poor creature.

The mob shouted and ran towards them.

"Now!" the young man said. "Or they'll kill us both."

"Give me that knife!" Juliana didn't wait, but snatched it from the sheath in his boot. While the mob approached, she sliced the bottom hem of her dress at the front and back, and then she ripped the dress all the way up to her waist.

"Now, what are *you* doing?" he asked.

"Protecting the horse." She sheathed the knife, took pins from her hair, and fixed the torn sides of her dress around her legs like breeches. Then, finally, she let him grab her hands and haul her up, and she slid into the saddle behind him.

"Take those reins," he said, pointing at a horse to her left. She grabbed the horse's reins, knowing there was no time to ask why.

They rode off, flanked by an extra horse on either side. The preacher's assistant held the reins of the horse on their right. He yelled at the other horses, trying to get them to follow, and a couple of confused-looking horses actually did trot after them.

She looked back over her shoulder as they rode out of the horse tent. The loose, wandering horses were slowing the crowd's pursuit.

They turned onto the muddy road, riding north along the Mississippi River, toward St. Louis. The two extra horses they'd captured galloped alongside them, making annoyed sounds at being woken and forced to run in the rain. Two additional horses followed at a distance, not eager to run but apparently not wanting to miss the party, either.

She heard the sounds of engines cranking.

"Maybe we should have taken one of those cars instead!" Juliana shouted to be heard over the pounding rain and the commotion behind them.

"Those can't go anywhere but roads. We wouldn't be able to escape. Drop those reins!"

Juliana released her captured horse, and so did he. He shouted "Yah!" at them a few times, and then turned and rode off along what looked like a muddy deer path into the woods. No truck or car could follow them here.

He slowed a little when they were out of sight of the road. "Any luck, they'll follow those other horses down the road before they figure out they've lost us."

"Where does this trail go?" she asked.

"I wouldn't know, we're just passing through town."

"Where are you from? Do you have a name?"

"I do." He leaned forward and shouted, "Yah!" The horse picked up speed, galloping away from the trouble behind them.

Juliana held tight to the boy's waist. Her fingers wanted to trace the shape of the muscle under his shirt, and she let them explore as much as she dared.

As they rode through the rain, under the bright harvest moon, she couldn't help noticing how she felt bounding against him again and again with each stride of the horse's leg, with only her rain-soaked underpants separating her from his scratchy woolen trousers.

She snuggled her arms tighter around him and rested her cheek on his strong back. Despite the rain, she hoped the ride would never end.

# Chapter Six

Jenny stood in her studio, staring at the mannequin. It was an androgynous, hairless, waist-up model clamped in place by a sawhorse. She'd carved and painted all kinds of symptoms into it, dark sores and dripping wounds. She'd glued ugly plastic black flies here and there all over the body, and cut out magazine pictures of people with horrified expressions and pasted a dense collage of them over the mannequin's heart.

She could never show it to anyone, for a number of reasons, but she had no desire to share it. It was a confession of her evil, a splattering of all the haunting memories of death and suffering that crawled inside of her. The point was in the making of it, in doing something with the guilt fed by the horror movies that never stopped playing inside her mind. If she didn't find a way to let them out, they would eat her up. She'd seen her dark side, with Alexander, and she wasn't going to be that person again.

Jenny touched a hand to her stomach. No heavy bleeding yet. The little starter baby was still swimming around in there like a tiny fish. She felt bad for the doomed creature, but she avoided thinking of it as a person. It wouldn't live long enough for that.

Seth knocked on her door, and Jenny turned down her stereo. She had to listen to Patsy Cline on a digital music app now. She missed her mother's record collection, still back home with her dad. She missed her dad every day, too. She'd lived with him for eighteen years, then vanished, and it was almost certain that she would never see him again. She couldn't risk returning to the United States.

"You busy?" Seth asked, leaning in the door.

"Busy-ish." Jenny gestured toward the mannequin. "Just working on this stupid thing. Want to go out for oysters?"

"I've got some bad news. There's something you should probably see."

"Okay..." Jenny reluctantly followed him out of the room. She didn't need more bad news. She could already feel their Parisian magic carpet beginning to unravel beneath their feet.

The living room was filled with autumn sunlight from the giant picture window. Seth dropped onto the antique settee, where his laptop was set up on the round oak table in front of him. Jenny sat beside him and snuggled up against him, enjoying the feeling of his hand resting on her hip. Being close to him made her feel safer, even though she would be the one dealing death if anyone attacked them.

"Here we go." Seth maximized a video to fill the screen, then pressed play.

Melodramatic, echoing music played, clearly trying to be spooky, almost a rip-off of the *Twilight Zone* theme song. An animated logo popped up: the planet Earth, slowly rotating. The view zoomed out to show that the Earth was actually inside of a snowglobe clutched in a gray three-fingered hand. Lightning struck the Earth, and then the text appeared in glowing letters: *Conspiracies of the Unknown*.

Jenny laughed and elbowed him. "Seth, you really had me scared, you fuckface."

"Just keep watching."

The video showed a man, hugely overweight, with a goatee and thick glasses. He was sitting in what looked like a basement or garage, with a handmade *Conspiracies of the Unknown* sign tacked to the wall behind him. From the video quality and angle, it was clearly a webcam.

"Hi, everyone. Rudley McGhee here again, with the latest in what *they* don't want you to know."

"Oh, come on," Jenny said. "Isn't this the guy who says aliens shot JFK?"

"Blue lizard aliens. Sh, keep watching."

"I have a *Conspiracies of the Unknown* special edition for you tonight, now that Beauford finally finished editing the footage." Another chubby guy, balding on top but with long hair at the back, leaned into the frame and waved. "Move over, Beauford, you're in the shot! Okay, folks, listen up. What if I told you that there was a little town, right here in the U.S.A., just a regular place like my town or your town, with a Wal-Mart and everything...But in this town, over two hundred people *mysteriously disappeared*!"

"It's gnarly crazy," Beauford said.

"Beauford, you're still in the frame, home skillet! Ugh. Like I was saying, people, that's a huge disappearance, all on the same day. That's right, the same day! And this isn't some Roanoke Colony thing from three hundred years ago...though I have a theory about *that*, too...No, this just happened! Like, a year and a half ago!"

"It basically just happened!" Beauford added.

"Dang it, Beauford, this isn't your show, it's my show! If you want your own show, go make one with your mom or something!"

"I'll make a video with your mom!" Beauford snickered. "Maybe I already did."

"You did not!" Rudley shoved his way up out of his chair, looking enraged. The video skipped, and then it was Rudley in his chair again, sweaty now. Beauford was not in the frame. "So Beauford and I took the Rud-mobile and the Conspira-cam and went to this town to investigate! It's called Fallen Oak, South Carolina." He held up a road map. "See it? There it is. Really small, right there. Roll the footage, Beauford!"

"Holy shit," Jenny said, sitting up straight. Seth wasn't joking.

"Yep," Seth replied.

The video cut to Rudley standing between a rusty El Camino and the rotten old "Welcome to Fallen Oak" sign, waving his hand gleefully, dressed in a Hawaiian shirt like a tourist. "We drove all the way from Crawley, West Virginia. Took us ten hours, plus a nap at a rest stop," Rudley's voiceover told them. "Beauford's hemorrhoids were flaring real bad, but we made it."

The video then showed Rudley standing in what Jenny first thought was a weedy, overgrown field, until the camera zoomed out and she realized it was the Fallen Oak town green in front of the courthouse. It was shocking to see it like that, with weeds high enough to brush the underside of Rudley's belly. Apparently nobody was bothering to keep it up.

"You see a lot of towns like this, driving around," Rudley said in the video as he looked at the boarded-up businesses. "You wonder what it was like, when a place like this was really alive. You wonder where everybody came from, and where they went, and why they just left this husk of a town behind like a...like a hermit crab changing shells."

"Hey, that's deep, Rudster," Beauford said from off-screen. Apparently, he was the one shakily operating the handheld camera.

"Beauford, dang it, don't interrupt my talking!" Rudley scowled at the camera for a minute.

"What are you waiting for?" Beauford asked.

"Just waiting to see if you're done running your mouth or not."

"I'm done."

"Because if you got something to say, Beauford, go ahead and say it so we can get on with the dang show."

"I ain't got nothing say."

"Yeah, you didn't have nothing to say when you ate the last Twinkie in the box, either, did you? Remember? Right about the North Carolina state line? Didn't even ask me if I wanted that last Twinkie."

"You been sore about this since North Carolina?"

"That was my Twinkie! You ate two more than I did! Can't you do no math?"

The video jumped again, showing Rudley from a different angle, calm again, still on the town green. "Anyway, sad little town. And, according to some stuff I read on the internet, it was right here that all two hundred people just vanished into thin air. No explanation. Homeland Security even took over the town for a while. And guess what the official story was? This is the kicker, listen! They said there was a little toxic leak from some old dye factory, which had been closed for like, what, forty years?"

"Fifty-six," Beauford told him.

"Dang it, Beauford....Think about it, folks at home. Two hundred people, vanished all at once. A government cover-up. No explanation. Are you thinking what I'm thinking? Because I'm thinking...*abduction*. I'm not saying it's aliens..." Rudley glanced around nervously. "...but I think it was aliens."

"Oh, that's a relief," Jenny said. "Nobody's going to take this seriously. How did you even find this?"

"Somebody linked it to Fark. Mainly to make fun of these two guys, but still. If they know something strange happened, other people could, too. And watch this next part."

Rudley sat in a front parlor, the sort of room some people's parents kept well-decorated and unused. He was facing a very unhappy-looking couple in their late forties or early fifties.

"Wait a minute!" Jenny said. "Aren't they..."

"Mr. and Mrs. Daniels," Seth said. "Bret Daniels' parents. I've spent the night at their house before."

Jenny briefly remembered killing the jock using a cloud of pox spores in front of the courthouse.

"...never made any sense to us," Bret's mother was saying. "He just drove off on Easter, and we never saw him again! They said there was an accident...some people died...but we never saw him or his...his..."

"His dead body?" Rudley asked helpfully, and Bret's mother cried out as if stabbed. The father just stared at the floor, stone-faced.

"Nobody would tell us anything," Bret's father said, without looking up. "Not a thing."

"Did you see any strange lights that night?" Rudley asked. "Were there any crop circles in the morning?"

"He left a daughter behind," Bret's mom added. "With his high-school sweetheart, Darcy Metcalf."

"They weren't exactly sweethearts," Bret's dad mumbled.

"Don't say that! He wouldn't have done *that* with a girl unless he really loved her. He was such a sweet little boy."

Bret's dad shrugged.

"We almost never see our grandbaby," Bret's mom continued. "Darcy up and moved to Columbia, and now she's living with a..." Her voice dropped to a whisper. "...a *Mexican*. Our little granddaughter, growing up in the city with a bunch of Mexicans. Probably eating burritos as we speak!"

"Judge says we can't do a thing about it," Bret's dad said.

"Back to the bright lights over town," Rudley said. "Did you see any? Or any glowing objects at all, perhaps parked in a cow pasture?"

"Didn't see nothing like that," Bret's dad mumbled.

"Well, I do have a little self-help brochure I wrote, for people who've been abducted, and for the families of the abducted, too. It's normally $5.99, but I'll let you folks have one for free." Rudley handed over a thick booklet with a flying saucer on the cover.

"What is this?" the crying mother asked.

"Aliens?" Bret's dad scowled. "Is that it? You come here to talk to us about aliens?"

"Well, yes, sir," Rudley told him. "There's an epidemic of Americans being abducted and studied by extraterrestrial visitors, you see...they're not from our dimension. They're from a different Earth, in the ninth dimension."

Mr. Daniels stared at him for a second, then stood up, raising his fists. "Get out! Get out of my house!"

"Sir, you should know there are alien-abduction support groups—" Rudley began, before Mr. Daniels punched him in the mouth. The man threw a punch at the camera, too, and it blacked out.

The video skipped back to Rudley in his basement.

"Okay, well, that's all the footage *Beauford* bothered to edit this week," Rudley said. "Check this website again for future updates about our trip to Fallen Oak...where the alien visitors got a little too greedy for their own good, methinks!"

"No, please, no future updates," Jenny said. "That was bad enough."

"I know." Seth closed the laptop. "What if other people, not I-have-a-webcam-show-in-my-basement types, start looking into it?"

"There's still no reason to come looking for us," Jenny said. "We died in the fire at your house, right? We're dead."

"Except we're not."

"Nobody knows that."

"Plenty of people know it, Jenny."

"Then what do you want me to do about it?" Jenny was surprised to hear herself scream. She made herself speak more calmly. "I mean, there's nothing we can do."

"I just thought you should know about it."

"Now I know about it. Now what?" Jenny chewed her lip, worried. She grasped his hand in hers.

"We could make out," Seth suggested.

"Maybe."

"You could tell me what happened to us."

"What do you mean?" she looked at him.

"The carnival, the tent revival. Did we get away? The last I heard, I'd done this really awesome thing, rescued you and carried you away on horseback, and it made you super-horny."

"Maybe I should keep more of my thoughts to myself," Jenny said.

"And then you ripped your dress in half for me." Seth grinned.

"It wasn't for you, it was for the horse."

"Gross."

"Do you want to hear the story or not, Seth?"

"I want to hear it. I like stories where I'm the hero."

"Maybe I should stop where we were," Jenny said, laying her head on his shoulder. "Things go downhill, just like all our lives."

"Sounds promising. Too much happiness is boring, right? Make sure you talk more about how much I turned you on."

Jenny took a deep breath and continued the story.

# Chapter Seven

Juliana and her mysterious, sexy, handsome rescuer rode on through the night and the rain, Juliana holding him tight. After a long and cold lifetime without touching anyone, she couldn't get enough of feeling his warm body through his wet shirt.

They followed a small stream westward from the Mississippi, staying in the wilderness. He finally stopped the horse in a meadow full of tall grass and wildflowers and climbed off. Juliana smiled as she let him help her down. The rain had slowed to a misty drizzle, and the horse soon found his way to a copse of trees, which protected him from the raindrops while he nibbled flowers.

The boy stood by the stream in his muddy boots and looked at the dark water glinting in the moonlight.

"Are we safe now?" she whispered.

"Maybe. The horse needs a break."

"I don't hear anyone." Juliana could hear the gurgling of the stream, the pounding of her heart, and a cheeping chorus of night bugs, but no horse hooves. She looked at him, studying his handsome face, though it was shadowy under the moonlight. He had a familiar look to him, though she was sure she'd never seen him before today. "Why did you do that?"

"Horse was tired, like I said."

"I wasn't asking why you stopped. I was asking why you started."

"Why I grabbed you and ran out? What else was I supposed to do?" he asked with half a smile. "Those people were ready to kill you, after hearing about the devil all day."

"But you weren't."

"I think I might understand you better than most people."

"You're the one with the healing power, not the preacher," Juliana said. "Why do you let everyone think it's him?"

"I'm just the assistant. I don't need everyone staring at me." He winked, then held out his hand. "Let's see it."

"See what?"

"You know."

Juliana cautiously let her take his hand, still not used to the idea of anyone touching her without suffering. He held it in his own, watching as she summoned the demon plague, letting dark blisters burst through her fingers and palm. He didn't seem scared. Instead, he lifted her hand to his lips and kissed each one of her fingertips, making the blisters disappear. The feeling of his lips on her fingers was almost too much to bear. She wanted to scream, or run away, or fling herself at him, so she just stood where she was, gaping at him like a fool while her whole body trembled.

"All better," he said. He released her hand, but she didn't lower it from his face.

"Will you ever tell me your name?" she whispered.

"Sebastian. And what do I call you?" He looked down along the front of her ripped dress, then quickly looked away.

"Juliana."

"Where do we go now, Juliana?" He smirked a little. "I don't think the good reverend will want me back after I helped you. I'm tired of making him look holy, anyway."

"Why did you do it in the first place?"

"I don't know, it's not a bad job. Lots of travel, helping people who need it. You meet lots of interesting people, too, like mysterious pretty girls with a lethal touch."

"Have you met many of them?" she asked, and he laughed. He looked her over, and his gaze warmed her body.

"Have you had this your entire life?" He touched the palm of her hand.

"Yes."

"Me, too. But yours must have been a little more...difficult."

"I've survived."

"You live here in Missouri?"

"No, I'm with a carnival." She smiled. "I'm the freak show special attraction. The World's Most Diseased Woman."

"I've heard about your carnival. I've been meaning to go, but the boss won't give me a break..."

"We can go now! If we circle back south." She looked up at the dark sky. "I have to perform tonight, anyway. Can you take me?"

"I've got no job and a stolen horse," he said. "A man can't be more free than that. We can go wherever you want."

"Thank you."

"Are you sure that's what you want? Staying with the carnival?"

"Why not?"

"It just seems like you'd get tired of people staring at you, like you're some kind of..."

"I'm a freak whether I'm in the show or not. I might as well get paid for it. It's better than stealing for a living."

"Sure, but there must be other work out there."

"Like what? I can't work with people, can't even touch animals. In the sideshow tent, I can see people all day and not worry about whether they're going to brush against me. Being a carnie is the most honest work I can manage."

He laughed. "Honest work as a carnie."

"And what were you doing? Helping some guy run a revival-tent scam."

"It wasn't a scam," he said. "People actually got healed."

"And I really am the world's most diseased woman. You're just lucky you were born with something that actually helps people."

"We're exact opposites, you know that?" He stepped closer, looking down into her eyes. "That's what I thought, when I saw the disease taking him over. Another person like me, but opposite." He took her hands in his. "It's in our touch. I have to touch people to fix them."

"I can't touch anyone," she whispered.

"You can touch me all you want," he said. From his twisted grin, she knew he was trying to joke, but his words made her tremble. She released his hands and reached up to his face, then his neck. His skin felt hot beneath his uneven stubble. His hands found their way to her waist.

"Have you never kissed anyone?" he whispered.

"Never."

Without another word—or bothering to ask permission—he lowered his face to hers and gently kissed her lips. She felt like she'd been set on fire, her body glowing with heat.

The kiss lasted a long time. When he drew back, their eyes were locked on each other. Something had happened. She could feel a deep sense of connection with this boy, like it had been waiting there all her life, just waiting to wake up.

"We'd better keep moving," she whispered.

"If that's what you want." He gazed at her for another long moment before turning toward the horse.

She touched her lips. Her hand was shaking.

As they rode on, she held tight to him, but reminded herself that she'd only just met him. She couldn't trust him, not yet, no matter what intense feelings he brought up inside of her. He'd helped her, but she began to realize that he was also the only person in the world who could hurt her. Without the demon plague, she was defenseless against him. The thought was scary but thrilling.

The horse walked into the fairgrounds just before dawn, and they stabled him with the Wild West horses. Inside Juliana's tent, she heaved the blankets from her cot onto the canvas floor, and they lay together. Juliana knew it wasn't proper, but she was far too tired to find him a different spot. Fortunately, he was far too tired to try anything, if he'd intended to.

She slept with her back against him, his arm around her, and his hand just happened to lay across her breasts as he fell asleep. She smiled to herself.

# Chapter Eight

Dr. Heather Reynard worked late in her office. It would cost more with the babysitter, but budget committees needed their reports. Life in academia wasn't exactly the pastoral, leisurely life she'd imagined when she'd left the Centers for Disease Control, but there was a lot less flying into war-torn regions to live in a tent surrounded by the sick and the starving. Everything had its trade-offs.

She emailed the report to her department head, then stood and stretched, ready to jump into Atlanta traffic for the slow ride home. She'd been extremely fortunate to get a post at Emory University, not far from her home in the Virginia Highlands, even if it was only a part-time associate professorship. Her commute ranged from three minutes to half an hour, depending on the time of day and the never-ending road construction.

She glanced out the window and smiled at the sight of a boy and a girl next to each other on the grassy lawn below. Studying their biology texts while thinking about each other's personal biology.

The door to her office opened. A man in a black suit entered without knocking, and despite the smile on his face, something about him chilled Heather. He was in his late forties or early fifties, his dark hair graying and cropped close and neat, military-style. His dark green eyes seemed to glow with a wicked mirth.

"Dr. Heather Reynard." He looked over her crowded bookshelves and saw her Newton's Cradle, each ball painted a bright pattern of purples, red, oranges, and greens. They were meant to represent different icosahedral viruses, like influenza and rotavirus. A gift from Dr. Schwartzman, her former boss at the CDC, on her last day there after resigning.

Her visitor raised the ball at one end and released it, letting the row of them clack back and forth.

"I'm sorry, can I help you?" Heather remained where she was, standing behind her desk.

"I believe so." He advanced into her office, his smile as warm as winter in Siberia. "We need to talk, Dr. Reynard."

"You know, I have an appointment right now, actually," Heather said. "So maybe you can call our receptionist tomorrow, set up a time for a meeting."

"Appointment?" The man held up what looked like a Blackberry phone. "No, I don't see anything here. You made a note to pick up eggs and milk, don't forget that."

"You hacked my phone?" Heather glanced at the bottom desk drawer, which held her purse. "Who are you?"

"I'm the man you've been waiting for."

"Excuse me?"

"Surely you've been expecting someone to come along, one day or another. There are a few too many loose ends, aren't there, Dr. Reynard?"

"I don't know what you're talking about." Heather reached for her drawer. She wanted access to both her phone and her pepper spray. "I really have to get going."

"Fallen Oak," he said. "Over two hundred dead. Extreme symptoms of biological illness, but with no known source, no known vector. No virus or bacterium ever isolated. All evidence incinerated. On your recommendation, Dr. Reynard."

"I'm not free to discuss specific cases or investigations," Heather replied. "You'll have to contact the CDC public information office."

"Don't be absurd. I've already read all your reports, patchy and inconclusive as they are."

"And who are you, again?"

"Why don't we sit down?" he asked.

"Why don't I call campus security?" she replied.

He smirked. He was jaw was squarish, his lips bloodless and thin. He almost had a case of missing mouth syndrome, until he bared his teeth in a smile.

"Here." He showed her a laminated badge with the seal of the Department of Defense—a golden eagle clutching arrows and an American flag shield—and his own photograph. According to the badge, his name was Ward Kilpatrick, and he was a lieutenant general.

"Then you should know that the details of Fallen Oak have been classified by the Department of Homeland Security. You'll have to speak with them." Heather pulled her purse over her shoulder and stepped around her desk. Ward stood between her and the door, blocking her way with the help of Heather's own bookshelves, boxes, and clutter. "If you'll excuse me," Heather added.

"I'm sorry, Dr. Reynard. You won't be leaving yet." Behind him, in the hallway, two more men emerged from either side of her door. They were much younger, dressed in dark suits and sunglasses, clearly his assistants, or his muscle. "Close the door, Buchanan. We're having a private conversation."

One of the men shut Heather's door without saying a word. They would remain outside, but clearly, Heather wouldn't get far if she tried to leave. Her heart pounded in her ears. She was trapped.

"Dr. Reynard," he said. "Because of your years of federal service, I'm going to level with you. I'm currently the director of a defense intelligence agency whose name you would not recognize, nor could you find it in any official budget or organization chart. We have been here since the earliest days of the Cold War, watching, studying...Our focus is on identifying threats and opportunities that lie outside the typical military paradigms. Homeland Security? To us, they're just the courtesy officer tooling around your local mall in a golf cart."

"They have all the information," Heather said. She was scared, but she made an effort to look calm. She didn't want him to see her tremble.

"Why did you resign from the CDC?"

"I was tired of being away from my family all the time."

"Oh, yes." Ward took a framed family picture from her desk. "Liam. And little Tricia, five years old. She was dying of leukemia, wasn't she? Until, one day, she wasn't."

"She's in remission."

"Oh, no. We've reviewed her records. She's cured. Like she never had it at all."

"No one's ever really 'cured' from cancer. There's always the possibility—"

"Nobody except your daughter and several other children on the same ward, at the same time," he said. "Miraculous, isn't it?"

"We're very grateful for her improvement—"

Ward smashed the family picture on the corner of her desk, and Heather jumped as fragments of glass sprayed everywhere. He threw the broken frame on the floor.

"Don't give me that," he growled. His green eyes burned bright. "The probability is off the charts. What happened at the hospital that night?"

"It must have been God," Heather said. "That's what everybody tells me."

"God." Ward smirked at her. "I don't believe in God, Dr. Reynard. But I believe in the devil. I believe he's in all of us, that he *is* us..." He stalked closer to her, and Heather backed up until she bumped against her desk. His voice dropped to a whisper as he leaned in close, his breath hot and sour on her cheek. "Tell me, Heather. What is the source of Fallen Oak syndrome? Why did you want every victim, and every inch of that old mansion, incinerated?"

"The pox," she said. "It had to be stopped. It could have become an epidemic overnight. Virulent. Contagious. Airborne."

"No," he said, stepping even closer, until she could see nothing in the world but his face. "I want the whole story."

"Get back," Heather whispered. She eased her hand toward her purse. Three-star general or not, he was going to get eyeballs full of pepper spray if he didn't step out of her personal space.

He grabbed her head in both hands and stared into her eyes. Heather's hand dove inside her purse, but then she felt like she was twisting and falling, suddenly lost in her own memories. She could feel him penetrating deep inside her brain, and she had no way of stopping it.

She flashed through her initial epidemiological investigation of Fallen Oak, the interviews with Darcy Metcalf and other locals, the tissue samples....Then she saw the true source of the outbreak, a small, sad-looking girl named Jennifer Morton....Not an immune carrier, as it turned out, because there *was* no biological vector. Combined with the zombies caught on video in a Charleston morgue, Heather was reluctantly realizing that the situation had to be supernatural, contrary to all her own beliefs....

...and then Seth Barrett, healing Tricia's leukemia. And then Heather standing by the blazing ruin of Barrett House, promising to help Jenny and Seth, to report them dead and strongly recommend that everything be incinerated...And the next day, Heather watching from a truck as men in biohazard suits loaded corpse after corpse into an incinerator truck. The demolition of the burned-out old mansion, the earth scorched with flamethrowers.

"Jennifer Morton," Ward said. "And she's still alive. Where?"

Heather gasped as the man stabbed deep into her brain, scouring it for information that wasn't there.

"Where?" he shouted again, shaking her. "Where?"

"I don't know!" Heather screamed.

Ward released her and stepped back as Heather sank to the floor, weeping uncontrollably. Her brain felt like someone had torn through it with a claw hammer. Her head would ring and ache for days.

"Thank you, Dr. Reynard," he said, adjusting his tie. "I suppose that was as helpful as you could be. Should you get the urge to tell anyone about my small, unimportant visit, I'll remind you that you falsified your reports on this matter and helped a mass murderer escape. We'll be monitoring your communications to ensure you remember to keep quiet. A little added service from me." He winked as he opened the door. "Have a pleasant evening, Dr. Reynard."

Heather remained sitting on the floor while she watched him leave, her skin crawling with horror. She barely understood what had just happened, but she felt painfully violated.

When he walked out into the hall, Heather crawled across the carpet, slammed the door, and turned the lock. She leaned against the door and tried to get herself together. It was a long time before she felt safe leaving her office and walking to the parking deck.

# Chapter Nine

In Fallen Oak, the front gate to the Barrett House property was secured by lengths of chain and padlocks. Ward's assistants, Buchanan and Avery, made short work of them with bolt-cutters, and then pushed open the heavy steel gate doors, which were flanked by very old stone lions.

Ward walked along the brick driveway, followed by the two younger men. Beyond a few ancient, mossy oaks near the front of the drive, the place looked like a wasteland. A huge amount of earth had been scorched black, any trees or grass long gone. In the year since Homeland Security had razed the place, spindly purple and pink flowers had colonized the vast burn scar.

The house itself was nothing but rubble, but from the few blackened hunks of brick wall that remained, Ward could see it had been an impressive structure at one time.

"They worked it over pretty good," Ward said, kicking a cracked piece of the driveway. "Didn't leave much for us to find, did they?"

"Sir," Avery said, "As far as we can tell, the boy's parents are at their house in Saint Augustine."

"I know," Ward told him. "The bad news is that his mother's name is Iris Mayfield Barrett, the niece of Senator Junius Mayfield, who sits on the Armed Services Committee. That could get tricky. Good news is the senator just recently had a stroke and he's in critical condition. If the old bastard would hurry up and die, we'd have less to worry about."

"Should I put in a call?" Avery asked.

"Avery..." Ward sighed and shook his head. Buchanan had half a brain, but Ward just regarded Avery as extra muscle. "I will never tell you to make a call like that about a person like that."

"Yes, sir."

"We're going to focus on softer targets for now," Ward told them. "The Morton girl's father, and any other witnesses who might have something useful. I don't think we'll find much here..." Ward looked at a distant brick structure on a low hill, back behind where the house had stood. "What is that?"

"Looks like a walled garden, sir," Buchanan said, squinting his eyes.

"It's the only thing standing. Might as well check it out. We're not going to find anything in this rubble." Ward led the way around the foundation of the house and on through the torched remains of what might have been an orchard or a stand of decorative trees. Large slabs of dark gray granite led up the hill to a tall wrought-iron gate, which stood wide open. They had to step high, as if the stairs were meant for larger beings than humans. They reminded Ward of old megalithic structures he'd seen on the History Channel, where some moron was always claiming Stonehenge was built by aliens.

If extraterrestrials were visiting the planet, Ward's agency would have known about it. The Anomalous Strategic Threat Research and Intelligence Agency (ASTRIA) was not known to the public. Their mission, dating back to the Eisenhower administration, had generally been to focus on "unknown unknowns," in the words of a more recent Secretary of Defense. Originally founded in response to reports that the Soviet Union was investigating the use of psychics for intelligence-gathering and other strategic purposes, ASTRIA had looked into matters ranging from the supernatural to the extraterrestrial...almost never finding anything of importance to national security. Almost.

They walked through the open gate. Inside, there tall blocks of dark granite, arranged in rows, many of them inscribed with names but not dates. Each row had a generation of people named

JONATHAN SETH BARRETT, followed by a Roman numeral. The most recent date that had been carved belong to the boy for whom they were searching: JONATHAN SETH BARRETT IV. It had a birth year, but no death year. Next to it was CARTER MAYFIELD BARRETT, born a few years before Seth, dead at the age of fourteen.

"What is this place?" Ward muttered.

"Looks like a graveyard, sir," Avery replied.

"I can see that. Looks like a graveyard for generations of people who haven't been born yet. Fucking rich weirdos," Ward muttered.

The earth in front of Carter's grave was churned up like something had dug its way in or out. As Ward continued walking, he saw all of the graves with death dates were like that.

"What the hell happened here?" Ward asked. "Don't see why Homeland Security would dig up all these graves."

"Maybe they didn't, sir," Buchanan said. "It could be like the security video from the morgue in Charleston. The walking dead, sir."

"The walking dead." Ward frowned. They even had the "zombie master" on video, for what it was worth. A grainy image of a tall guy in dark sunglasses with longish hair. "How many paranormals are we talking about now? The little diseased girl, the healing rich kid, and some zombie master guy? I believe we have stepped into some shit here, gentlemen." One of the dark granite slabs near the back was labeled JONATHAN SETH BARRETT. "This must have been a hell of a guy, this first Jonathan Seth Barrett. They planned to name unborn generations after him. What kind of freaks are we dealing with?"

Buchanan wore a thoughtful look. Avery blew his nose into a handkerchief.

"Getting a cold, Avery?" Ward asked.

"Must be allergies, sir." Avery wiped his eyes.

"Get it together, Avery," Ward said. He looked around the churned-up graveyard one more time. "There's nothing for us here. Let's move on to the next objective."

They returned to their black Chrysler 300C sedan, which was modified with armored plates inside the body panels and bulletproof glass for the windows. It was faster and quieter than when it had arrived from the factory, and loaded with heavily encrypted communications equipment that was a bit more advanced than what was available on the open market. Despite all this, it looked like a perfectly normal car, at least to the casual observer.

They crossed through the decaying, boarded-up town. The largest remaining employer in the area, Winder Timber Processing, had shut down a year earlier. It had belonged to the mayor of Fallen Oak, who had died along with his wife and daughter the day little Jenny decided to kill a crowd of people. The records showed Mayor Winder's relatives had inherited the business, taken one look at the books, and closed it down and sold off the machinery. Fallen Oak's population was shrinking rapidly now. Ward doubted if anyone would still live here in ten years, except maybe a handful of elderly types with Social Security checks and nowhere to go.

The sedan's information system had a few features that OnStar didn't, including instant access to anyone's financial, medical, criminal, and military records. It guided them to the red-dirt driveway of a rickety old house half-hidden in the woods outside town. A rusty dodge Ram squatted in the driveway. Darrell Morton was home.

"So this is where our little monster grew up," Ward said from where he sat in the back seat. Avery and Buchanan were up front. "What a pathetic hellhole."

Avery hurried to open Ward's door. Ward led the way to the sagging boards of the front steps, automatically glancing in every direction, including up at the roof, watching for any sign of danger, anyone who might be hiding among the dense autumn leaves of the branches overhead. This was second nature to him. The leaves crunched under their shoes—otherwise, it was a quiet afternoon.

Inside the house, a man in a ragged t-shirt approached the screen door and looked out. The front door had already been open, indicating a possible lack of any centralized climate control. Ward knew this man could barely afford to get by month to month. He wondered how growing up in such an environment might have shaped Jennifer Morton's mind.

"Darrell Morton," Ward said as he climbed the creaky steps, followed by the two other men.

"Yeah?" The unshaven man in the dusty jeans looked out at them suspiciously. He was in his forties, but looked older.

"I'm Special Agent Ward Adams. Federal Bureau of Investigation." Ward held up the Department of Justice badge, which was only half-fake. Anyone who called up the FBI to ask would be told he was a real agent, though almost nobody bothered to check once they saw the badge. "We just need to ask you a couple of quick questions, and then we'll get out of your way."

The man froze where he stood. He obviously knew exactly why the FBI would be visiting.

"What's the trouble?" Darrell Morton asked in a shaky voice.

"We're looking into some events that happened here in town last Easter," Ward said. "Chemical leak from an old factory. Lots of people dead."

"Um..." Darrell looked confused. "I don't know much about that."

"We understand your daughter was involved," Darrell said. "She was among the deceased, is that right?"

"Yeah. I mean, no. I mean, yeah, she died, but it was in a fire at the old Barrett house. About a year ago." He was looking away and avoiding eye contact. Lying, and not very good at it.

"The fire at the Barrett house is also of interest to us," Ward said. "You see, Mr. Morton, your daughter's remains were not found. She may still be alive."

Darrell's widened and he took a step back from the screen door. "No, she was there. If she was still alive, she'd be back home. I haven't seen her since the fire."

"That's our concern," Ward said. "It's possible she could have been injured or kidnapped. Perhaps even suffered amnesia. We just won't know until we piece together what really happened the night of the fire, will we, Mr. Morton?"

"I don't want to dredge all this up," Darrell Morton said. "If she was alive, I'd know it." He started to close the wooden front door inside the screen.

Ward opened the screen door and blocked him from closing the inner door.

"Mr. Morton, if there's even the smallest chance your daughter is still alive, wouldn't you want to know about it? I have three kids of my own, and as a parent, I just can't understand your reaction." Ward actually had no children, and was not even married.

"I know what happened," Darrell said, still trying to close the door as Ward held it open. "Please. You can't stir up all this."

"Mr. Morton." Ward gave the door a hard shove, swinging it wide open and sending the man stumbling backward into his own house.

Darrell caught himself on the arm of a worn old sofa.

Ward advanced into the house, followed by Buchanan and Avery.

"Hey, you can't come in here! This is private property," Darrell said. "You got to have a warrant."

"If you want to be picky about it, yes," Ward said, moving closer still to the scared man. Ward's hand eased toward the shoulder holster hidden beneath his coat. It held a rare German machine pistol, the VP70M, a classic piece that had cost him a chunk of money, but he loved it. He rarely got to use it, unfortunately. He had no intention of shooting Darrell Morton today, but country dwellers sometimes had impressive arsenals in their homes, and it was best to be ready for it.

"Get out of my house," Darrell said quietly, folding his arms. "Unless you got a warrant."

"There is a slight problem with the warrant situation," Ward said. "You see, we're not actually from the FBI."

Darrell turned and ran toward the hall—probably to his bedroom to grab a firearm, Ward assumed. Ward drew his pistol and fired a three-round burst into the ceiling above Darrell's head. The man ducked low, slowing enough that Avery and Buchanan had no trouble grabbing him and hauling him back. They turned him to face Ward.

This was exactly why Ward traveled with two men instead of just Buchanan. Two trained soldiers were capable of restraining just about any normal individual so Ward could concentrate on his own special work.

"Mr. Morton," Ward said. "You must know that your daughter is a mass murderer. You must know that she is a potential threat to national security. Your own wife ran away after her birth...or did she run away at all, Mr. Morton? What about that fire at the county hospital, Mr. Morton? A doctor and a nurse both dead. It was twenty years ago, right about the time little Jenny was born...am I right?"

Darrell just stared at him.

"I think Jenny killed your wife, didn't she?" Ward spoke in a lower voice, moving closer to Darrell. "And you hid it. All to protect a baby who would one day grow up and kill your town. And what will she do next, Mr. Morton? How many more people must die? Why do you protect her?"

"She's dead," Darrell said. "There's nothing I can do."

"Don't lie to me!" Ward punched the man in the mouth, hard enough to draw blood from his lip. "I can't stand liars, Mr. Morton."

"I got nothing else to say to you," Darrell said. He spat blood in Ward's face.

Ward charged as a blind fury descended over him. He pounded on Darrell's face, then punched him in the stomach. By the time Ward regained his senses, he had Darrell lying on the floor and was repeatedly kicking the man's ribs with his steel-toed leather loafer, with additional assistance from a chuckling Avery.

"Stop, stop," Ward said, shaking his head. "Need him alive. For a few more minutes, anyway."

Ward squatted on the floor next to the groaning, bleeding Darrell Morton.

"We know your daughter is alive," Ward told him. "We need to know where she is before she kills again. This is your last chance."

Darrell blinked and didn't say a word.

"All right, Mr. Morton." Darrell seized both sides of the man's head and shoved his way inside, ripping through terabytes of the man's memory. He found the earliest that interested him: Darrell's wife, Miriam, dying horrifically as she gave birth to Jenny. The doctor and nurse that had ended up dead from Jenny's touch, too. Darrell setting the place on fire, taking his baby and his deceased wife with him. The wife had been buried under a stone cairn right here, in the woods on the Morton property. Darrell's struggle to raise his daughter without touching her, using gloves and even ski masks. Like a man caring for a pet scorpion, pouring his love onto something hideous. Pathetic.

Darrell knew that his daughter had killed a large number of people in town, that she'd faked her own death with the fire, that she was still alive somewhere.

Unfortunately, Darrell did not know where. He only knew that it was being handled somehow by the Barretts, the rich, connected family of Jenny's consort, Seth Barrett. The family Ward couldn't risk disturbing, not while Senator Mayfield remained alive. It made perfect sense, and it was damned inconvenient for Ward.

Something unexpected jutted out from Darrell's memories. The night of the riot in Charleston, a young man with dirty blond hair and odd gray eyes had broken into Darrell's house and attacked him. He'd seized Darrell's arms and filled him with mind-shattering nightmares. The next clear memory was of Darrell waking up in the hospital and leaving, turning down the recommended psychiatric evaluation, partly because he had neither the insurance nor the money to pay for it.

The boy had a touch that spread fear. Darrell did not seem to know anything else about him.

Ward released the man's head, letting it thump back onto the warped hardwood floor.

"Watch him," Ward told his men. He walked down the hall, pulling on a pair of green biohazard gloves, its molecules woven so tightly that even the smallest scrap of a virus couldn't pass through.

He passed a bathroom and glanced without interest into the open door of the man's room. Another bedroom door stood closed. Jenny's room. Ward turned the handle.

The room was small, with a single bed, a record player and a box of records. Clothes were spilling out of the dresser drawers and scattered on the floor as if the girl still lived here. A bookshelf held some ragged paperbacks, mostly cheap horror novels and some poetry, as well as homemade attempts at pottery. A picture of Jenny's long-dead mother on the wall. Faded posters featured old country singers like Loretta Lynn.

One poster showed The Cure, the sissy English band kept alive by generations of sissy teenagers. Ward snorted, taken back to his teenage years in East St. Louis. He and his buddies had once stomped a few frilly brats outside a Cure concert. Later in life, he'd joined the Army, which he saw as the best way to escape the dying city and do a few important things in the world.

From the start, Ward had been nothing like the average soldier. He'd seen most of the recruits around him as either idealistic do-gooders or clueless kids, born without Ward's instinctive understanding of power, or his paranormal edge.

With a touch, Ward could see anyone's past. His ability to extract information from anyone had landed him a job with military intelligence. Ward had always employed textbook interrogation tactics as a performance for his commanding officers, but they were just for show.

He'd also learned he could he advance his career quickly by gathering dirt on his superiors. A well-placed comment or two would make it clear that he knew the officer was embezzling, cheating on his wife, or had a vast collection of boy porn at home.

He'd gone through Officer Candidate School and quickly scaled the bureaucracy, even gathering secrets on American politicians who were deemed obstacles to national security. He'd taken over the top-secret ASTRIA—where he was able to operate with an unusual lack of oversight, as the agency was both classified and no longer of great interest to the Pentagon—out of a desire to find others like himself. It looked like that choice was starting to pay off.

Ward marched back up the hall.

"Pack it up," he told his two men. "Everything in the girl's room, every stick of furniture. I want it all for analysis."

"You can't take Jenny's things," Darrell protested weakly, from where the two men held him to the floor. "That's all I got left of her."

"So sad," Ward replied. "Tie him up and stuff him out of the way."

"Sir, we might need a van or a truck to move the furniture," Buchanan said.

"Then call for one. And nobody goes in there without gloves and a mask. Place is probably crawling with toxins," Ward told him.

Ward stepped outside while Avery tied up the man, who was so badly beaten he could barely protest as Avery shoved him into the coat closet.

Buchanan joined Ward on the front porch.

"There's a fourth one," Ward told him.

"A fourth paranormal, sir?"

"Might be the most dangerous of all. His touch spreads fear."

"Do we have a name, sir?"

"Just a face. I'd need a sketch artist to render it. We have a lot to do, Buchanan, but it's all turning into dead ends down here. We need to talk to the Barretts. Let's pray God sees fit to let Senator Mayfield die. Until then, we'd better get back to Virginia and crunch what we've learned here, get our data miners working. Determine our next step. Now, call someone for me."

"Yes, sir." Buchanan made a call.

Later, a team arrived with a small truck and full-body hazardous material suits. They picked Jenny's room clean, taking everything from her bed to the small picture of Jenny and Seth Barrett tucked into the corner of her mirror. Ward wanted to see what a biochemical analysis might reveal, and to find whether Jenny had left him any clues to her next destination.

When Jenny's room lay bare, and all the other men had left the house, Ward opened the coat closet door. Darrell Morton, though bound, gagged, bruised, and bloodied, gave him a defiant look.

Ward cut away the rope from his hands and mouth.

"Mr. Morton," he said, "There is no reason you should tell anyone about our visit today. If you do, you will be punished. We'll be watching and listening from now until the end of your life, which could be very soon, or could be many years from now. Think about that."

Ward stood and walked out the door.

# Chapter Ten

Jenny ate an unspeakably delicious slice of mushroom pizza with a rich, spicy tomato sauce, sitting alone at an outdoor table at L'Oraziano, directly across the street from the high glass facade of the economics school. She had a weird craving to smear a glop of peanut butter on top of the pizza, but she didn't have a jar handy. As best as she could tell, she was about three months pregnant, and she was starting to feel it.

Mariella Visconti had not bothered her again, but Jenny had continued thinking about the girl as the weeks passed. It made Jenny uneasy to know that another of her kind might be right here in Paris, one who was searching for Seth and already knew where Jenny lived.

Jenny was allegedly shopping for Thanksgiving dinner. Of course, in Paris it was just another Thursday, but it would be nice to have something that reminded them of home.

This was the third day she'd slipped off to spy on Mariella. So far as she could tell, Mariella had told the truth—she did live in a student apartment building near the Sorbonne, where she attended classes at the Broca Center, the business school, as well as the Saint-Charles Center, which housed the school of art and cinema. Today, she'd come to the economics building, which was far from the rest of the campus. Jenny watched and waited for her to come out.

If the girl was like her and Seth, then she posed a serious threat. Jenny couldn't stand not knowing. She had to determine whether the girl had a supernatural touch like her, and what it was, and what the girl's intentions might really be. Watching Mariella go to class or hang out with other students at cafes and wine bars wasn't telling her much, unfortunately.

Jenny had a sense of growing urgency, as if time were short. She tried to pretend that it didn't have anything to do with the baby growing inside her, or her insane wish that the baby could live, that she and Seth could start a family. Thinking about it only led to pain...but still, she couldn't help feeling more worried and more alert to danger.

Jenny decided not to wait any longer.

She wolfed down her food, to the disgust of two women at the next table, and then hurried out.

When Mariella emerged from the front door of the building, Jenny just happened to be strolling slowly along the sidewalk, and she just happened to glance up and make eye contact with Mariella. A look of recognition flashed across Mariella's face, followed by excitement. Jenny acted surprised to see her, then wrinkled her brow as if trying to remember who Mariella was.

"Have you seen him?" Mariella asked, looking up and down the street. Mariella wore gloves, a long jacket, and a scarf, and most of her hair was gathered into a soft cloth hat. Like Jenny, Mariella bundled up before going out in public.

"I'm sorry, who?" Jenny replied.

"The boy. Do you not remember me?"

Jenny looked at her for a few seconds. "Aren't you that girl who came by my apartment? Looking for some guy?"

"That is me." Mariella's smile faded as she realized Jenny hadn't come to tell her she'd found Seth. "How did you find me here?"

"I was just having lunch." Jenny pointed across the street. "I was walking by, and I had a feeling that I should stop here. So I did." Jenny shrugged.

"Do you get strange feelings sometimes?" Mariella's voice dropped to a whisper, and she glanced over her shoulder, as if afraid a student or teacher would hear her. "About the future?"

"I get strange feelings about everything," Jenny said, and Mariella surprised her by laughing. "Can you see the future?" Jenny asked. "Does it happen when you touch people?"

"How could you know this?" Mariella's eyes widened, and she looked at Jenny's hands, gloved in powder-blue silk. "We should walk away from the school."

They went south down Boulevard de l'Hopital, along a broad sidewalk decorated with stands of trees gone skeletal in late November. The baroque and Art Noveau architecture gave the entire evening a dreamlike atmosphere as the glowing spheres of the streetlamps came to life.

"Tell me what you know," Mariella whispered.

"About what?"

"About anything. About all of it."

Jenny looked at the girl's earnest face and almost felt sorry for her.

"You tell me," Jenny said. "You touch someone, you can see the future?"

"Just the future of that person, which keeps things fuzzy," Mariella told her. "And the future can change if you tell them about it, but it rarely does. I see their futures whether they want me to or not. Even if I don't want to see—that's why I wrap myself up in public. If I don't, I'm overwhelmed with glimpses of everyone's future. And that can be very sad and depressing. But here, I'll show you." Mariella took off a glove and reached for Jenny's hand.

"No!" Jenny pulled back quickly.

"I'm sorry." Mariella smiled. "Not everyone wants to know their future."

"Well...that's true," Jenny said, taking advantage of the excuse Mariella had just provided for her. "I don't think I'd want to know." The exact opposite was true. Jenny was eager to know what lay ahead, especially for the baby. "Can you see your own future?"

"That's the most difficult," Mariella said. "Because, when you see your own future, you react to it in the present, and that changes the future. Over and over. My own is almost entirely a blur. Only a few things stand out clear and strong."

"What kinds of things?"

"Like the boy I told you about." She gave a glowing smile at the thought of Seth, which did not make Jenny very happy at all. "I can see him in my future. I knew I would meet him in Paris. This is why

I came to school in France."

"What...kinds of things do you see?"

"It is more of a sensation. An aching here..." Mariella touched her chest. "Almost like being lovesick. It is ridiculous, but...do you believe in reincarnation?"

Jenny, who could remember lifetime after lifetime stretching back tens of thousands of years, shrugged. "I suppose anything is possible."

"What if he is my soulmate?" Mariella asked. "Maybe that's why I have such...passionate dreams about him." The girl blushed and giggled, and Jenny resisted the urge to smack her across the face, pox and all. "I just wish I could find him. I know that when I do, my life will finally start to make sense."

Jenny didn't have much to say about that. They approached *Place d'Italie*, a ring of parks centered on a fountain. Jenny could hop onto the Metro and escape here. She wasn't sure she was ready to hear more about Mariella's passionate dreams of Seth.

"What about you?" Mariella asked. "What's your secret?"

"Who says I have one?"

"You can tell me." Mariella bumped her arm and snickered, almost as if they were friends. "You know about me. What can you do? There's something in your touch, too, isn't there?" She reached for Jenny's hand again.

"Don't." Jenny tucked her hand in her jacket pocket.

"What happens to you when someone touches you?" Mariella asked.

"Nothing," Jenny said. "Nothing happens to me at all."

"Am I misunderstanding something?" Mariella frowned at her. Her full lower lip made a cute little pout when she frowned, which made Jenny want to upgrade from smacking her to scratching her. "You seemed to know me. I thought..." A sad look crept into her bright green eyes, and she looked away.

"What did you think?"

"I thought you were someone like me. How did you know so much?"

"I'm not like you," Jenny said.

"Did you once know someone like me? Is that it?" Mariella looked hopeful. "Maybe you have seen the boy I need?"

"There is no boy."

"I have to go," Mariella said, checking the time on her phone.

"Can we talk again? Over a nice bottle of wine, maybe? I would like to hear more of your thoughts. Although you must think I am out of my mind now." She gave a small, awkward smile.

Jenny looked over the pretty Mediterranean girl in the pricey high-fashion clothes. Part of her already hated Mariella for her interest in Seth. Another part of her felt bad for the girl, who'd clearly stumbled through life without meeting anyone like herself, something Jenny fully understood. Now Mariella was trying to reach out to her own kind—unfortunately for her, most of their kind tended to be wicked, ruthless, and deceptive. Jenny herself had always been a powerful evil force. She was working her hardest to change that, but very few of her past-life memories gave any guidance on how to live with the pox and still be a good person.

Yet another part of Jenny recognized that the girl could be tricking her in any number of ways. Maybe she was another Ashleigh, capable of charming people while plotting to ruin them. Jenny decided to listen to that part of her, the one that said to trust no one and avoid contact with others as much as possible. It was how she'd survived her life so far.

"Do you want to give me your mobile number?" Mariella asked as Jenny approached the escalator that would take her underground to the Metro station. Mariella had a look in her eyes that bordered on desperation.

Jenny's heart almost went out to her, but she stopped herself. The only safe choice was to run the girl off forever. Jenny glanced around to make sure no one was looking at them, and she peeled off her gloves.

"Do you know what my touch does?" Jenny asked her, stepping on the escalator. "It brings pain and death. That's all I've ever been to anyone."

Jenny held up her bare hands. For a moment, she unleashed the pox, her hands and face rippling with gory disease. A look of terror filled Mariella's face as Jenny descended out of sight.

Jenny drew the pox back inside her and turned to face forward down the escalator. She heard the girl scream, and she smiled. Her past-life memories *did* provide plenty of tricks for striking fear into people. She'd always been good at that.

With any luck, she'd scared Mariella all the way back to Italy.

* * *

The bed in Jenny and Seth's apartment was a rococo-style antique with curving posters at the foot. The high headboard was carved with intricate little grapevines and cupids armed with love arrows., and the mattress was stuffed with goose down. Jenny had never slept in a more comfortable bed in her life, but lately she was having trouble sleeping at all.

She looked at Seth, who dreamed the night away beside her, his bare chest painted silver by the moonlight, a crooked, happy smile on his lips. What did he have to worry about? He didn't know she was pregnant, or that the baby was doomed. He didn't know that another one of their kind was trying to track him down.

She was fighting panic. Mariella claimed to see the future, and in that future, she saw herself and Seth together. Jenny wondered if it was true. How would Seth react if she told him she was pregnant, and then the pregnancy reached its inevitable, bloody end? How would he feel about her? He claimed not to care about having children, but he was still young. His mind could change, especially if he learned he'd fathered a child, and it had died.

Jenny regretted how she'd threatened Mariella, remembering from previous lives that the more she used the pox, the more likely she was to miscarry. Her moment of trying to scare the girl could have cost the baby's life. But the baby had no future anyway, so why should she worry about that?

Her thoughts kept swirling and pounding against the inside of her skull. She could sense everything going wrong, the magic carpet tearing beneath them.

Seth's eyes drifted open.

"What's wrong?" he mumbled.

*More than I can tell you,* Jenny thought.

"Nothing," she whispered. "Bad dreams."

"Sucks," he said. His eyes were barely open, and his blond hair stuck out in every direction. He put an arm around her.

Jenny had been having bad dreams, too. Telling Seth about their most recent life had stirred up those memories like angry hornets, and they kept intruding on her waking thoughts as well as her dreams. Alexander had purposely tried to block her memories of her most recent lives, while restoring hundreds of others. He'd wanted the old, evil Jenny back, not the new, slightly-less-evil version she'd become as she spent her recent lifetimes with the healer, Seth, instead of the dead-raiser, Alexander.

"There's more I didn't tell you about our last life," Jenny said. "The more I tell you, the more I remember."

"I thought we ran off with the circus and lived happily ever after."

"If 'happily ever after' lasts only a few weeks."

"It's over now. Long time ago." He turned away from her, leaving Jenny to stare up at the ceiling. She couldn't stop thinking about that life, which wasn't surprising, considering the specific things she was dealing with in the present. It seemed immediate to her, as if none of the problems from their previous life had been resolved, and they were all waiting to come back and haunt her.

Jenny closed her eyes, but she couldn't sleep.

# Chapter Eleven

Juliana stripped away her robe for the eight men who'd crowded into the back of the sideshow tent, smoking cigarettes and drinking whiskey from paper cups. They shouted and whistled as she bared herself—all of them except one. He stood watchfully in the back corner, his fedora pulled low, arms folded. He wore a suit instead of the frayed overalls and work shirts of the other men, and he wasn't drinking.

Juliana did not try to make her show alluring—the carnival had a special "model show" tent for that, where men could leer through a thin, gauzy curtain at women wearing little or no clothing. Still, on occasion, there would be a man who came back to her show day after day until the carnival left town, eyes hungry to see Juliana's pale, exposed body turn rotten with disease.

She did her best to avoid those men, who sometimes waited around outside the tent wanting to talk to her. She did not want to talk to them. This man was most likely one of those. He'd now come to see her three days in a row, ever since the carnival had arrived at the busy fairgrounds in Anderson County, South Carolina.

She gave the man no special notice at all as she slowly turned, letting the weeping, pus-dripping sores bloom slowly all over her.

The drunken men shouted and jostled each other, impressed by the apparent circus trick.

The man in the corner didn't join in the drunken laughter and applause. He had a shaggy beard and sharp eyes, and the squarish bearing of a police officer, which troubled her. Carnies always had to watch out for cops and usually had to pay "patch money" under the table to avoid being harassed. It wasn't normal for local cops to hit up individual performers for bribes, but anything was possible.

Juliana finished her show, and Radu ushered the men out. She sighed and let her aching legs rest a moment, then changed into a light dress made of cheap, lumpy cotton, and she tied her hair back with a scarf. She slipped out through the back of the tent and circled around behind game booths, emerging far down the midway, in case her obsessed fan in the fedora was looking for her.

She emerged from behind the Wheel of Chance and hurried across the midway, which grew dark as each booth shut down for the night, like clusters of stars vanishing from the sky. The stragglers wandered toward the gates. Only the grab joints remained open, selling off the last of their hot dogs and fried dough to the departing visitors.

She nodded at One-Eyed Filip, the middle-aged man who ran the haunted house. He claimed to have lost his eye in the war, but Juliana had heard it was actually from a knife fight in Budapest. He played it up as the host of the haunted house, rubbing black makeup around the hollow eye to make it seem even larger and darker.

He smiled, showing several missing teeth, and waved her into the haunted house through the tall front door, painted to look like an arched medieval gate surrounded by lurid green skulls.

She walked quickly through the dark, twisting corridor, ignoring the sounds of chains and screams. Little windows on either side of the hallway offered views into different "scary" rooms: a mortuary where a bloody arm reached out of a casket, a dungeon where skeletons and one very decayed body hung on the walls, a red-lit "Hell room" with devil mannequins around a tinfoil fire. In that room, other clumps of tinfoil glittered in "fireplaces" around the wall, which was decorated to look like a volcanic cave. Horned red bats with pointy wings flapped up and down near the ceiling, and the wires that held them up were almost impossible to see.

She looked in through another window at a "mad scientist's"

laboratory, decorated with jars full of disgusting items like fetal pigs, giant spiders, and a small monkey, all preserved in formaldehyde. A body lay under a sheet on the lab table. It slowly sat up, moaning with the agony of the undead, and the sheet tumbled down to reveal Sebastian, his face painted green, bolts glued to his neck. He rose stiffly from the table, holding his giant green hands out in front of him.

"Argh! Beware Frankenstein's monster!" he groaned at her, waving the big green hands in her direction.

"The monster doesn't talk," she reminded him.

"Argh...argh!" He staggered toward her and reached out his oversized, overstuffed green gloves to grab her through the window. "The monster is hungry!"

"The monster doesn't eat girls, either." She stepped back along the hall, out of his reach.

"Argh!" The big green hands retracted into the window. She waited for him to come out. And waited. He'd been working the haunted house for a couple of weeks, on top of general work as a roustabout. It had been his idea to add the movie monster Frankenstein to the exhibit of gross jars.

"Sebastian?" she asked. The haunted house had gone quiet, including the hidden phonographs. Filip was shutting down for the night, like everyone else, which meant the last paying customer was gone.

She heard footsteps, but they were from the wrong direction, back toward the front door.

"Filip?" she asked. "Is that you?"

Nobody answered. The footsteps came closer, approaching through the dim, twisting hallway.

She thought of the large man with the fedora and the wild beard. If he'd seen her, he might have followed her inside, slipping past Filip while he was busy closing up shop, or maybe knifing Filip to get him out of the way. He seemed like the kind of man who wouldn't think twice about killing someone.

She returned to the window and looked into the laboratory, but Sebastian was gone. A pickled pig fetus stared back at her from its jar.

"Sebastian?" she whispered as loud as she dared, and then someone grabbed her from behind and hauled her back off her feet.

She could feel the brushy beard against the back of her neck. He smelled like mothballs.

She screamed as she twisted herself back and forth, trying to wriggle and kick her way free, but his arms were strong and clutched her tight.

"Unhand me!" she shouted, letting the pox boil up to her skin. She clawed her nails across his leathery face and ripped out a fistful of his beard, but he only laughed.

"Unhand me?" He laughed harder, releasing her as he doubled over. "That's what you said! 'Unhand me!' Yes, right away, Your Majesty! I shall unhand thou!"

Juliana scowled. She'd known it was Sebastian the instant she'd heard his voice. He'd changed into a hairy werewolf mask, which she'd mistaken for a beard. She grabbed the mask off his head.

"Yow! You pulled my hair." He clapped an oversized hand to his head and looked pained. He still wore his green Frankenstein makeup, complete with fake stitches on his forehead.

"I think you will survive the injury," she said.

"Oh, sure. I can already feel the hairs growing back."

"Braggart." She looked around and saw that he'd pulled her back through a hidden door into the room with the devils and bats. "You've dragged me into Hell. What do you intend to do here?"

"We'll punish your sins." He pulled off the big green Frankenstein gloves and walked towards the biggest fireplace in the cave.

"I avoid sinning," she told him.

"Up the chimney you go. Victims first." He gestured inside the fake fire.

She leaned her head inside and looked up. The inner structure of the haunted house was bare here, the wooden beams and columns roped together where the different chunks of the house had been assembled after they were unloaded from the train. Exposed wooden rungs formed a ladder to the roof.

"We're climbing up?" she asked.

"Yes, Your Majesty, now that I've unhanded you, you may climb."

"You first." Juliana smiled. She watched him climb up through the dark space, then opened a trap door at the top, revealing a square of starry sky.

"Come on up," he called down to her. "The roof ghosts are in a friendly mood tonight."

"So long as the roof ghosts don't mind." Juliana climbed up after him.

They stood on a narrow wooden platform behind the plywood dormer windows, painted to look like cracked shingles and boards. The roof ghosts were just balls of rag cloth mounted on sticks, with sheets tied over them to flap and billow in the wind. From here, she could see the darkened midway spread out below.

"This carnival has everything backwards," he told her. "They put the freaky girls in the model show, and the pretty girls in the freak show. It makes no sense."

"You're dangerously close to being charming."

"I know. There's always danger in the air when I'm around."

"Are you going to kiss me or not?"

"That's an easy choice." He drew her close and gave her a long kiss, while her hands clasped behind his neck. The feeling of his body pressed against her made her shiver. Since joining the carnival, he'd slept in a cot in the crowded roustabout tent, but she was often tempted to invite him back to her personal tent instead. Tonight, she was in a very tempted sort of mood.

After a few minutes, she pulled back and smiled up at him. Her cheeks felt like they were caked in mud, and when she touched them, her fingers came away green.

"You got Frankenstein makeup all over me!" she said.

"Now you look like the Bride of Frankenstein."

"Frankenstein doesn't *have* a bride."

"Poor Frankenstein. One of my favorite picture shows."

"I would love to see a picture show with you." She rose on her tiptoes to bring her face closer. He kissed her again, but this time one of his hands slipped down her back to caress her bottom through her dress. She let out a delighted, surprised squeal into his mouth and pressed herself against his broad chest. Her body was flushed and heated. She tried to work up the nerve to whisper a suggestion in his ear, that they should both go to her tent.

Bright yellow light flooded the space behind her closed eyelids. She opened her eyes, blinking at the flashlight pointed at them from the ground below. They'd been caught, and anyone left on the midway could see them now, embracing, green Frankenstein paint smeared on her face.

"What are you kids doing up there?" Filip shouted.

"Ah..." Sebastian replied.

"Get down here! There's someone needs to talk to you. I'll unlock the front door." The flashlight swooped down to the entrance of the haunted house.

A minute later, the two of them emerged from the front door, looking sheepish. Filip shook his head at the sight of them.

"This man needs a word," Filip told them. He pointed his copper flashlight at a large man standing beside him, who had a thick beard and wore a suit and fedora.

Juliana jumped in surprise, then grabbed Sebastian's hand. It was her repeat customer, the man who stared at her a little too hard. He lit a cigar with a match.

"He's got a special offer for you," Filip said. "A side gig. Sounds like it pays well." Filip tapped a folded dollar bill jutting from his shirt pocket. The bearded man had clearly seen Juliana enter the haunted house and paid an entire dollar just for Filip to stick around and help him.

"I don't do private performances," Juliana said.

"Are you the ones who caused all the ruckus at the tent revival about a month ago? In Missouri?" the stranger asked.

"We don't know what you mean," Sebastian said quickly.

"In that case, I must be the country's worst detective," he said. "After interviewing all those witnesses and tracking down this carnival. If you were the ones I was looking for, I know a man who'd like to meet you. He'll pay you for your time. A sawbuck. Each." He held up a pair of bank-crisp ten-dollar bills.

Juliana's eyes bulged at so much money. Perhaps she *did* give private performances.

"Ten dollars for what?" Sebastian asked.

"We should take a walk." The man led them out to the center of the midway and strolled down it, away from the performance tents and toward the front gate. Filip departed in the opposite direction.

"I'm a private investigator," he told the two of them. "Currently on retainer for a man—an association of men, in fact—looking for people with...how do we say it? Unusual abilities. The 'supernormal,' they call it. Supernatural, even." He smoked his cigar, looking them over as if measuring them. They were out of earshot of the last remaining carnies, who were closing down the grab stands.

"Why?" Juliana asked.

"Explaining beyond that isn't my job. What I can tell you is that one of them lives here in South Carolina, and like I said, he's offering you ten dollars each just to sit and talk with him. You might get a good meal out of it, too."

"And what will we talk about?" Juliana asked.

The man shrugged.

"Is he here in town?" Sebastian asked.

"No, he's in a much bigger town, Fallen Oak. About two hundred miles southeast."

"Two hundred miles! We'll be gone for days." Juliana shook her head.

"That's what you might think, but I have a Ford Model 18. It has *eight* cylinders, can you imagine that? If we set out tomorrow at sunrise, we can be in Fallen Oak by lunchtime, you can be back to the carnival by dusk. Twenty dollars richer."

Sebastian and Juliana shared a look. It was a difficult offer to turn down.

"Personally, I don't know whether you two are 'supernormal' or whether you're just plain old hucksters," the detective added. "The man's made up his mind to see you. If I were you, I'd take the cash."

"What's his name?" Sebastian asked. "This man who wants to see us?"

"Jonathan Barrett. He's a big-timing banker around here. This association I mentioned, it involves a lot of men like that, bankers, businessmen, politicians...You could do well for yourself with them, if you're sharp." The detective stopped walking. They'd reached the end of the midway, and he looked over the padlocked sugar shack with its peeling painted clowns. "I'd say there's room for improvement in your future. These days, we all gotta watch for any chance we can get."

"Ten dollars is a lot of money..." Sebastian said. He gave Juliana a questioning look. She hesitated, then nodded.

"We'll go," he told the detective.

"Sunrise tomorrow," the detective said. "I'll meet you right here."

Filip was waiting by the locked front gate to let the detective out. Juliana watched him climb into a long black automobile with running boards beneath the doors. He cranked it up. The round headlights flared to life, like the glowing eyes of some demonic creature opening in the night, and the engine growled as the Model 18 pulled away from the fairgrounds and drove off down the dirt road.

"Fallen Oak," Juliana said. "That sounds like a creepy place."

"All of it sounds creepy," Sebastian said. "Whatever this banker guy says, we just say 'no' and pocket the money. Agree?"

"I agree," Juliana said, watching the lights of the car disappear through the trees.

"Wise choice," Filip said.

"Have a good night, Filip," Juliana said. She walked back into the fairgrounds, Sebastian at her side.

"Ah, Sebastian," Filip called after him. "I can see you've forgotten, but you did not help close down the house for the night. We still have work to do."

"Oh, sorry, Filip." Sebastian turned to Juliana and kissed her cheek. "Good night," he whispered in her ear.

"Good night," she whispered back. She watched the two of them return to the haunted house.

She glowed as she walked back to her tent, still feeling his lips on her face.

# Chapter Twelve

"Oh, come all ye faithful, joyful and triumphant...sing it, Nevaeh!" Darcy said, bobbing her head to the Casting Crowns CD as she strung lights on the tree in her apartment. Nevaeh, almost fourteen months old, rose onto her feet, giggling, and grabbed onto the strand of glowing, teardrop-shaped electric bulbs. She yanked them from the tree and tried to stuff the bright bulbs into her mouth.

"Nevaeh, stop that!" Darcy knelt and pulled the string of lights away from her.

The little girl screamed, her face turned red, and she grabbed insistently for the lights.

"Nevaeh, no! You'll shock yourself!" Darcy held the lights even farther away, and Nevaeh shrieked again, slapping Darcy in the face. "Nevaeh!" Darcy gasped.

Decorating the apartment for the holiday had been a struggle all along, from Nevaeh trying to eat the cotton lambs from the nativity scene to Darcy trying to figure just what in Juniper she was supposed to do with all the Catholic stuff Ramon's mom had given them, like statues and candles of saints.

She was Darcy Espinoza now, a clerk at Patterns & Pins in Columbia, but she thought she could make assistant manager in a few months if she played her cards right, and if Bernice retired when everyone expected her to. Her husband Ramon was a cook at a MexiCarolina fusion place. Ramon's mother lived here in Columbia, too, and she watched the baby a lot, which gave Ramon time to study culinary arts during the day. It also gave Darcy time to attend praise-based Christian aerobics class four times a week.

Darcy liked their little apartment in the city. Life felt like an adventure here, far away from all the misery of Fallen Oak. It was a pretty safe little adventure, and she liked that, too.

Darcy picked up Nevaeh and touched their noses together, looking into her baby's flat brown little eyes. They were just like her father's, Bret Daniels from Fallen Oak. Ramon wanted to have more babies, and Darcy hoped for a little boy next time, one she could give a pretty Spanish name.

"Oh come, let us adore Him," Darcy sang into her little girl's face. "Oh come, let us adore Him..."

A fist banged on her front door, startling her. Nevaeh began screaming and ripped at the little ribbons in her hair.

"Sh! It's okay...sh!" Darcy went to the front door and looked out through the lens. In a big city like Columbia, with over a hundred thousand people, it wasn't safe to just go and open the door to anybody.

She saw three men outside, all in dark suits, one of them many years older than the others. He stood at the front of the group, staring at her door. They looked important, like police officers.

"Hello?" Darcy asked through the door.

"Darcy Metcalf?"

"Espinoza," she added.

"Excuse me?"

"Darcy Metcalf Espinoza. I'm married, you know. My husband will be home soon."

"Mrs...Espinoza," the man said. He held up a badge. "I'm Constable Ward Brown of the South Carolina State Law Enforcement Division."

Darcy gasped. The state police! She hoped Ramon wasn't in some kind of trouble.

"What can I do for you?" Darcy asked.

"You can start by opening the door, ma'am," he said.

"Oh, Goonies! I'm sorry!" Darcy hurried to unlock and open it.

Nevaeh immediately charged on hands and knees toward the open door, determined to escape the apartment. Darcy had to block her with her leg, and the toddler responded by screaming and pounding Darcy's knee with her fists.

"We need to come in and ask a few questions," Constable Ward Brown told her.

"Yes, sir. Come on, Nevaeh!" Darcy scooped up her daughter, who responded with screaming, kicking, and pulling Darcy's hair. "Okey-dokes, I guess you can come inside. Sorry about the mess everywhere." Darcy nodded at the open boxes of decorations and wrapping paper scattered through the small living room. "Just trying to deck the halls a smidge! 'Tis the season, you know!"

"Uh, yes," Ward said, following her inside. He nodded back at his two men, and they stayed outside, closing the door after him. He was clearly the boss, Darcy thought.

"You can sit on the couch, but watch out for the glitter and ribbons!" Darcy warned. "Can I get you anything? Fruitcake? Christmas Krispies? I make them with Rice Krispies, you know, and food coloring."

"No, thank you." Ward glanced at the gift-wrapping flotsam that covered the couch, and he sat in the easy chair instead.

Darcy frowned, thinking Ramon wouldn't like some stranger sitting in his favorite chair. She sank down to the couch, where Nevaeh immediately grabbed double handfuls of ribbon and stuffed them in her mouth.

"Nevaeh, stop it!" Darcy barked. "I'm sorry, officer. What did you want to ask about?"

"Mrs. Metcalf—"

"Espinoza." She held up her left hand, displaying a wedding ring with a tiny flake of diamond.

"Mrs. Espinoza, after the Easter events in Fallen Oak...I'm sure you know which Easter I'm talking about...you gave a very interesting interview to a doctor from the Centers for Disease Control. Isn't that right?"

"Oh, Gobstoppers, that was so long ago," Darcy said.

"You said two kids from your town, Jennifer Morton and Jonathan Seth Barrett IV, were most likely responsible for the event. You made a reference to witchcraft."

"I know, it sounds crazy," Darcy said.

"Why did you believe they were involved?"

"Just all the witchy things they did. Nevaeh, put that down!" The little girl had opened a can of gold and tinsel glitter, which spilled everywhere as Darcy tried to wrestle it away from her. Nevaeh screeched and cried.

"What kind of witchy things?" Ward asked, ignoring the wailing baby completely.

Darcy, while struggling with Nevaeh, managed to tell him about the time the tractor had fallen on Jenny's dad, and he should have died, but Seth healed him in front of a small crowd of people. That was when everyone had started talking about witchcraft. Then, on Easter, Darcy and some other girls had seen Jenny afterward, at Ashleigh's house.

"She killed Ashleigh until she was nothing but bones and junk," Darcy told Ward. "I know, because I buried her. And then Jenny jumped in the pond and had to've drowned, but then she was alive and perfectly okay after that." Nevaeh smacked Darcy in the face a few times, and Darcy lowered the girl so she could crawl around on the carpet. "I know this might sound strange to you, because not everyone is a believer, but I think God and Satan had a showdown in Fallen Oak. It looked like the devil won at first, but then really God won. I'm still glad to be away from that place, though."

Ward leaned forward and touched the back of her hand.

"I'm a believer, Darcy," Ward said. "You can tell me anything, especially about Jenny Morton."

"Oh, whoosh! Big relief," Darcy said. "You never know, with so much atheism these days. So, anywho, I think Jenny and Seth were on the devil's side, and then Ashleigh and us were on God's side."

"Why do you say the devil won, and then God won?"

"First, Jenny defeated Ashleigh, and then Ashleigh was dead. But later, God sent Ashleigh back with the angels, and whatever she did must have worked, because Jenny was pretty much gone after that. I only saw her like one more time. Nevaeh!"

Nevaeh had crawled back to the tree and plucked a bright red ornament, and she was currently attempting to eat it like an apple. She squalled when Darcy took it away from her.

"You say Jenny defeated Ashleigh. That was Easter?" he asked.

"Uh-huh." Darcy picked up the crying Nevaeh again and held her.

"Explain the part about Ashleigh and the angels?"

"Oh, I can try. You see, these two angels came to me. One of them pretended to be Ashleigh's cousin at first, he even looked like her, same gray eyes. The other one was Mexican-looking, but I guess angels aren't really from Mexico or America or anything. Anywho, this angel brought Ashleigh's soul back, and Ashleigh had to use my body for a while. To finally defeat Jenny, I guess. Like she couldn't finish her mission in life, so I had to help her."

Ward was just staring at her, his eyebrows raised.

"Aren't you taking notes or anything?" Darcy asked. "I thought cops took notes."

"Don't worry, I'll remember everything you say. How was it that Ashleigh finally defeated Jenny?"

"I dunno. That big riot in Charleston must have been part of it. Because Ashleigh's spirit left me after that, and I woke up in a hotel room and didn't remember too much."

"I spoke with your parents in Fallen Oak, Darcy," he said. "They told me you were friends with Jenny, at one point."

"Nah, that must have been Ashleigh's soul working through me. Tricking her, maybe. I don't really remember what all happened, because it was like I was asleep while Ashleigh was in me."

Nevaeh wailed, snot pouring down from her nose.

"That's a lovely baby you have there." Ward stood and touched Darcy's shoulder. This time, his touch was like ice water, flowing through her shoulder and up to her brain.

For a moment, Darcy relived her memories—the two angels sitting in her room, then Ashleigh's soul filling her up, a quick flash of Ashleigh's face...and then, weeks later, waking up in the hotel room, her purse missing. Finding out she'd checked in under her dad's credit card, which he'd reported stolen. Having no ID and going to jail.

Then, months later, Jenny and Seth coming to the Taco Bell and giving Darcy the PayPal card from Ashleigh's charity. A couple of days after that, Darcy heard both of them had died in the fire at Barrett House.

"That was another thing I wanted to ask about," Ward said. "How did you come to administer the funds raised by Ashleigh Goodling? Why did she give you all that money?"

"So I could hand it out to everyone. I did it, too. An equal amount to every girl. That was another witchy thing about Jenny, all those girls getting pregnant."

"But it was Jenny who gave you the money? That surprises me. I thought you said she was evil."

"Even the devil is ruled by God, you know," Darcy said. "Maybe she had to give it to me for some reason. I dunno. But I did what I felt like I was supposed to do."

Ward nodded, backing away from her.

"That's a very...unexpected story," he said.

"It's all true!"

"I know it is. That's the strangest part of all." Ward shook his head. "You've been both less and more informative than I expected."

"Well, I'm sorry and you're welcome, I guess!" Darcy smiled, and Nevaeh punched her in the mouth. The little girl shrieked and cried even louder.

"Sure. It would be best not to mention we were here, Mrs. Espinoza. Not to anyone. That could be construed as interfering in our investigation."

"Oh, golly! I won't tell anyone, pinky promise!"

"Right. Have a good evening, Mrs. Espinoza." Ward opened her front door and stepped out to the hall.

"Merry Christmas, officers!" Darcy shouted at him and the two police officers outside, but nobody said "Merry Christmas" back. Darcy wondered whether the constable was really a believer or not.

\* \* \*

"Five, six," Ward said, as Avery and Buchanan trailed him through the apartment building's breezeway, toward the concrete steps. "One of them's dead, but she can possess the living. Another one can communicate with the dead. And we have another appearance from our friend with the fearful touch and gray eyes. I wouldn't be surprised if he turned out to be the mastermind. If Senator Mayfield doesn't do us a favor and die tomorrow, our next move is track down 'Tommy' and a Latino girl named 'Esmeralda'...no known surnames."

"That doesn't sound like much for the data miners to go on, sir," Buchanan said.

"The rare eye color might help us identify the male," Ward told him. "Search police and prison records, all the usual."

Avery held the door as Ward climbed into the car. When they pulled out of their parking spot, Ward said, "It looks like there are two factions. This Esmeralda, Ashleigh, and Tommy were one—Tommy is probably the ringleader. Jenny and Seth are another."

"What about the zombie guy?" Avery asked.

"We don't know where he fits, do we? But I believe the events we've seen—the Easter plague in Fallen Oak, the riot in Charleston, the Barrett House fire—are all simply side effects of their conflict. They leave a path of destruction behind them."

"Sounds like somebody ought to neutralize 'em," Avery said.

"Acquire or neutralize, that's our objective," Ward said. "This 'Tommy' has a particularly dangerous power. We find him first. If we can bring him over, his entire faction might follow their leader."

# Chapter Thirteen

Jenny stood in front of the little wall mirror in her studio, her shirt off, turning side to side as she examined herself. At four months, her belly was really starting to pooch out. So far, she'd kept to wearing loose, bulky shirts and sweaters, and she'd joked about how the French cheeses and chocolates were fattening her up, but it was clear that she would have tell Seth the truth pretty soon. She was shocked the pregnancy had already lasted so long, but she hadn't used the pox at all, except to frighten Mariella once, which she regretted. Besides that, she'd done what she could to keep the developing baby safe.

She opened a door to a cabinet where she kept her art supplies, and she reached all the way to the back of the bottom shelf. Even as she picked up the bottle, she cursed herself. It was empty, and she'd meant to buy another one, but it had slipped her mind.

She gave it a shake anyway, but there was nothing inside. Jenny had started taking the prenatal vitamins about a month ago, despite knowing the baby was almost certainly not going to live. She wasn't sure why she'd started doing it, and she tried not to think about it too much. Clearly, she wanted the baby to live, but it was useless to desire impossible things.

Jenny heard the loud squeal of tires on pavement, following by an ear-shattering crash. She hid the pill bottle and walked out to the living room, where Seth was playing a Nintendo Wii game that involved racing and crashing big monster trucks.

"You can take the boy out of South Carolina..." Jenny said.

"Ha ha. You can drive Grave Digger if you want to race."

"I think I'll pass. I have to run to the store."

He paused the game. "Why? What's up?"

"Nothing. I just have to get some cream and, uh, nutmeg. For the eggnog."

"Don't worry about the eggnog. It's Christmas Eve already, everything might be closed."

"No! I mean, it doesn't really taste like Christmas without eggnog. My dad always had some."

"I'll go with you." Seth stood up.

"You don't have to." It would be hard to buy prenatal vitamins without Seth noticing, Jenny thought.

"It's icy out there, and it's almost dark, too."

"What do I care about the dark?" Jenny asked. "I almost feel bad for anyone who tries to attack me."

"Why would you feel bad for them?"

"I said *almost*." Jenny bundled up in a scarf, knit hat, coat, and gloves, and she grabbed her purse. "Do we need anything else?"

"Wine. You keep forgetting to buy it. And bourbon for the eggnog, if you want to get lucky tonight." He winked at her. "It could lower my inhibitions."

"Seth, you don't have inhibitions."

"What do you mean?"

"I seem to remember you hooking up with some random blond girl at the festival in Charleston..."

"Oh, come on, that was Ashleigh's fault. She was possessing Darcy, and she forced me to do that."

"It looked like you were suffering pretty badly. The way her boobs were in your face. Lots of pain involved there."

Seth sighed and rubbed his eyes. "You know Ashleigh was trying to drive us apart. First possessing Darcy and pretending to be your friend, then making me hook up with some random hottie and making sure you caught us—"

"You did *not* just call her a 'hottie.'"

"That's not what I meant...What happened, Jenny? Why are you in a bad mood tonight?"

"Not a bad mood. Reflective, maybe. See you in fifteen minutes, if I don't have to kill a mugger or anything." Jenny walked out the front door and down the hall to the elevator. She hadn't meant to bite Seth's head off, it was more of a ruse to keep him from joining her. She was a little flushed and angry, though, thinking how she'd discovered Seth that night, his mouth open and eyes glazed as the other girl rode on top of him. Even if Ashleigh's wicked, loving touch had been involved, it still made Jenny angry sometimes.

In the plush lobby, filled with the sound of old jazz, Jenny waved at the security guard at the front desk. As usual, he wore his burgundy-and-brass uniform coat and gave only a very slight nod as she passed.

Then she was outside in the cold December night. A thick snow had fallen on Paris this year, blanketing the city in white and hanging icicles from trees and window ledges. Their apartment was located in *Le Marais*, a district full of centuries-old mansions that had mostly been converted into museums. There were also a number of cabarets and nightclubs, where Jenny had made Seth take her to a couple of drag shows.

Her favorite corner shop was already closed, so Jenny had to continue on several blocks to the big Monoprix supermarket. The streets were mostly empty as a fresh flurry of snow tumbled down among the beautiful old buildings. Music played from a couple of bars she passed, but nearly every shop was closed. Jenny smiled, feeling for a moment that she had all of Paris to herself.

Then she passed through glass doors into the Monoprix, where a crowd of last-minute shoppers were checking out before the store closed. Jenny automatically drew her arms close around herself, even though her gloves and coat ensured she wouldn't touch anyone.

She found the prenatals in the pharmacy area, and then paused in an aisle full of baby supplies. Bottles, diapers, pacifiers, little toys and pajamas and tiny pairs of socks. Her baby wouldn't be needing any of this, she thought. Then she barely managed to stop herself from crying in front of everyone. The pregnancy seemed to make her emotions spiral out of control fast, for the stupidest reasons.

She hurried to the check-out, then out the door.

Jenny was halfway home before she remembered that she was supposed to buy eggnog ingredients. She cursed under her breath, then doubled back to the store.

When she'd finished her second visit to the store, she walked down the narrow *Rue Vieille du Temple* alone, hearing her footsteps echo back from the masonry and closed windows above her. The walk back seemed somehow less pleasant. She was aware of being alone, of the sunken doorways and dark windows around her. She felt a twinge of childhood fear, the kind that fully believed monsters could be hiding in every shadow, waiting to snatch her with a clawed hand. She shivered.

Her sense of fright only grew worse as she approached her apartment building, as if something evil and twisted waited for her inside. There was danger in the air, even though she couldn't see anything out of the ordinary.

She waved to the security guy as she passed through the lobby, and he nodded once, very slightly, in return. Everything seemed normal.

Her sense of dread grew worse as the rattling elevator carried her up to her floor. She could feel her heart beat in her chest as she inserted the key into the lock.

*Stop being paranoid, Jenny*, she told herself. Then she opened the door.

Seth was on the couch, but he was no longer playing the Wii. He faced a girl with deep red hair, almost black, and a long leather jacket who now sat beside him. Her back was to Jenny, but Jenny could see that they were gripping each other's hands, and Seth's eyes were closed. His eyes opened as Jenny stepped in through the front door.

"Jenny!" Seth said, with a goofy smile on his face. Then he seemed to notice that he was holding hands with the other girl, and he disentangled himself and stood up. "This is Mariella."

Mariella turned toward Jenny, and a look of shock crossed the Italian girl's face.

"You!" Mariella said.

"Me," Jenny replied.

"I'm confused." She looked from Seth to Jenny. "You said you did not know him."

"Wait, you know each other? Now I'm confused," Seth added.

"It's a confusing night," Jenny said. "Strange things happen when you go out for eggnog. Looks like you two were having fun."

"She was reading my future," Seth said.

"Really? And?" Jenny asked.

"We're all in a lot of trouble," Mariella said.

"Yep. Especially Seth." She walked into the kitchen to put away the groceries, and Seth followed her. She'd already tucked the vitamins into a coat pocket.

"Where did you find her?" Jenny asked.

"She came to the door. She said she's had visions of meeting me in the future, and they led her here," Seth whispered.

"And you believed her?"

"She knew things about me. She knew about my healing touch. I had to see what she wanted, or if she was a danger to us."

Jenny put the nutmeg in the spice cabinet, in front of the other nutmeg that was already there, and slammed the cabinet door. She turned to face Seth. "So. She tells you she's like us, and you think it's a good idea to let her touch you? What if she was like Ashleigh and made you her little slave? Did you think of that?"

"How could she do that when her power is seeing your future?" Seth asked.

"Why did you trust her enough to take the risk?"

"I...you..." Seth stared at her for a moment, clearly fumbling for an answer. Then he asked, "How do you already know her?"

"She showed up at our front door one day, looking for you."

"She did? What do you know about her?" Seth whispered.

"She's a student here in Paris. Working towards degrees in art history and economics...and Google tells me that her family in Milan are crazy rich. Fashion, media, banking. Your parents would love her."

Seth scowled a little at that.

"She wears gloves all the time, even when she doesn't know I'm watching," Jenny said. "She's either like us, or she's going to a lot of trouble to pretend she is."

"So you knew there was another one of us right here in Paris, and she knows where we live, and you never thought that was worth mentioning?" Seth asked.

"Excuse me," Mariella said. She stood at the edge of the kitchen, pointing back over her shoulder at the front door. "Should I be leaving now, or...?"

"That might be a good idea," Jenny said.

"Wait," Seth said. "I think you should stay for a minute."

"Do you?" Jenny asked him.

"We should talk about this," Seth said. "Figure out what the hell's going on. Let's have some wine."

"Sorry, forgot to buy any," Jenny said. "Let's go back to the living room. It's getting crowded in here."

Seth and Jenny took the settee, while Mariella sat alone on the loveseat and brought out a golden pack of Fantasia cigarettes and a lighter.

"You can't smoke in here," Jenny said. "You can smoke if you leave."

"I am sorry." Mariella tucked the cigarettes back into her purse. She sat with her hands in her lap, her knees bouncing nervously in her tight designer jeans. She looked like nothing so much as a kid in trouble at school, waiting to see the principal. "Can I ask...why didn't you tell me about him?"

"About Seth?" Jenny asked.

"Is that his name? Seth," Mariella said, as if trying it on, and she smiled warmly. Jenny wanted to stab the girl with her own stiletto heel.

"What do you expect me to do?" Jenny asked. "Some girl shows up at my door, so eager to meet my boyfriend she's practically ripping her panties off, and what am I going to do? Introduce you to him?"

"Oh." Mariella's face fell, and she looked at the floor. "He is your boyfriend."

"What did you think we were? Roommates?" Jenny asked.

"I have not had time to think about it." Mariella frowned deeply, which pouted out her lower lip. "This makes no sense to me."

"I know, he's kind of goofy, but I stick with him anyway," Jenny said.

"Wait, somebody was ripping their panties off?" Seth asked.

"Quiet." Jenny knocked her knee against his leg, and she hoped it hurt. "Why did you come back, Mariella? Have you been stalking us?" She asked the question self-righteously, as if Jenny hadn't stalked Mariella herself.

"No, I wanted to see you," Mariella told her.

"Right. Why would you want to see me, after last time?"

"What happened last time?" Seth asked.

"It took time to work up the courage," Mariella said. "But, I kept thinking...maybe she is like me, and scared. Maybe she has never met another person with strange powers, either. Maybe it frightens her, and so she is defensive."

"I'm not as scared as you think," Jenny told her.

"I thought...with who else can I talk about these things? I've never been able to talk with anyone. The priest, he told me I was making it all up, when I was a child. He told me never to speak of it."

Jenny folded her arms. "You're saying you came here because you wanted to be...*friends* with me?"

"Is that so strange?" Mariella gave a small shrug. "I thought, we have some things in common. We could talk about...shopping for gloves, perhaps? I know many fine places to buy gloves in Paris."

In spite of her angry mood, Jenny couldn't help laughing. She quickly covered her smile, but the damage was done. Mariella had broken Jenny's stern glare.

"I am very sorry how this turned out," Mariella said. "I did not know he was yours. You could have told me."

"I thought it was better to get rid of you," Jenny said.

Mariella looked hurt, her eyes shimmering.

"You have to understand, though," Seth told her. "We've met others like us—"

"You've met others?" Mariella sat up. "Where? Can we speak to them?"

"—but we aren't very nice, as a group," Seth continued. "I mean, we're mostly psychopaths. Present company excluded, as far as I know."

"The ones who caused us the most trouble are already dead," Jenny added, raising her eyebrows just a little.

"What could the others do?" Mariella asked. "Do we all have different powers? Where do they come from?"

"They're all different," Seth said. "We come in pairs. Opposites, like me and Jenny. Healing and plague. Love and fear."

"Then I must have an opposite somewhere," Mariella said. "If I can see the future, then he would...what? See the past?"

"That's not very useful." Seth snickered.

"It could be, if there's something in your past you want to hide," Jenny said.

"That's a little more useful," Seth conceded.

"Would he be a boy?" Mariella asked. "How could I find him?"

"Let's go back to the sociopath-slash-psychopath thing," Seth said. "If someone like that is out there, odds are you *don't* want to meet him."

"Give me your hands again." Mariella stood up and approached him with her palms out. "I need to see something."

Jenny watched as Mariella took his hands and closed her eyes. Seth sat there awkwardly, trying not to look at Mariella at all.

"There are many possibilities," Mariella said. "The future is always shifting and changing. But one thing I see clearly for Seth is the man who will hunt him down."

Jenny sat forward. Mariella might or might not be able to see the future...but if she could, it didn't mean she was telling them the truth. Jenny thought of Ashleigh's intricate, destructive little plots and tried to imagine what Mariella might be scheming.

"I really don't like the sound of 'hunt me down,'" Seth said. "Like kill me?"

"Take you. Kidnap you," Mariella replied.

"Who is this guy?" Seth asked.

"He is older. Some gray hair." Mariella's already-closed eyes squinted, and she clutched Seth's hands tighter, as if she were concentrating hard, or maybe trying to pass a kidney stone. "American. He has soldiers...influence...I think he has a touch like ours. I'm not certain of his power, but his eyes are..." Mariella's eyes opened wide and she released Seth, hurrying back from him and shaking her head. "He has my eyes."

"Your opposite," Seth said, and Jenny wanted to scowl at him. She wasn't sure whether they should be helping the girl or not. "Sometimes we have the same eyes."

"Like yours." Mariella stepped forward, looking at Seth, then at Jenny. "Blue. The same beautiful shade of blue..."

"When is he coming?" Jenny asked.

"I'm sorry?" Mariella shook her head as if she'd been momentarily hypnotized, looking into Jenny's eyes. "When is who?"

"The guy we were just talking about. The one who's going to hunt Seth down? When is that going to happen? And where?" Jenny asked.

"Right here," Mariella said. "Not far into the future."

"We can change that," Seth said. "Right? We can pack up and move somewhere else, hide ourselves better."

"It is possible." Mariella held out her hand, and Seth reluctantly took it again. This time, she gazed into his eyes instead of closing her own. Seth stared back. It made Jenny uncomfortable.

"Where would you go?" Mariella asked.

"The French Riviera might be nice," Seth said.

"That changes nothing," Mariella told him, shaking her head.

"I don't know. England?" Seth suggested.

"No. He finds you there."

"Eh...Berlin?"

"Definitely not," Mariella said quickly.

"Italy?" Seth asked, and Jenny gave him a little scowl, which he didn't notice.

"No...no....Wherever you go, he finds you. This cannot be avoided." She continued gazing at Seth, and continued holding his hand.

Jenny felt suspicious. This would be the trick, convincing them that they had to move in order to be safe. Then the girl would conveniently know exactly where they needed to go. Jenny couldn't imagine her motivation, but if it was a scam, that had to be her intent. Mariella would want the two of them to go somewhere with her, she suspected.

"Then what do I do?" Seth asked. "Stock up on guns and ammo?"

"That would likely lead to your death," Mariella replied.

"If anyone comes for Seth, I'll just pox the shit out of them," Jenny said, staring hard at Mariella. "Where am I in all of this?"

Mariella closed her eyes, gripping Seth's hand tight. Her brow furrowed. After a long minute, she sighed.

"I can't see you at all," Mariella said. "Jenny...it's like you're not even there."

"Where am I?" Jenny asked. "Can you ask, um, future Seth?"

"It's not that." Mariella opened her eyes. "I can't see your future at all. Perhaps because I cannot touch you. Pain and death, you said."

"Yep," Jenny told her. "Pain and death. Fast, too." Jenny noted that Mariella was still holding Seth's hand. "Let me ask you something. You have a big family in Milan. Tomorrow's Christmas. Why aren't you home?"

"Oh, no. Like you say...a very big family. With too much drama this year." Mariella shook her head. "I thought I would spend Christmas in Paris. Then I thought of you, Jenny...I wondered if you might be alone on Christmas, too." She looked from Jenny to Seth. "I was wrong."

"You're going to be alone tomorrow?" Seth asked. Jenny frowned, thinking *I'm going to kill him if he invites her*— "You could come here if you want. Jenny's making some French dish with a duck. Then I'm going to heal the duck back to life and let it fly around our apartment."

"That's really sick," Jenny said.

Mariella looked at Jenny, then down at the floor. "I don't want to get in the way."

Now Jenny started feeling bad for the girl. If she was telling the truth, she was lonely, she'd only just found the only people in the world who were like her, and they were basically rejecting her. Or Jenny was, anyway. She thought of her dad back home, having Christmas without her, and felt a little sad. She wondered how Rocky was doing. The last time she'd seen her dog, he was much more comfortable around people, much less frightened. That could be dangerous, if Jenny ever saw him again. Which, she reminded herself, she probably wouldn't. She nearly burst into tears, thinking about her father...the stupid pregnancy hormones striking again.

"Just come, if you want to," Jenny said. "There's going to be too much food, anyway."

"You don't have to invite me over," Mariella said.

"Seriously," Jenny said. "I want you here. Freaks like us should stick together, when we're not too busy trying to kill each other." Jenny sighed to herself. Even if the girl was deceiving them about anything, it was better to keep an eye on her until Jenny could figure out what she wanted. *Friends close, enemies closer*, Jenny thought.

Besides, Jenny thought she was beginning to remember this girl from their last life. Keeping her around would clarify those memories.

"Who wants eggnog?" Seth asked.

\* \* \*

Later, after Mariella had gone home, Jenny lay awake in bed. She still couldn't be sure whether she'd made a new friend or met a new enemy, and it worried her. Even if the girl was telling the truth, that meant Seth was in danger, while Jenny's fate, and that of the baby growing inside her, remained unknown.

"I think I remember her," Jenny whispered.

"Her?" Seth asked, his eyes opening easily. He hadn't been asleep, but he'd been trying, or maybe faking to avoid Jenny's inevitable teasing about the other girl. Jenny was holding that in reserve for now, though.

"Mariella," Jenny said, as if he didn't know who she'd meant. "I think she was in our last life. Maybe there's unfinished business."

"What kind of unfinished business?" Seth rose up on his elbow, facing her. His hand went to her hip, then down along the waistband of her soft flannel pajamas. "I can think of some unfinished business we need to take care of."

"I'm serious," Jenny said, though she did nothing to stop Seth from hooking a finger under her waistband and sliding it down her hip. "Maybe her opposite's involved, too. The one who's hunting you?"

"Right. Like I'm hunting you right now." He leaned in close to the exposed curve of her pale hip, his mouth open like he meant to bite her.

"Stop being cute," she said.

"Can't help it."

"Listen, if she's telling the truth, we could be in a lot of danger. You don't know what happened last time."

"No, tell me. I'll be down here listening." Seth kissed his way from her hip to her lower belly, tugging her pajamas down as he went.

"This is important, Seth. You should, you know, arm yourself with knowledge."

"Arm yourself with knowledge?" Seth looked up at her, laughing. "Really? That's almost as bad as the time you said 'unhand me'!"

"And when did I say that?"

"It was..." His eyes scrunched up as he struggled to remember. Then he smiled. "The haunted house! Right? On our first date?"

"The haunted house where you worked."

"Right. The haunted house where I...but when did I do that?"

"A lifetime ago. Your memories are bleeding through."

"Do they have to be 'bleeding' through?" Seth asked. "Can't they be nicely, gently drifting through?"

"I'm still having trouble with our most recent lives...Alexander didn't want me to remember those, because of my memories with you."

"That bastard," Seth said quickly.

"But our last life is coming together slowly. If I tell you what happened, maybe you'll start to remember, too. And we won't miss anything, like whether your new girlfriend might be planning to ax-murder us, any details like that."

"She's not going to ax-murder us," Seth said.

"You're right. She'll probably use those high heels. And I'll be in my sneakers, unarmed."

"You'd just hit her with flying plaguey-pox."

"That's true," Jenny said. "And she'd do that pouty frown thing until it ate off her lips. Now, listen, I have to catch you up on the story."

"Are you sure? There's an interesting story unfolding down here, too, you know." He tugged her pajamas down to her hips, and she wasn't wearing anything underneath. His lips traveled downward, between her legs.

"Stop!" Jenny squealed.

"Usually squealing doesn't mean 'stop,'" Seth pointed out.

"First, my turn," Jenny said. "Then yours. Now, listen."

Seth rested his chin in his hand and looked at her. Handsome boy, she thought, for the millionth time.

# Chapter Fourteen

Fallen Oak was a large, thriving town, with a tall brick cotton exchange, a crowded stockyard, and a textile mill, plus a large Postal Telegraph Company office and a railroad spur connecting the town to the rest of the world. As they rode through in the detective's Ford Model 18, Juliana and Sebastian sat in the back seat, looking out at the busy little downtown, full of shops, with a two-story department store on one corner. The courthouse had a marble facade engraved with the figure of Justice, blindfolded and wielding a sword, overlooking a neatly manicured town green with a bandstand. There was also a sparkling white Baptist church on the central square, facing the green. Despite the Depression, Fallen Oak seemed to be bustling and growing.

"Looks like such a pleasant place to live," Juliana commented.

"We should bring the carnival," Sebastian said. "These people seem like they have money to spare."

Juliana laughed. "You're thinking like a carnie already."

They drove eastward out of the downtown, past fields of cotton. Thin, hungry-looking black laborers in patched clothing worked the fields under the scorching sunlight. They didn't seem to be receiving too much of the town's swelling prosperity.

They arrived at a three-story mansion on a hill, largely obscured behind ornamental trees, the entire property protected by a tall, spiked wrought-iron fence. The detective pulled up to the locked front gate, reached out the window, and rang a bell on a rope.

"This is where we're going?" Sebastian asked, amazed. "This Jonathan Barrett must have heaps of dough."

"I told you that," the detective replied. "You should listen to his offer."

"What will he offer us?" Juliana asked.

"I wouldn't know."

A gray-haired black man in a dark suit and high, starched collar opened the gate for them, and the detective drove up the brick driveway to park in the circular turnaround, centered on a flower garden and a water fountain. The driveway was flanked by ornamental gardens full of more blossoming, cheerfully bright flowers. Towards the sides of the house, the flower beds turned into kitchen and herb gardens.

The man who'd opened the gate glanced at Sebastian and Juliana, then nodded at the detective.

"He's expecting us," the detective said.

"Yes, he is. This way." The man led them up the front steps and opened the heavy front door. They entered a two-story entrance hall dominated by a massive granite fireplace that lay cold and dark. The room was paneled in dark oak, and heavy draperies blocked the large windows. A wide Persian rug occupied the parquet floor, and a grand staircase circled up along the wall to the second story. A few candles burned in the glittering crystal chandelier overhead, but the room was left in darkness and shadows. Juliana felt as though she'd stepped into a massive, finely appointed tomb.

They followed the man deeper into the house as the front hall narrowed and darkened. The place didn't smell like a tomb, at least— it smelled like baking bread, green vegetables, and spices. Juliana's mouth watered. In these difficult times, she was lucky to eat one meal a day.

The servant led them straight through to the enormous back porch, shaded by the equally large veranda above it. A fine dining table had been set out, with a dozen hand-carved wooden chairs facing a dozen place settings with spotless white china and silver.

The long dining table was empty except for a man who sat at the head. He wore a black suit with a white silk shirt, tailored perfectly to his lean, fit body. He was immaculately groomed, like a king, every hair in place, his fingernails spotless, his golden cufflinks glittering. Two very dark-skinned young women in skimpy dresses waved large paper fans, which cooled him from the South Carolina heat and blew away the countless tiny insects that swarmed in the air.

Juliana had a strong visceral reaction when his dark, deep eyes looked at her. It wasn't clearly a good or bad feeling—it was delicious and guilty at the same time, like the times when she'd let Sebastian reach his hand under her dress.

"This is Jonathan Barrett," the detective told them. "Mr. Barrett, those kids I've been looking for. Sebastian, Juliana. Those are their stage names, anyhow."

"You've brought my guests. Good work," Jonathan Barrett said, rising from his chair. He looked over Juliana and Sebastian, then gestured to chairs on his left side. "Just in time for dinner, too. Please sit, both of you. Are you hungry?"

Juliana nodded. The answer to that was always "yes."

"They'll serve you in the dining room, if you'd like anything," Barrett told the detective, who tipped his hat and returned inside. Barrett looked them over again, slowly, as if absorbing them into the darkness in his eyes. "Did you have a good journey?"

Sebastian and Juliana looked at each other, neither wanting to speak first.

"It was good," Sebastian finally said. "I've never ridden in such a fast automobile."

"Excellent." As Barrett spoke, two large, much older black women brought out food in such copious amounts that Juliana could have drooled all over the table. A basket of puffy rolls the size of her fist, a cake of cornbread, a pot of boiled greens with peppers, slabs of ham preserved in salt. They filled wineglasses with a strange orange-colored drink. Barrett raised a glass of it. "I should warn you, this punch is made with real Caribbean rum, nearly impossible to find with the absurd dry laws. We add the juice of watermelons and peaches grown right here." He nodded out to the sprawling land beyond the back porch.

The back yard sloped down to a peach orchard with small irrigation canals, where workers were picking the last fruits of the season. Beyond that, a hill rose up behind the house, where some kind of construction was underway. Juliana squinted her eyes, trying to see better. It looked like they were erecting a brick wall around several rows of tall, thick granite columns. She couldn't fathom what they were building. It clearly wasn't a barn or a smokehouse; the materials were far too heavy and expensive. A church, maybe.

"My family necropolis," Barrett said, with a sharp smile. Juliana found the smile unsettling and strangely appealing. The man radiated an aura of power, as if his presence charged the air around him with electricity.

"What is a necro...necro...one of those?" Sebastian asked. His eyes kept darting from Barrett to the plate in front of him, which one of the women was piling with freshly cooked food. Clearly, Sebastian was struggling not to grab up the meal by the double handfuls and cram it into his mouth.

"Are you familiar at all with Egyptology?" Barrett asked, looking from Sebastian to Juliana. They both shook their heads. "It's a fascination of mine. An indulgence, really. The study of such ancient civilizations. How do you suppose they built those pyramids, so many thousands of years ago, without the benefit of modern industry? It seems impossible."

"One rock at a time, I suppose," Juliana said, which earned her a powerful smile from Barrett.

"True. All things must be built that way, mustn't they, from the humblest home to the widest empire." Barrett cut a slice of ham, which Juliana and Sebastian took as the signal to start eating as fast as they dared. The food tasted even more delicious than it smelled. Juliana knew they would both eat until they were ready to burst, and then try to smuggle more home with them for later. She'd never had such a bountiful meal placed before her.

"What impresses me about the Egyptians was the scale of their ambition," Barrett said. "A pyramid hundreds of feet high, just to serve as a tomb for a single king. They outfitted them with everything the king would need in the afterlife. Gold, food, clothing, servants....They believed all of this went with them to the other world."

"Sounds expensive," Sebastian said.

"If they wanted to destroy a dead pharaoh's soul, they destroyed any image of him, every painting and statue. They struck out his name wherever it was carved. Removed him from history, as though he had never existed."

"There's an Egyptian strong man in the carnival," Sebastian told him, biting into a floury biscuit. "Cheopus the Magnificent. Shaved head, pony tail. He can bend bars of iron."

"He's not really Egyptian," Juliana said.

"I don't think the bars are really iron, either." Sebastian sipped the rum punch. "This is so good. Try it, Juliana."

Juliana took a drink. It was so sweet she could barely taste the rum. It was cool, too, probably from sitting in an icebox somewhere. She nodded and smiled. "I'll have to be careful not to drink too much."

"Drink too much? Such a thing is not possible." Barrett raised his glass and took a long drink.

"Mr. Barrett, sir." A middle-aged black woman emerged onto the porch, with a scrawny, big-eyed white boy of six or seven clinging to her skirt. "Jonathan Junior wants to go and see the pigs."

"The pigs!" Barrett glared at his little son, who tried to hide behind the big woman. "Are you sure you don't want to see the *horses* instead?"

The boy shook his head, not saying a word. He looked scared.

"Pigs!" Barrett shook his head. "Go roll in the mud and be a swine. What else are you good for?"

The boy looked like he would cry as the woman led him away.

"Scared of horses, scared of goats, scared of his own shadow." Barrett shook his head.

"Is there a Mrs. Barrett?" Juliana asked. Sebastian looked at her as if he didn't like the sound of that question.

"She's upstairs, not feeling well. She had to take laudanum."

"Is she sick?" Juliana asked.

"She gets sick if she doesn't take her laudanum," Barrett said. "I've lost my appetite, and it's time we talk about why you're here." He stood and walked past them into the house. Juliana and Sebastian waited until he was out of sight, then crammed their pockets full of biscuits and salted ham before following him.

Barrett's study was a spacious room at the back of the first floor, the walls hung with animal heads: a lion, a wolf, a leopard, and a jaguar, among others, all of them angled so that they seemed to snarl at visitors as they entered the room. A wall of wooden filing cabinets and pigeonholes ended at a 19th-century, saloon-style liquor cabinet in the back corner. The black petrified-wood slab of his desk held a heavy Comptometer mechanical calculator, as well as a telephone and a teletypewriter.

Barrett sat behind his desk, checking a printout. He quickly put it aside when they entered, and he directed the older black man from the front gate, who stood at his elbow, toward the liquor cabinet.

"I have Canadian whiskey," he said to Sebastian. "Like one?"

"Yes, thanks."

"I would, too," Juliana added.

"A woman who drinks whiskey," Barrett said. "I'm starting to like you already."

Juliana did her best not to blush at his smile.

The older man poured the illegal drink into three very old, handmade glasses. He placed a cigar box on Barrett's desk, gave the man a cigar, and lit it for him with a match.

"Cuban tobacco." Barrett smiled as the smoke curled out of his lips. "At least they still allow us *some* indulgences. Have one." Barrett nodded at Sebastian, who reached for a cigar, then sat awkwardly as the servant lit it for him. He coughed miserably at the smoke. Barrett smiled at Juliana again. "Does the lady smoke cigars, too?"

"She does not," Juliana replied, giving him a coy smile she did not actually intend. She didn't know where it came from. Sebastian regarded her over his smoldering cigar—he'd clearly seen it.

Barrett made a slight gesture with his cigar, and his servant left the study, closing the door behind him.

"To the future," Barrett said, raising the glass. Juliana and Sebastian joined the toast, though they weren't sure exactly what he meant by it, and then they drank. The Canadian whiskey had bite, but was much smoother than most of the liquor she'd tasted, like moonshine and bathtub gin. She tried not to let the men see her shudder as the whiskey kicked her in the stomach.

"Mr. Barrett, what is it that you do?" Sebastian asked, looking around the office, which was an odd mix of bland accounting décor and African safari.

"For work? Just tedious things. Farming, banking, shipping. The grunt work of civilization, really, but it must be done. I won't bore valued guests with such talk." He puffed his cigar and stood, looking out over the sill of one of the room's high windows, which left the lower half of the room in shadow. "Egyptology is not my only avocation, nor is it my primary one. I do share with the pharaohs an interest in legacy, a desire to leave a sizable mark on the world before I pass on. My own little piece of immortality.

"That town down the hill is my playground. My family has been here since the beginning. Soon, we'll have paved roads and a modern water system. We're even digging a reservoir, with a little pocket money from the Roosevelt administration. The town will grow into a city. It's well-positioned, right at the crossing of two of the busiest roads in the area. People have been meeting and trading here for two centuries. Now the telegraph line from Charleston runs right through Fallen Oak and on to Columbia, where it hooks into the main New York-New Orleans line. Add that to our railroad spur and our cotton exchange, and we're looking at a prosperous future."

He sat down, facing them again, and had more whiskey. "But that's small-time, isn't it? Just a little personal project of mine, this town. I'm involved in much larger things. Have you ever heard of the International Human Evolution Congress?"

Juliana and Sebastian shook their heads.

"I have the quarterly newsletter here somewhere," Barrett said, but he made no move to find it among the stacks of papers on his desk. "It's an organization of men influential in academia and the sciences, as well as simple business folk like me. We are committed to improvement of the human species. Already, our research has led to public health policies implemented by states like Virginia and California. The recently elected government in Germany has embraced our work enthusiastically, and is committed to funding and advancing our research."

Juliana just nodded. She and Sebastian had little idea of what was happening in a place as exotic and distant as Europe. Or even California, for that matter.

"What kind of policies?" Sebastian asked. "In Virginia and California?"

"Most of our work focuses on identifying and combating genetic disorders," Barrett told them. "For the benefit of posterity. On the other end of the spectrum, though, is the truly interesting work, and that's where the two of you fit in. We are constantly searching for those who possess, not disorders, but supernormal DNA. Those at the forward edge of human evolution. We want to encourage the progress of humanity."

"Encourage how?" Juliana asked. She sipped the whiskey again. Her head was starting to grow cloudy with the rum and whiskey, but the liquor also emboldened her to talk and ask questions.

"First, through research. We must understand how humanity is evolving and what new abilities might be emerging. The many talented scientists in our organization would be eager to study the two of you...provided that your powers are genuine, and my detective has not simply been fooled by your carnival tricks."

"You want to know if we're genuine?" Juliana smirked drunkenly and stripped the ratty cotton glove from her left hand. The open air felt cool on her sweaty fingers. "Watch me."

As Barrett watched, Juliana summoned up the demon plague within her, causing blisters and welts to erupt all over her exposed hand. They dripped blood and pus onto Barrett's petrified desk.

"Does that look genuine to you?" Juliana asked him, her voice sharp and challenging. The drink had her riled up, and she was ready to fight with someone.

"It appears genuine, of course," Barrett replied.

"I can infect you, if you like." Juliana reached across the desk toward him.

"Juliana, don't!" Sebastian pulled her back.

"What? You can just heal him," Juliana said.

"I'd rather not be the test monkey for this one, thank you," Barrett replied. He walked past them, cracked open the door, and whispered to someone outside—the older male servant, Juliana assumed. Barrett returned to his seat and smiled at Juliana, saying nothing.

After a minute, the servant led the detective into the study.

"Good," Barrett said. "Now, don't open that door again until I specifically call for you. Understand?"

The older man nodded and quickly left again, closing the door.

"What's the problem?" the detective asked.

"No problem yet, Emil," Barrett told him. "Roll up your sleeve and hold out your hand."

"Why would I do that?"

"Just a quick test," Barrett replied, nodding at Juliana.

The detective shook his head, moving out of Juliana's reach. "Not me. Test her on one of your Negroes!"

"And have them whispering about sorcery and witchcraft for

years to come? I don't believe I will. Hold out your hand," Barrett insisted again. "If they're just grifters, she won't hurt you. And if they're truly supernormal, the boy will heal you right away. You're risking nothing. And I insist that you do it. On behalf of the entire association."

The detective glared at him. "This will cost you extra."

"I assumed that much," Barrett replied.

The detective looked among them. Gritting his teeth, he shrugged off his coat and rolled up the sleeve of his left arm, then he looked at Juliana.

"Can you keep it small?" the detective asked her. "Don't turn me into a leper like you did the preacher. I've heard the horror stories from people who were there."

"I'll keep it small." Juliana giggled drunkenly. She reached her bare hand toward him, then touched her index finger to his forearm. She dragged her finger down toward his wrist, and dark sores opened in the wake of her touch.

The detective shouted and jerked his arm away from her. "It's real," he told Barrett. "Oh, God, it's real. You! Fix it!" He held his diseased arm in Sebastian's face.

"Wait," Barrett said. He stood and leaned over his desk, reaching cautiously toward the infected arm. "Is it contagious?"

"Only if you touch me." Juliana gave him an intoxicated smile and offered her hand. "Want to try?"

"No, thank you." Barrett inspected the sores on the detective's arm, then looked at Sebastian and nodded. Sebastian made all the sores vanish with a sweep of his hand, and the detective sighed, his eyes half-closing in pleasure at the sensation of being healed. Then he shook his head, as if coming to his senses, and glared at Barrett.

"Are we done?" the detective asked.

"Remarkable," Barrett said. "But it could still be a trick."

"It's no trick. That hurt," the detective told him. "Like my arm was on fire."

"Good. But before I can recommend them for our research program, I'll need to try just one more test." Barrett opened his desk drawer and took out a revolver.

"Hell, no!" The detective hurried toward the door as Barrett raised the gun and fired. The bullet struck the detective in the left shoulder, and the man howled and tumbled to his knees. He leaned against the wall, screaming and bleeding.

Barrett turned to Sebastian, grinning as he pointed the smoking gun at him. "Well? Are you going to do anything about it?"

Sebastian rose from his chair, looking warily at the gun in Barrett's hand, and walked backwards holding up his hands until he reached the suffering detective crumpled in the corner. He touched the man's head and closed his eyes. The detective stopped screaming and gave another contented sigh as the healing energy flowed through him.

The detective stood up, looking healthier than they'd ever seen him, with a kind of golden glow to his flesh. Sebastian had touched him long enough to heal him fully—not just the immediate damage to his arm, but any other health problems the man might have possessed, down to the slightest headache. The detective gave Sebastian a big, goofy smile, which looked completely out of place on the gruff man.

"Congratulations, Emil," Barrett told the detective. "It seems you've found two supernormals for us. As agreed, that's a hundred-dollar bonus for each."

"Good." The detective looked Sebastian over again before turning to Barrett. "Now you're done with me, Mr. Barrett?"

"Don't leave just yet," Barrett told him. "You can wait in the library, or the parlor, or the music room. Have my colored girls play piano for you, they know an extraordinary range of songs. They listen to all the newest phonographs. Are you a jazz man?"

"I'll find my way." The detective tipped his hat as he left.

Barrett smiled at Juliana and Sebastian, who simply gaped at him in shock, Juliana gripping the arms of her chair, Sebastian frozen in the corner. After a moment, Barrett seemed to notice the revolver still in his hand, and he put it away in his desk drawer as he returned to his high-backed chair.

"Sebastian, feel free to join us," Barrett said, gesturing at the empty chair. "I am sorry for all the drama, but I had to be sure before I could send you on."

"Send us on to where?" Juliana asked, while Sebastian cautiously sat beside her again.

"Tell me something. Have you ever wished to understand your powers? To gain greater control of them?" Barrett asked. "What about you, Juliana?"

"That's why I went to the revival," Juliana said. "I thought the preacher could heal me. I didn't mean to hurt him."

"But he couldn't heal you," Barrett said.

"No, it was Sebastian that had the healing touch, even though he was just the assistant. And he couldn't heal me. But his power protects him, so he's the only person who can touch me without getting infected." She took Sebastian's hand.

"Isn't that a pity?" Barrett asked. "A pretty girl like you should be free to touch anyone she likes."

"That's all I want," Juliana said. "I want to know how to make it stop, so I don't hurt anybody. Unless I need to hurt them."

Barrett laughed. "And that's what I'm offering you. The chance to finally have your abilities studied scientifically. To give you both the greatest possible understanding and control."

"You're saying I'll be able to go through life without infecting anyone?" Juliana asked.

"I'm saying that you have the opportunity to be studied by the finest scientific minds in Europe. Physicians, biologists, geneticists, even physicists. You will never again have a chance like this. If it is possible for you to turn off your ability, Juliana, they will discover the means."

Juliana felt her heart pounding. It was exactly what she'd been searching for all her life. She looked at Sebastian, but he didn't seem so excited.

"Europe?" Sebastian asked.

"If you agree, I will send the both of you to Berlin, where some of today's greatest scientists live. I mentioned that the German government is now sponsoring research programs in collaboration with the International Human Evolution Congress, as many high German officials are already members of our group. They will provide comfortable accommodations and all living expenses. And they will apply modern science to understanding your supernormal abilities."

"I don't know. I'm not sure I want to be studied like that. It could be...strange." Sebastian shook his head.

"Sebastian." Juliana squeezed his hand tightly. "You don't understand what it's like for me. Your touch is good for people. Mine...I can't continue living like this, avoiding everyone, always afraid of killing anyone who comes near me. My whole life has been a nightmare. If this could end all of it, then I need to do it, Sebastian."

She and Barrett both looked at Sebastian, but he seemed at a loss for words.

"The girl's right," Barrett said. "This is a necessity for her."

"And I don't want to go all the way to Europe without you," Juliana said. "Please. I need you."

Sebastian looked at the floor and rubbed his temple, as if thinking it over was a strain on him.

"You don't have to decide immediately, of course," Barrett said. "Take the day to think it over. You can stay here, eat, drink, listen to music, walk the gardens, and let me know your answer in the morning. If you decide not to do it, we can have you working at the carnival again by tomorrow night. If that's what you'd rather do with your life." He reached for the telephone. "Now, I have some of that boring old bank business to cope with. Make yourselves at home. I'll have the staff prepare rooms for you upstairs. If you see the detective, tell him he can go. We'll make other arrangements if you decide to rejoin the freak show tomorrow." Barrett placed the earpiece of the phone by his head and began talking to the operator.

Juliana clutched Sebastian's hand as they left the room, her mind swirling with excitement and fear. She knew that getting control of the demon plague was the right thing to do, and the only way she could ever hope to be a good person, but the idea of being examined in a laboratory day after day terrified her. If Sebastian was with her, that would make it all bearable. Without him, she would be alone, with no one who understood her.

Without speaking, they walked outside into the gardens, toward the peach orchard and the elaborate graveyard under construction. They didn't speak for a while. Both of them had plenty to think about.

# Chapter Fifteen

Juliana and Sebastian tried to enjoy an afternoon running free on the Barrett grounds. They avoided the darkness of the house, instead visiting the stables to view Mr. Barrett's horses, including a champion racehorse, which the horse groom was happy to discuss.

Barrett slaughtered a pig in their honor, outside by the smokehouse. He made a show of cutting the squealing animal's throat himself with a butcher knife, which sent his young son screaming and crying into the house. It roasted in a pit until long after sunset, filling the grounds with the smell of hot pork.

Sebastian and Juliana waited for supper in the library, where Sebastian continued to "taste" Mr. Barrett's Canadian whiskey again and again, while Juliana read aloud from a collection of poems by Percy Shelley. Barrett had made a number of notes in the margins of "Ozymandias," but she couldn't decipher his handwriting.

When she looked up from the book of poetry, she saw that Barrett's small, timid son, also named Jonathan, had crept into the room to listen to her. He stood behind a stiff wing-backed chair near the door, as if hiding while also making sure he could escape fast. Sebastian, drowsing off in his own chair while looking out at the gardens, hadn't even noticed him.

"Hello," Juliana said to the little boy, who cringed.

"Do I have to leave, ma'am?" he whispered.

"No, you can come and sit. Do you like poetry?"

"I like listening to you read it, ma'am." He tiptoed around the wing-backed chair and sat down on the edge, tentatively, as if he expected to be attacked at any moment.

"You don't have to be scared," Juliana said.

The boy looked at her and started crying. She could not touch him to comfort him, so she tried the softest voice she could manage: "Why are you upset?"

"He killed my pig." The boy rubbed his running nose on his sleeve. "My favorite pig."

"Your father?"

"Yes, ma'am."

"I'm sorry." She felt terrible for him. She could imagine how a boy might get attached to an animal. "He probably didn't know it was your favorite."

"He knew! That's why he killed her. Because she was my friend." The boy turned red and cried harder.

"What's happening?" Sebastian asked, startled awake by the boy's bawling.

"His favorite pig died."

"Because he hates me! That's why he did it," the boy said.

"I'm sure your father doesn't hate you," Juliana said.

"And he could have brought her back to life, but he cooked her instead. And now you're all going to eat her!"

"I don't think he could bring her back to life," Juliana said.

"He could! He can bring the dead back. He showed me one night, in the Negro graveyard. He made one climb right out!" The boy was blubbering. "My father's evil. I think he's the Devil. Or he's worse."

"I'm sure your father isn't evil," Juliana told him.

"You don't know anything!" the boy shouted. He ran out of the library.

"Kid liked that pig," Sebastian said.

"I couldn't even hug him or anything. It breaks my heart. Where's his mother, anyway?" Juliana asked.

"Upstairs with the laudanum, remember?" Sebastian said.

A servant collected them for supper, where Barrett drank heavily

and regaled them with stories of nights he'd spent in New York and
London, sometimes meeting famous people, about whom he gossiped
freely. Some of the stories had Juliana laughing into her punch,
though all the alcohol she'd consumed certainly helped her find the
humor in his jokes. He came across as well-educated, well-traveled,
and just plain wealthy, but with a deep fondness for the little town
where he'd grown up.

Neither Barrett's son nor his wife made an appearance during the
meal. Neither Seth nor Juliana had the nerve to ask what his son
might have meant about him bringing the dead to life, and with the
drinking, the subject was soon forgotten.

* * *

In the morning, Juliana felt ill from so much drinking. She ate
one of the fluffy, buttery biscuits served at the dining room table,
along with a slice of fresh-cut peach, but she didn't touch the eggs or
sausages. She drank plenty of coffee.

"Have you had time to consider my offer?" Barrett asked when he
joined them. He was already washed and dressed for the day, which
made Juliana feel disgusting with her matted hair, wearing yesterday's
clothes. At least she'd slept well, in a beautiful room on the second
floor with nautical paintings on the walls, the bed made from old ship
timbers, the curtains cut from sailing cloth. Sebastian had slept in a
different room up on the third floor.

"It's certainly interesting," Sebastian said. He sat next to Juliana
and gave her a long look. Juliana had made it clear to him how much
she wanted to do this, even if Barrett himself grew stranger the more
they learned about him. She would almost certainly never get another
chance to free herself from the demon plague.

"You sound uncertain," Barrett said. "How else can I convince
you?"

"I'm as convinced as I'll ever be," Sebastian told him. "I don't
really want it for myself, but I'll have to go for Juliana's sake. Make
sure she doesn't slip up and kill everybody there, you know?"

"I would not!" Juliana said, smiling at him. "You'll go to Berlin?
Truly?"

"I can't stay with the carnival, can I?" he asked. "They're about
to lose the star of their freak show. Things could go south from

there."

"I'm sure the carnival will manage to survive. They did for thirty years before I joined. Oh, thank you!" Juliana threw her arms around Sebastian's neck and held him close.

"That makes an excellent start to the morning," Barrett said. "I'll telegraph my colleagues in Berlin, and phone my office manager in Charleston to arrange your transportation across the Atlantic. We'll find you a nice, modern ship that makes good time. The accommodations must be suitable for a fine lady." He smiled at Juliana, and she did her best not to smile back too widely. She would be much more comfortable once she was out of Mr. Barrett's unsettling, magnetic presence.

After breakfast, Barrett instructed his staff to draw a warm bath for Juliana, a process that involved boiling buckets of well water, hauling them upstairs, and pouring them into the claw-footed tub. After giving the order, he retreated to his office.

Juliana declined when a servant girl offered to "bathe" her, an offer that made her uncomfortable on many levels. She instead invited Sebastian to join her in the bathing room, provided he sat in a chair with his back turned and promised not to look. Partly this was to tease him, partly it was a peace offering—she'd gotten a lot of glares from him for her inappropriate drunken flirting with Mr. Barrett. Mostly, she did it to ensure Sebastian himself bathed before she spent days holed up in a steamship with him.

When Juliana whispered this suggestion, Sebastian gave her his first real smile since they'd arrived at Barrett House.

In the bathroom, she closed the door and turned the key, then slid a wooden chair from the corner to face the door.

"Sit here," she told him.

"The view won't be as pretty over here. And I won't be able to wash your hair for you or anything."

"I think I can do that myself," she told him.

He sighed and took the chair, shaking his head as he stared at the closed door. Juliana backed away from him, almost to the tub, and then she pulled her dress up and over her head. She unhooked and removed her cotton undergarments, then stood by the tub, naked from head to toe. She shivered with the forbidden delight of being unclothed in a room with him, her nipples stiffening as she looked at his broad shoulders and his unkempt hair. She almost hoped he would turn around and look at her, but he unfortunately remained a gentleman.

"So, this Barrett fellow, he's a little strange, isn't he?" Sebastian asked, still looking at the door.

"He's going to help us." Juliana slipped into the warm water. It felt delicious on her bare skin. She soaped her body. "He's certainly got the dough. A real butter and egg man."

"Now you're making me hungry again," he said, and she laughed. "Don't you think it sounds suspicious?"

"Of course. I've always been a suspicious girl." She dunked her head underwater, then soaped her hair. "Never trust anyone, that's what I say. But, still, a free holiday in Europe sounds nice, doesn't it?"

"It doesn't sound like a holiday. They'll probably cage us up like rats in a laboratory."

"If they do, I'll kill them."

"Europe is a dangerous place."

Juliana laughed. "We're not going to Tasmania. Europe's more civilized than we are."

"When they're not slaughtering each other with wars."

"The last war ended when we were both little children." Juliana rinsed out her hair. "Nobody wants war anymore. The world is saner now. Everyone agrees peace is important."

"I hope you're right."

Juliana quickly finished her bath. She stood up in the tub, letting herself drip for a moment, just in case he decided to peek. She would, of course, pretend to be angry if he did. He didn't look, though, so she reluctantly toweled off, stepped out of the bath, and put her dirty clothes back on, since she didn't have anything else to wear.

"Your turn in the bath," she said.

"I don't need one." He quickly turned to face her, and his face showed a little disappointment at seeing her fully dressed.

*Should have been faster, boy,* she thought. She said: "I disagree. Who knows when we'll get another chance to bathe?"

"I'd rather not."

"I insist."

He got out of his chair and grinned at her, unbuttoning his shirt to reveal the lean muscles of his chest and stomach. She wanted to reach out and place a hand somewhere low on his belly, but that could make things dangerous fast. He unbuckled his belt, and she turned away to look at the door.

"He really likes you, doesn't he?" Sebastian asked behind her back. The water sloshed as he entered the tub. "Mr. Barrett."

"Are you feeling jealous?" she asked him.

"He must be, what, ten years older than us? Twenty? Do you think he's twenty years older?"

"You are jealous!" She glanced back over her shoulder to see him in the water, and he quickly covered himself with his hands.

"Do you have no modesty?" he asked, though his voice wasn't exactly angry.

"None." She turned away again, smiling to herself.

"There's no reason for me to feel jealous. If he touches you, he dies. Right?" Sebastian asked.

"Yes." She was glad he couldn't see her frown. "Of course."

"So, flirt all you want. I don't have to worry about anyone else."

"I don't belong to you, you understand that?" Juliana asked, still looking at the door. "I'm not your property."

"Yes, you are," he said, grabbing her by the waist and lifting her into the air. She squealed, kicking her legs. He must have eased quietly out of the water and tiptoed up behind her.

"Let me go!" she demanded.

"Why would I let you go now?" He turned her and lowered her against him, pressing his lips to hers. He was still wet, naked, and, judging from the hard pressure against her thigh, very aroused.

"Put me down, Sebastian," she whispered. "You're making my dress wet."

He raised his eyebrows.

"Don't you say a thing!" she told him. She kissed him again. "We have to go."

Reluctantly, he returned her to the floor. He took his time getting dressed again.

* * *

Barrett led them out along a brick path to the stables. Juliana stayed close to Sebastian, holding his arm. It was a hot, sunny day, and she was glad her hair was still wet enough to help keep her cool.

"We don't mind taking the train to Charleston," Sebastian told

Barrett. "You don't have to send a wagon all day."

"You're in luck," Barrett told them as he approached a small shed next to the stable. "I have a mountain of work to do in Charleston myself."

He lifted a loose horizontal board and opened the wooden door it had pinned shut. Inside, where Juliana had expected a wagon or buggy, there was a long, sleek, maroon and black Cadillac convertible, its creme-colored cloth roof laid back to expose the leather interior. It had a gleaming spare tire mounted behind each of the front wheels, just ahead of the running boards. The hood ornament was a silver goddess with wings.

Juliana looked at Sebastian, who was gaping at the polished luxury automobile. It was like something in which a king might travel during a parade, waving to the crowd.

"I may as well drive you there myself," Barrett said. "It's the fastest way. Besides, the two of you will be my greatest contribution yet to the Evolution Congress. I want to make sure every moment is as fully pleasurable for you as possible." He winked as he opened the front passenger-side door. "Ladies ride in front, of course."

Sebastian shook his head and opened one of the rear doors. He gave her a grin as she sank into the soft leather seat in front of him. Jealous or not, he was clearly going to enjoy the ride.

"Thank you," Juliana said to Barrett. "I believe this is the finest automobile I've ever seen. Will we really travel all the way to Charleston in this?"

"It won't be a long ride." Barrett grinned as he dropped into the passenger seat and cranked the motor. The entire car thrummed and vibrated.

"You don't have a servant to drive you?" Sebastian asked. He'd clearly expected Barrett to ride in the back with him.

"I suppose I could pay a servant to drive my car for me," Barrett said. He slid a pair of very dark sunglasses over his eyes. "I suppose I could pay someone to eat, drink, smoke, and dance for me, too, but where's the fun in that?"

Sebastian didn't look happy, but he moved to the center of the back seat, sprawling out his arms and legs as if pleased to have so much room to himself. He forced a smile and did a horrific attempt at an English accent: "Then drive us, good sir!"

Barrett looked back to give him an annoyed look while punching the accelerator. The car shot out of the shed at high speed, across the brick path and toward the peach orchard. Barrett didn't even look where he was going.

"Watch out!" Sebastian shouted, ducking. Barrett laughed and wrenched the car around, kicking up grass and dirt as he fishtailed back onto the paved path, more or less, and then gave the car even more gas, charging past the house and into the circular turnaround in front of it. Juliana screamed as he slid sideways in front of the house, his back tires squealing and smoking, and then he whipped onto the driveway and roared past old magnolias and oaks on the way to the front gate.

Juliana looked back over her shoulder, her heart crashing in her chest. A cloud of dust and burnt-rubber smoke hung like a veil in front of the house. In a third-story window, Juliana caught a glimpse of a woman with a very pale, thin face and unkempt hair the color of pine straw. The face vanished quickly. Juliana wondered whether Barrett had even told his wife and son that he was leaving for the day.

The car roared through the open gate and flung up another long cloud of dust as it spun onto the road. They moved east, toward the sun and the countryside, leaving the town behind. The state highway was paved for the initial stretch, so Barrett pressed the accelerator to the floor. The Cadillac moved unnaturally fast, turning cotton fields and cow pastures into a green and white blur on either side of the road. The speed pushed Juliana back against her seat and sent her long, dark hair streaming across her face.

She looked at the round speedometer dial and saw the needle touching 100 miles per hour. She didn't know anything could move that fast, except maybe airplanes.

Barrett swerved around the very occasional wagon or farm truck without slowing. At each turn, Juliana had to grab the door and the edge of her seat to avoid being slung back and forth, or possibly out of the car altogether. It was frightening, and far more exhilarating than any ride at the carnival. Juliana felt a little bit in love with the car.

Then the highway turned from pavement to dirt, and Barrett had to slow down because of the dips and washout gullies that bounced the car.

"That was fantastic," Juliana breathed, her skin flush from the long, unexpected blast of speed.

"Must be one of those eight-cylinder cars like the detective had,"

Sebastian said, trying to sound bored.

"*Sixteen* cylinders," Barrett told him, beaming. "They don't make many like this, because most people are too dull to want a car like this."

"It doesn't seem possible for a person to drive so fast," Juliana said.

"You could do it," Barrett told her.

"I don't believe so! I've never operated any automobile before."

"Is that true?" Barrett slowed to a stop, pulling over to the right side of the road next to a barbed-wired goat pasture. The creatures stared at them as he climbed out of his seat and motioned for Juliana to slide over behind the wheel.

"No, you don't want to do that," Juliana said. "I'll wreck us."

"I'll drive the car," Sebastian offered, but Barrett ignored him.

"You will not wreck us, Juliana. Take the wheel," Barrett insisted. He crossed in front of the car, around to the passenger side.

"Are you joking?" Juliana looked at the dials and levers.

"All the things in the universe are in a state of decay," Barrett told her. "It's a law of thermodynamics."

"What does that mean?" she asked.

"It means time is always wasting. The time we spend arguing could be time you spend flying down the road." He opened her door, standing over her, blocking out the sun. "Move on, or it's going to get crowded on this side."

She laughed and slid over behind the wheel, touching it hesitantly with her gloved hands. The engine rumbled ahead of her, sounding eager to move.

Barrett placed one of her hands on the wheel and the other on the long gear stick that jutted up from the floor. Though he knew of the demon plague within her, he seemed to have no fear of leaning his face close to hers, or touching her through her thin summer dress. Juliana found herself blushing a little, and her breaths grew shorter as he positioned her feet on the clutch and the brake pedal, explaining how to use them. His hands brushed her legs a few times, and once his hand happened to linger on her lower thigh as he explained when to shift gears. She wanted to slap him, but she wanted to do a few other things to him, too.

She was grateful that the plague took the choice out of her hands. If she were free to touch Barrett all she liked, she might have been in danger of betraying Sebastian. She could feel guilt on her face as she glanced back at him. Sebastian simply stared at her and said nothing, but he had an angry glint in his eyes.

"I think you're ready to drive," Barrett told her.

"I'm not sure..." Juliana said, but she moved the stick out of its parked setting and operated the pedals and wheel as he'd demonstrated, and the car lurched forward and began rolling.

"More gas," he said, and she stepped hard on the pedal. The Cadillac surged forward, spraying dust behind it. Juliana couldn't help crying out in excitement as she felt the power surging under her and the wind blowing back her hair. Her fear quickly turned to joy, and soon she drove as fast as the road would allow.

"I'm doing it!" Juliana shouted at Barrett, over the roar of the engine and the high wind that filled her ears. "I'm driving!"

Barrett grinned and patted her on the back. He let his arm linger at her shoulders a little too long, and it almost gave her goosebumps to think of him so near, so willing to risk death just to touch her. His hand was dangerously close to brushing against the bare flesh of her neck. He only withdrew the arm when Sebastian leaned up between them and kissed her on the cheek.

"Don't kill us!" Sebastian suggested.

"I'll do my best!" Juliana put on more speed. "I could drive all the way to Charleston, Mr. Barrett! Just tell me where to turn."

"All you need to do is follow the telegraph line." Barrett pointed to the cables strung alongside the road, held high above them by wooden poles with crossbars. She remembered a story she'd read in a musty library book when she was a child, about a slave uprising in ancient Rome. The slaves had lost, and thousands of them had been crucified on wooden crosses like these, all along the road to Rome.

For a moment, she could *see* the bodies crucified along the road. It wasn't the blocky woodcut image from the old book, either, but real people nailed up and dripping gore, their faces contorted from long, painful deaths, as if she had been a witness to them, traveling along the stone road in the aftermath.

She gazed at Barrett beside her and felt something dark and ancient between them, as if they'd ridden side by side countless times, drawn by fast horses here and there across the world. Later, she would learn the term *déjà vu* and understand its meaning immediately, thinking of this moment.

Then the moment passed, and she was simply driving again, feeling the sun and the wind on her face. She looked forward to the next stretch of pavement, where she could press the accelerator all the way down and feel the car's full speed.

# Chapter Sixteen

Jenny and Seth slept late on Christmas. Jenny awoke first, made a pot of coffee and took a small, rich square of chocolate with her to the frosted front window. The short but brightly lit tree by the window filled the apartment with the golden scent of living pine. Outside, a thin, fresh frosting of snow had fallen, decorating the trees, ledges, and balconies with spotless icy fluff.

She thought of her father again, back home in Fallen Oak. Maybe he wasn't even home at all, but over at June's apartment. Jenny hoped they were still seeing each other. She hated imagining him at home, by himself, accompanied only by the dog and pictures of his lost wife and daughter. She wondered if he'd started drinking again.

Jenny busied herself by getting a start on Christmas dinner. She was attempting a few French dishes, including a *bûche de Noël* for dessert, a rolled-up cake with chocolate cream filling. The fun part would be carving the outer layer of icing with a fork to make it look like the bark of a Yule log.

Her digital Christmas song list played at random on the stereo, jumping from Bonnie Raitt singing "Merry Christmas Baby" to John Lennon's "Happy Christmas."

She made hot chocolate, another smell that reminded her of

Christmas. Her father had made it for her, usually by mixing Valu Time chocolate-flavored syrup with Piggly Wiggly brand milk and heating it in the microwave. He did that even in those years when December in South Carolina had felt like early summer. Now she made it with fresh-grated dark and white chocolate from *La Maison du Chocolat*. She wished her father were here to try it.

Jenny looked out at the boulevard below, where thousands of tiny golden lights glowed on strings as far as she could see and the lamp posts were hung with green garlands. The sun slid out from behind the clouds, making the city's blanket of snow sparkle. Few cars passed, and everyone who walked by seemed beautiful to her, even the hacking old man hunched over his walker, escorted by two excited young kids who must have been his grandchildren.

She heard Seth approaching in his sock feet, probably trying to sneak up on her. He found that hilarious for some reason.

"Merry Christmas," he said, sliding his arms around her waist. He felt strong and warm against her back.

The sky darkened, and their ghostly, transparent reflections appeared in the window pane. Jenny found herself looking at her own face and Seth's sleepy, smiling face behind her. Their child growing inside her.

*This is it*, Jenny realized. *This moment is the happiest I'll ever be. The baby will die, and I'll hate myself, and Seth will probably hate me, too, if he finds out. Nothing will ever be the same.*

Jenny watched her own eyes fill up with tears, until her vision turned blurry and she had to wipe them. Stupid hormones.

"What's wrong?" Seth asked.

She turned to look at him, smiling as she touched his face. "Merry Christmas," she whispered, and she kissed him. Then she leaned in against him, hugging him with all her strength, as if she could stop the future from coming if she clung tightly enough to the present.

"Are you sad because we haven't opened presents yet?" Seth asked, which made her laugh.

"I was just thinking about my dad." She wiped her eyes again, and she'd managed to swallow back the tears and put on a smile.

"Yeah, that's hard." He hugged her back just as tightly. "I think about my parents waking up in a silent house on Christmas morning. They've lost both their sons now, Carter and me."

They were quiet for a minute, holding each other. Then Seth

asked, "So...can we open presents now?"

"Yes, please!" Jenny dropped to her knees by the tree, looking over the bright packages and ribbons.

"Me first," Seth said, joining her and picking up a present, which he handed to her. "By which I mean you first."

Jenny smiled as she tore it open. The cardboard box inside held a wide selection of DVDs, all of her favorite holiday movies, from the old stop-motion *Rudolph the Red-Nose Reindeer* that she had watched on TV every year, to the *Muppet Christmas Carol*, all the way to *Scrooged* with Bill Murray.

"Awesome!" Jenny said. "I missed seeing these last year." Their first Christmas in Paris had caught them almost by surprise, and they'd done little to remind themselves of home.

"And I remembered you saying that." Seth tapped the side of his head. "Thoughtful. Good listener. Yep."

"Here, open this." Jenny handed him the biggest package with his name on it.

Seth ripped it apart, revealing a box full of plain socks.

"Remember how you complained about wanting more socks last Christmas?" Jenny asked.

"Did I?"

"See if there's anything else in there."

Seth moved the socks aside and found the new Kindle Fire hidden underneath. "Oh, cool!"

"Now you can read any book you want, anytime you want," Jenny told him.

"This is the one that plays movies, too, right?"

"I guess."

"That makes me want to give you this one next." Seth passed her a small box wrapped in satiny red paper.

"Looks sexy." Jenny unwrapped it—it *was* sexy, a very revealing piece of lingerie held together by thin, lacy black straps. "Ooh, a dominatrix outfit!"

"It is not!"

"Just add leather," Jenny said. "And I'll need handcuffs."

"I even got the size right this time. I checked your underwear drawer first."

"And how long did you spend in there?"

"Ha, ha. Why don't you try it on?"

"I'm sure you'd like that," Jenny snickered.

"No, seriously." Seth leaned back on his elbow and eyed her.

"Mariella's going to be here soon."

"Just a quick look." Seth winked.

Jenny felt a growing sense of panic. She could stave him off for now, but there was no way she could wear this without Seth seeing her swollen belly. It was hard enough keeping concealed in heavy sweaters around him, turning off the lights before she took off her clothes, and remembering to lock the door when she showered.

"I'll help." Seth reached for her very oversized red sweater, and she pulled away from him. He jumped at her, seized her, and playfully wrestled her down, then he climbed on top of her, his weight pushing her whole body against the floor.

"Careful!" Jenny shouted. "I'm pregnant!"

"You're what?" His eyes flew wide open, and he rolled off her and sat up. "What did you say?"

The phone in the apartment chimed, the special sound it made when a visitor downstairs wanted to be admitted to their apartment.

"Jenny?" he asked. "Did you just say—"

"I win!" Jenny jumped to her feet and scampered to the door, where she flicked on the tiny video screen. Mariella, dressed in thick layers with a hat, scarf, and gloves, appeared in black and white, and Jenny buzzed her in. "Looks like your girlfriend's here."

"Why do you keep saying that?" Seth followed her to the door. "She's not my girlfriend. I've never done anything with her."

"You will."

"What do you mean?"

Jenny sighed and shook her head. It all fit together now. Jenny and Seth's baby would die, the strain would ruin their relationship, and he would end up with Mariella. If Mariella was really seeing herself and Seth together in the future, then that would probably be the way it happened.

If Jenny and Seth weren't going to break up, then Mariella's vision could only mean that Jenny would die, which didn't exactly fill her with hope for a better tomorrow.

"Jenny..." Seth hesitated. "Did you just say you were pregnant?"

"We'll talk about it later."

"So you are?"

"No. Maybe."

"Maybe?" He gaped at her. "Did you take a test?"

"I...um..." Jenny saw Mariella arrive through the door lens and opened up before Mariella had a chance to ring the bell. *"Bon jour! Joyeux Noël!"*

*"Joyeux Noël!"* Mariella replied with a bright smile. Her green eyes seemed to glow, helped along by her matching dress, which she wore under her usual dark coat. She carried bright packages and an embroidered shopping bag into the apartment, and Seth quickly took them from her arms. Mariella leaned in to kiss Jenny's cheek in the typical French greeting, and Jenny automatically pulled back and covered her mouth, shaking her head. It indicated that she was refraining, not to be rude, but because she was sick and contagious.

Seth had no trouble accepting Mariella's kisses. He put the glittering wrapped packages on a side table, but Mariella reclaimed the shopping bag.

"Oh, no, you didn't have to bring presents," Jenny said. She spoke in English, since it was pretty obvious that Seth didn't know much French, while Mariella was fluent in English. "We didn't..."

"It's nothing, I promise," Mariella said. She held open the shopping bag, revealing three different bottles of red wine. "I did not know what you liked best."

"Oh, that's too much!" Jenny laughed.

Seth was giving Jenny a very serious look over Mariella's head. He gestured toward the bedroom, clearly wanting to talk privately about whether she was pregnant or not. That was the subject Jenny wanted to avoid most, at the moment, so she took Mariella's arm and led her into the kitchen instead.

"How can I help here?" Mariella asked, looking around at the multiple dishes in progress.

"You don't have to." Jenny set the wine bottles on the counter. She opened a Pinot noir and poured two glasses.

"Please, it does not feel like Christmas if I'm not a kitchen slave for at least part of the day," Mariella said. "You forgot to pour a third glass. I'll do it."

"No, I'm not drinking right now," Jenny said.

"Even on Christmas?" Mariella looked at Jenny's ridiculously baggy sweater, which reached almost to her knees. "Are you pregnant?"

"Sh!" Jenny said, and Mariella's eyes widened.

"He does not know?" Mariella whispered.

"You've been in my house for thirty seconds and you're figuring out all this? In five minutes you'll be telling me my own darkest secrets."

Mariella laughed. "How dark can they be?"

"You might be surprised."

"You can have a glass with us," Mariella said. "In Italy, women still drink a glass with dinner, and all is well. And we are very good at having babies. We've been doing it for thousands of years."

Jenny laughed.

"Do Alsatian women stop drinking wine altogether?" Mariella asked. "I thought only American women did that."

"I'm just being cautious."

"Be less so." Mariella poured a third glass, giving her a cheerful smile. "It's good for the heart."

"Red wine, or being less cautious?" Jenny asked.

"Both!"

They were laughing again when they rejoined Seth in the living room.

"Should you be drinking wine?" Seth asked when Jenny handed him a glass.

"Why shouldn't I?" Jenny asked him, but Seth just answered with a frustrated shrug and glanced at Mariella, not sure whether the other girl should know or not.

"You're Americans, aren't you?" Mariella asked.

"Stop doing that! Seth, I can't hide anything from her." Jenny took a long sip of wine.

"We should open our presents." Mariella carried her gifts to the couch and set them on the coffee table.

"No, really, we didn't get you anything," Jenny said. "I'll go shopping tomorrow, anyway."

"There is no need," Mariella said. "Unless you are inviting me to shop with you. The Christmas villages remain open another week."

"Maybe," Jenny said, giving her a genuine smile. She had to remind herself not to trust this girl too much.

Seth was already ripping open his small package. "Whoa!" he said.

"What is it?" Jenny asked.

Seth held up a stainless steel Cartier watch with a black dial.

"Look, Jenny. Now I can be one of those guys who wears a watch."

Jenny tried not to look shocked, but she knew the watch must have cost hundreds, if not thousands of dollars. She wanted to insist that Seth give it back, but there was not a polite way to do it.

"Please, it's too nice," Jenny said.

"Don't be silly. Now for yours." Mariella tapped another gift, and Jenny reluctantly sank to the settee and unwrapped it. Then she stared at what lay inside.

It was some kind of charm bracelet, made of gold with sapphires in the individual little charms, which included a heart-shaped lock, a miniscule rocking horse, an owl, a coin with the face of Victor Emmanuel III, the final king of Italy, and other tiny, glittering objects.

"Oh, no," Jenny breathed. She could tell it was unspeakably expensive. "You shouldn't give me this."

"It's nothing," Mariella said. "Just put it on. I think sapphires would look beautiful on you."

"I love sapphires," Jenny whispered.

"Then try it on. Or let me." She reached for the glove on Jenny's left hand and tugged it off, her fingers protected by her own soft kidskin glove.

"Careful!" Jenny pulled back. "It's too dangerous for you to touch me."

"Then you had better put it on yourself." Mariella reached for her hand again.

"Okay, I give up." Jenny slid the bracelet onto her wrist. The gold was smooth and bright against her skin.

"Do you like it at all?" Mariella asked.

"I love it," Jenny admitted. "But why did you...when did you even go shopping? The shops must have been closed by the time you left here last night."

Mariella laughed. "Don't trouble yourself too much. I stole the watch from my brother six months ago, because he was being mean. And the charm bracelet...I must have been eight or nine when I stole it from my sister. Swiping from my siblings has always been my favorite way to shop. Youngest child syndrome. With eight older brothers and sisters, there's always plenty of tempting loot around."

Jenny breathed a sigh of relief. "So these were just things you already had. You didn't go spend a fortune on us."

"Are you disappointed?" Mariella asked.

"No, now I'm definitely keeping the bracelet."

Mariella laughed and emptied the bottle of Pinot into their glasses. She gave Jenny a thoughtful look.

"I know we got off to a...how would you say it? An awkward start," Mariella said, with a brief side glance at Seth. "But I wanted to show you how important this is to me, knowing the both of you. I've never met anyone like us before. I hope you don't hate me already."

"Why would we hate you?" Seth asked, but Mariella just kept looking at Jenny, her green eyes hopeful, her lips twitching nervously.

"I don't hate you," Jenny said. "But I'm sure you understand, I'm still pretty bothered by what you said."

"What she said about what?" Seth looked back and forth between them. "What am I missing?"

Jenny and Mariella held each other's gaze. Jenny didn't exactly want to tell Seth what Mariella had said, about seeing herself and Seth together in the future, or Mariella's sweaty, hot dreams about Seth. She could only imagine the expression on Seth's face if they told him about that. As if they were sharing the same thoughts, she and Mariella burst into laughter at the same time.

"What's so funny? Jenny?" Seth asked, looking frustrated now. He drank down his entire glass of wine, then held it like a microphone. "Hello, can anybody hear me? Is this thing on?"

"You had a bad vision about Seth, too," Jenny said. "A man who was hunting him. Can you see anything else about that today?"

"I can try." Mariella pulled her gloves off and reached for Seth's hands.

"So, me getting attacked or killed, that was the funny thing?" Seth asked. "That's what you were laughing about?"

"Quiet, Seth, let her concentrate," Jenny said.

Mariella gazed into Seth's eyes, holding his hands tight. He kept glancing away, looking uncomfortable.

"I can see him," Mariella said. "He comes and takes Seth to a dark place."

"Does that mean I die?" Seth said.

"He takes you as a prisoner."

"What about Jenny?" he asked.

Mariella closed her eyes. A pained look crossed her face. "I can't see her future any better than my own. It's like a dark cloud. All I can think is that her power might block mine in some way. I certainly can't touch her."

"That's why I always have enemies among our kind," Jenny said. "Most of them can't even try to control me or use their powers against me, or they'll die from the pox."

"Jenny can't be tamed," Seth said. "She's like a wild animal."

"That's right," Jenny said.

"A badger, maybe," Seth said, and Jenny gave him a light punch in the arm. Seth pretended to cringe in pain. He asked Mariella, "So, I get taken prisoner. How? Why? For how long?"

Mariella shook her head, her eyes still closed, her teeth grinding together. "I...*can't*. It's never been so difficult, not with normal people."

"We're definitely not normal," Jenny said.

"I can see the man dragging Seth away...but everything's hidden behind a scramble of colors and a cloud of sleepy fog."

"What's 'sleepy fog'?" Seth asked.

"I don't know, that's just what I feel!" Mariella opened her eyes. "I must be involved, that's why I can't see much. Or Jenny is involved and I can't see her future. Or both."

"Involved how? You're helping him kidnap me?"

"No, of course not! I wouldn't," Mariella told him. "All I know is that you become his prisoner."

"Is that all you see?" Jenny asked.

"Maybe I'll see more later. The sooner something will happen, the clearer I see it. So we must have some time."

"How much time?" Seth asked. "Should I barricade the apartment or what?"

"A few weeks, a couple of months, maybe." Mariella bit her lip. "I'm sorry! I'm usually much better at this. Most people, I get more information than I ever wanted...and most people don't listen, either, even when I tell them they're moving toward disaster. And they never come back and admit I was right, either."

"No one believes you?" Jenny asked.

"Usually not. A few times, people have listened to me and changed their futures...but then they tell me I was worried about nothing, because they avoided whatever danger I saw." Mariella looked at Jenny's hands. "It must have been difficult for you, growing up. Avoiding the touch of everyone. It makes my problems look silly, people ignoring me and not believing me."

"I managed," Jenny said. "You try not to kill anyone, but sometimes you can't help it."

Mariella laughed, but there was a glint of fear in her eyes.

"I'm starting to think I might know who this man is, from the way you described him," Jenny told her. "I think I'm starting to figure out who you are, too."

"I've been honest with you," Mariella said, and then laughed a little. "Too honest, maybe."

"I don't mean in this life, but in our last one. You and him were both there...the oracle and the seer."

"Who?" Seth asked.

"That's what we've called them in the past," Jenny said. "She's the oracle. Her opposite is the seer, a very nasty soul."

"Are you talking about reincarnation?" Mariella asked. "I thought you didn't believe in that."

"I can remember hundreds of lifetimes," Jenny said. "I mean, not all at once, obviously. And the last few are the most difficult for me, because the person who opened my mind to my memories...Alexander...he didn't want me to remember those lives. So he blocked them, or kept me from opening them, or something. I'm working on unraveling the last one, because I think it matters now."

"I knew it!" Mariella said. "I've always felt that I've lived before."

"We all have," Jenny told her. "And you were part of the last one, and so was your opposite. That's why it's important we figure out what happened. It's the only way to figure out what the seer wants and how we can stop him."

Seth was raising his eyebrows at her, clearly surprised she'd told Mariella so much. Jenny shrugged. Let Seth judge for himself when he learned more about who she was, Jenny thought. Mariella's past life didn't necessarily tell Jenny who Mariella was in this lifetime, and it was always best to be suspicious.

"Can you tell me about my past lives?" Mariella asked.

"I will, if you feel like listening. The duck's going to roast another hour. I'll have to catch you up on the story so far...and this calls for another glass of wine, so let's pretend I'm drinking one." She slid her glass across the table to Seth, who drank it down like it was Jell-o shot. "You might as well open the next bottle, Seth."

He smiled and walked to the kitchen. Jenny's plan was to get Seth completely sloshed before Mariella left. Maybe she could put off the big pregnancy talk one more day.

"The last time we saw each other, it was the Great Depression," Jenny said, "1933."

# Chapter Seventeen

Just before they reached Charleston, Barrett took over the driving from Juliana, explaining that city driving was a little more complicated, and there were rules to learn.

The city of Charleston was full of life, with street vendors hawking everything from newspapers to fresh shrimp, trolleys crawling through the crowded downtown, music playing from open windows and balconies. It was a far more beautiful place than Juliana had expected, full of masterfully worked wrought-iron gates and fences, brick walls and high columns. Mr. Barrett must have brought in craftsmen from Charleston to build his mansion, Juliana thought, because the style was the same.

Massive old trees lined the streets, live oak and magnolias dripping with Spanish moss and wisteria. The towers of churches and cathedrals reached toward the sky on almost every block.

"I love this city," Juliana said. "You wouldn't even know there was a Depression at all."

"You can thank the United States Navy for that," Barrett told her. "They've expanded the shipyards and they're turning out battleships like clockwork. Good for jobs, good for business. I was even lucky enough to invest in some of the companies that provision the shipyard.

Really helps us weather the economy."

"Battleships?" Juliana asked. "Is another war coming?"

"The more battleships you have, the easier it is to keep the peace." Barrett honked at a slow, horse-drawn wagon loaded with vegetables blocking up the street ahead of them. "Remember, we have two big oceans to control, the Atlantic and the Pacific. That takes a lot of ships, and Charleston is proud to provide them."

They finally reached a four-story, colonial-style office building a few blocks from the wharf, its bricks painted a cheerful blue color, its windows trimmed in gold and white. The artfully carved and painted wooden sign by the front door listed several businesses, one of which was "Barrett Mercantiles."

"This is where I have to be dull and go through paperwork," Barrett told them as he got out of the car. He circled around to open Juliana's door, but Sebastian climbed out first and beat him to it, holding her hand as she stepped down from the running board. Barrett gave Sebastian a smirk, then handed Juliana a pair of twenty-dollar bills. "The city is yours. Buy clothes, a suitcase, whatever you want for your journey."

"Do we need to buy food for the trip?" Juliana asked.

"Of course not. You'll eat in the dining saloon, all expenses charged to my account," Barrett said. "You may want books and magazines. It's nine days at sea before you arrive in Hamburg. Meet me back here at sunset." He tipped his hat and walked up the brick steps into the building.

Juliana and Sebastian smiled at each other. Such a fantastic city to enjoy, and such an amazing amount of money with which to do it.

They explored the streets, shaded by the old trees and dappled with summer sunlight. Juliana bought herself new gloves and two dresses at a boutique, including a chiffon evening gown with flapper-style beadwork on the long sleeves—she felt like she should have something nice if she was traveling to Europe. She picked out a simple white collared shirt and trousers for Sebastian, after he vetoed a couple of fancier embroidered options.

They explored the city market, a few blocks of long, low sheds full of vendor stalls, the area marked by "Market Hall," a building that looked like an ancient Greek temple, complete with columns and a sculpted triangular pediment. Juliana was reminded of the impressive courthouse in Fallen Oak. Many of the merchants were black men and women in colorful clothing, who spoke among themselves in some sort of African language she couldn't begin to understand.

They ate a gumbo of shrimp, sausage, corn, and potatoes, served by a woman who called it "Beaufort Boil." It was so thick their spoons could almost stand up in the broth.

They went to a picture show, where Juliana hoped to see the popular new Mae West film, but the theater was showing a monster movie called *King Kong* instead, which Sebastian was pleased to discover. They held hands as the lights went down in the smoky theater. Juliana was impressed by the movie's special effects, but she spent most of the time kissing and caressing Sebastian in the dark.

At sunset, they met up with Mr. Barrett, who took them for supper at a tavern by the docks. It was a dingy, dark, and loud place and served some of the tastiest food Juliana had ever eaten—shrimp with a kind of barbecue sauce, crabs, and fried balls of cornmeal called "hushpuppies." Barrett talked a lot about the history of Charleston and South Carolina, but said little about Juliana and Sebastian's coming voyage.

Afterward, they went to a speakeasy where a live band played bouncing, brassy jazz that made Juliana want to dance. The place served Caribbean rum and didn't bother being discreet about it, probably because the Prohibition laws were crumbling—beer was already legal again, and there was talk that full repeal of the Eighteenth Amendment was on the way.

From their wobbly table in the back, Juliana watched the city girls dancing on the crowded floor, dressed in their extravagant feather hats and fringed dresses that left much of their legs bare. They drank, smoked, and flirted freely with the boys, and Juliana thought they were quite glamorous.

"Come and dance," Barrett said after a few minutes, reaching for Juliana's gloved hand.

"I can't! There are too many people," Juliana told him. "It's dangerous for you, too, Mr. Barrett."

"I very much prefer that you call me 'Jonathan,'" he told her, not for the first time.

"As you like," Juliana said.

"I would *like* for you to dance. You won't see great jazz bands like this in Europe. Enjoy it while it lasts." Barrett stood and held out his hand expectantly.

"I don't know..." Juliana looked at the crowded floor, then at Sebastian. He gave a shrug and raised his glass, acting indifferent.

"Come along, before the night grows old and dies," Barrett said. He took her arm just above the elbow, protected by her long-sleeved dress, which already had her hot and sweating in the crowded nightspot.

Juliana rose from her chair and swayed under the influence of dark rum as he led her to the dance floor. She did her best to imitate the swinging arms and wide steps of the other girls. Barrett himself was a skilled dancer and led her as best as he could. She laughed at herself but kept moving, unable to resist the fast-paced siren song of the nine-piece brass band and the beautiful dark-skinned lady who sang in front of them. The tunes were light, all about dancing and flirting, though they grew more ribald as the night flowed on.

While she was lost on the crowded dance floor with him and out of Sebastian's sight, Barrett stole a kiss from her, in spite of the danger, and her demon plague did not hurt him at all. Juliana would have slapped him, but she was too stunned at finding him immune to her power.

Much later, the three of them staggered out into the street, the stiff breeze off the ocean very welcome after the thick, smoky air of the speakeasy. They clambered into Barrett's car, and he swerved wildly as he drove them away. Juliana closed her eyes, enjoying the feeling of the wind.

Barrett's apartment in Charleston was the top floor of a regal old Tudor mansion with a walled courtyard full of flowers and wrought-iron staircases. He swayed heavily as he led them up to an apartment furnished with dark wood, the tall windows hung with thick curtains, creating the same tomb-like feeling as his house in Fallen Oak. Juliana had her own guest bedroom, while Sebastian slept on a long leather couch in the sitting room, which had to be more comfortable than his cot in the roustie tent.

Juliana lay awake for nearly half an hour, staring at the moonlit door to her room. She'd left it unlocked, in the drunken hope that Sebastian would be bold and impertinent enough to visit her in the night. He never came, and she eventually passed out.

She had confused but vivid dreams, in which Mr. Barrett was some dark-eyed king in ancient Greece, and she was his weapon, bringing the demon plague to a city he meant to conquer.

* * *

In the morning, Barrett had a large, dark woman in a bright dress come to the apartment and prepare a bracing breakfast of "grits," bacon, coffee and fresh-squeezed orange juice. It was the perfect cure for the slight hangover Juliana felt from the night before. It would have been much worse if she hadn't danced out so much of the alcohol.

He drove them to the docks and showed them the towering steel ship that would whisk them across the Atlantic like a seafaring locomotive. Its name was painted in huge black letters on the hull: *S.S. Eurydice.*

"I wish you both the best of luck," Barrett said, giving them their tickets. He took Juliana's gloved hand and held it. "Be safe."

"Thank you so much for everything, Mr....Jonathan," Juliana said.

"Mr. Jonathan?" Barrett laughed. "I'll accept it this time. Next time you see me, I expect to be addressed correctly."

"I don't suppose we will see you again, though," Sebastian said, with an 'ain't-that-a-shame' sort of smile. "Not for a long time."

"As it happens, I plan to visit Berlin myself in the near future," Barrett said. "A little more of that boring shipping business. With any luck, my friends in the Human Evolution Congress will invite me to see the advanced work they'll be doing with you. So we may meet again sooner than you expect, Sebastian."

Sebastian nodded, frowning, and didn't say anything.

"Until then, good luck and Godspeed to you both." Barrett held Juliana's hand, then slowly released her and offered his hand to Sebastian instead.

"Thank you for all your help, Mr. Barrett." Sebastian said, though his tone was cold. "We appreciate it more than we can say."

When Sebastian shook Barrett's hand, Barrett hissed and jerked his hand back. Barrett stared at his palm, and Juliana saw what looked like burn marks across his fingers.

"Did I squeeze your hand too hard?" Sebastian asked, clearly trying not to snicker. "I forget my own strength."

"The strength of your grip had nothing to do with it," Barrett hissed. He showed Sebastian the strange burn marks on his hand.

"Oh, let me heal that for you," Sebastian whispered, reaching for him.

"Don't touch me again!" Barrett tucked his hand into his coat pocket and glared at Sebastian with an ugly expression on his face, full of hate. Then it smoothed out into a businesslike smile. "I hope you enjoy each other." He tipped his hat and walked back toward his car, leaving them at the crowded ticket gate.

"What just happened?" Juliana asked.

"My touch hurt him instead of healing him. What a pity." Sebastian sounded almost delighted. "Come on, let's get onboard. I can't wait to cross the ocean."

The *S.S. Eurydice* was a multi-deck steamship with its hull filled with cargo—international mail, rum and tobacco from the West Indies, timber and cotton from the United States. A few hundred passengers rode on the upper floors.

Juliana had a stateroom on the highest deck, with a teak chest of drawers and matching wardrobe, a queen-sized bed, soft carpeting, and a private bath, lit by ornate sconce lamps and a row of curtained portholes. Seth's room was on the same hall, in a servant's nook, essentially just a cot in a narrow closet without a single window.

"How posh," Seth said, looking over his quarters.

"It's better than sleeping with four roustabouts in a tent on a summer night," Juliana pointed out.

"It's also better than sleeping in a sewer during a flood, or in a barrel of rusty nails. It's better than so many things."

"If you're pleasant to me this evening, I may let you sleep on the divan in my sitting room," she said.

"Or we could trade rooms," Sebastian suggested.

"I don't believe that will happen. Shall we watch the launch?"

"Won't it be crowded out on the deck?" Sebastian asked. He knew how being in a crowd terrified her.

"Not on the top deck," Juliana said. "Most passengers don't have access."

"Aren't we traveling in high style?"

They watched from the railing of the upper deck as the steamship chugged away from the terminal. Most of the passengers were crowded on the level below them, leaning over the railing and waving good-bye to a matching crowd on the dock, friends and family seeing them off. There was a festive mood, like the beginning of a party.

She spotted Jonathan Barrett among the crowd on the land.

Apparently, he hadn't driven off at all. He stood with his arms crossed, smoking a cigar, standing apart from the rest of the crowd. Even from this distance, she could feel his dark eyes picking out her form on the upper deck, watching the stiff, salty wind tousle her white dress and dark hair. She looked back at him, and her heart beat at a faster tempo. He was dangerous to her, even at a distance.

Sebastian circled an arm around her waist and drew her close.

"You have a look in your eyes," he said. "What are you looking at?"

She turned to face him, hoping he wouldn't notice Barrett watching from the dock.

"It's such a long way," Juliana said. "Aren't you scared?"

"I'm scared of sleeping in that little closet for nine nights."

"Then you'd better enjoy your days, hadn't you?"

"This one's already looking much brighter." He drew her close and gave her a long kiss, long enough to wipe out any thought of Jonathan Barrett until he was just a tiny shadow, lost over the horizon.

*I feel nothing for Mr. Barrett*, Juliana told herself. *Nothing at all.*

She and Sebastian explored the ship, which was filled with entertainments for the passengers. There was a tennis court, a restaurant, a lounge with a piano player and a singer. They amused themselves sitting on deck chairs and reading each other stories from the pulp magazines Sebastian had bought from a newsstand in Charleston. The magazines had lurid covers and names like *Amazing Stories* and *Weird Tales*, and they were filled with stories about aliens, ghosts, and detectives.

They ate steak with smoked mussels, accompanied by summer salad and a great deal of Spanish wine. In the lounge, they found themselves playing cards with a minor French diplomat on his way from New Orleans to France, accompanied by his strikingly attractive young mistress, a stage actress. Juliana tried to get them to talk about life in Paris, but he stubbornly returned to his favorite subject, horse breeding, which he discussed in long, graphic, and highly specific detail. When the music slowed, Juliana coaxed Sebastian into a dance, which continued for the next two songs.

Later, they walked the promenade deck, her arm tucked into his, with a billion stars glowing in the cloudless sky above. Their walk slowed considerably after they turned a corner and found themselves alone on a stretch of the deck. Jenny looked up at the stars. Rain was starting to fall, but it was warm, and neither of them ran for shelter.

"Do you think there's life out there, like in *Amazing Stories*?" she asked him.

"You mean three-eyed monsters with blue tentacles who fly around in metal bubbles and shoot rayguns?" Sebastian asked, referring to a story they'd read earlier.

"Just any life at all. It looks so dark and cold. And lonely."

"My mother told me that the stars were all alive. She said they were angels watching over us."

Juliana smiled. "Imagine something that's alive, but made entirely of light. Or darkness." She looked down at her hands, imagining the demon plague inside her, which she always pictured as a swarm of tiny, poisonous black flies.

"Beats the three-eyed tentacle alien," Sebastian said.

She looked up at him and traced her fingertip along his cheekbone. "Maybe there really are angels. How else could I have been fortunate enough to find you?"

"You make a good point," Sebastian told her. "I'm a pretty good find."

Juliana looked at him for a long moment, then said, "Walk me to my room."

They walked quietly down the passenger corridor. He opened the door to his narrow closet.

"Have a good night," he told her.

"You don't have to sleep in there!"

"That's right. I can curl up on the rug in your room. Sleep by the fireplace, which you probably have, too."

Juliana took his hand. Inside her stateroom, there was no talk of sending him to sleep on the couch or the rug. They kissed each other hungrily, and his hands explored all over her body, caressing her through the summer dress.

She stepped back from him, lifted her dress over her head, and tossed it on the carpet. He gazed at her, desire in his eyes.

"Are you sure?" he asked.

She didn't answer, but she walked to the bed, turning off all the lamps in the bedroom, and he followed. He took off his cotton shirt and dark trousers, and she could see him thick and hard inside his underwear. The two of them together, almost completely undressed now, made her shake in anticipation. She'd longed to get out of their clothes together, to let every part of him touch every part of her, skin on skin, a sensation she'd never experienced. She wanted it so much it frightened her.

The rain fell faster as he lay her across the bed, splashing against the glass and making the steel hull echo with thousands of tiny pings.

He kissed her slowly, touching the tip of his tongue against hers. His hands moved from her hips and across her stomach and ribs, not hurrying at all, as if he wanted to feel every part of her. He had the rough-skinned hands of a boy who'd grown up working hard for little money.

She sighed when his hands touched her breasts through her bulky, starchy cotton bra. She unlatched it for him, then shivered in delight when he touched her bare skin. He kissed her and she held his face close, unable to get enough. He tasted like sunlight on her lips.

His hands moved down her body, at a speed she found agonizingly slow. His fingertips brushed low on her stomach, beneath her navel and just above her cotton panties. Juliana traced her hand down the muscles of his abdomen and touched the erection that strained against his undershorts. She took a breath and reached inside, touching him without any cloth barrier. He felt scorching hot in her fingers, and he grew more rigid as she explored his length with her fingertips.

He slowly drew down her panties. They lay naked for a moment, looking at each other in the silver moonlight as a thunderstorm ripped across the ocean, rocking the vast ship around them. Juliana embraced him, kissing him hungrily and pressing her body against him. He wrapped his arms around her, and the feeling of their bodies wrapped in each other was better than she'd ever imagined. She wanted to stay just like this forever, his skin on hers, his breath on her lips.

"I was dead," she whispered. "You brought me to life."

Her fingers touched his lip, and his hand brushed down her side. They kissed again, and his fingers rubbed her gently at *just* the right spot between her splayed legs. Her body filled with a roaring fire, and a burst of lightning filled their cabin.

He climbed on top of her and slowly entered her. She bit her lip in pain. After a lifetime of solitude, the intimacy hurt almost as much as the physical loss of her virginity. She clung to him while he was inside her, and her breath came out in short, hot gasps. She had never felt so close to anyone.

"I love you," she whispered afterward, too low for him to hear over the rumbling thunder. She lay against him and let the ship rock them to sleep.

* * *

Eighty years later, telling the story to Seth and Mariella, Jenny would skip the more intimate details of their first night on the ship...but she would pause and give Seth a secretive smile, for reasons he didn't even remember.

# Chapter Eighteen

After a week of travel, which Juliana and Sebastian spent eating, drinking, dancing, and playing, the *Eurydice* reached Le Havre, France. They marveled at the massive number of ships from all over the world porting at the sprawling industrial city. Juliana wanted very much to visit Paris, but it was three hours each way by train, so they didn't have time.

The ship carried them into the cooler weather of the North Sea, around the Netherlands, then south along the River Elbe towards Hamburg, Germany. Farms and woodlands lined the wide river, and heavy boat traffic flowed both ways.

Juliana stood on the deck, gripping Sebastian's hand as the German port came into view. It was a beautiful city, full of canals, bridges, and symmetrical neoclassical buildings. Trees lined the streets, and the spires of cathedrals soared here and there along the skyline. The city looked both ancient and extremely modern, even futuristic, and it was situated in the center of Europe. It felt like they were arriving at the center of the civilized world. As their ship approached the busy docks, full of cranes unloading automobiles and railroad cars, a sudden stab of panic struck Juliana.

"What's wrong?" Sebastian asked, seeing the look on her face.

"What if this is a mistake?" she whispered.

"Then we'll go home."

"What if they don't let us?"

"Why wouldn't they?" He looked into her eyes. "This is what you've always wanted, a chance to be cured of the demon plague. It's why you came looking for me in the first place."

"You think we made the right choice?"

"We don't have much to lose, do we?"

Juliana thought about their life back home, scratching out a meager living as they traveled America in the middle of the Depression. Strange men paying pennies to leer at her diseased, nearly-nude body. Her body had thickened in the time since they'd met Mr. Barrett, and her ribs were much less visible.

"Not much to lose at all," she agreed.

"With modern science and the latest technology, they can find a cure, if there's one to be found," he said. "Mr. Barrett was right about that."

"I hope you're both right," she said.

The ship docked, and she drew very close to Sebastian as they descended the gangplank towards a dense crowd of people coming and going in every direction. She wore a hat and an unseasonable scarf, as well as her gloves, but she always worried. Maybe, she thought, the scientists of Europe really would cure her, and she would never again need to fear being around other people.

The vast concrete terminal struck her as overwhelmingly foreign—not just that most people in the crowd spoke German, or that the frequent, crackling loudspeaker announcements were in German, and all the signs, newspapers, and magazines were in German, but there was an overwhelming array of countless tiny differences, from the buttons on people's coats to the steamy pickled smell of the food sold by the vendors.

"Where do we go?" Sebastian wondered.

"Look there." Juliana pointed to a uniformed chauffeur holding up a placard with Sebastian's name on it. "He must be here for us."

They made their way through the crowd toward the young man, but as they got closer, Juliana realized that what she'd assumed what a chauffeur's uniform was actually black military or police wear, with a matching peaked cap and boots. He wore a brown shirt and a black tie underneath his jacket. The only splash of color was a red armband with a strange symbol, like a broken, twisted black "X" inside a white circle. As they made their way through the crowd, Juliana spotted a few other men in similar uniforms.

The young uniformed man saw the two of them approaching his sign. He whispered something to a tall, beautiful young woman who stood near him, and she turned to face Juliana and Sebastian. She had a similar uniformed look, a black coat and dress with a starched, high-collared white shirt. The two of them looked similar to each other. Their eyes were gray, the boy's the color of a dark stormcloud, the girl's much lighter and clearer. They had blond hair—again, the boy had a darker, dirtier shade, while the girl's hair looked like spun gold.

*"Heil!"* the young woman greeted them, smiling, as they arrived. "You are the two sent by Herr Barrett from America? What are your names?"

Sebastian told her, and she gave a short, crisp nod, as if verifying she had the right people. She took Sebastian's hand for a moment and looked into his eyes, and an odd, glowing smile spread across Sebastian's face.

"I am Alise," the gray-eyed girl said. "This is Niklaus. I am your...welcoming committee." She smiled. Her English was hesitant but perfectly clear. "Welcome to the new Germany. We will go this way. Niklaus!"

When she said "Niklaus!" the boy immediately reached for Juliana's new suitcase. Juliana instinctively stepped back, holding her suitcase close.

"No, no," Alise said. "He can carry it. Boys should carry." She gave Juliana a bright, heartwarming smile, as if she were desperate to win Juliana's approval.

"Hmm..." Juliana smiled, then handed her bag to Niklaus. "Maybe boys *should* carry."

The gray-eyed boy touched the brim of his hat and gave Juliana a very slight nod. He had a solemn, serious expression that didn't change. Juliana noted that he wore black leather gloves, while Alise wore none. Alise looked at Juliana's gloves and frowned, but said nothing.

As they passed through the cavernous building at the terminal, which echoed with the sounds of dockworkers hoisting and dropping large shipping containers, Alise fell into step beside Juliana, while the boys lagged behind with the luggage.

"We have all been so excited to meet you," Alise told her. "Especially me."

"Why is that?"

"Because there are so few girls who are truly...like us." Alise covered her mouth and giggled a little. "I shouldn't have said that."

"Like us? What do you mean?"

"You have the touch," Alise said. "Yes? It moves through touch."

"What do you know about me?"

"I read telegrams, letters." Alise smiled.

"Are you in the research project? Are you a scientist?"

"Scientist..." Alise turned the word over in her mouth, and then laughed. "No! Not a scientist. More of...administrator? I apologize for my English, I will study more of it for you."

"You don't have to do that. I'll learn German."

"I need the practice, thank you," Alise said. She glanced over her shoulder, and then whispered, "What I read about you, I recognized. You both have the touch, you and Sebastian. Disease and healing. Opposites. Sometimes, people like us are opposites. Like Niklaus and me."

"You are?" Juliana looked back over her shoulder at the gray-eyed boy. "What does his touch do? What does yours do?"

"Sh! Already I am saying too much. General Kranzler and Dr. Wichtmann may not want us to speak of such things."

"Who are they?" Juliana asked. They approached the crowded railroad terminal by the port, which looked like a modernist castle, complete with arches and a clock tower. The city teemed with life, people hurrying everywhere, and the air smelled like industrial smoke and grease.

Instead of answering her question, Alise turned back to face the boys. "Do we move too fast for you?"

"What have you been whispering about?" Sebastian asked as he and Niklaus caught up with them.

"I am hoping your journey was comfortable." Alise touched Sebastian's forearm, drawing another smile from him. He brightened up a little too much at her touch, Juliana thought.

"It was nice. I could use a beer, though," Sebastian said.

*"Yah, bier."* Niklaus nodded as he spoke his first words since their arrival. He also gave his first hint of a smile.

*"Nein!"* Alise snapped at him. Then she turned a sweet smile on Juliana. "We go to the rail station now."

"For Berlin?" Juliana asked.

Alise shook her head.

"Mr. Barrett said we were going to Berlin," Sebastian said.

"Herr Barrett does not know about the new laboratory," Alise said. "In the Harz mountains, very pleasant. You will like it there!" She smiled. "I promise."

Sebastian and Juliana traded worried looks, but there wasn't much they could do but go along with whatever Alise told them.

They rode in a spacious, first-class car, divided by heavy curtains into private areas with plush seats. A porter secured Juliana and Sebastian's luggage above them, then left the group alone.

Niklaus tapped Sebastian's shoulder and pointed down the aisle, toward the club car. *"Bier?"*

*"Yah, bier!"* Sebastian replied, already learning two key words of German. He glanced at Juliana, who shrugged. The two boys left for their drinks. Alise looked toward the ceiling and shook her head.

"What can we expect when we get there?" Juliana asked her. "What will they do to us?"

Alise smiled. "First, they treat us all very well. Good food, nice rooms. There is radio, books, and even a small projection room. Sometimes we watch Hollywood movies!"

"That sounds nice."

"Of course, they test our powers. They do these tests on me, too, and Niklaus."

"What kind of tests?"

"For you, it is very dangerous," Alise said, then shook her head. "Your *touch* is very dangerous. So...animals?" She shrugged.

Juliana frowned.

"It is necessary science," Alise said, nodding firmly. "They will use microscopes to study your blood, skin, hair. And, if you are like me, they will find nothing!" She laughed, almost looking proud of it, but Juliana felt her heart fall.

"They find nothing?" Juliana said. "Why not?"

"Because the touch is a mystery." Alise raised her hand and wiggled her fingers. "Even for the best scientists."

"What does your touch do?" Juliana asked again.

Alise glanced at the empty aisle, then out the window, as if she expected someone to be spying on them. A bell clanged, and the train crept forward.

"My touch," Alise whispered. "Makes people feel...happy."

"Happy?"

"Happy." Alise touched her heart and smiled wide. "Sometimes *too* happy."

Juliana laughed, trying to imagine a room full of people feeling "too happy." Would they be dancing? Singing? Kissing?

"Yes, happy," Alise said. "We should talk no more on this until we arrive. It is not public information, we must keep it very quiet."

Juliana nodded. If Alise filled people with happiness, it explained Sebastian's comically large smile whenever Alise touched him, but that didn't exactly make Juliana feel reassured. She looked out the window and saw long, stiff vertical banners hanging at regular intervals along the platform. They billowed as the train picked up speed. They were red, with a white circle and the black twisted-cross design in the center, the same one that was on Niklaus' sleeve.

"What are those?" Juliana asked. She tried to imitate the strange shape with her fingers. Alise quickly covered Juliana's gloved hands and shook her head. Then, probably remembering that Juliana's touch was deadly, she snapped her hand back away from Juliana.

"It means National Socialist party," Alise explained.

"Is that a...political party?" Juliana didn't know much about European politics. She knew that Germany had been an enemy of the United States during the Great War, but that had been old Germany ruled by a king. They were a democracy now, so they were probably more peaceful.

"They are the only party that matters anymore," Alise said. "They are raising Germany up, up from darkness." She raised her hand high above her head, as if measuring rising water. "Creating a better future for us. My father has helped the party for years—he was one of the first to see they were Germany's best defense against the Communist threat. I personally helped to organize *Bund Deutscher Mädel in der Hitler-Jugend*." She smiled proudly.

"The what?" Juliana asked.

"League of German Girls...Hitler Youth," Alise translated.

"What is a Hitler?"

"Sh!" Alise looked cross, and glanced into the aisle to check if anyone had heard Juliana. "The leader of the National Socialists and of Germany. You will need education."

"I suppose," Juliana said. "I'm sorry, I just don't know these things."

"Politics," Alise said, then pretended to yawn, and Juliana smiled.

The boys returned with beer for everyone, and they kept the conversation light after that. They learned that Alise was the daughter of a duke, making her "nobility." Though Germany was a democracy, belonging to the old aristocracy seemed to still count for something. Niklaus was her first cousin, which explained the strong resemblance between them. Alise was twenty-five, while her cousin Niklaus was nineteen.

Juliana gathered that Alise was the truly influential one, and she had pulled strings to have her cousin Niklaus made into an officer of the *Schutzstaffel*, apparently some kind of elite police force. His main job, as far as Juliana could tell, was acting as Alise's bodyguard, driver, and all-around footman.

Though she reminded herself not to trust Alise, or anyone else just yet, Juliana felt relieved to have a girl about her own age to explain things to her—in English, especially.

The train left the city of Hamburg and picked up speed across the green countryside, rushing them towards the mountains and their uncertain future.

* * *

They had to change trains at a mountain town called Wernigerode, which had a number of impressive Gothic buildings with pointy spires, including a castle overlooking the town from a hilltop. They moved to a special narrow-gauge track built for the steep curves and narrow passes of the mountains. The view out the window became both lovely and terrifying, full of steep gorges dropping away toward lakes and waterways far below the narrow tracks.

Juliana felt relieved when they finally disembarked at a tiny, unidentified station in the mountains, guarded by a pair of S.S. officers in black uniforms. Nobody was coming or going here except Juliana, Sebastian, and their two escorts.

Niklaus loaded their suitcases into the back of an old black Brennabor sedan, the only car in the small lot. The car coughed and chugged its way up a newly paved mountain road, which passed through a solid wilderness of old, mossy spruce and thick banks of fern. The mountain forest was unbroken until they reached a fork in the road. They stayed to the right, while a smaller road branched off to the left.

The steep road took them up toward a brick wall with square towers at each end. As they drew closer, Juliana saw guards in the watchtowers, partially shielded by metal-grill walls, with machine guns mounted below the grillwork. A coil of wire ran across the top of the brick wall, and the gate was made of steel doors. Juliana had imagined a place that looked sort of like a college, set among trees and mountain streams, but this looked more like a prison than any kind of research lab.

"Do not fear," Alise told her, seeing the look on her face. "It is all for our security. The inside is nice."

"Okay," Juliana replied. She couldn't think of anything else to say. She had a sudden urge to announce that she'd changed her mind and wanted to go home right away.

Guards were posted at the gate, and they spoke briefly to Alise before opening up for them. Niklaus drove them inside.

Juliana didn't think the interior was at all nice, either. The brick wall was actually a big square perimeter, with a guard tower at each corner. There were four low, squarish buildings, single-story and made of plain concrete, and a long brick building like a warehouse along the western wall. She saw some smaller structures that she took for strangely tall brick water walls, circular and with slanted tin roofs mounted a few feet above them. As they passed one, she saw that it had a whirling electrical fan inside, and seemed to be sucking down a large quantity of air.

Niklaus parked in front of one of the squat concrete buildings and climbed out of the car.

"We're not staying here, are we?" Sebastian asked. "We're just stopping here for a minute, and then driving on to the real place. Right?"

"This is the end of your long journey," Alise told him. Niklaus opened the door for Alise and held her hand as she stepped down.

"I knew we couldn't trust that Barrett guy," Sebastian whispered to Juliana.

"Then why did you come?" Juliana whispered.

"To watch out for you. I knew you wouldn't turn down a chance to find a cure."

"I don't have as much hope for that now. This place feels wrong." Juliana sighed. Niklaus opened her door and offered his hand, but she shook her head at him as she climbed out.

They carried their luggage inside the low concrete building, where a single guard sat at a desk in front of a heavy steel door, like the door to a bank vault. He exchanged a few words with Alise as he stood and unlocked the door, and then he grunted as he hauled it open.

Juliana and Sebastian leaned forward, curious. Beyond the door, a wide concrete staircase descended deep underground, lit on both sides by a row of electric bulbs.

"Down here." Alise smiled and led the way, her polished black flats echoing with each step.

Juliana and Sebastian held hands as they followed, Sebastian's suitcase bumping as it dragged along the stairs. Niklaus followed, and the guard heaved the door shut behind them. It slammed with an echoing clang, like the door of a prison cell.

The stairway took them to an underground hallway, as brightly lit as a hospital and wide enough to drive a truck through. The floor was concrete, but the walls were plastered white and hung with huge pictures. Some depicted German historical events Juliana didn't recognize, mostly large battles. Others were different pictures of the same man, an odd, stern-looking person with a Charlie Chaplin mustache. From the German text on the posters, Juliana guessed this was the politician who so excited Alise, Chancellor Hitler. Stormy classical music echoed from somewhere.

"Boys," Alise said, pointing to the right. Then she pointed to the left and said, "Girls." She smiled at Juliana, while Niklaus returned Juliana's suitcase to her.

"Sebastian and I can't stay together?" Juliana asked.

"We stay on separate halls," Alise said. "Men and women together on the same hall would be *too* much fun."

"Can't we just stay together for the first night?" Sebastian asked. "While we get accustomed to this place?"

"You will accustom fast," Alise said. "We will see each other again at dinner, very soon. Maybe even screen a movie tonight, to celebrate that you are here?"

"That sounds nice," Juliana said.

"This way. No need to fear." Alise started walking away.

Juliana gave Sebastian a quick hug and a kiss.

"Are you going to be okay?" Sebastian asked.

"I hope so." Juliana gave him a smile, though she was feeling scared and lost. "I'll see you at dinner, I suppose."

He hugged her again. "If anybody gives you any trouble," he whispered in her ear, "Just kill them."

Juliana laughed as she reluctantly stepped away from him and followed Alise down the corridor.

"Girls' hall," Alise said as she opened a pair of double doors. The short hallway, with five doors on each side, was carpeted and hung with pretty pieces of art, like paintings of flowers and sunset landscapes. The lighting fixtures were encircled with colored glass, and the walls themselves were painted gentle pastel colors. The classical music was louder here, echoing from somewhere up ahead, where the hall ended at another set of double doors.

"Oh, this *is* much nicer," Juliana said. "I thought you were joking."

"I always tell the truth," Alise said. "Even when people don't like to hear it, which is nearly always."

Juliana laughed, and Alise showed her to an open door. Alise knocked on it as they entered.

The dormitory room was wide with a high ceiling. A bed occupied each end of the room, with plenty of open space in between them. Drawers, cabinets, and bookshelves were built into the walls, many more than Juliana could imagine needing for herself.

One side of the room was empty, the walls bare except for the built-in shelves, the bed made up with a colorful quilt thrown on top of it, which looked like it had been made by somebody's very talented grandmother. The other half of the room was plastered with pictures of Hollywood movie stars cut from magazines and newspapers. A girl lay on the bed there, reading a paperback, and she quickly sat up when Alise and Juliana entered.

*"Heil,"* Alise greeted the girl, then spoke to her in a language that was neither English nor German—French or Italian, maybe. She gestured to Juliana and mentioned her name, and the girl slowly nodded, glancing nervously at Juliana. Her hair was a dark burgundy, almost black, and her eyes were sea-green. Her skin was olive, and she looked very exotic to Juliana. She wore a long black skirt and a

white blouse edged with scraps of bright color. Her hands were gloved almost to her elbow, Juliana noticed.

"Juliana," Alise said. "This is Mia. She will room with you and help you find your way around. She is from Sicily, but knows a little English."

"Oh...that's good." Juliana smiled, feeling uneasy. "Hello, Mia."

"*Piaciri di canuscirvi.* Hello, Juliana." The girl waved and tried to smile, but her face showed that she was just as nervous as Juliana felt.

"Oh, you're going to love each other!" Alise said. "I'll make sure of it. I have to report to General Kranzler and Dr. Wichtmann now, so they know you and Sebastian arrived safely. We'll talk more at dinner! Any special food requests?"

"Anything to eat would be great. I'm starving," Juliana said.

"I'll make sure the cooks give you plenty!" Alise winked as she left the room.

Juliana and Mia looked at each other awkwardly.

"Your bed," Mia finally said, pointing to the empty side of the room and nodding.

"Thank you." Juliana carried her suitcase to the bed and sat down. There was another long, awkward pause. She looked at the pictures pasted around Mia's bed.

"You like movies?" Juliana asked.

"Yes!" Mia said, with an exuberant grin, probably just happy to have something to talk about. She pointed to one of the pictures, an advertisement for the film *Red Dust* with Clark Gable and Jean Harlow locked in a passionate embrace. "I lived in Rome for a time, many films. You like Clark Gable?"

"Yes, he's very handsome," Juliana said.

"Handsome." Mia nodded and pointed again. "Douglas Fairbanks?"

"Yes, also handsome."

"Charlie Chaplin?"

"Very funny!" Juliana said. "I love him." She looked over the girl's pictures. "You like Mae West?"

"Mae West, yes!"

They shared a smile—Mae West was bold, flirty, and fearless, which, as a woman, made her controversial and the talk of much scandal. A modern, outspoken woman who just happened to be gorgeous and glamorous.

"How long have you been here?" Juliana asked.

Mia concentrated. "Many days. One...week? Or is it month?"

"I'm not sure. Do you have a touch?" Juliana raised her hands and nodded at the gloves Mia wore. "Like me?"

Mia leaned forward, raising her eyebrows like she was about to share some good gossip. "I see your future." Mia stripped off her gloves and stood up, striding towards Juliana, closing the door along the way. "I can show you."

"No, wait! I'm poisonous."

Mia hesitated in mid-step. "Poisonous?"

"Yes. I can't help it." Juliana took off a glove and spread her fingers. She called up the demon plague, letting her hand fester into open sores.

Mia gasped and stumbled back to her own bed, where she pulled up her knees protectively. Juliana started to regret bringing up the subject of their powers.

"I am sorry," Juliana said. "But you should be warned. No touching me, for your own safety."

"No touching." Mia shook her head, staring warily at her now.

"I am sorry," Juliana told her again. She lay back on her new bed, looking up at the pastel-pink ceiling. She'd felt the possible beginning of a friendship with the girl, but now she'd scared her away. Everyone else had something useful: Sebastian could heal, Alise could make people happy, Mia could see the future. Only Juliana had a useless curse, one that could only hurt people.

Even among the freaks, she was a freak.

# Chapter Nineteen

Ward approached the grimy concrete building housing the nightclub, as well as a bail bond place and a pawn shop that had both closed until morning. The club was in the half-buried basement of the strip mall, and its entrance was at the back, not visible from the road. Broken bottles littered the gravel parking lot, which was crowded with cars even though it was the day after Christmas.

Two doors led into the basement. One of them had been surrounded by chainlink to form a smoking pen, where a few kids in spiked, dark mesh clothes smoked cigarettes. A boy whose earlobe had been stretched to grotesque proportions was making out with a girl who had a long needle through her eyebrow.

His target, Tommy, sat on a stool by the other door. It was propped open, and the sound of a loud band slamming their instruments pulsed out from inside the dark club.

Ward approached Tommy, flanked by Buchanan and Avery, who stayed a half-step behind him. They all wore thick leather gloves tonight, and he'd warned them not to touch Tommy at all if they could avoid it. The boy's touch could shatter a man's mind with fear.

Tommy looked them over sullenly as they approached, studying their dark suits and ties. He smelled like he hadn't bathed in a couple of days, and his long hair was dirty and tangled.

"I don't think this is really your scene, guys," Tommy said as they stood before him. "Somewhere in Orange County, an Applebee's is calling your name."

"We didn't come for the music or ambiance, Mr. White," Ward said.

Tommy sat up on his stool, and his eyes widened. He glanced among the three of them, probably realizing that he couldn't win a straight fight, and would need his power if he wanted to escape. Ward didn't want him running just yet.

"Settle down, we're not here to hurt you," Ward told him. "That is your name, isn't it? Thomas White? Also known as Thomas Krueger? Currently going by Thomas Voorhees. Cute."

"Who are you?" Tommy asked.

"We are with the Department of Defense," Ward said. "We know you escaped from a maximum-security penitentiary in Louisiana, and the guards there would just love to have you back. We also know that you killed your foster father, Ben Tanner, just before you went and caused that riot in Charleston. Your foster mother says you were a very disturbed boy."

"You talked to her?" Tommy asked.

"She's doing well with Mr. Tanner dead, I'd say. Spent some of the life insurance money on a candy-pink Le Baron convertible. Didn't you think she looked well, Buchanan, in that red Christmas dress?"

"Yes, very healthy," Buchanan replied.

Tommy shrugged, as though indifferent to his foster mother's fate.

"Have you ever played Monopoly, Tommy?" Ward asked. "I'm offering you a little orange Get Out of Jail Free card. We can expunge your entire criminal record, make you a free man. No more scurrying around in the dark."

"In exchange for what?" Tommy asked. He had a cornered-rat look in his eyes, still deciding whether to fight or flee.

"In exchange, you serve our country. You apply your fear-inducing ability toward protecting American interests around the world. Surely you don't want to do this for the rest of your life." Ward pointed inside the dark, loud club.

Tommy shrugged. "This job's okay."

"It's *okay*? Son, you have a tremendous power inside you. You've got to have some ambition, don't you? You could be out there making the world safe for America. You could be a hero instead of a criminal. Wouldn't you like that?"

"What's it pay?" Tommy asked.

"Pay?" Ward shook his head, exasperated. He was ready to punch the kid in the nose. "We're talking about you finally doing something worthwhile with your life. You've got to look at the bigger picture here."

"So the pay sucks," Tommy said.

"It has to be more than you're making here," Ward said. "Room, board, medical, and we'll pay you what we pay the Special Forces guys. Is that good enough? Or do you want to sit on this goddamn stool collecting dollar bills from drugged-out kids until it's time for you to go back to prison with an extended sentence? What the hell are your plans for your life?"

Tommy sank on his seat, looking like a petulant child.

"Wake up, kid," Ward said. "This is your only chance. You've got to see that."

"I'll think about it." Tommy scratched his head.

Ward shook his head in disbelief. What was the kid's problem?

"We want your girl to come, too," Ward added. "Esmeralda, the one who can speak with the dead? We want both of you. Go and talk to her about it, too."

"You want Esmeralda, too?"

"Isn't that what I said?" Ward glared at the dirty, long-haired kid and tried to keep his temper under control. "Go and talk to her about it," he repeated.

"I guess I will." Tommy shrugged.

"You've got twenty-four hours," Ward said. "It shouldn't take you twenty-four *seconds* to make this choice. At your age, it's time to stop being a slacker and start being a man." Ward handed him a plain white business card—no logo, no name, just a single phone number. "We'll be back tomorrow. Call if you come to your senses before then." Ward turned and walked away, followed by his two assistants.

"I'm not working tomorrow," Tommy said.

"You're barely working now," Ward replied without looking back. "Don't worry, we always know where to find you. Just don't do anything stupid between now and then."

When they returned to the car, the wheels in Ward's mind were turning. He'd believed that Tommy had been the leader of a small group of paranormals, but he was starting to doubt that assessment. The kid could barely lead himself to the bathroom to take a piss. The faction must have had a different leader...maybe the zombie-master guy, but he was dead, according to Heather Reynard's memories. Killed by Seth's healing power, somehow.

So, Ward reasoned, maybe Tommy and Esmeralda didn't have a leader anymore, they were just wandering without any direction at all. Ward was prepared to give them one.

Their next stop was a motel not far from Tommy and Esmeralda's apartment, just off the interstate. They would listen to the device Buchanan had set up, a laser listening system pointed at the apartment window. The laser translated glass vibrations back into sound, creating a clean way to bug a room without ever entering the premises. They would be able to hear what Tommy and Esmeralda's thoughts might be regarding whether to serve their country or not.

"Kid looks like a real loser," Avery commented as they pulled out onto a busy boulevard.

"We'll see," Ward replied.

* * *

"You have to come with me," Tommy said. He'd already crammed half his clothes into a duffel bag, and he was trying to shove more into it.

"The only thing I have to do is catch the bus," Esmeralda told him, buttoning her blouse. It was seven in the morning and Tommy's eyes were open, which meant he'd skipped sleeping after he'd gotten home from work. He looked disheveled, with a sheen of nervous sweat. "Why don't you take a bath?" she asked him.

"You're not listening, Esmeralda. They're going to delete my prison record. If I don't do what they want, they'll probably send me back to prison. I don't have a choice."

"You could ride away," Esmeralda said. "Go hide somewhere new."

"If I did that, would you come with me?"

"I can't, Tommy. I have school, and my mother. And you know how much trouble I had finding another job after I ran away last time." She pulled on a pair of dark slacks. "And that crappy new job is where I need to be in thirty minutes."

"This is our big chance to really do something with our lives. Don't you want that?" He reached for her arm, but she shook him off.

"I am doing something with my life," Esmeralda told him.

"What, putting make-up on dead people?"

"I like dead people. They tell interesting stories."

"Don't you want an interesting *life*?" Tommy asked. "Instead of just watching what dead people did with their time?"

"If you want to go off and be an assassin or whatever they want, that's your choice. Staying here and living my own life, that's mine." Esmeralda trembled, feeling fear tinged with hope. Maybe he would go. Maybe this was finally it. He made her feel protected, but also miserable. Without him, she would be vulnerable and free.

"Then maybe I'll go without you," he growled, narrowing his eyes. "Maybe you'll never see me again."

Esmeralda stared back at him, feeling the war inside herself between the part of her that craved him and shivered at his touch, and the smarter part, the one that knew he would only destroy her life if they stayed together.

"You don't have anything to say?" he asked.

Esmeralda sighed and folded her arms. "You need someone to order you around, don't you, Tommy? Somebody in command, like Ashleigh, always telling you what to do. I give you your freedom to be anything you want to be, and all you do is piss yourself away."

He glowered at her, his jaw grinding inside his cheek. He looked like a mad dog.

"So you think I'm worthless. Anything else?" he snarled.

"I did not say that."

"You basically did."

"I have to work, Tommy." Esmeralda started for the door.

"I might not be here when you get back," he called after her.

Esmeralda resisted the temptation to turn around and say anything. She walked out the door, closed it firmly behind her, and started down the concrete stairwell.

When she returned from work that evening, Tommy and his clothes were gone. So was the gold 1908 Indian-head coin he'd given her when they'd first met as children. She didn't know if he was keeping it as a reminder of her, or taking it away to show her that they were finished.

Either way, at least her mother would be pleased to hear that Tommy was gone. Maybe she would start talking to Esmeralda again.

# Chapter Twenty

Jenny awoke the day after Christmas to find Seth sitting up in bed, staring at her with a very serious look on his face. Bad sign. He usually slept much later than Jenny. She wondered if he remembered—

"Are you really pregnant?" he asked.

Jenny hesitated. "Yes."

"Are you sure?"

She pushed her blankets off, then lifted up her nightdress and threw it on the floor. She took his hand and placed it on her swollen belly.

"Feel that?"

His eyes widened. "How pregnant *are* you?"

"Between four and five months, is my best guess. You haven't noticed me getting bigger?"

"A little, but I thought it was all the, you know, cheeses and chocolates and heavy French sauces..."

"You thought I was getting fat."

"I wasn't going to say anything. Four months? Have you been to a doctor? Why haven't you said anything?"

"I told you why. I can't have children, they almost always

miscarry. The few times that hasn't happened, the baby dies on the way out. They can't handle my poxy birth canal."

"Okay...but isn't there another way, where they take the baby right out?"

"A C-section," Jenny said. "I've thought about it, but it's very rare that my baby even lives long enough to try that."

"But it's possible," Seth said.

"I don't know. The technology's never been there before." She shook her head. One bad thing about having so many past-life memories was that she tended think of her present options as being limited by her past experience. "We could try, but it still probably won't be safe enough..."

"But I'll be there," Seth said. "If the baby needs healing, I can do it." He stroked her stomach, and Jenny felt the warm glow of his healing touch, passing right through her and into the baby. The baby stirred in response, and feeling it move nearly broke her heart. "He's not going to die if I can do anything about it."

"Or she," Jenny said. "Or...it's better not to think of it as 'he' or 'she.'"

"Can't the doctors tell by now?"

"I guess they could. That's not my point, Seth. You're getting your hopes up, but I have lifetimes of experience showing me it's hopeless. It's better to just accept that."

"No." He shook his head. "I might not have all your memories, but I know we can change. We're not stuck with what happened in the past. Jenny, I think we can make it work."

Jenny dared to consider whether he might be right.

"If the baby doesn't survive, you're going to hate me," she said.

"No, I won't."

"But you'll realize that being with me isn't the best thing for you. You could be with someone else and have a much easier, happier life. Someone like..." *Mariella*.

"Someone like who?" Seth asked. "It doesn't matter. I love you, Jenny. I always will. And I want to have this child with you." He took her hands.

"Seth..." Jenny suddenly found herself sobbing, and she buried her face in his shoulder. "Stupid pregnant hormones."

"Even your hormones are pregnant?"

"Yep." She looked up at him. "Do you mean it? You want to

try?"

"I want to try." Seth put an arm around her and kissed her. "We're going to make it work."

"I love you so much." Jenny put her arms around his neck and leaned against his chest. His hand remained on her hip, a river of golden warmth flowing through her flesh and deep into her womb.

* * *

In the evening, they met Mariella at one of the wooden Christmas villages that sprang up all over Paris during December, as if bands of Santa's elves had emigrated from the North Pole like itinerant gypsies setting up camps in the city. Instead of gypsy tents, the villages were made of wooden chalets that looked as if they'd been transported from some enchanted place high in the Alps.

Christmas carols played everywhere, naturally, and the chalets offered a dazzling array of colorful merchandise, from chocolates and Christmas candies to wine, caviar, and artisan cheeses. They sold holiday decorations and handmade toys, clothes, and organic cosmetics.

Jenny, Seth, and Mariella walked slowly down the Champs-Elysees, looking over the cheerful scene. Jenny and Mariella were both heavily bundled against the cold, Mariella to avoid getting lost in flashes of the future from everybody in the crowd, Jenny to avoid killing anyone. Jenny and Seth drank hot cider, while Mariella drank a cup of hot wine.

"You should do yoga," Mariella was telling Jenny. "My sister Stefania did it every day her last two pregnancies, and she said they went much easier than the first."

"I don't know. A yoga class?" Jenny asked. "That's kind of risky for me, all those people in workout clothes."

"I will show you," Mariella said. "In your own home. I am a black belt in yoga."

"I didn't know they gave black belts for that," Seth said.

"It is only a joke. But I can teach you, Jenny."

"It can't hurt," Jenny said. "It'll give me something to do besides watch Seth play that *Walking Dead* video game."

"I'm going to beat that game one day," Seth said. "Watch."

"I'm sure you will, Seth," Jenny told him.

"Here." Seth stepped toward a booth and picked up a plush rabbit, stitched together from several kinds of material to create a quilt pattern. "We should get this for him. Or her."

"We can probably find some cute Christmas clothes here, too," Mariella said. "So you'll be ready next year."

"Enough!" Jenny said. "We don't even know..." Jenny decided she didn't want to say *We don't even know whether the baby will live*, so she fell quiet.

"We have to prepare, Jenny," Seth said. "We have to believe. And I'm buying this wittle wabbit." He paid the toymaker.

Jenny shook her head. She didn't need the pressure.

"So, lunch," Seth said. "Are chocolate-covered waffles okay with everyone?"

"Ugh. Baguette for me," Jenny said.

"I'll just have a soup," Mariella told him, nodding at a chalet that sold both soup and baguettes.

"You two stalk a place to sit. I'll be right back." Seth headed toward the food vendors.

Mariella approached a wooden bench with carved, cartoony reindeer heads for its arms. Three teenage boys sat there, drinking wine and joking with each other, but the beautiful, smiling Italian girl quickly caught their attention. She spoke with them in French, explaining that her friend was pregnant and needed to sit.

The boys fell over themselves to do what she asked. Mariella waved Jenny over, and the two of them sat down. Mariella thanked the group of boys and waved good-bye, and they reluctantly trudged away.

"Being pregnant does have some advantages," Mariella told her. "You should enjoy them."

"They didn't move because I was pregnant, they moved because you're pretty," Jenny said.

"Boys can be shallow. That's something else worth taking advantage of."

Jenny laughed and shook her head.

Mariella's smile faded, and a hard look came into her eyes. "So. You and I were roommates at a Nazi death camp."

"You could say that," Jenny said.

"You gave me the worst dreams last night. Swastikas, fire, screaming, execution chambers..."

"I'm sorry."

"It isn't your fault." Mariella paused, as if thinking something over. "Juliana. Mia. These names did feel very familiar, when you said them. So I was Sicilian? Have I just been bumming around Italy since the Renaissance? Or maybe the Roman Empire? Don't I get to travel?"

"I'm sure you do," Jenny said.

"Is it possible that I could remember my past lives, as you do?"

"Anything's possible."

"What is it like, all those memories?" Mariella asked. "It must be like a thousand voices in your head."

Jenny laughed again. "Not exactly. It's more like...Have you ever had something happen, maybe you taste something or hear a song, and then suddenly you remember a moment from your past that you'd completely forgotten? Like a childhood moment you haven't thought about in years?"

"Yes, I know what you mean!"

"It's like that, when you remember your past lives. Only lots and lots and lots of that. You really can't remember everything at once. Just like you can't remember your entire lifetime all at once. You have to focus. And also..."

"Also what?" Mariella was leaning forward, a hand on Jenny's arm, intently soaking up every wood.

"Also, most of it's not good."

"How do you mean?"

"It's warfare, murder, deception," Jenny said. "That's what our kind love. The human race are just pawns to us. When you find out all the evil you've done in the past...it's just not good. It's hard to separate yourself from that. You have to learn that you can change, and not let your past trap you."

"Warfare, murder, and deception," Seth repeated, arriving with their food. "Is that near the cheese chalet?"

"More like the merry-go-round," Jenny said. "Over and over again, life after life."

"Oh, sorry, didn't know we were having a heavy talk." Seth sat down next to Jenny, scrunching her in the middle between him and Mariella. He passed out their food, which smelled delicious, fresh-baked bread and warm tomato bisque to fend off the cold.

"Apparently, I've been giving Mariella nightmares," Jenny said.

"Oh, you, too?" Seth asked Mariella, and Jenny nudged him playfully. "No, seriously," he said. "All these jumbled memories from the past. I keep dreaming about them, but they don't make any sense. Like nothing happens in order, it's just random scenes. Real horror-movie stuff, too."

"I guess I'm helping you remember," Jenny said. "Mariella, can you see anything else about Seth's future yet?"

"I'll look." Mariella slipped off a glove and reached across Jenny's lap to take Seth's wrist. She looked deep into Seth's eyes. Seth made faces back at her. "Stop it!" Mariella snickered, and she closed her eyes instead. "He's there. Taking Seth into the dark. Everything's still confused, covered in a fog...But the danger is there. He's coming."

"How soon?" Jenny asked.

"I still can't tell."

"Should we stock up on guns? What do we do?" Seth asked.

"I don't think we can buy guns in France," Jenny said.

"That's too bad. In South Carolina, you could practically buy them at the gas station."

"I can't say what to do," Mariella told him. "We can better prepare if we know more about him. We all need Jenny's memories." Mariella looked at her. "Jenny. Did you not say that someone helped you remember your past lives?"

"Alexander," Jenny said.

"Could you not do this for us? For Seth and me? So that we can all be prepared?"

"I don't know. We ate these mushrooms, psychoactive mushrooms. He guided me. I couldn't do that now, with the...baby."

"But Seth and I could." Mariella had a pleading look in her eye. "And you could guide us without taking them."

"I could try, but I could mess it all up," Jenny said. "Besides, where are we going to get magic mushrooms around here?"

"I *am* an art student," Mariella said, which made Seth laugh. "Tell me what these mushrooms looked like, and I'll see what I can do."

"It's risky," Jenny said. She thought about it for a minute. "But so is knowing that General Kranzler is coming for us, and not doing anything about it."

"General who?" Seth asked.

"*Gruppenführer* Kranzler," Jenny said. "A general in the Nazi

S.S. Yep. I'm pretty sure that's who's after us. The question is: what does he want this time?"

"What did he want last time?" Seth asked.

"Supernormals. That's what he called us. He thought we were on the front edge of human evolution. He thought our powers came from our DNA."

"But they don't?" Mariella asked.

"They're in our souls, not our bodies," Jenny said. "But, like everyone else, Kranzler tried to fit us into his own myths. In the ancient world, it was easy, because everyone believed gods and demigods were everywhere, so we fit right in. By the Middle Ages, we had to watch out for witch trials. But the Nazis were crazy about eugenics—I mean, they were crazy about a lot of things, but that was their biggest obsession. So they saw us in terms of biology and evolution, instead of anything supernatural."

"But supernatural is more correct?" Mariella asked.

"Definitely," Jenny said. "So they got more frustrated the more they studied and tested us..."

"I remember!" Mariella sat up as if she'd been zapped with electricity, and she gripped Jenny's hand tight. "I remember...oh, the poor goats."

"The poor goats," Jenny agreed.

"What goats? I think I saw some marshmallow goats at one of the candy chalets," Seth said.

"Maybe we should let Mariella tell you," Jenny said.

"I don't know that I could remember it all correctly," Mariella told her.

"I'll help. We'll start by telling Seth what happened after we met. Just tell what you remember, and I'll fill in the rest."

Mariella drank her hot wine, then closed her eyes and concentrated.

# Chapter Twenty-One

Mia, Juliana's new roommate, showed her around the girls' dormitory area. The double doors at the end of the hall led to a "community room" with comfortable chairs, a radio, a record player, and sewing supplies. A side door there opened to their group bathroom.

They ate in a military-style mess hall, located down a long hall and up a flight of stairs. The little buildings up top, it turned out, were just doorways into different areas of a vast underground complex with many levels. The walls were rock or concrete, and the carpeting and cheery colors didn't reach beyond the girls' dormitory.

The diners fell into easily recognizable groups. The S.S. in their black uniforms took the largest table at the center. Scientists and doctors sat along one side of the room, while nurses and secretaries took the table near the front. Test subjects like Juliana and Mia sat at the back.

The food tonight was German, lots of sausages, cheese, and pickled vegetables, with dark beer to drink. Juliana and Mia shared a long table with the others from her hall. Alise sat at the head, excitedly introducing Juliana to everyone. She wasn't shy about discussing their supernormal abilities, either.

The girls included Vilja, a Swedish girl with extremely pale skin and white-blond hair, who claimed to see "energy spirits," which apparently included angels, demons, ghosts, gnomes, and fairies. A Polish girl named Roza, whose face was framed by a thick braid on each side, had what Alise called "far-sight," the ability to see distant events as they happened. There was a small Slavic girl, Evelina, with very dark eyes and short black hair, who sat apart at the end of the table and didn't even look up from her food when Alise introduced her.

"And what does she do?" Roza asked, pointing at Juliana.

"Her touch spreads the plague," Alise said in a loud whisper, as if confiding a secret to the entire room. All the girls leaned back from Juliana.

*Thanks so much, Alise*, Juliana thought, but she nodded.

"It's true," Juliana said. "You're perfectly safe as long as you don't touch me."

"I don't think we will forget!" Roza said, looking disgusted.

The conversation was difficult, everyone trying to speak in a patois of German, which they'd been studying since they arrived, and English, and their own native languages. Juliana gathered that they'd each been recruited by agents of the Evolution Congress, which included scientists, businessmen, and politicians from all over the Western world. Evelina, the Slavic girl, did not speak at all, and Juliana wondered whether she was shy or was just having language difficulties.

Sebastian, Niklaus, and another boy approached their table, but Niklaus continued on without acknowledging them and sat at a table with the S.S. men. Sebastian sat by Juliana and hugged her. Alise cleared her throat and shook her head, as if affection shouldn't be shown here.

The other boy smiled at the girls, and sat next to Vilja. The ghostly Swedish girl looked uncomfortable at his grin and shifted away from him.

"Who's he?" Juliana whispered to Sebastian. "Your roommate?"

"Why would I need a roommate?" Sebastian asked. "There are only three guys on our hall, and Niklaus has the biggest room to himself because he's the hallway *fuehrer*. That means he's the guy in charge of watching us and enforcing the rules, I think."

"I see you talking about me," the boy told them, in accented but fluent English. "What are you saying?"

"She was just asking who you were," Sebastian said. "Juliana, this is Willem. He's from, uh..."

"Holland," Willem said. He had short blond hair and blue eyes, and he gave off a nervous energy, fidgeting in his chair, his fingers restlessly tapping. He kept stealing glances at Vilja,who ignored him. "They must be growing desperate for subjects, if they're looking as far away as America."

"There don't seem to be many of us here," Juliana agreed.

"That's because we're only looking for the truly extraordinary," Alise told them. "The supernormal. We're selective."

"There just aren't many of us, are there?" Willem asked. "Supernatural gifts are rare."

"What is yours?" Juliana asked him.

"I start fires." Willem gave her a wicked grin.

"With your hands?" Juliana asked.

"With my hands?" He smirked. "Anyone can start a fire with their hands. I start them with my *mind.*" He touched the side of his head.

"Your power doesn't involve touch?" Sebastian asked.

"He has no power," said a soft voice at the end of the table. Evelina, the small Slavic girl, speaking for the first time. She didn't look up from the plate of pickled vegetables in front of her, though she wasn't eating, just stirring it with a fork.

"What?" Willem scowled, leaning towards Evelina. "Are you calling me a liar?"

Alise took Willem's arm and spoke softly to him in either German or Dutch, Juliana couldn't tell. Willem gazed longingly into her eyes, like a small boy falling in love for the first time. When she released him, Willem sank back in his seat, wearing the same kind of goofy smile that had appeared on Sebastian's face when Alise touched him.

Alise saw Juliana looking at her and gave a big smile. "See? We can all get along peacefully," Alise told her.

Juliana looked at Willem, who stared at Alise with his mouth open, starting to drool. Juliana realized that Alise's "happy" power might be more dangerous than it sounded.

"You will all be happy to learn that, in honor of our two new friends from America, we have obtained permission to use the screening room tonight," Alise said, and everyone seemed to brighten at this news. "We'll watch 'She Done Him Wrong' with Mae West and Cary Grant."

Juliana and Mia immediately looked at each other and smiled.

"We have selected this film because Juliana expressed an admiration for the actress," Alise added, with an extra smile at Juliana. Juliana smiled back. Mia must have mentioned it to Alise, though Juliana wasn't sure when that might have happened. The American movie would certainly help them feel at home.

All of the subjects went to the screening room after the meal. Alise quietly made it clear to Juliana that hand-holding and kissing in the darkened room was not allowed. Juliana and Sebastian had to sit with an empty seat between them. Still, Juliana enjoyed the movie.

Things became much less pleasant the next day.

Juliana's morning started with a physical examination in a laboratory. She had to strip down while a couple of German nurses, not much older than her, weighed her, measured her, took her pulse, and drew samples of her blood and cut lengths out of her hair, which they placed into labeled test tubes. They wore surgical masks and gloves and acted wary around her, as if they'd been warned about her touch. Juliana gave them an extra warning, but she wasn't sure if they understood. She was tense throughout the physical.

Eventually, the doctor entered, and the two nurses moved to the side of the room, where they stood with their hands folded and backs straight, like soldiers at attention. Juliana, sitting naked on the steel exam table, hurried to cover herself with her arms. She cast a desperate look at the two nurses, wanting to know whether she could put her clothes on again, but they didn't even look at her.

The doctor's nose was buried in a file folder, and he kept reading for a few minutes after he entered, saying nothing at all to Juliana or the nurses. He was a very pudgy man, balding, with a fat, clean-shaven face but a thick neck beard under his chin line, like he was trying hard to look eccentric, or desperately wanted to look like a lion. His eyes flicked back and forth behind his horn-rimmed glasses as he read.

"Hello?" Juliana finally said to him.

The man glanced up and eyed her coldly. "Yah?"

"Can I get dressed?" she asked.

He grunted and took a pen from the breast pocket of his lab coat. "You are Juliana?"

"Yes."

"Hm. Severe infection caused by physical contact—not the only case of transmission through touch we've seen here." He looked up from the file again. "Background questions. Age?"

"Twenty."

"Any allergies, chronic illnesses, past surgeries, anything at all in your medical background?"

"No, sir. I've almost never been to the doctor, and I've never been sick."

"Never sick?" He scribbled in his file. "Nothing? No common cold? No minor infections of any kind?"

"No. Can I get dressed now?"

"Not until exam is over."

"Do you have a name?" she asked.

"I am Dr. Franz Wichtmann," he said, sounded impatient. "I am the project director here. Tell me about this deadly touch of yours. How long have you had it?"

"All my life."

"Have you ever harmed a person with it?"

Juliana hesitated.

"You can be honest," Wichtmann said. "All is confidential."

"I have, but only when they attacked me first," Juliana told him.

"Have you ever killed anyone with your touch?"

Juliana hesitated again, looking down at her bare feet. Her whole body seemed pale and sick under the harsh surgical lights overhead.

"We are scientists, not police," Wichtmann reminded her. "And we are not even in your country. We are here to promote human evolution, and we have no wish to put our test subjects in prison. If we are to study your situation, we must have the facts."

"Again...it was only when they attacked me."

"Then you have killed human beings with your touch?" His eyebrows were raised, but he seemed more curious than horrified.

"Dr. Wichtmann, I grew up on the streets, alone," she told him. "Sometimes, a man would see a vulnerable young girl and attack. I had no choice but to protect myself."

"How many?"

"How many?" she asked back.

He sighed. "How many men have you killed, Juliana?"

"I don't know, I try to block it out...Five? Seven?"

"Five or seven?"

"Yes."

He noted this down. "Does your power spread only through touch? Can it become airborne?"

"No, I don't think so. It's only happened through my touch."

"Hm. And is your touch harmful to nonhumans? Animals, plants?"

"Animals, definitely. Plants resist it better...but if I stand on a patch of grass too long, it will eventually turn brown and die."

"How long does it take to kill a person or animal?"

"If I just touch them, they usually get away with an infection that fades in time. If I hold on for a minute, they'll die." Juliana squirmed nervously. His questions made her feel even more exposed than she already was. "I try not to kill people, honestly! Sometimes I can just threaten them away."

"And people believe your threats? What do you tell them?"

"I don't have to say much. I just..." Juliana held out her arm, and dark sores opened from the crook of her elbow all the way to her fingertips. They spread up to her neck, then ruptured open along one side of her face, turning her eye the color of diseased blood. One of the nurses in the corner screamed. "You don't really have to tell people not to touch you, if you look like this."

Dr. Wichtmann gaped, then pulled his surgical mask from his neck up to his face. "Are you certain it isn't airborne?"

"I've worked at a freak show for years, showing these things off to crowds in a small room at the back of a tent," she told him. "No one's ever gotten sick, or I would have stopped doing it."

"You can exhibit symptoms at will?" Wichtmann asked. He wrote much faster now, his eyes bugging behind his glasses.

"Sure." Infected wounds and blisters opened all over her body, turning her into a mass of disease and gore. Both the nurses gasped at the sudden transformation, as did Dr. Wichtmann, who took an extra couple of steps back from her, even though he'd kept a good distance between them since he'd arrived. He turned his head and barked orders at the nurses in German.

One of the nurses crossed her arms and shook her head, but the second nurse grabbed the first one's arm and pulled her along. They reluctantly approached Juliana and took samples of the dark fluid and blood leaking from her sores, the inflamed cluster of pustules on her cheek, the sticky bile that leaked out through the leprous decay of her stomach. They took what seemed like an endless series of photographs.

"Does it cause pain?" Dr. Wichtmann asked.

"I guess it's a little itchy."

"Not for you, I mean for others."

"Oh. I think so. They usually kind of hiss and pull away, and then they have lesions wherever I touched them."

"And you can make them heal at will, too?"

"I can heal myself." Juliana's disease symptoms closed and vanished, leaving traces of blood and other fluids here and there on her skin. "I can't heal anyone else, though."

Dr. Wichtmann scribbled more notes. "I have determined that your supernormality may be genuine. You will have testing this afternoon. Until then, you have two hours lunch and recreation." He turned away.

"What kind of testing?" Juliana asked, but he left the room without answering. After he'd been gone a few seconds, the two nurses raced out the door, casting fearful glances at Juliana and whispering as they departed.

Juliana quickly dressed herself. A guard in an S.S. uniform escorted her to the mess hall, which was still mostly empty because she was early. She sat alone at the usual table in the back. She'd hoped to see Sebastian at lunch, but none of the other test subjects were here, just a group of S.S. men at the center table. Three young nurses arrived, but one of them pointed at Juliana and whispered to the others, and all three immediately turned and left without eating.

As Juliana was the only female in the room, she drew repeated looks from the S.S. men eating their early lunch. It made her uncomfortable, so she hurried through her beef stew and chunk of bread, then returned to her room.

In the afternoon, she found herself standing alone in one of the big concrete laboratory rooms, facing a row of six cages, holding six live goats that stared at her with their creepy eyes. A video camera whirred, recording her on fat spools of film. The room had a high ceiling, like an airplane hangar. Dr. Wichtmann and several younger scientists observed her from sealed glass windows far above her.

"To your right," Dr. Wichtmann said to Juliana, his voice crackling over an electronic speaker. She looked at the row of cages and approached the one on the far right. She'd had a sick feeling in her stomach since the moment she'd walked into the room and seen the animals in their narrow cages.

"What do you want me to do?" Juliana asked, though she was afraid she knew. She was just stalling.

"Touch the first one," the doctor told her.

"It will get sick."

"That's what we want."

Juliana frowned as she stepped toward the first cage. The goat stepped toward her and made a bleating sound.

"Go ahead," Dr. Wichtmann ordered. "We have a tight schedule."

Juliana forced herself to move closer to the goat, but she couldn't bring herself to touch it.

"Don't make me do this," Juliana said, looking up at the fat doctor in the window. "There must be something else we can use...like snakes or lizards. Or spiders, I can kill spiders."

"Those are no good for us," Wichtmann said. "You must do this if you ever want to gain control of your power. Is that not your stated purpose in being here?"

*I'll just touch it for a second*, she told herself. *It will heal from that.*

Juliana tried to ignore her feelings as she reached through the cage bars and brushed her fingers lightly across the goat's back. The animal squealed and twisted away from her as bloody blisters erupted along its spine. The goat turned in circles inside the cage, kicking its hooves against the walls. The other goats began echoing its fearful bleats.

"Very good." Dr. Wichtmann was looking through binoculars, as were two other scientists, for a close-up of the goat. She realized that all these men were frightened of her, and that was why none of them were down here with her.

"The second stall," Dr. Wichtmann called out. "Now, you are holding onto the goat for ten seconds. I will time."

"Ten seconds could kill an animal that small." Juliana looked at the second goat, who was shaking and trying to escape, alarmed by the cries of the first goat. "Can't we at least use animals that are already sick or dying?"

"Other illnesses would only confuse the data," Dr. Wichtmann insisted. "We must be certain they begin in good health. Now, ten seconds. Now!" All of the faces stared down at her coldly, making her feel she had no choice.

Juliana forced herself to walk toward the second goat, who squealed and backed away from her, but it didn't have very far to travel inside the cage. She steeled herself, then reached inside and wrapped her fingers around its hind leg, the farthest she could get from any of the poor animal's vital organs. That would give it a better chance of surviving, she thought.

It shrieked as the dark blisters spread up its leg and across its torso. The skin of its face bubbled and burst, blood trickling down across its small, wooly chest. It slammed its head repeatedly into the wooden wall beside it, leaving smears of blood thick with lumps of rotten flesh. Its lower lip rotted away, revealing its lower teeth as they sank into the black, mushy remains of its lower jaw, like stones sinking into a swamp.

"Time!" Dr. Wichtmann called. Juliana immediately released the goat, and it collapsed on its hindquarters. The leg she'd held had broken apart like a rotten sponge, and now the three-legged goat flailed helplessly on the ground, squealing in agony.

"I'm sorry!" Juliana whispered to the thrashing goat. "I wish I could take it back. I wish I could...Sebastian!" she screamed up to Dr. Wichtmann. "Sebastian needs to heal this animal. Where is he?"

"*Nein*," Dr. Wichtmann replied.

"Please!" Juliana called.

"We must study the disease to understand it," Dr. Wichtmann told her. "This is necessary."

Juliana tried not to cry at the sound of the wailing, plague-ravaged goat. While she'd never been sick from any disease, she now had to fight her desire to throw up in front of everyone. She needed this test to end. She wished she'd never agreed to it.

"And now the third goat," Dr. Wichtmann said. "This one, thirty seconds."

"It won't live!" Juliana said.

"Now," Dr. Wichtmann said. "Thirty seconds."

Juliana bit her lip as she eyed the third goat, its eyes rolling in terror at the screams of the other two. She forced herself to reach for it, and this time she grabbed it around the neck, thinking to make the animal's death as quick and merciful as possible.

She imagined the demon plague pouring out of her hands like a swarm of poisonous black flies, burrowing straight toward the center of the goat's brain. It bleated, and blood poured from its eyes, mucus and brain fluid from its mouth. Its head fell apart, and the portion of the neck she held in her fingers rotted away.

The headless goat fell to the floor of its cage with a sickening splatter sound. A wave of dark sores rippled across its front legs and abdomen, but stopped halfway along its body, because the goat was dead. Its back half still looked perfectly healthy, except for the blood slowly seeping its way through the goat's fur.

Juliana stepped back, shaking, with bits of deteriorating skull and brain dripping from her bloody fingers. She looked at Dr. Wichtmann and shook her head. She didn't want to do it again, and three more goats remained.

"That is enough," Dr. Wichtmann said. "The other three goats are controls. You may..."

Another scientist tapped Dr. Wichtmann's shoulder and pointed. A small group of S.S. officers appeared in the window beside the scientists, led by a man with poison-green eyes and close-cropped hair the color of burnt copper. His face was all hard slabs, and his colorless lips pressed together, almost too small to see. His black military cap had a small eagle and a skull and crossbones on the front, and he had oak leaves on his lapel, signifying some kind of rank. Two younger men in black uniforms stood a step behind him.

Dr. Wichtmann saluted the man with his palm out and conversed with him in German. Then Wichtmann turned toward Juliana. "This is Group Leader Kranzler, the man in charge of the base. He wishes to inspect the results of your test," Wichtmann explained.

Kranzler looked down at her, and then he and the two S.S. men stepped back from the window. Less than a minute later, the laboratory door opened, and Kranzler marched inside, right toward Juliana. The two men who accompanied him followed very slowly, as if they were afraid to go near her like everyone else. Kranzler's eyes bored into her as he approached, and he did not look scared at all. He looked like he meant to crush her in one of his large fists.

He stopped to look her over, then looked at the goats. The first one had stopped panicking and gone into a kind of shock. The second lay on its side, groaning and vomiting as it died. The third lay completely still, its head just a lumpy, dark puddle on the cage floor.

Kranzler surveyed them carefully, then spoke to Juliana in

German.

"*Gruppenführer* Kranzler would like to know why the second one dies more slowly, when its wounds extend all over its body. The third goat died before the infection fully spread," one of the younger S.S. men translated. Both of them remained near the door, ready to run away.

Juliana shrugged. "I guess I concentrated it. Like a cannonball." She pressed her hands together, in case that made anything clearer.

Kranzler listened to the translation, then muttered in German. The other S.S. men laughed, followed quickly by the scientists above.

"What did he say?" Juliana asked the translator.

"He says, the Reich no longer needs an army. We can simply place you alone on the battlefield."

"I would not recommend it," Juliana told him. Kranzler himself laughed when he heard the translation, and everyone hurried to join in. Then he spoke to her at length.

"The *Gruppenführer* wishes to convey his great joy at having such a valued guest as you," the translator said. "He asks whether your accommodations have been pleasant, or whether you lack for anything."

Juliana could have said that she didn't want to kill any more animals, but she didn't think her opinion would matter much. She realized that this man held the true power here, and he was trying to decide how he might use her. The thought made her more than a little uneasy. His face was like iron...despite what his assistant said, he did not look like a man feeling great joy, or deeply concerned about her comfort.

"Tell him my accommodations are fine, thank you," Juliana said, eager to escape Kranzler's powerful, penetrating gaze.

Kranzler touched the brim of his hat, then crisply turned and walked away, followed by his two assistants, who quickly closed the door behind them.

"This test is concluded," Dr. Wichtmann announced when the S.S. men had left the lab. "We will study the results and design more for you tomorrow. Leave now and return to your room."

* * *

Juliana scrubbed and scrubbed herself in one of the four sinks in the bath area on her hall, but she couldn't quite erase the taint of red from her hands. The animals' dying shrieks kept echoing inside her skull, tormenting her. She didn't know if she'd ever felt so horrible or hated herself so much.

She wanted to simply curl up on her bed and speak to no one, but she learned that every evening during the week, the girls had to meet in the community room for "culture hour," to be led by Alise, since she was their hall *fuehrer*.

Alise sat on the deep, comfortable couch in the girls' community room, flanked by Roza, the Polish girl with the large braids, and Vilja, the Swedish girl so ghostly-pale she seemed on the verge of fading out of existence. The three of them had also made chocolate cookies and an apple-cider punch in the community room's small kitchen corner, and these now sat on the card table in the middle of the room.

The three blond girls formed a kind of clique, from which Juliana's roommate Mia seemed excluded. Evelina, the short, dark Slavic girl, was all but ignored by the group. She sat in a chair in the corner, while Juliana and Mia sat in rocking chairs next to each other. Juliana thought it was silly to have cliques based on hair color, but that almost seemed to be the idea. In that case, Juliana and her long black locks properly belonged with Evelina instead of Mia.

"First, some good news," Alise announced. "We will no longer be herded into the mess hall with everyone else. Instead, we subjects will have a private dining room on our own level! They'll send the food down by dumbwaiter, and we'll just send our dishes back up."

"It's because of her, isn't it?" Roza looked at Juliana, with a smile that wasn't particularly friendly. "They're scared of her. They don't want to get contaminated."

"Roza, let's try something original and be nice to the new girl," Alise said, touching Roza's arm. The look in Roza's eyes immediately softened, and she turned to gaze lovingly at Alise.

"If you want," Roza breathed.

"Good. Now, Juliana, since you're new, allow me to explain cultural hour, my favorite hour of the day," Alise told her. "It is my job to instruct you in German language and history, so we can all speak and understand each other better. We also study proper female arts, such as sewing..." She indicated the sewing machines. "Or we read from the great German writers, or listen to true German music."

"That sounds fun," Juliana said. She didn't mind learning

history, and she liked the idea of learning a new language, especially if there were cookies involved.

"I knew you would like it!" Alise said. "You should begin by learning your German numbers. Do you know any yet?"

Juliana shook her head.

"It's easy." Alise held up one finger at a time as she said, *"Eins, zwei, drei..."*

*"Eins, zwei, drei..."* Juliana repeated, as did all the other girls in the room except for Evelina. The small Slavic girl just watched them with a distant frown.

# Chapter Twenty-Two

Ward, his assistants Avery and Buchanan, and Tommy hitched a ride on a military plane hauling crates of supplies bound for U.S. Army installations in Schweinfurt, Germany. From there, they rode north in a helicopter, toward the research center in the Harz mountains.

"There it is." Ward pointed down through the window. "What do you say, Tommy?"

Tommy looked, and Ward could have laughed as his face fell. The old base didn't look like much—a few sunken concrete pillboxes and rattling ventilation wells in a weedy yard enclosed by a high brick wall and rusty coils of wire.

"What are we doing out here?" Tommy asked.

"Just what I told you, testing and training."

"At the town dump?" Tommy asked.

"It doesn't look interesting at all, does it?" Ward asked. "Certainly not worth a second look if you happen to notice it by airplane or satellite. Just old World War II ruins surrounded by chainlink, with signs warning about hazardous conditions inside, just in case any hikers or campers stumble their way up here. We're in the middle of a national park, so nobody lives nearby."

The helicopter dropped them down inside the brick wall, onto a helipad painted to blend with the dirt and weeds around it. Ward instructed the pilot to refuel immediately, and then he led Tommy away from the helicopter and toward one of the old concrete buildings.

Inside, the floor was cracked and full of dead weeds and scattered trash. A small, sleek structure of black steel, obviously much more recent, stood in the center of the room, with a pair of sunken double doors like an elevator. Ward stepped up to the circular lens beside it and let the security system scan his retina. There was loud *thunk*, and then the steel doors slid apart.

"After you." Ward nodded at Tommy.

Tommy stepped forward. Inside the doors, a long escalator, activated by their arrival, flowed silently down a steep tunnel made of old concrete reinforced with bright steel ribs. Bars of fluorescent lights hung at evenly spaced intervals all the way down.

"What's down there?" Tommy asked him.

"Your future," Ward replied.

Tommy lifted his overstuffed duffel bag and stepped onto the escalator. It took them down, down, down...

"What is this place?" Tommy asked.

"A research base. Originally built by the Nazis before World War II, for the Yggdrasil Project...which, as far as we can tell, was about finding and breeding humans with 'supernormal' abilities, to create a race of super-soldiers."

"Is that what you're trying to do?" Tommy asked him.

"We're not interested in breeding projects, only national defense," Ward said. "This base fell into Soviet hands after the war, and they did God knows what with it until the 1980s, when they realized they were losing Germany, cleared the place out, and sealed it up. The modern German government has no use for it—they were going to demolish it, but now it's under lease to the U.S. government. My agency, specifically."

They reached the bottom of the escalator and stepped into a wide corridor with gleaming white tiles on the floor and walls. When Ward had first scouted the location, the walls had been either concrete or raw rock from the natural cave system. It had looked like an underground bunker, but with the new walls, floors, and lighting, it now felt more like a proper research center.

"How big is this place?" Tommy asked, clearly impressed.

"Several levels deep," Ward said. "It had everything we could wish for—dormitories, huge reinforced laboratory bays, an independent supply of mountain spring water, ventilation, hydroelectric power from a couple of nearby waterfalls. German engineering. You have to hand it to the Nazis, they really knew what they were doing sometimes."

Tommy snorted laughter and smirked.

"Here's our observation deck." Black double doors opened automatically at Ward's approach. They entered a wide, dimly lit corridor lined with clear windows, which looked down into high-ceilinged concrete laboratories, some of them just bare bones with just fluorescent lights and huge steel sinks, others jammed with chemical testing or medical equipment. One had an MRI machine. The workday had ended, so the observation deck and the labs below were deserted.

A digital workstation sat in front of each window, allowing observers to monitor the lab from above. A long table with more workstations ran along the center of the corridor. Little square flags hung here and there, depicting the "union" of fifty white stars on a blue field from an American flag. As an agency with no official existence, ASTRIA had no official insignia or seal, either, but it had used the starry blue as its unofficial symbol since the 1950's.

"This looks really familiar to me," Tommy said. "Like I've been here before."

"That's because you made the right choice," Ward said. "You belong here. This is where we'll use the latest technology to unravel just how your power works, and how it can best be applied to national defense. It's quiet now, so let's go to your new room."

Ward led him through more tunnels, toward the dormitory area for test subjects. Along the way, they passed a pair of security officers in black uniforms ribbed with light body armor. Their uniforms were blank, with no insignia, badges, or other designs to indicate what organization employed these men. Like all the security staff at the base, they were not soldiers, but specialists from Hale Security Group, a Virginia-based multinational that provided operatives under contract to the Defense and State Departments, the CIA, and other sensitive agencies, and they did similar work for an assortment of other national governments, including the UK and Saudi

Arabia. These men were former Special Forces or intelligence agents from across the Western world, highly trained killers who knew how to keep a secret.

Because they were mercenaries and not soldiers, they did not salute Ward, but simply nodded their heads in recognition.

Ward opened the double doors to the short dormitory hall for male test subjects. Tommy gaped as he stepped into the first room, the largest on the hall.

"This seems familiar, too," Tommy said. "It's weird. You ever get the hairs on the back of your neck standing up?"

Ward had felt that same cold tingle of recognition before—when he'd first toured the facility when scouting locations for a research center. He'd known immediately that this was the place he wanted.

"It can happen," Ward said. "You'll see we've modernized, got you a flat screen TV with satellite feed. Climate control panel. At the end of the hall, you'll find the common room and the bathrooms. You've got the place to yourself for now."

Tommy sank slowly onto the bed, looking dazed.

"The scientists might come here to meet you," Ward told him. "If not, you can go to the mess hall for dinner." Ward gave him directions through the underground complex.

"Are you leaving?" Tommy asked.

"I'll have to jump back to America to deal with a certain situation," Ward said. "But I'll be returning soon. Very soon, if things go well. Are you all right here?"

Tommy nodded, but made no move to unpack his duffel bag. The kid seemed out of it, but he had tonight to rest.

Ward left the dormitory hall, followed by Buchanan and Avery.

"You think he'll work out?" Avery asked.

Ward ignored the question. "Buchanan, didn't we see transactions between Barrett Capital and Hale Security Group?"

"A few, sir. It looked like standard private-sector work, risk assessment for investments in India and East Asia."

"Of course, it *looked* like nothing interesting. Hale isn't run by idiots. But didn't those transactions begin around the time Seth Barrett disappeared?"

"I believe so, sir."

"Tell me, Buchanan, if you were some rich guy, and you wanted to hide yourself...or hide your son...from the United States government, would Hale be a good company to hire?"

"Of course, sir," Buchanan replied.

"Those rats!" Avery said.

Ward considered it. He'd automatically seen Hale as part of "his" team because he'd staffed up the research center with their security officers. He'd had Buchanan check into the payments from the Barretts, of course, but the story had sounded normal at the time. It hadn't occurred to him that his own security people could be hiding the targets for whom he was searching.

Ward slowly smiled. Hale had a multimillion-dollar contract with his agency, ASTRIA. He had plenty of influence with them, and he could even threaten to have their security clearance revoked if they didn't play ball. That would cost them most of their revenue, destroying the company. Their piddling payments from Barrett Capital were nothing compared to their government contracts.

Also, Ward felt like he had the current Hale CEO, Edward Cordell, in his pocket. He'd shaken hands with the man on many occasions, and so he knew all about Eddie's twenty-two-year-old mistress and the Manhattan apartment he rented for her. He also knew that Eddie hid things from his wife by keeping the apartment on a Hale corporate account, lightly embezzling from the company to protect his secret. Ward would have almost no trouble getting him to cooperate and tell him where to find Seth Barrett and Jenny Morton.

There was only one remaining obstacle, and it was time to square that away.

* * *

Senator Junius Mayfield woke in his hospital bed on the fifth floor of a private hospital in Maryland to find a ghostly apparition staring in through his window. His heartbeat kicked up until he realized it was just a barn owl perched in the tree limb outside, its dark eyes and ghost-white face turned toward Junius, watching him. The owl's stare was unsettling, and he would have liked to yell at it and chase it off, but he couldn't even get out of bed.

"Go on, fly on, leave me be," Junius said, but it sounded like "Ooh ah, faya, lemma buh." His voice came out as a whisper, barely audible above the beeping of his heart monitor.

The owl, clearly not intimidated, stayed where it was, staring into his window.

The left half of Junius' body was frozen solid, and the right half moved as slowly as a stiff old mule in the dead of winter. His staff had done their best to keep the full extent of the stroke damage from the news media and the public, but his prolonged absence from the Senate floor spoke volumes about his true condition. Already, his enemies back in Tennessee were pushing for a special election to replace him.

Junius thought about calling in the nurse and getting her to close the blinds so the owl couldn't stare at him, but it seemed like a pathetic request. Instead, he clawed his right hand toward the side of the bed, thinking he would find the TV remote and discover what kind of programming the Golf Channel offered at three in the morning. Probably the women's tour, he thought.

His hand couldn't find the remote, so he turned his head, and then he saw the three men in his room, all of them wearing dark suits and lab coats, but they weren't any doctors he knew. The one in the lead was the oldest, his sandy-red hair going gray and cropped close. One of the two younger men held Junius' remote, smirking at him. Without it, Junius couldn't summon help.

Junius didn't recognize any of them. He flipped through his mental catalog of enemies, trying to figure out just who would bother having him killed when he was already down for the count. He couldn't think of anyone. Junius had the sort of enemies who relished the chance to give a speech at his funeral, where they could damn him with faint praise. On reflection, Junius wasn't sure he deserved much more than faint praise, anyway.

"Senator Mayfield," the oldest man said. "I'm General Ward Kilpatrick. I'm looking for your niece's son."

Junius tried to snarl at them, but he had very little control over his face. So it was about *that*. Junius had hoped he would die before the Seth ordeal raised its head again. *I told Iris not to marry into that Barrett family*, he thought. *Told her they were trouble.*

Junius had known the first Jonathan Seth Barrett briefly, a lifetime ago. The man had a heart like black smoke, and in his prime, they said he could charm the horns off the devil. Barrett had started out as a small-town banker and landowner, but managed to work himself up into a minor player on Wall Street and a titan of Southern industry. Fortunately for the world, the South wasn't all that

industrious, or Jonathan Seth Barrett could have been the next J.P.
Morgan. Instead, Barrett had eventually shriveled up and faded away,
going crazy inside his big house with all his money.

The sound of Ward's voice brought Junius' wandering mind back
to the present.

"...can do this quick and easy or quick and painful, Senator,"
Ward was saying. "Where are Seth Barrett and Jennifer Morton?"

"Don't know," Junius said. *Doh nuh.*

"I find that hard to believe, Senator," Ward said. "Did you not
help to hide them? Did you not help the White House to bury the
entire situation?"

Junius didn't speak, but he felt relieved. He didn't personally
know where Seth was, that hadn't been part of the arrangements.
Only one or two people inside Hale Security Group knew the answer
to that one.

"Senator, I'm afraid we'll need the answer immediately," Ward
said.

"What do you want with him?" Junius asked, and it sounded like
*Wah ooh ooh ah wah heh?*

"You're not making much sense, Senator. But that's all right.
Just think about your grandnephew for me." Ward grabbed Junius'
right hand. Junius tried to pull away, but he had no strength in his
arm. All he could do was make his hand tremble like a frightened
mouse.

Junius found himself thinking of the arrangements they'd made
with Hale. Jenny and Seth would live in a location known to almost
nobody, but the family was assured it would be quite pleasant there.
A tropical island, maybe.

"You really don't know." Ward dropped his hand back onto the
bed. "But Hale Security knows, don't they? And it just happens that
Eddie Cordell is a friend of mine, so I'll go ask him where to find
Seth. Good night, Senator." Ward started for the door.

Junius kept his face as stoic as a poker player's. He didn't want
to signal that the man was on the right trail, although he was. Junius
retreated into silence, usually the best move when you didn't know the
score. He didn't know who this man was, what agency he
represented, or what his intentions might be toward Seth. Junius
would need to make some phone calls after Ward left.

Ward halted and turned back to him. "Oh, Senator, there is just one more little problem. Eddie Cordell might continue protecting Seth out of fear of crossing you, a senior member of the Armed Services Committee. We've been waiting for you to die, Senator, but you're taking too damned long. Avery?"

One of the younger men, the one not holding Junius' remote control, drew a small sheath from his inner coat pocket and slid out a syringe filled with clear liquid. He approached the bag of fluids hanging over Junius' bed, which fed right into Junius' arm.

Junius squirmed weakly, but he was helpless to stop the man. He tried shouting with as much power as his lungs and vocal cords could manage, but that wasn't much.

"Please, Senator, consider dying with some dignity," Ward said, while Avery injected the poison into Junius' fluid line. "You'll feel some pain, but if I were you, with your history of sin and corruption, right now I'd mostly be worried about the devil waiting for me on the other side. Good night, Senator."

Junius felt a cold burning in his heart as the three men left. He reached for the remote, now dangling from its wall cable, and managed to catch in his arthritic fingers. He dragged it up onto the hospital bed with him, and he lay a finger on the red EMERGENCY button. Before he could press it, his heart stopped and his eyes glazed over.

Outside, the barn owl took flight.

# Chapter Twenty-Three

On New Year's Eve, Jenny, Seth, and Mariella took the train west across France, traveling to the small town of Carnac on the coast of Brittany. The place was a tourist destination in the summer, but in January it was freezing cold, and much of the town lay empty and quiet.

Jenny had suggested they find very old ruins, since Alexander had taken her to an ancient Mayan pyramid half-swallowed by the jungle when he'd helped Jenny recover her past-life memories—the ones he'd wanted her to remember, anyway, the lifetimes she'd spent as his consort.

Mariella had suggested the standing stones of Carnac, the oldest known structures in all of Europe, built about five thousand years earlier. Thousands of stones, some of them more than twice as high as a tall man, were arranged in straight rows that stretched for half a mile or longer. Their original prehistoric purpose remained unknown, but might have been related to religion or astrology.

Carnac itself was a pretty little village of centuries-old houses and cobblestone streets. A "campground" near the standing stones offering camping sites for tents, but also rental apartments and mobile homes. Seth rented a two-bedroom trailer for their stay, joking that it made him feel like he was back home in South Carolina.

They dropped off their overnight luggage in the rented trailer, including paints and canvases, which would provide their cover story if local authorities caught them among the standing stones late at night. Tonight was a full moon, providing plenty of light for painting, and Jenny thought the full moon might even help with their real purpose, too.

They ate at a local restaurant, enjoying a thick stew called *Pot au Feu de Homard*, full of lobster, scallops, shrimp, oysters, and mussels, all locally caught. Jenny peppered Mariella with questions about her life in Milan, and was rewarded with stories of lavish parties at her family's palazzo, crowded with Italian politicians, film directors, and fashion models—sometimes exciting, often tedious, according to Mariella, but it all sounded insanely glamorous to Jenny. Mariella had quietly offered "palm readings" to those who wanted them, just for fun, but her parents strongly discouraged it, as did their priest.

They walked through the little village during the sunset, browsing the shops and playing tourist, and later returned to the "campground" to pass time on the water slides at the heated indoor pool, an unexpected treat on a cold winter night.

When it was late enough, they sat in the living/dining area of the trailer, and Mariella placed a large camera bag on the table, with a sticker warning that it contained exposed film that should not be exposed to the light. She opened it up and took out a camera, followed by a plastic bag full of pointy, dark brown dried mushrooms.

"He told me the name of these, but I forgot," Mariella said. "They were supposed to be the strongest ones the guy could get."

The sight of the mushrooms made Jenny a little frightened, remembering how intense her previous experience had been. She was glad she wasn't taking any tonight.

"I also brought some smoke, in case we need it to take the edge off." Mariella tossed a half-ounce of shaggy purple marijuana buds onto the table next to the mushrooms. "And I brought wine, because...just because."

"Looks like a wild night for you two," Jenny said.

"So what do we do now?" Seth asked. "Is there a ritual? Do we have to chant or strangle a chicken or something?"

"The chicken sacrificing doesn't start until later," Jenny told him. "Y'all just eat the shrooms, they take a while to kick in. Then we'll go walking."

Seth picked up one of the brown mushrooms. "They look like...little shriveled brains."

"Does that make them more appetizing to you?" Jenny asked.

He put in his mouth, chewed, and gagged, looking disgusted. "They taste like shit."

"They grow in shit, so it makes sense." Mariella curled her lips as she placed one in her mouth, then took a swig of wine. She and Seth passed it back and forth, washing the mushrooms down with more wine.

"Okay," Jenny said. "Now we wait. Who wants to go to the beach?"

They walked from the lighted campground out to the endless darkness of ocean, where they shivered in the icy wind off the water.

"Who feels like swimming?" Mariella asked.

"Or freezing and dying," Seth said.

"At least we have the beach to ourselves," Jenny pointed out.

"Let's make the most of it." Mariella took a joint from her coat pocket and lit it up. She and Seth passed it back and forth, coughing, while Jenny watched the dark waves roll in under the shimmering night sky.

"Tell me something, Jenny," Mariella said as she exhaled blue smoke. "You have the memories. What are we, really? I mean...we have something supernatural, but obviously we're not, um...vampires or werewolves or...zombies..."

"I'm a werewolf," Seth said. "I've just never mentioned it before. But with the full moon, I think I should warn both of you."

Jenny tried to figure out how to answer Mariella's question. She pointed out at the sky over the ocean. "What do you see up there?"

"Stars," Mariella said.

"Beyond that?"

"Nothing. Darkness."

"The darkness beyond the stars," Jenny said.

"What does that mean?"

Jenny thought about it. "In almost every ancient myth, the universe begins in darkness and chaos, and then order and light take over."

Mariella nodded quickly. She'd attended a Swiss boarding school, Jenny knew, so she must have studied classics there. Jenny had studied classics herself, in the actual classical age.

"Imagine..." Jenny closed her eyes. "Imagine the entire universe is just a single mind. At first, it's all alone, and it knows nothing, and there's no one else to explain anything, so for a very long time, it's just confusion, fear, nightmares, lost in its imagination. But, after a very long time, a small little portion of the mind sorts itself out and becomes....sane. The little patch of light grows, turning the raw chaos around it into order. An ordered universe begins to emerge."

"Man," Seth said, pulling on the joint, "Are you sure you haven't smoked any of this?"

"Quiet, Seth. So, there are these isolated bits of chaos left scurrying around in the new, orderly universe," Jenny said. "That's us. Have you ever read any H.P. Lovecraft?"

Mariella shook her head. She was listening intently.

"It doesn't matter," Jenny said. "So our kind had nowhere left to go but to infiltrate the living. And here we incarnate again and again."

"But why?" Mariella asked. "Do we have a purpose?"

"Our purpose is to destroy the new order and bring back the original chaos, where we thrived instead of scurrying around like rats in the basement," Jenny told her.

"That's all we want? Destruction?" Mariella asked.

"We don't have to be that way. We have a choice," Jenny said. "Many times, I used plague as a weapon of war...some king or emperor would send me to destroy the armies or the cities of their enemies. And it was fun, to my old self. But I will never do that again, not for anyone. No man will use me as his weapon again."

Mariella nodded, thinking things over, the moonlight making her green eyes glow like a cat's. Seth was gaping silently out at the waves.

"It's all waves," Seth whispered. "One after another, it's all just waves, waves in the universe of the ocean...or the ocean of the...what was I saying?"

"I think the mushrooms are starting to work," Jenny said, and Mariella laughed. She kept laughing, and Seth started laughing, and Jenny shook her head, watching them stumble around the beach, laughing so hard they toppled over into the cold, wet sand.

"Okay, kids," Jenny said. "Let's go back in time. We're trespassing, so try to keep quiet."

A wooden fence surrounded the nearest field of standing stones, but a few boards were missing, so they were able to slip right through. That was lucky, because Jenny doubted Seth or Mariella could climb a fence in their current state. They kept bumping into each other and giggling.

"Sh!" Jenny whispered. She pointed to the small farmhouse on the far side of the field. "Someone might be home. Stay quiet."

"I wonder who lives there," Mariella whispered.

"Old French ghosts," Seth whispered, and they both laughed, and Jenny had to shush them.

They found themselves in the middle of nine perfectly straight rows of tall standing stones stretching away into the distance, where Jenny could make out the remains of what looked like a megalithic house, with a few gigantic stones for walls and equally large stone cross-pieces across the top. She wondered why Stone Age people had built such things.

"Stand over here, next to each other, and look at me," Jenny said. She thought back to the few previous lives in which her memories had been fully awoken.

"You're glowing, Jenny," Seth said. "You're glowing blue."

"That's just the moonlight. Concentrate," Jenny said. "Close your eyes, both of you. Imagine...imagine there's a door right behind you."

"What kind of door?" Seth asked.

"You tell me," Jenny said. "What do you see?"

"My door's made of colored glass and crystal, and sunlight is glowing through it. It's so beautiful," Mariella sighed.

"Good. What about you, Seth?"

"My door's *awesome*. Like a big castle door, with big spikes and torches all over it."

"Okay...This door leads to all your past-life memories," Jenny said. "Imagine it slowly opens, and through it, you see a long hallway of doors. Each door on that hall opens to one of your past lives. Now, open your eyes, turn around, and step through into the hall."

"Ooh!" Mariella gasped as she turned and opened her eyes.

"I can see it," Seth said, looking at the long rows of standing stones that stretched out of sight. "I can see the doors! Are there supposed to be ducks?"

"Open the first door you see," Jenny told them.

Seth and Mariella each took a step forward and touched one of the tall stones, which now represented doors to them.

"Oh, I see it!" Mariella told them. "I see both of you...and General Kranzler...and..." Mariella's chest hitched and she gave a loud sob. "Oh, Jenny..."

"Barrett," Seth said. "He betrayed us. I *told* you I had the worst great-grandfather in history."

"Now imagine all the doors opening, all the way back to the beginning," Jenny said. "Don't hold anything back. Don't hide anything from yourself."

They kept walking, touching one stone after another as if looking into each door, sometimes running away in horror, or laughing at some long-forgotten moment of happiness, or crying at some tender memory. She watched as they awoke to themselves, overpowered by all that they'd forgotten.

"Good," Jenny said, though neither seemed to be listening to her anymore. "You're doing fine. Just take it easy, don't rush..."

"A jester?" Seth laughed, shaking his head as he stared at the blank face of a standing stone. "I was a court jester, can you believe that?"

"Yep," Jenny said, catching up to him.

Mariella cried out in horror as she stared at a tall stone ahead of them.

"What's wrong?" Jenny hurried to catch up with her, then hesitantly took her by the arm. "Mariella? Tell me what you see."

"I...see..." Mariella's face turned ashen. "Plague, suffering, war..."

"Keep talking," Jenny encouraged her. "Remember, it's in the past, it's not happening now."

"There are men in armored masks, plates, chains, they have swords and hammers..."

"Do you know where you are, or when?" Jenny asked.

"It must be medieval Europe..." Mariella's eyes closed. "I think those are the Alps in the distance. I serve a minor prince. He's going to war with his brother, who has conquered a lot of territory and never been defeated in battle...I am his witch. I touch the prince I serve and see his future." Mariella's lips twisted in disgust. "In the future, I see his armored men in rows for the battle. His brother, the ruthless war-maker, has his own witch, and she casts a spell. My liege's men begin to die of the plague. They rot on their feet, the tattered flesh dropping between the plates of their armor, blood running out from the slits in their face visors...This witch, I tell him, is the reason his brother has never lost. He listens to me and sends assassins to his brother's camp the night before the battle, to kill the girl with their crossbows."

"I remember," Jenny said. "I was drinking a cup of wine, and the bolt hit me in the throat. I died fast."

"The next day, your prince tried to surrender to mine, because he couldn't win without you, Jenny," Mariella said. "My prince defeated yours and carried his head on a pike until it rotted. His own brother." Mariella looked sadly up and down the row of stones. "So many lives, full of so much suffering and death, so little love."

"That's true," Jenny said, touching her arm. "It's hard, but it's better to know the truth. It's up to us to make our lives different now. Don't let your past trap you."

Mariella nodded and wandered toward the next stone, looking dazed, but Jenny had successfully calmed her. Far ahead, Seth let out a high scream, loud enough to wake the French farmer on whose land they were trespassing.

"Seth! What's wrong?" Jenny ran to catch up with him. He was gripping one of the standing stones and leaning against it, his eyes closed. She took his hand. "Seth, talk to me."

"You tortured me!" His eyes flew open, and his mouth curled into a snarl. "You tortured me, Jenny."

"Can you be more specific?" Jenny asked, thinking of too many past lives that he might be seeing. "Sorry."

"Egypt," he said. "I was an Egyptian swordsman, the best in the kingdom. I'd come home from battle without a scratch, and so would the men around me. But then you...and *Alexander*...invaded from Persia..."

"Cambyses," Jenny remembered. "That was Alexander's name. Son of Cyrus of Persia, the king of kings."

"Cambyses and the famous 'immortal' swordsmen of Persia," Seth said. "They were immortal enough. Undead. Not very skilled at fighting, but relentless and almost impossible to kill through their armor and shields. Thousands of them came into Egypt with you and Alexander. He conquered and declared himself pharaoh, making all the Egyptians worship him."

"That's very Alexander," Jenny said.

"I didn't know my touch would damage his zombies," Seth said.

"You and Alexander eventually hunted me down. You tortured me for months, letting me heal up each time, before you finally killed me. By then, I was begging to die."

"I'm sorry, Seth." She touched his face, but he pulled away and continued on down the row.

Mariella passed by, absorbed in her own vision. Jenny watched both of them wander ahead, absorbing their long line of past lives.

Something small and fast shot past Jenny's eyes like a comet trailing smoke, and she gasped, getting a lungful of cold gas. It ricocheted from the stone beside her and landed in the grass between her feet. She had a quick glimpse of something like a kid's smoke bomb, and then the gas rolled up over her legs like a fog.

Jenny ran towards Seth, trying to hold her breath, but she'd already taken a lungful of the stuff. Mariella was lost in her trance, but Seth saw Jenny coming and started toward her.

"No...not this...not this way..." Jenny said, but she couldn't speak above a whisper. She felt like she was trying to run in quicksand, her legs dragging, all her muscles shutting down. More of the smoke-bomb devices rained down around her and around Seth. They weren't actually smoke bombs, because smoke bombs didn't come loaded with powerful tranquilizer gas.

A fog rose around Seth, and he staggered and slowed, then fell to one knee.

"Jennifer Morton," a stern male voice said. "Don't bother running. We've got you." Men approached from the shadows of the stones with electric devices crackling in their hands, prepared to zap Jenny if the tranquilizer didn't take her out.

Jenny tried to continue on toward Seth, but she lost her balance and toppled to the ground. As she lost consciousness, her last thought was a hope that the gas wouldn't harm the baby.

# Chapter Twenty-Four

Ward walked the observation deck at midnight, alone. The only lights were the dim glow from computer screens, which reflected in the armored glass windows overlooking the concrete bays of the laboratories below. Soon, things would really start to heat up around this old place.

He felt the sense of satisfaction that came with completing a difficult but necessary task. After he'd killed Senator Mayfield, it had only taken the shortest of talks with Eddie Cordell from Hale Security to make the rest of the arrangements. They'd monitored Jenny and Seth in their Paris apartment, learned of their planned trip to Brittany, and decided an ambush would run much more smoothly and quietly in the village of Carnac than in the center of Paris. Hale's operatives had even helped in the capture of Seth and Jenny.

Now Ward had them all here: Tommy, already cooperating. Jenny and Seth, captured. As a bonus, he had a fourth paranormal, Mariella Visconti, who had the power to see a person's future, according to the conversations Ward had heard in Jenny and Seth's bugged apartment. It was a sticky bonus, though, because her family was influential in Italian politics. The last thing Ward needed was a complaint about his activities brought before some NATO panel by the Prime Minister of Italy. He would have to keep things quiet and work hard to gain Mariella's cooperation.

They'd also captured Esmeralda Rios. Ward had tried on his own to convince her to join Tommy, but she'd refused, so they'd been forced to drug her and covertly transport her to Germany. Six paranormals, including himself, were now together under this roof, and it was time for his real work work to begin.

ASTRIA was not generally viewed as a desirable command. While the agency's mission had been considered very serious between its founding in the early 50s and into the 1970s, it had become a dumping ground for dead-end careers by the end of the 1980s, when not even Nancy Reagan's astrologer was taking the idea of Soviet psychic spies seriously anymore. Ward had no trouble getting himself appointed head of the agency, though it had required the small matter of also getting promoting to a lieutenant general. He could have used his unofficial, blackmail-based influence to gain himself almost any command around the world, but he had chosen the neglected Cold War agency instead.

Under his command, he'd been able to swell the funding from the Pentagon while giving only the vaguest description of his intentions, enabling him to build the research center of his dreams. Ward had one goal: to study others like him, those with a paranormal touch, in order to gain greater control and understanding of his own power without having to put himself under the scientists' microscopes and scalpels. Whatever they learned from the other five, he could determine for himself how it might apply to him.

At the same time, he might succeed in obtaining powerful new weapons. He could imagine sending Tommy into a city to cause a riot...or, better, sending Jenny in to kill everyone in a targeted area. Esmeralda could gather secrets from the dead, including enemy spies and leaders. Seth's healing power would be extremely useful on dangerous missions, to himself and others in his unit. If Mariella could see the future, that would be extremely valuable for gathering intelligence.

He could imagine using all of them, but it remained to be seen which of them might cooperate.

Ward looked through the window at the lab he'd designed just for Jenny. She was down there in the dimness, asleep in a hospital bed, already connected to her monitors—the computer screen in front of the window told him that her heartbeat, blood pressure and breathing were normal, and her EEG showed delta waves, deep sleep. When she awoke, she would find herself trapped like a spider in a bottle. It wasn't the best way to recruit a person, but after the mass death she'd caused in Fallen Oak, he wasn't taking any chances with her. Surely, she would come to understand his logic.

Ward felt suddenly dizzy, and he pressed a hand on the window to steady himself. He felt a strange prickling sensation as goosebumps swelled all over his body and the little hairs on his arms and neck spiked out. He felt a crushing headache, and then a feeling of vertigo, and he thought he might black out. He closed his eyes and clenched his jaw, trying to get hold of himself.

He felt like he was falling...and then he was walking along the same corridor, the observation deck, but the computers were replaced by file cabinets and typewriters, and there were many more people coming and going in this one room than Ward employed at the entire complex. The walls floor was bare concrete, instead of the white tiles he'd added.

Everyone wore black, even the typists and secretaries in their slim black skirts and jackets. He also couldn't help but notice, everywhere, the swastikas—on the arms of men in black military-style uniforms, on lapel pins, on the flags that hung along the hall.

Ward himself wore a black uniform, coat, and cap. He walked along the corridor slowly, accompanied by a tall, attractive blond girl in a black-skirted uniform with a white shirt and black tie. Her eyes were a strange gray color, like clouds on a rainy day. She touched his hand frequently as she spoke, and each touch sparked an intense feeling of affection and desire inside him. He wanted her to keep touching him.

She spoke in German, yet he understood her perfectly.

"Has there been any news with Willem?" she asked. They paused in their walk to look down through a window into a lab. A young man in his early twenties sat on a stool, facing a metal barrel filled with bits of newspaper, wood scraps, and sawdust, a mixture intended to be highly flammable. Three researchers watched him from the side of the lab—a chemist, physicist, and a doctor—and wires were plastered all over Willem's bare torso, connecting him to loud, clunky monitoring machines around him.

Willem stared intently at the barrel of tinder and kindling, rubbing the sides of his head with both fingers. After several minutes, nothing happened.

"I suppose you'll continue testing him?" asked the gray-eyed girl, whose name was Alise.

"No," Ward heard himself say. "He's a fake. He must have tricked our investigators when they found him. Under controlled conditions, he does nothing."

"What shall we do with him, sir?" Alise asked.

"Get rid of him. I don't want him eating one more meal at the Reich's expense. And I don't want him talking to anyone."

"Consider him gone, sir," Alise said.

They moved on to look into the next lab, where a small, dark-eyed Slavic girl named Evelina stood over a gray, gunshot corpse, touching it and talking while a young typist took notes. The corpse had recently been a leader of the Communist party in Germany, which had been outlawed but continued underground. Evelina was meant to learn about any secret plots the Communists might be planning.

"This is an interesting case," Ward said. "The Slav seems to have a genuine power, but of course she may not be acceptable for breeding. She doesn't look Aryan at all. I don't think the Fuehrer would accept her as an example of advanced human evolution."

"Then what should we do with her?"

"Keep her, study her, use her. But we can't introduce such racial inferiority into our supernormal program. It's bad enough we have an Italian girl."

At the next lab, they looked down on the American girl, Juliana, small and pale with long, dark hair. She was currently stripped to the waist, also hooked into loud, thunking monitoring devices, making sores and blisters appear and disappear on her skin while a biologist in gloves and a gas mask examined her.

"Her power is clearly real," Ward said. "But her background...does she look Jewish to you?"

"Greek," Alise said.

"I suppose if we're taking Italians, we'll take Greeks," he said in a resigned voice. "We can always make reference to the empires of antiquity, if pressed by the Party leadership."

"Clearly, the Hellenes and the Romans must have had much Aryan in them, to conquer so much and build such a culture," Alise said.

"It seems obvious to me that she should be bred with the other American, the healer boy," he said. "Anyone else who touches her will die, and we should assume the same about their genetic material."

"Juliana is already pregnant," Alise said.

"She is? Why was I not informed?"

"Because I told them I wanted to inform you myself." She gave him a stunning, radiant smile. "I knew it would please you, and you know I like to please."

"Is Sebastian the father?"

"I believe so, based on their intimacy when I met them," Alise said. "Unless she is a slut, he must be the father. And, as you just said, who else could touch her?"

"We must find out for certain."

"I will speak with her for you. She's more likely to speak freely about such things to another woman."

"And now we must discuss you," he said.

"You want to talk about me, *Gruppenführer* Kranzler? Don't you know that's the direct path to any woman's heart?" Alise giggled, touching his hand, setting off another fiery wave of desire inside him.

Ward understood that his name was now Kranzler, at least within this strange dream.

"We must breed you like the others," he said. "We may have to cross you with Sebastian as well. We have a shortage of males in our stable."

"Ugh, after he's been with that diseased girl?" Alise asked. "I don't want to catch an infection from her."

"He is immune to her. He will not transfer any disease to you."

"How can we be sure? I don't want to be the test subject for *that* experiment, Herr Kranzler."

"You and your cousin Niklaus are clearly the most Aryan of the supernormals we've identified, the most racially pure."

"Thank you, Herr Kranzler." She gave him an alluring smile.

"I proposed breeding the two of you together, but Dr. Wichtmann says there are too many risks, you're too closely related."

"What about you, *Gruppenführer* Kranzler?" Alise touched his hand again and leaned closer to him.

"You must be bred with a supernormal. That is our program." The girl's touch did stir certain hungry, aggressive feelings inside him, but he tried to resist them.

"And are you not a supernormal, Herr Kranzler?" She batted her eyelashes, playing at being extra-innocent. "I have seen you draw information from people many times. They don't even have to say it aloud—you just touch them and *know*. I have seen you work your magic, Herr Kranzler. I am a careful observer."

Kranzler looked around the crowded corridor to see whether anyone appeared to be listening to them, but everyone was busy, and the room was loud with clanging typewriters.

"We should not discuss this here," he replied in a low voice.

"Perhaps in your office, sir?" Alise suggested.

He took her arm and marched her out of the observation deck, toward a suite of offices in the northeast quadrant of the underground complex. His office was the largest. He closed the door tightly behind them, while Alise crossed to his desk and leaned against it, in a manner clearly intended to make her breasts and hips prominent inside her tight black uniform.

"I am not mistaken, am I, sir?" Alise asked, with a knowing smile, as if she were quietly laughing to herself.

"I am not registered as a supernormal, and I do not wish to be," Kranzler said. "If you repeat what you just said in front of anyone else, I will kill you."

"Your secret is safe with me, sir, forever. But it does not matter to me whether you are registered, only that you do possess a power like mine. Imagine our powers combined into a child...a son...he would be the son of a supernormal S.S. officer, a true Aryan of the future. Imagine it!"

"We could not raise him as our own," Kranzler reminded her. "He would belong to the Reich."

"I know this better than anyone," Alise said. "I do not wish for a family—the Reich is my family, the Party is my family. I wish to do this as my gift to the Reich, my act of devotion. I want to personally present the Fuehrer with the first child of this project, the first of a generation of German supermen who will conquer the world." She approached him, taking his hands, her gray eyes locked on his. "Do you not want the same? Do you not want me?"

Kranzler wanted it all. He wanted a son who could lead armies and destroy every enemy in his path. Though he rarely indulged in fleshly pleasures, he wanted the young, pretty Aryan girl currently offering herself to him. It was difficult to think of anything but his own desire when her hands were on him.

"You must tell no one," he whispered.

She placed her hands on his broad shoulders and rose up to kiss him. Kranzler lifted her up onto his desk, and she lay back on her elbows, smiling at him with a surprised look in her eyes.

"Here?" she asked.

"It may take several attempts." Kranzler, an efficient man, lowered his black trousers just enough to free himself, already erect from her repeated touching. He turned her onto her hands and knees and bent her over the desk, then flipped her long black skirt up over her hips. She wriggled her ass in her white silk panties and laughed, until he reached a wide, muscular hand into the space between her legs.

"These aren't regulation undergarments for women," he said.

"And how would you know that?" She smiled back at him over her shoulder.

He grabbed her expensive, inappropriate underwear and ripped it away, leaving her bare. She gave a shocked little gasp as he stripped her, and then another as he pressed his fingertips against her.

"We should hurry," he said. "I have a busy schedule."

"Go ahead. I'm not here for romance."

Ward entered her, and she bared her teeth and shrieked in pain. She was golden, a beautiful daughter of a wealthy nobleman, while he'd grown up as a dirt-poor peasant with calloused hands from tending his father's sheep, and he was old enough to remember when the difference between peasant and noble truly mattered, before the Great War. It gave him pleasure to make her suffer. He grabbed her long blond hair and pulled hard, getting another scream from her.

"You're a good German girl," he said as he took her again and again. "You should lie in my bed every night." He slapped her ass, hard enough to leave a blood-colored handprint.

She snarled at him, baring her teeth, which only aroused him more.

"I can see your past," Ward said, squeezing her waist in his large hands. "So many flirtations with fancy little aristocrat boys. Many of them...consummated."

"You don't care about my past," she whispered. "You love me."

"I do," he said, then he shoved her face down against his desk and pinned it there with his hand, raising her hips higher so he could slide more deeply inside her. He deposited his seed quickly and backed out. She lay on his desk, naked from the waist down, looking battered, a look of disgust in her cloud-gray eyes.

"Make me a son," he ordered as he buckled his belt. "Fix yourself up. We have a lot of work today. We can do this again tomorrow."

He closed the door as he left the office.

# Chapter Twenty-Five

Tommy lay on the bed in his room, smoking cigarettes and watching an *A-Team* rerun on some satellite channel. Smoking wasn't allowed inside the base, except for one specially ventilated room, but he didn't care. He didn't think they would throw him out for it.

In the past few days, he'd learned that using his power raised his body temperature by a degree or two and heated the air around him. It caused an explosive spike of activity in a part of his brain called the right temporal lobe. He'd been meaning to look up brain parts to figure out what the hell that meant, but he wasn't provided internet access. The underground research facility had a small science library, and he could probably find out there, but he hated libraries and kept putting it off.

He'd also learned that he could scare the hell out of mice and chimpanzees. He assumed human tests were next. That could be fun.

Things looked hopeful for him here—General Ward Kilpatrick clearly had big plans for Tommy's future.

Tommy already ached to see Esmeralda again and felt terrible for leaving her, especially since they'd parted angry at each other. He wanted to think of her waiting for him back home, and imagined himself coming back to her, finally a success and not a loser. He knew that he was no good for her, that he only held her back and sometimes made her miserable, but he still loved her and wanted to be with her. When he came back a better, more successful person, then she would understand why he'd left.

He flipped the gold coin in his hand. It had belonged to old man Tanner—*Pap-pap*, as Tommy and the other children had been required to call him—and Tommy had stolen it the night he met Esmeralda. He'd given it to her as a present, and she'd kept it all these years.

He'd been a little surprised that Esmeralda hadn't wanted to come with him and learn how to use her power for the greater good of the world. She seemed content to spend her life arranging funerals and applying makeup to dead people, but Ashleigh had taught Tommy to reach for bigger things in life. It hurt that Esmeralda had turned down the idea so quickly, and she had seemed to care so little when he left.

For a moment, the room seemed to shift around him, as if he'd had a glimpse of other walls hidden behind the ones around him, drab olive instead of white. All of the small hairs on his body stood up, from his legs to the nape of his neck, and he shivered as if a ghost had passed through him.

The sense of *déjà vu* permeated the place for Tommy, whether he was doing tests in the lab, eating at the cafeteria, or even sitting here in his room, where the feeling seemed at its strongest. It was like being in the most haunted house in the world, every room crowded with ghosts he couldn't quite see. Sometimes, like now, the feeling filled him with a strange, paranoid terror.

Tommy left the television on as he left his room and walked down the deserted hall. He wondered about the people who'd originally occupied the rooms on this hall. Nazis had lived here, he reminded himself, and he broke out in nervous sweat.

He walked to the common room, where there was a big-screen television, multiple game consoles, surround-sound stereo, a foosball table, and a pool table, along with bookshelves full of military action movies and video games. They seemed to expect more residents in the future. Tommy doubted they'd provided all this stuff just so he could play with himself.

He turned out the light, lay down on the couch, and blasted an "Arena Rock" music station over the television to drown out his thoughts. The bad feelings weren't so strong here, and he thought he might be able to sleep.

In that halfway region between wake and sleep, still aware of himself lying on the couch and hearing Guns N' Roses at painful volume, he had a strange waking dream in which he saw himself walking down the same dormitory hall and entering the same room, but the walls were drab olive, and all the entertainment gear had been reduced to a bulky wood-cabinet radio and an old-fashioned phonograph player with a big funnel amplifier.

Tommy wore heavy black boots in his vision, which echoed on the wood-tiled floor of the boys' hallway and common room. Within the dream, he somehow knew that this was the boys' dorm, and there were, elsewhere, both a girls' hall and a conjugal hall for the eugenics portion of the project.

In his vision, the common room had more spartan furnishing, and a Wagner record had replaced the sound of Guns N' Roses. Tommy reasoned that he must be completely asleep now, because he could only hear the television very distantly.

A boy was in the common room, reading a book on ancient Roman wars—the bookshelf in the room was stocked only with books about Germany and war. Tommy knew the boy was from Holland and his name was Willem, that he was twenty-two years old, while Tommy was only nineteen in this dream, but Tommy had authority over him. Tommy's authority stemmed from the black uniform jacket he wore, and the black boots.

"Willem," Tommy said. "It's Saturday night, we should have some fun."

"Do you mean it?" Willem adjusted his thick glasses and sat up. He was a squirmy, fidgety, awkward kind of guy. He seemed awed that Tommy would approach him. *Niklaus*, Tommy thought. *To him, I'm Niklaus.* "What do you have in mind? Can we leave the base?"

"That's exactly what I had in mind." Tommy, or Niklaus, leaned against the door, lit a cigarette, and blew smoke at Willem. "I have an automobile parked just outside the wall. We could drive to a town, drink at a pub, go dancing."

"I am not so good at dancing."

"You'll have to learn fast. I invited Roza and Vilja to come with us."

"You did?" Willem jumped to his feet. He was enamored of the pale, wispy Vilja, the quiet Swedish girl who claimed to see ghosts and demons. Though Willem had never spoken about his feelings, they were obvious to Niklaus, whose job included paying close attention to the male supernormals living here. Willem was often seen trying to work up the nerve to speak to Vilja, but he was awkward and hesitant when he managed to talk to her.

"The girls wanted to get out, too. We've all been cooped inside too long," Niklaus said. "They're ready for a good time. You don't mind that I invited them?"

"No, no. Alise doesn't mind if we take the girls out?"

"Are you scared of my cousin?" Niklaus snickered.

"I'm not afraid of a woman! When do we go?"

"Now," Niklaus said. "The girls are already waiting for us with a bottle of wine for the drive. You may want to put on a fresh shirt...something with buttons. And a tie. You want to look smart."

Willem ran back to his room to get ready. Niklaus loaned him some cologne, laughing inwardly as he watched Willem splash it all over his neck and face.

"Keep quiet as we leave," Niklaus whispered as they walked down the hall. "We don't want anyone getting mad at us for not inviting them, but the car only seats four."

Willem nodded and winked. He meant it to be sly and conspiratorial, but it was so exaggerated that Niklaus laughed at him. Niklaus led the way out into the main corridor and up the very long flight of steep concrete stairs to the exit. He had a key that allowed him to unlock the door from the inside.

They passed through the concrete bunker housing the door, where Niklaus exchanged quiet nods with the S.S. officer on guard duty at the desk. Niklaus had already spoken with him earlier to ensure he and Willem were not added to the official record of entries and exits.

They left through the west gate, the supply gate that opened onto a loading dock, which was dark under its high tin roof. Niklaus jumped down to the newly paved road, and Willem only a hesitated a moment before jumping down after him. They walked along the road.

"Where is your car?" Willem asked, looking from the high brick wall to the forest across from it.

"Just ahead. What will you say when you see her?"

"Vilja?" Willem cleared his throat. "I will tell her she looks beautiful...in the, in the...moonlight."

Niklaus snorted laughter. "Here." He stepped off the road into a grassy fire break carved through the trees.

"It is parked in the woods?" Willem stopped, looking worried.

"Of course. You will see why, I promise."

They walked into the dark woods, lit only by occasional patches of moonlight. Niklaus smirked each time he heard Willem stumble over a branch or stone behind him, and laughed when Willem tripped and fell on his face.

"It's like watching a clown perform," Niklaus said, as Willem pushed himself back to his feet and wiped dirt from his mouth.

"How much farther? Why is it so far away?" Willem asked.

"It's by the creek. Can you hear it?" Niklaus led him down a narrow trail to an overgrown creek bank. At this altitude, the creek was only a thin sheet of icy water, spread over a bed of sharp rocks.

"I still do not see a car," Willem said, fidgeting hard now, shifting back and forth on his feet. "Where are the girls?"

"They're just across the creek." Niklaus pointed to the deep woods. "I told them you would signal them by starting one of your magic fires with your mind."

"What? No, I can't just do that right now. I must prepare..."

"You can't do it at all, can you, Willem?" Niklaus asked. "You tricked the German scientists who came to study you."

"Niklaus, what are you saying?" Willem shivered hard now. "Why would you say such things?"

"Don't lie to me, Willem. You tricked them. You aren't going to lie to me again, are you?"

"Please, Niklaus!"

"Why would you do that?"

"I didn't...I only...it was a trick, I performed it in the street for money," Willem said. "I learned the right materials for a very slow fuse, and how to time it just right, so it appeared that, it appeared that..." He swallowed hard. "I could create the fire with my mind. I tried to make a stage act of it."

"But why trick the scientists, Willem?"

"I was hoping they would take me to a university to study me, and I could take classes...Please, Niklaus, you must tell no one!"

"Everyone knows, Willem. Even the typists and the janitors know. You haven't done a thing since you arrived here."

"Everyone knows?" Willem turned stark white. He looked at the woods across the creek. "The girls aren't here, are they?" he whispered.

"You're of no use to us, Willem," Niklaus said. "And you know too much for us to let you go."

Willem was trembling now. "What are you saying?"

Niklaus drew the Luger pistol from his belt and pointed it Willem's face, aiming for the reflection of the moon in the left lens of his glasses.

"Oh, no!" Willem gasped. "Oh, God, Niklaus, no, you don't have to—"

Niklaus shot him through the head, shattering the glasses and blasting out the back of his skull, and Willem tumbled into the shallow, cold stream. Kranzler had stressed that he wanted it done with a single shot, to keep things quiet.

Niklaus watched as the boy lay bleeding in the creek, his remaining eye staring lifelessly at the stars. When he was certain Willem was dead, he holstered the pistol and walked back to the base.

# Chapter Twenty-Six

Mariella awoke slowly, the tranquilizer gas still floating in her brain like leftover wisps of fog. Her eyes crept open, revealing drab gray walls, a single steel door with a small, clear window, a sink, a toilet. The ceiling had a sickly glowing fluorescent panel and the sort of tiny black inverted dome that usually housed a security camera.

Her bed was hard and narrow, like a prison cot. The entire place looked like a prison cell, in fact, and there was no handle on her side of the door.

She tried to remember where she was and how she'd gotten there. Slowly, her memory came back. They'd been among the stones at Carnac, and someone had captured them. Her precognition had failed to protect them—she'd thought they might have more time before the man that Jenny called "Kranzler" came to capture Seth. It looked like he'd captured Mariella, too, which was probably why her vision of the event had been so fuzzy. It was hard to see her own future, and even harder when perception-distorting mushrooms and sleeping gas were added to the mix.

Then she remembered *everything*. Before they'd been captured, Mariella had fully remembered dozens of prior lifetimes—not all her past lives, because the process had been interrupted, but plenty of them. She was the ancient soul called the oracle, and Mariella Visconti was just one of many masks she'd worn and discarded over the millennia.

Another such mask was Mia Ruggieri, the poor, clueless peasant girl from Sicily whose reputation for seeing the future had attracted the interest of the German scientists. They'd offered her a sizable amount of money for joining their research, enough to provide for her parents and six brothers and sisters for years to come. Under strong pressure from her parents, Mia had accepted the offer, turned all the money over to her father, and traveled off to Germany with the strange foreign men.

She stood, stretched, and walked to the door to peer out the window. All she saw was a concrete corridor and a similar steel door across from hers. She touched the blank area on the door where the handle should have been. She pounded her fist on the window, but nobody came.

With nothing to do, Mariella eventually reflected on her past dealings with Kranzler and the others, trying to prepare for whatever might lie ahead. Looking into her own future, she only saw a dark blur. Even her visions of love and passion with Seth had deserted her. She didn't know whether to feel relieved or disappointed, or maybe frightened—it could mean that one or both of them were going to die, and so the anticipated future was gone.

Within an hour after she awoke, a voice crackled from somewhere in the ceiling above. "The general wants to see you."

A man in a black uniform appeared at the window in her door. She nodded and gave him a small wave.

"I should warn you," he said. It was odd to watch his lips move in front of her but hear his voice electronically amplified above her. "We're all armed with X3 TASER guns. We won't hesitate to take you down if you give us trouble."

"There's no need to expect trouble from me," Mariella said. "I promise. I wish to see the general as well."

The guard nodded. There was an electronic buzz, followed by a mechanical thunk, as her door unlocked. The guard pulled it open and let her out into the hall. Two other guards were there, with their hornet-yellow electrical stun weapons drawn and pointed at her. She held up her hands and gave them a reassuring smile.

She noticed that the guards wore armored black uniforms without no flag or logo, as if the organization that employed them did not want to be associated with their actions. Two wore thick helmets, face shields, and gloves, as if specifically prepared to deal with paranormals. Mariella wouldn't be glimpsing any of their futures.

They led her down the corridor. She noticed Seth through one of the narrow windows, still unconscious on a bed in his own cell. She didn't see Jenny in any of the cells, though, just a Latino girl she didn't recognize, sitting on her cot and staring into space.

The guards took her through another, larger steel door at the end of the hallway, which had to be unlocked with a plastic ID card. They turned down another corridor and passed through another secure door, then rode an elevator up a level.

As they took her down a narrow side corridor to a suite of offices, Mariella felt her skin prickle. She recognized where she was—the colors had gone from gray and green to white, making it feel more like a modern research lab and less like a military base, but beneath that, everything was still the same. It *felt* the same.

Memories from that past life bubbled everywhere in the underground base. Why not? They were gathering back in the same place—herself, the plague-bringer, the healer, the seer. She wondered whether the Latin girl in the other cell just happened to be the love-charmer, or perhaps the dead-speaker.

The setting and characters might have been the same, but Mariella intended for the story to end differently this time.

The guards took her to exactly the office door she expected, the largest office. Inside, a burly man in a general's uniform stood behind his desk, and she barely had to look at him to recognize that this was the man from her vision, the man who'd been searching for them. She also knew that, in a past life, this man had been a Nazi S.S. officer named Helmut Kranzler. There was no mistaking his heavy, menacing presence.

He smiled and offered his hand, his green eyes eerily like her own. There was a strange energy in the room between them. They were opposites, but not exactly the sort who fell in love like Jenny and Seth. She wondered if he had any of his past memories, or if he were limited to the gnat-sized viewpoint of a single lifetime.

"Miss Visconti, my name is General Ward Kilpatrick, United States Department of Defense." He shook her hand, and she noticed he wore gloves, maybe to protect himself from her power. "Thank you for meeting with me."

"I wasn't aware I had a choice, General," Mariella said.

"Please, ma'am, have a seat. You can relax now." He dropped into his chair and waved the guards away. "You can go, boys, she's not violent."

"We'll be right outside." One of the guards closed the door.

Mariella slowly sat down opposite him. "Where am I?" she asked, though in a sense, she knew perfectly well. Germany. The Harz mountains.

"You are at a top-secret defense research facility," Ward said. "I apologize for bringing you here under these circumstances, ma'am, but you were in the company of a wanted mass murderer. Jennifer Morton. I'm not sure what name she might have told you."

"Genevieve? She can't be a murderer."

"Oh, yes." Ward turned his computer screen toward her and summoned images of bodies in clear plastic bags, disfigured and twisted by horrific diseases. "Two hundred people, right in her own hometown. Kids from her school. The pastor at her church. The mayor." He scrolled through more and more pictures, intestines poking through rotten flesh, eye sockets full of tumorous gore, until Mariella had to stop herself from being sick. "She did this *to her own*, Miss Visconti, not to some foreign enemy. Can you imagine a person who would inflict that on her own people?"

"I can't." Mariella shook her head. "Are you sure she did it? She seems so nice."

"She did it. Her touch spreads a deadly infection...you already know all about that, Miss Visconti. We overheard you have a secret of your own, don't you?" He leaned forward, grinning and speaking in a conspiratorial whisper. "What is it like, Miss Visconti? Seeing other people's futures?"

"You know about that?" Mariella faked a surprised gasp. "I tried to keep it secret for so long."

"Your secret will remain safe with me, don't you worry." Ward leaned back. "Miss Visconti, you're a law-abiding citizen from a good family. How did you get tangled up with these criminals, Jenny and Seth?"

"I only met them a few weeks ago, honestly," Mariella said. "If you've been spying on them, you must know that, don't you? Whatever terrible crimes they've committed, I want you to know that

I was not involved, I barely know these people, and I just want to go home." Mariella's voice cracked, and she teared up. "I just want to see my family. That's all."

"Oh, no, wait." He sat up, taken aback by her sudden outpouring. "You don't need to be afraid as long as you cooperate. You see, this project ultimately affects the entire Western world. We hoped that, given your family's prominence in Italy, you might be willing to work with us, on the side of law and order."

"Work...with you? How?" She looked up at him, wiping her eyes.

"We'd begin with basic scientific tests, studying and measuring your precognitive ability, and unraveling what makes it tick. Wouldn't it be nice to understand yourself better?"

"I suppose it could." Mariella nodded and gave him a weak smile.

"In time, you might have assignments. Protecting NATO interests, including Italy. We might send you to read the future of a specific influential person, for example."

Mariella thought it over. "So...I would be a spy?"

"Essentially. But we would need your absolute loyalty."

"I've always wanted to be a spy. Is that silly?" Mariella gave an embarrassed giggle.

"Not to me. You would be on our side, the good guys working against the evil in the world. Secret missions, traveling in disguise. Would you like that?"

"Oh, yes!" Mariella's eyes lit up, and she tried to sound as naive and impressed as possible. "Do you mean it? You want me for that?"

"We think you would make an excellent agent," he continued, really laying it on thick. "Young, intelligent, well-bred, educated...and a very useful power in your hands. Will you work with us?"

Mariella gaped at him for a long moment.

"Is that a yes?" he finally asked.

"Oh, yes, please, of course, sir!" She bounced in her chair as if she couldn't contain herself. "What's my first mission?"

He laughed. "Decorate your room. We're moving you out of the cellblock and into more comfortable quarters. We have your overnight bag from Carnac waiting for you. Just let us know what else you need."

"Egyptian cotton sheets."

"Excuse me?"

"At least twelve hundred thread count, and they must be organic, or it's just not comfortable," Mariella said. "I'll make you a list of everything I need once I see the accommodations."

Ward rubbed the side of his head. "Not a problem."

"Do I get a secret spy name? Or a code number?"

"I'll let you know."

"What kind of spying will I do?"

"Your first job is to call your parents and let them know you're safe," he said. "Tell them you took a semester off to study Alpine folk music, or whatever bullshit you have to tell them, so they aren't calling every police agency in France searching for you."

"Oh, yes, sir! I'll come up with something. Something *very* clever." She winked.

"Good. The guards will show you to your new room. Any more questions?"

"Only a million!" Mariella said. "But I can wait, I see you're busy." She bounced out of her chair and smiled over her shoulder as she approached the door.

The guards brought her to the largest room on a dormitory hall that had no other residents. They showed her the common area and bathroom, both of which she had to herself for now. She was certain that she was being monitored with hidden cameras. The general was treating her well, but that didn't mean he trusted her. She certainly didn't trust him. He was probably just worried about her family's influence. If they learned an American agency had kidnapped their daughter, it would only take one phone call from her grandfather to elevate the complaint to NATO...which explained why the general was being so nice to her.

She sat down on her new bed as the three guards left, snickering to herself for insisting on organic Egyptian sheets. She'd give him a laundry list of luxury items, playing the spoiled rich girl. If he thought she was shallow and empty-headed, he'd probably find her less suspicious.

Her mind boiled over with strong memories from this same hall. This room had belonged to Alise, not to her. Mariella supposed she was now the hallway *fuehrer*.

Mariella had once shared a smaller room down the hall with Jenny, when their names were Mia and Juliana. She smiled to herself at the memory. She could almost hear Duke Ellington's orchestra echoing softly in her ears, tinged by the scratchy crackle of a phonograph record.

She smiled as the memory welled up inside her.

* * *

"Juliana," Mia whispered, shaking the sleeping girl's arm with her gloved hand. It was a Saturday, a few minutes after midnight. "Juliana, you have to wake up!"

"What's happening?" Juliana's eyes opened just a sliver. The room was dim, lit only by a single small lamp in the corner. Without it, the underground chamber was dead black.

"I have to tell you something," Mia whispered.

"What is it? Are you hurt?" Juliana leaned up on elbow to look at Mia, who knelt on the floor by Juliana's bed.

"No, but I have to show you something." Mia crawled over to her bed, reached underneath, and found the paper-wrapped package. She carried it over to Juliana.

"What is that?"

"Burgundy!" Mia whispered, unwrapping the bottle.

"You have wine?" Juliana sat up now, brushing long hairs from her face. "How?"

"I sweet-talked a kitchen steward. He swiped it from the officers' wine cellar for me! Can you believe it?"

"Good job!" Juliana said.

"I've been saving it for tonight. You've been so sad ever since the...poor goats..." Mia bit her lip, wishing she hadn't said it, but the thought had slipped out.

"The poor goats." Juliana frowned and looked at the floor.

"So, I think we must drink. Let's go the common room. We can play music there."

"We'll wake everyone up."

"Not if we play it *softly*." Mia took her gloved hand. "Please. It's so boring here."

Juliana laughed.

They crept down the hall in bare feet, Mia in her nightgown, Juliana wearing the baggy cotton nightshirt that she'd originally bought for Sebastian, but he'd only worn it a few nights on the ship before she stole it. Juliana had blushed as she told Mia about it.

They eased through the double doors to the common area, and they tiptoed past the bathroom door to the lounge area with the bookshelves and phonograph. Mia played a jazz record, Duke Ellington, and uncorked the bottle. She took a long sip and passed it to Juliana, then watched uneasily as Juliana drank from the bottle's mouth.

"I won't get sick if I drink after you, will I?" Mia asked, and Juliana gave her a sad, hurt look.

"No, you're fine," Juliana whispered as she passed the bottle back.

"So what do you hate most about this place?" Mia asked.

"You don't sound happy to be here."

"I know you're not, either," Mia said. "I can see it in your face."

"I just don't like killing the animals. I hope they don't do that again, I don't think I can handle it. And I miss Sebastian." Juliana took the bottle back and drank more.

"You see him at meals," Mia said.

"*Only* at meals. I used to see him all the time. On the ship, we were together all day and night, dancing, or reading stories, or secretly making fun of the other people onboard..." Juliana and Mia both laughed. "What I really miss is the kissing, so much kissing."

"Was it just kissing? Or more?"

Juliana bit her lip, then giggled. "More."

"A little more, or a lot more?"

"A *lot*," Juliana said, and they laughed again. "I miss him so much."

"You must. He's so handsome."

"Do you have anyone? Back at home, maybe?"

"No one who's going to wait for me," Mia said. "I don't even know how long I have to stay here."

"Can't you leave whenever you want?"

"I wish." Mia explained how she'd accepted money to be a lab rat for the Nazis, and how her family had pushed her to do it. "There was a boy I liked, during the time when I ran away to Rome...but I don't know if I'll ever see him again. He'll be with someone else. He was never with me, anyway." She drank more, then put the bottle down on the table and hopped to her feet, holding out her hand. "We can dance. We don't need boys for that."

"Don't get too close to me," Juliana warned, but she let Mia pull her to her feet.

They danced to the fast, heady music, and soon they were trying to outdo each other with silly moves. Mia couldn't stop laughing. It was the first good time she'd had since leaving Sicily.

They jumped up on the couch, and Juliana showed off some of her American flapper moves, lifting the hem of her long shirt and kicking to show a lot of bare leg. Mia imitated her, and soon they were trying to out-sexy each other instead. Juliana laughed so hard she lost her balance, and the couch cushion slid out from beneath her. Mia thought nothing of catching her, then holding her hands and dancing with her. She knew Juliana's touch was death, but she was filled with the combined confidence of wine and youth. Dancing with death made her feel alive.

A female voice shouted, and the needle was ripped from the record, scratching it terribly.

"I said, what is happening here?" the voice demanded in German. Mia and Juliana were both learning the language while they were here, but between themselves, they spoke in English, the language of Hollywood movies.

Alise had entered the room, flanked by her two blond cohorts, Roza and Vilja. They were wrapped in robes or blankets and glared indignantly at the two girls cavorting to jazz in their night clothes.

"We're dancing," Mia said. "Want to join?"

"No music after ten o' clock," Alise said. "The rules are clear!"

"But it's Saturday night," Juliana protested.

"And unauthorized wine!" Roza said, pointing. "Look, Alise. Nobody else gets to have wine. The scientists forbid it."

"Thank you, Roza. Who gave you permission to drink? Where did you get that wine?" Alise demanded.

"Oh, Alise." Mia's words were slurred. "We're just having fun."

"There is plenty of room for fun within the rules," Alise said.

"I think someone's taking their hallway *fuehrer* job a little seriously," Juliana said, and Mia laughed.

"Rules must be followed!" Alise barked so hard that locks of blond fell into her face, and her serious tone only made Mia and Juliana giggle more. "That is not a proper use of the common area seating! Get down now!"

Mia and Juliana stepped down from the couch, still holding hands and giggling.

"You are both on administrative restriction," Alise told them.

"How could this place get any more restricted?" Mia asked through her drunken giggles.

Alise narrowed her eyes at Mia and leaned in close to her. "Try me if you want to find out. Back to your rooms immediately. I will be filling out an incident report for Dr. Wichtmann." She turned on her heel and marched out of the room.

"Oh, no, an incident report!" Juliana said, and Mia laughed.

"You're both in a lot of trouble," Roza said, crossing her arms. "I hope you know that."

"They might kick us out," Mia said. "How terrible!"

Juliana and Mia couldn't stop snickering as the blond girls herded them down the hall and back into their room. The two of them lay on Mia's bed, whispering and making fun of the other girls, and laughing and shushing each other, until they fell asleep.

# Chapter Twenty-Seven

Jenny woke feeling stiff, sick to her stomach, and full of cramps. She lay in a hospital bed under dim lights. Someone had replaced her clothes with a thin hospital gown and pasted small circular sensors all over her arms and chest. She could feel them on her neck and face, too, but when she reached up to touch them, she discovered her hands were chained to the bed. So were her ankles. The steel chains were thin but heavy, and allowed only the smallest movements—she couldn't even scratch her nose if she needed to do that. Naturally, her nose started itching immediately.

She was alone in a cube-shaped cell with clear walls, a clear ceiling, and no furniture. The larger room outside her cell was a concrete bay that looked like the hangar for a small airplane. Dark windows looked down on her from high on one wall.

Jenny recognized it immediately as one of the laboratories at the underground complex in the Harz mountains. For a long, strange minute, she wondered whether she'd somehow traveled back in time...or maybe all her different lives were really happening at once, in some way, and she could move  between them.

Then she saw the bank of digital monitors lined up outside a clear wall of her cell, remotely reading the sensors all over her body, spitting out moving graphs of her heartbeat, breathing, blood pressure, brain waves, and other metrics she couldn't identify, all her inner biological activities displayed and tracked, and probably recorded. They must have gathered their data remotely from the sensors glued all over her body.

This definitely was not the 1930's, but she was back in the same place. They'd all been captured by the unavoidable man Mariella had seen in Seth's future, whom Jenny believed would turn out to be the Nazi officer Kranzler, the seer who could reach in and find people's memories, Mariella's opposite.

Jenny immediately began to worry about Seth, and about Mariella, too. Where were they?

She looked up at the clear roof of her cube, where a pair of fan units each connected to a ventilation duct that reached away to the laboratory ceiling high above, keeping Jenny's air separate from everyone else in the underground complex.

Between the fan units, which were located on opposite ends of the cube, a small black dome watched her.

"Hey, I'm up!" Jenny shouted at the camera that had to be inside the dome. "Anybody want to take these chains off?" She waved her hands as much as the restraints allowed.

She looked out through the transparent wall of her cube, toward the steel doors that led out of the lab. Fifteen or twenty minutes passed before one of them opened.

The man who entered bore some resemblance to Kranzler—dark red hair tinged with gray, a broad and stocky build, flat nose, feral green eyes. He wore a dark blue military uniform with a starched white shirt and black tie, and he was followed by three guards in biohazard facemasks and body armor. The guards wore black from their helmets to their boots, with no flag or any other decoration.

This incarnation of Kranzler stepped up to the monitor bank just outside the wall, ignoring her and looking at the machines for a moment. He looked like some kind of *Star Wars* villain, she thought, with the masked stormtroopers standing in a razor-straight row behind him.

"Jennifer Morton," he eventually said, still looking at the EEG machine. "We've been looking for you."

"Who are you? And where are we?" Jenny asked, although she was certain she knew the answers to both questions.

"I am the one who finally caught you." He looked up at her, smiling. "You make for dangerous prey, Jennifer. I hope you'll forgive our use of tranquilizers."

"Where are Seth and Mariella?"

"Safe. Secure. No need to worry about them."

"I want to see Seth. And you can take these chains off me, I'm not going to attack you."

"I'm supposed to take your word for that? I've studied the Fallen Oak outbreak, Jenny. I've seen what you do to those who get in your way. And, you may not believe me, but I respect it, I truly do. Because the world is shaped by one thing, Jennifer: force."

"The Force?" Jenny asked, still thinking how the guards looked like stormtroopers.

"Force!" He slammed a large fist into the clear wall. "You have it inside you, but force must be used intelligently. It must have purpose and direction. I can provide that."

"I don't need purpose or direction," she told him. "I *need* to scratch my nose."

"Nobody's ever died of an itchy nostril."

"How long are you going to keep me in this bed?"

"As long as we wish. We have to keep our technicians and medical staff safe from you, don't we?"

"Why are we here?"

"To protect the United States against all enemies...foreign and domestic." He smiled. "You're a threat to security, Jennifer. We can't just have someone like you running wild, leaving hundreds of dead people in your wake simply because you don't like them."

"That's not what happened! I don't want to hurt anybody."

"I've seen many photographs that say otherwise."

"They were attacking me...and I've changed since then."

He gave a cold laugh. "Changed how? Found Jesus? Born again? Or maybe those Mormon kids with the bicycles knocked on your door and changed your life? I'd like to hear the tale."

"You couldn't begin to understand it."

"I'm sure it's all very convoluted and dramatic. But I'm not so much interested in what you've done, Jennifer, as where you're going now. You can work with us. I'm prepared to offer you that."

"Doing what?" she asked.

"Serving your country."

"Serving *you*. I know you, Kranzler. You're a monster. I don't know how you climbed so high in this lifetime, in this world. I guess cockroaches know how to survive in any environment."

She could tell he hadn't heard anything after the world *Kranzler*. He looked stunned for a moment, then shook his head as if to clear it.

"You must work with us," Ward said. "Let us test you. Let us examine how your ability works. Your power could reach its full potential with my help."

"I don't *want* to reach my full potential. I don't want to use the pox ever again."

"Your choice is to accept your place and work with us, or to stay locked up in this cell for the rest of your life. All we want now is to test and learn. We'll table any discussion of national defense applications until you're comfortable talking about that. Do we have a deal?" He folded his arms and watched her face.

"I can't do any testing now, anyway," Jenny said. "With all these whirli-gizmos attached to me, I'm sure you've noticed I'm slightly pregnant. I can't use the pox, it's not safe for the baby."

"You're only half-term. We can't wait months to begin testing."

"Then I suggest you don't go around kidnapping pregnant women."

"Everything I do is for the greater good," Ward told her. "When you see that, you will join us."

"Whose idea of the greater good? Yours?"

"You will cooperate with us, Jennifer." His eyes seemed to grow dark as he stared at her. "You will submit to testing when I order it."

"I'm sorry, General, but like I said, my hands are tied." Jenny raised her cuffed hands.

He glared at her, then shook his head as he turned away. The guards followed him out and slammed the steel door behind them.

Jenny looked around the concrete lab. They hadn't bothered to provide her with anything to read or a TV, but she had plenty of past-life memories to watch. This place crawled with them. She wondered if she was in the exact same lab where they'd tested her so many times. She looked around at the concrete floor, but she didn't see any bloodstains.

* * *

Juliana felt a wave of relief as she stepped into the lab. No animals today, just more beige machines full of dials and knobs. They hadn't made her touch any more animals since the goats, and she hoped they'd decided not to do that anymore, after seeing how much it upset her. She didn't mind letting them monitor her and swab samples from the gory lesions she summoned to the surface of her body, and photograph her naked as Dr. Wichtmann kept insisting, but she had resolved not to kill any more animals no matter how much they pressured her. They would have to adjust their testing to that. Maybe they already had.

She stood near the exam table and looked up at the windows high above. They'd dimmed the lighting on the observation deck, so the windows looked like black mirrors. She had no idea whether anyone was watching her.

A few minutes passed, and she grew more and more uneasy. By now, the biologists and doctors should have been here in their gas masks and elbow-length rubber gloves, poking and prodding at her. The room felt unusually cold today, too, and she shivered in her light dress and folded her arms in around herself.

A steel door opened, and two uniformed S.S. men in black gas masks entered, rolling a surgical gurney. A man was strapped to it with wide leather belts, his mouth bound with a cloth gag. He lunged his shoulders and hips uselessly, grunting and screaming against his gag. It was hard to tell his age, because his face and head had been carelessly shaved with a straight razor, leaving them cross-hatched with cuts and scrapes. He was stripped to his stained underwear, and deep lash marks were carved all over his body. It was clear he'd been tortured, and starved as well, his ribs jutting out through his skin.

The S.S. men rolled him to the center of the room, then turned and marched toward the door without a word to her.

"Wait! What's happening?" Juliana asked.

They ignored her and hurried out, locking the door behind them, leaving her alone with the tortured man squirming on the gurney. His head flopped toward her, his eyes wide, and he made some desperate pleading sounds against his gag.

"Please hurry." Dr. Wichtmann's voice sounded over the intercom.

"Hurry? What do you expect me to do?" Juliana asked.

"You know what we expect you do," Wichtmann replied.

"You want me to infect him?"

"Death is preferred."

"I can't do that!"

"Do not fear, Juliana." Kranzler's deeper voice spoke now. "This man is a convicted criminal. He will die whether you are the instrument or not."

"He is?" Juliana looked at the suffering man. "What was his crime?"

"Treason."

Juliana had been hoping to hear he was a raper of women and a murderer of children. "What kind of treason?"

"I cannot disclose that. Rest assured, he is the lowest sort of mongrel, barely a man at all," Kranzler said.

"We are on a schedule," Wichtmann's voice added.

Juliana shook her head, backing away. "I can't."

"You can," Kranzler said. "We are in a war, Juliana, of civilization against barbarians. In a war, you must kill."

"I'm not at war with anyone," Juliana said. "And I'm not German, so if you guys are planning a war, that's your problem. You have to get this man a doctor right now!"

"You do not give orders in my lab!" Wichtmann snapped. "Apply the touch."

"No!" Juliana folded her arms and walked to the door. "Let me go. Let me go *home*. I want to return to America, right now. I'm not staying here and doing this."

There was a muffled conversation, as though someone had covered the microphone, and then Dr. Wichtmann spoke in a resigned voice: "Testing is concluded for today. You may return to your quarters."

"I don't want to return to my quarters, I want to get Sebastian and leave this place. And that's all I'm going to do."

"Juliana, please relax yourself," Kranzler said. "We cannot make transportation arrangements immediately. If you still wish to leave in the morning, we will happily put both of you on a train."

Juliana took a deep breath and tried to calm down, but the bleeding, screaming man wasn't going to allow that. His face and voice would echo in her mind for the rest of her life.

"Fine. Thank you," Juliana said. "We'll be happy to take a train in the morning. Now, please, somebody help this person!"

"The medical staff will enter when you leave," Dr. Wichtmann said. "No one wishes to be exposed to your condition."

"I'm going, I'm going, just send them down." Juliana stepped out through the door, past a couple of armed S.S. guards, and hurried along the corridor toward the dormitory. The guards trailed her at a distance until she reached her hall.

She spent the rest of her afternoon sitting on her bed, knees to her chin, and shaking.

Eventually, Mia came home from her own testing, and she hurried over when she saw the horrified look on Juliana's face.

"What's wrong?" Mia asked, taking one of Juliana's gloved hands. "What happened? Tell me."

"They wanted me to kill somebody," Juliana whispered.

"Are you serious?"

"He was strapped to a table. Everyone acted like it was no big deal, like I wasn't even supposed to care about killing some helpless person."

"Why would they think that?"

"Because I'm a monster." Juliana laid her head on her knees. "Just a monster who can't touch anyone. Death in a white dress." Juliana pulled her hand away from Mia's. "You shouldn't touch me."

"You're not a monster." Mia rubbed her arm through her sleeve. "You're the only sane person here. I'm so glad you came, Juliana. I felt like I was losing my mind."

"I'm not glad," Juliana said. "I mean, I'm glad I met you, but this place is just...scary. I told them I wanted to leave. They said they'd put us on a train in the morning."

"Oh, no!" Mia's face broke down, and she covered it with both hands. "You're going to leave? You're leaving me here?"

"You can come with us. To America, if you like."

"I can't!" Mia was already crying. "Juliana, my father sold me to them. They'll go back and punish my family if I leave."

Juliana's shoulders sagged. She didn't know what to do now, and she wondered how the people running the base would react.

She found out a few hours later, when Alise stopped by their room just before dinner, while Juliana and Mia were quietly reading.

"How are you two today?" Alise asked. "Anything exciting happen?"

They both shook their heads.

"You look so cute today," Alise told Mia. "New make-up? Or did you change your hair?"

"Same old everything," Mia told her.

"Well, you look beautiful. Listen, I need to speak with Juliana in private for a minute. Want to go on to the dining room, and we'll see you there?"

"I suppose I could..." Mia rose slowly from her bed, but she looked uncertain. "Are you going to be all right, Juliana?"

"I'm fine," Juliana nodded her head, though she didn't feel fine at all. She felt repulsive and evil. "See you at dinner."

Mia trudged out of the room, clearly not wanting to leave Juliana alone with Alise. Alise closed the door behind her, then turned her gray eyes on Juliana, who still sat on the bed.

"Let's talk, Juliana." Alise sauntered towards her, then pulled out the chair from Juliana's writing desk and sat just a few feet away. "You can be honest with me. Are you unhappy here?"

"They wanted me to kill someone today."

"Oh, he was only a common criminal," Alise said. "You have to understand, Juliana, that with your touch being so...medical, they have to test the effects on people. Why not criminals? It's not like we'll ever run out of them, unfortunately, and the Reich has already sentenced them to death. So their death should at least have value, shouldn't it? Add something to the knowledge of humanity? Like how your power works. That's worth the life of a man already sentenced to die, isn't it?"

"I'm not going to kill anyone for them. You can tell them I said that when you report back."

"Juliana, I'm here because I'm worried about you."

"I doubt that," Juliana said.

Alise glanced at the door, as if concerned someone might be spying on them. Then she leaned closer and whispered, "I want to show you something. About me and my power. But you must promise to keep it secret. Will you?"

"If you want." Juliana shrugged.

"This might seem strange, but be calm and watch." Alise took in a deep, slow breath, filling her lungs all the way, her gray eyes fixed on Juliana's face. When she exhaled, she breathed out a cloud of what looked like tiny, pink, fluffy flower petals. Juliana flinched as they landed all over her face, neck, and arms...but then she felt much, much better.

The delicate little petals melted into her skin like sugar cubes in hot tea. A few of the pink flakes drifted into Juliana's gaping mouth and landed on her tongue. They reminded her of cotton candy from the fair, and every sweet thing she'd ever tasted.

Juliana sighed and relaxed. The world had a beautiful golden glow now, radiating from Alise, the girl she loved with all her heart, even if she hadn't realized it until just now.

"You're so sweet to come see me," Juliana said. "You're so...perfect."

"I know. Are you happy now?"

"I am happy when you're near me."

"And you trust me, don't you? You know that anything I ask you to do is for the good?"

"Of course." Juliana beamed. At that moment, she would have jumped off a cliff in the desert if she knew it would make Alise happy. Her heart had never felt so alive and so vulnerable. "You're a good friend, Alise. I want us to stay friends."

"Why wouldn't we?" Alise look puzzled.

"Weren't you mad at me when you got here? You were mad about...something." Juliana couldn't remember. All she could think about was Alise, beautiful, fascinating Alise. "Let me think..."

"I know what it was. You said some silly thing earlier, to Dr. Wichtmann. You said you wanted to quit the research, leave the base, and go back to America. That's not true, is it?" Alise looked as if she were about to tear up and start crying, just like Mia had. "Oh, no, I can't lose a friend like you. Promise me you'll never leave me, Juliana."

"I wouldn't leave you." Juliana's heart ached sweetly, just knowing that Alise felt the same way about her. "I couldn't leave you, Alise. I...I think I might love you."

"I love you, too, Juliana." Alise stood and winked. "Let's go have dinner. I'm glad we could talk things over. I'll walk you to your lab tests in the morning, if you like."

"I'd like it very much." Juliana beamed at her as they left her room, toward the small dining room where the test subjects had been segregated ever since Juliana's arrival.

It had never been easy for Juliana to make friends, so she couldn't believe her luck, having a friend like Alise who lived just down the hall.

# Chapter Twenty-Eight

An electronically amplified voice woke Seth from his sleep: "The general is here to see you."

"Huh?" Seth sat up, his hair sticking out in clumps. He tried to get his bearings. He was on a very small, uncomfortable bed in a concrete room like a prison cell. He faced a steel door where a young man in a black uniform looked at him through a thick pane of glass. "Where the hell am I? Is this Alabama?" Seth asked.

"You are in a classified research facility." A hard, gruff voice took over. The young man in the window moved aside and was replaced by a man in his late forties or early fifties, with bright green eyes and close-cropped red hair, going gray. "You and Jennifer Morton have been taken into custody because of the mass death in Fallen Oak."

*Oh, shit, that again*, Seth thought. "So...Alabama, then?" he asked.

"You are very far from home, Seth. My name is Lieutenant General Ward Kilpatrick, U.S. Department of Defense. We're very concerned about the threat to national security represented by you and Jenny...especially Jenny."

"Jenny's not a threat to anybody," Seth said.

"How can you say that, after witnessing the slaughter in Fallen Oak?" Ward asked. His voice crackled from the ceiling, slightly delayed from the movement of his lips.

"Those people were trying to kill her. And me. So my sympathy is kind of limited," Seth said.

"Were they not people you knew personally? Teenagers and teachers from your school? Your church pastor? Your mayor?"

"I did know them," Seth said. "A lot of them were assholes."

"But did they deserve to die?"

Seth shrugged. "Once you say it's okay to murder somebody, aren't you kind of saying that it's okay for somebody to murder you? I mean, fair's fair."

"You have no remorse?"

"I wish it hadn't happened, but I've had plenty of time to get over it." Seth smiled. He realized that he was something...*more* than he'd been before. He remembered scores of past lives, and he was now the sum of thousands of years of experience and knowledge. He was no longer just Seth Barrett from Fallen Oak, he was the healer, veteran of many human lives.

And he knew all about the man who stood before him.

"Where's Jenny?" Seth asked. "I need to see her."

"I'm afraid she's in isolation at the moment," Ward said.

"You have to take me to her." Seth walked toward the window, looking Ward in the eye. "Right now."

"You are not in charge here, Seth. Seeing Jenny is a privilege you'll have to earn."

"Earn how? By obeying you? Being your pet dog?"

"I'm giving you the chance to redeem yourself by serving your country, Seth. I'm only going to offer it once."

"I'm not going to work for you, General Kranzler. I'm not going to kill for you."

Ward's eyes widened at the name. "What did you call me?"

"I called you General Kilpatrick," Seth said. "That's your name this time around, isn't it, Kranzler?"

"You said it again." Ward's voice was a low growl. "Why? Where did you get that name?"

"Do yourself a favor, Kranzler, or Ward Kilpatrick, or whatever you think your name is," Seth said. "Let me and Jenny go now. You'll wish you had, I promise. And I do keep my promises, lifetime after lifetime. All of them."

"You're in no position to threaten me!" Ward snapped.

"Maybe you're the one who doesn't understand your position, Kranzler." Seth stepped even closer, looking hard into the man's eyes. "Because it looks to me like you're the one who's trapped. Like Alexander. The same life, again and again."

"Who is Alexander?"

"He's dead, so it doesn't matter. I killed him. It was a long time coming...but, like I said, I keep my promises." Seth grinned at Ward through the thick window.

"You just blew your only chance." Ward's face turned a dark crimson.

"My one and only chance?" Seth asked, even as Ward and the guards departed down the hall. "Not like my last one and only chance, in 1933? Or my next one and only chance, when you bring us all back to the same place again in another hundred years? How many times are you going to set up this same situation, Kranzler? Hello? Is this thing on? Where's Jenny, Kranzler?"

Ward and his guards continued on out of sight.

"That went well, I think," Seth said, wondering if the man could still hear him. He looked around the room, wondering whether he'd been in this exact cell before. It didn't look like it had been cleaned since 1933.

Seth felt a giddy high from having so many of his memories restored, as if he'd been sleepwalking all his life and finally woken up. He could see how Kranzler, or Ward, was trapped in the same drama, creating the same situation again, apparently unaware that they'd all been here before. Jenny, and their unborn baby, had to be here somewhere. To understand the present, he needed to study carefully his memories of the past...

\* \* \*

Sebastian walked into the dining room where the test subjects ate at a long table. Evelina, the dark, quiet Slavic girl, sat alone at the end, and he greeted her, as he did every time. She mumbled something back without looking up from her boiled beef and potatoes, which was actually a big response from her.

He thought the tests were going well. He'd healed animals and human subjects with a variety of afflictions, and he'd even healed Dr. Wichtmann of a persistent bladder infection, though that wasn't an official test. The scientists seemed pleased with the work but still clueless about how his touch actually worked, except that it put out a lot of heat and electromagnetic energy.

The worst part was how rarely he saw Juliana—just meals and the occasional film night, no private time. He hoped he would be included in the girls' activities more now that Willem had apparently returned home to Holland over the weekend. Niklaus was always on his official duties and still took his meals with the other S.S. officers, so Sebastian found himself spending hours alone on his hall at night. Not that he particularly wanted to spend more time with Niklaus—the guy had a strange, threatening way about him, but at least he always had beer or schnapps. The scientists had instructed Sebastian not to drink alcohol, but what else was he supposed to do with all his time?

Sebastian took a platter of potatoes and beef from the open dumbwaiter, then sat at his usual place near the middle of the table. He greeted Roza and Vilja, who flanked the head of the table where Alise would inevitably sit. The blond girls waved back at him and whispered to each other, giggling.

Mia, Juliana's roommate, arrived and hurried over to sit next to Sebastian.

"Hi, Mia. Where's Juliana?" Sebastian asked.

"She'll come." Mia leaned close to him and whispered. "She's very upset today. I hope you can comfort her."

"They didn't make her do more animal tests, did they?"

"No, they just..." Mia frowned. "They wanted her to...kill a man. With her touch." She placed her hand on Sebastian's, as if to demonstrate.

"Are you serious? What kind of sick people are these Nazis? Is she in her room?" Sebastian began to stand, but Mia grabbed his arm.

"Alise is talking to her now," Mia said quietly. "God knows what she's saying. They should be here soon."

Sebastian pulled his arm free and started for the door, but then Juliana and Alise entered the room. Despite what Mia had said, Juliana had a broad, glowing smile and a drifting-on-a-cloud look in her eyes.

Sebastian smiled and reached out to hug Juliana, but she looked right through him. She trotted after Alise like a loyal puppy and sat down next to Roza, on Alise's end of the table. Roza gave Juliana a disgusted look and scooted her chair away, but Juliana didn't seem to notice. She gazed droopy-eyed at Alise, with a drunken smile.

"Alise touched her, didn't she?" Sebastian asked, taking his seat again. "How could Alise touch Juliana without getting the plague?"

"I don't know, but it looks like she did."

Sebastian shook his head. Alise had only touched him a few brief times, but her power was clearly strong. Even those brief touches had made him feel intoxicated, and a couple of times, had left him with painfully swollen erections that wouldn't go away for hours.

"I have an announcement," Alise said. "Now that both halls are together."

Sebastian tried to catch Juliana's eye, but she hadn't even looked his way since entering the room. Either Alise had dosed her pretty heavily, or Juliana was angry at Sebastian about something.

"Orders have come down that we will no longer tolerate music, film, or literature corrupted by Jewish, homosexual, Communist, or liberal influences," Alise continued. "No more degrading Hollywood filth, no more records of music by the lower races. We will enjoy only civilized film and music, promoting proper German virtues."

"No!" Mia said. "Please, Alise!"

"Excuse me? Do you have a problem, Mia?" Alise stared at her, and Roza and Vilja copied her cold look. So did Juliana, as if she'd become part of their clique. The four girls seemed to be trying to intimidate Mia.

"I have to agree with Mia on this one," Sebastian said. "We really need our entertainment around here."

"You're taking *her* side?" Juliana scowled at him.

"It's not about sides, it's about not losing our music and movies," Sebastian told her.

"Juliana, I read there's a new Mae West coming out," Mia said. "Called *I'm No Angel*. Don't you want to see that?"

"It sounds exactly like the kind of degenerate film we're trying to avoid," Alise said. "We'll be collecting all unsuitable records from the common rooms. You will still have the records of many fine German composers."

"This is ridiculous," Sebastian said. "We should at least keep the records we have."

"We are not debating the new rule, I am simply telling you what it is," Alise said. Juliana, Roza, and Vilja all nodded, as if Alise had made an excellent point.

"Why are you doing this?" Sebastian asked.

"I am responsible for guiding all of you toward healthy bodies and healthy morals, too," Alise said. "This may shock you, Sebastian, but we caught Juliana and Mia together on Saturday night, drinking wine and dancing to Negro music in a very lewd manner."

"You did? Where was I?" Sebastian grinned at Juliana, but she was still imitating Alise's withering glare. It was as if the Juliana he'd always known had vanished, and a new minion of Alise had taken her place.

"The behavior was unacceptable and violated several dormitory rules," Alise said. "*Gruppenführer* Kranzler and I agree that the corrupting influence of foreign, racially inferior music is to blame."

"American music isn't foreign to us!" Sebastian said.

"Sebastian, please don't fight with Alise," Juliana told him, her blue eyes frosty and hard. "She has a difficult job looking out for all of us. We should support her and listen to her. If she wants to remove corrupting influences, then we should help her instead of arguing."

"Hi, I'm not sure we've met," he replied. "My name is Sebastian."

"You can't be serious about this," Mia said to Alise.

"The new rule goes into effect immediately," Alise said. "Roza, Vilja, and I will review the appropriateness of records and books in both common rooms. Juliana, would you like to help?"

"I'll be happy to," Juliana said. "I'm sorry Sebastian is giving you problems."

"Don't worry, he's just a boy," Alise said, and Juliana laughed, as did Alise's other little followers. Sebastian cast a look of disbelief at Juliana, but she ignored him.

"I think I'm done." Sebastian stood and returned his slightly-eaten meal to the dumbwaiter. The little rope-powered elevator would return their dirty dishes up to the kitchen.

"So am I." Mia followed him out to the hallway, though she hadn't eaten at all.

"Have fun, you two," Alise said, and the other blond girls snickered.

"It's like she's under a spell," Sebastian said quietly to Mia as they walked down the hall, away from the dining room and back toward the dormitories. "I mean, I've felt Alise's power before, and I know it's very..."

"Sexy?" Mia asked, and he couldn't help laughing.

"Yeah. Strong. Like opium. It feels like Juliana's completely out of touch with herself. And me."

"Don't worry, I'm still here." Mia smiled. "I'll talk to her. And she'll come back to her senses...Alise has touched me before, and it does wear off eventually."

"It's good you're here, Mia," Sebastian said. "Without you, I'd be going crazy."

"You might still be going crazy." She smiled as they reached the double doors to the girls' hall. "I'll see you at breakfast. Don't worry about Juliana."

"I'll try." Sebastian reached out and hugged her, without thinking about it. He'd never hugged her before. She leaned her face against his neck, wrapping her arms around him tightly and holding him much longer than he'd expected, while his healing energy seeped into her body. She gave him a dazed smile as she finally pulled herself away and stepped through the door.

# Chapter Twenty-Nine

Esmeralda stood in the high concrete room and stared at the dead body on the gurney in front of her. A sheet covered him to the chest, hiding the bullet wounds that had killed him. She'd been told nothing about him, but he looked Arabic to her, or maybe Pakistani.

Two scientists, two U.S. military intelligence officers, and General Ward Kilpatrick watched her from across the room, as did a digital video camera.

"Anytime, Miss Rios," Ward said.

Esmeralda sighed. She didn't want to help this man, who'd had her drugged and kidnapped from her home. She had no idea where in the world they were, and there were no windows anywhere to give her any clues. The lack of windows made the place even more creepy and sinister. She had a constant bad feeling, as if the place were haunted by angry ghosts. At night, in the dark, she spent hours laying awake in terror, expecting something to grab her.

Her kidnappers belonged to some kind of secret government agency, the same people who'd recruited Tommy. Ward had approached her in person a week after Tommy left, asking if she was ready to join him, but Esmeralda had turned him down. So he'd had men kidnap her instead.

Now she was cooperating reluctantly, out of fear of what he might do if she didn't. She kept asking him to let her see Tommy, but Ward just smirked and said she had to "earn" a visit with him. This involved reading bodies that Ward brought to her, while his researchers monitored her through sensors attached all over her body.

Esmeralda took a deep breath, placed her hands on the corpse, and closed her eyes.

Immediately, she saw flashes of life in a city of bombed-out and blackened buildings...Afghanistan. He was Pashtun, not Arab.

"I see Kabul," she told them. "Now, another city, Herat, full of ancient towers, not so destroyed...He traveled back and forth, buying and selling...Dishes? Dishes and teapots from Iran. He preferred Herat. He died in Kabul."

"He brought weapons from Iran to Afghanistan," said one of the intelligence officers who'd brought the corpse to the base. "A gun dealer."

Esmeralda's forehead wrinkled as she concentrated. "No...I don't see anything like that."

"He has to be the guy. We worked hard to track him down. A paid informant assured us he was a gun runner."

"Maybe you should ask for your money back." Esmeralda opened her eyes.

"We were told he was involved in guns and heroin," the officer told her.

"No. He did make a sport of sleeping with the wives of other men. Perhaps that is why someone wants him dead."

The intelligence officers looked at each other.

"This girl's a fake," one of them said to Ward. "She doesn't know anything."

"Is she?" Ward asked. "Or are you trying to cover your own ass?"

"We didn't make a mistake," he said. He looked at Esmeralda. "This is the right guy."

"Thank you, gentlemen. Your response is noted. I think we're done here," Ward told them.

The dead Pashtun was wheeled away, and the two visiting intelligence officers left.

"He sold teapots, huh?" Ward asked her.

"Teapots." Esmeralda shrugged.

"Guess they aren't sending the high-value targets for our tests."

Ward shook his head, chuckling as he left the lab. Guards in black uniforms escorted Esmeralda away, down the elevator, and back to her room in what they called the cellblock. She sat on her bed as the steel door of her cell clanged shut. She was cooperating now, but was still treated like a prisoner because they knew she didn't want to be here.

Esmeralda shuddered as the dark, fearful feeling washed over her again, more strongly ever before. Goosebumps rose all over her. Every shadow and shape in her concrete cell suddenly seemed threatening, as if it were all stage dressing concealing a dark, dangerous evil.

She tried to push back the tide of dark feelings, but they overwhelmed her, drowning her. She felt a flood of memories of another life, like when she touched a person who had died, but somehow these were her *own* memories.

She stood in the lab again, looking at a different body, a middle-aged man with a long beard. There were scientists in white coats again, as well as uniformed men with red patches and swastikas on their sleeves. She knew that she was terrified of them, especially their leader, a man with dark red and gray hair and evil green eyes. *Kranzler.*

"Go ahead, Evelina," said a balding, fat man with neck beard. *Dr. Wichtmann.* "Tell us what you see."

She took a breath and reached out, touching the dead man's cold, stiff shoulder. She told Wichtmann about the last months of the man's life—he was a rabbi who'd spoken against the National Socialists, and even published pamphlets against them. This was the reason he was dead.

"He was involved in a plot against the state," one of the men in black uniforms said. "We want to know details—time, place, the kind of bombs they will use. All you can tell us."

Evelina concentrated for several minutes, trying to find what they wanted. Then, slowly, she shook her head.

"There is nothing," she told them, in her hesitant German. "Writing and speaking, yes, bombs, no."

One of the uniformed men exploded, shouting at Kranzler, speaking too fast for Evelina to follow. Though she did catch the words "filthy Slav," clearly referring to her.

"Evelina," Kranzler growled as he approached her. "You must tell us about any conspiracies. You cannot protect anyone."

"I am protecting no one, only telling the truth. If there was terrorism, he was not involved."

"We are talking about plots for the future!" shouted the S.S. officer who'd called her a filthy Slav. He must have been the one who'd captured the man. "Not events that have already passed."

Evelina shrugged. "This man was involved in no such plots."

"What about the larger Jewish conspiracy?" the officer asked. "The banks? The gold?"

"I don't know what you mean," she replied.

"Look again!"

She sighed and touched the dead man for another minute. "I don't see what you're talking about. Gold? Banks?" She shook her head.

"You lying dirty whore!" the officer shouted. "Kranzler, she is a fraud. She is of no use to us."

"Evelina, this is your last chance," Kranzler said. "No more lying to protect the Jews."

"I am not lying!" This was the first time Evelina had raised her voice, or done anything but whisper, nod, and cooperate.

"She is a dirty animal and should be tied up!" the S.S. man yelled. "She speaks nothing but lies."

"Evelina, tell us about the Jewish plots!" Kranzler said.

"There are no plots! Why are you all too stupid to understand that?" Evelina shouted back at them. She immediately regretted her words—they were sure to get her in trouble—but it was too late to take them back.

"Guards," Kranzler snarled, "Let her spend a night in the cellblock. Perhaps that will convince her to stop protecting Jewish conspirators."

S.S. men seized her and carried her out of the lab. She didn't struggle as they brought her down to the floor beneath the dormitory hall, to a guard station with two armed guards. One of them opened the steel door to the cellblock, and they escorted her to a concrete cell and locked her inside.

She didn't mind being in the cellblock—this was where the Germans had housed her first, after she'd refused to come with them and they'd responded by forcibly taking her. After cooperating for a time, she'd been allowed to move up to the residential dorm with other test subjects, provided she kept quiet and complained about nothing.  She'd kept almost perfectly silent the entire time.

While it was better to be upstairs with the others, a night or two alone in a cell would at least give her a respite from Alise's cold, gray eyes boring into her, filled with suspicion each time they saw each other.  In her own way, Evelina thought, Alise seemed almost as sinister as Kranzler himself, even if everybody else seemed to love her.

# Chapter Thirty

Ward remained seated as Mariella entered his office, but he smiled at her. He nodded at the Hale Security guard who'd escorted her, and the guard closed the door to wait outside.

"Miss Visconti," Ward said. "Thank you for coming to see me."

"Of course, sir. Is this about..." She dropped her voice to a whisper. "...spy work?"

"It is. Have a seat. Coffee?" He reached for the button on his telephone.

"No, thank you." Mariella kept her posture perfectly straight as she sat. "What can I do for you?"

Ward found Mariella to be a typical rich ditz, underneath her air of education and culture. She'd already ordered thousands of dollars in clothing, since she had almost none with her, as well as furnishings for her dormitory room, but that was a small price to pay keep her happy, considering the hellstorm her politically connected family could raise on her behalf. He was relieved to have her on his side, even enthusiastic to follow orders, but he still needed to test her loyalty and dedication.

"I think you can help us streamline our operation," Ward told her. "We now have five paranormals at this facility, and three are cooperating with us—you and the boy Tommy most of all. The Mexican girl, the one who can speak to the dead, she does what we say, though she clearly doesn't share your enthusiasm or your understanding of the importance of our work."

"But Jenny and Seth are not cooperating, sir?" She looked puzzled, as if this news made no sense to her.

"Exactly."

"Jenny is pregnant, sir, so she may not be entirely rational." Mariella gave him a big smile. "You know how we women are— erratic, emotional, impulsive. When a woman's pregnant, multiply that by a hundred. Let me speak to her, and I'll help her understand what she needs to do."

"I want your help with the boy."

"Seth?"

"He won't listen to me, but I think he'll be more willing to listen to a pretty little thing like you," Ward said. He didn't see how any red-blooded American male could ignore her, with her high cheekbones, dark red hair, and dancer's body.

"I could talk with Seth, too, if you like," she said.

"Don't just talk to him, convince him. I want you to redirect his affections."

"I don't think I understand, General Kilpatrick."

"You understand. Stroke his ego, stroke his cock if you have to, do whatever it takes to change his mind. Make him switch his allegiance from the plague girl over to you."

Mariella gasped and even blushed a little. He just watched her coolly.

"Are you serious?" she whispered.

"You said you wanted to be a spy. It's not the movies, it's not ninja fights and poison darts hidden in your wristwatch. It's about gaining people's trust. And this is the way you're going to do it. Female spies use every asset they have, including their feminine wiles."

"My feminine wiles?" Mariella giggled.

"I assume you have some. This is your first assignment. The first test of your ability to act as an intelligence operative."

"I like the sound of that." She beamed. "I do know boys, sir, and how to use their feelings."

"Then you think you can handle that?"

"Please, he's not a challenge. He's very immature, even for an American boy."

"Good. Go to his cell tonight. The guards will let you in."

"I'm excited!" The girl was practically bouncing in her chair before she recovered herself and tried to look proper. "I mean, I'll do it, sir! But I could still talk to Jenny for you, too."

"Not just now," he said. "I have special plans for Jenny."

Mariella sat in her chair, smiling at him, her eyes practically glowing—her eyes, the same green hue as his own, as if they were mirrors reflecting his own gaze. She might be useful, but her presence made Ward uncomfortable, stirring up the prickly-flesh feeling that had turned into a strange hallucination last time. He probably needed psych meds, but he wasn't about to tell anyone that his brain might be slipping. Once something like that got added to a file, Ward's enemies in the Pentagon could use it against him. As a man who'd primarily gotten ahead in life through blackmail, he knew there were a number of top brass who wouldn't mind seeing him retired, one way or another.

"You can go now," Ward told Mariella, and she hopped out of her chair with another "Yes, sir!" and bounced to the door. As she left, he watched her shapely ass, framed in the two-hundred-dollar Armani jeans he'd paid for out of his agency's budget. He felt a powerful urge to grab the spoiled rich girl, throw her across his desk, and rip off that tight denim...

He didn't know where the thought had come from. It wasn't attraction, it was a need to dominate. He wanted to knock her down, put her beneath him. He couldn't stop thinking about it, until it became like a painful throbbing in the right side of his head. He closed his eyes, but all he could see was the same scene...but in his imagination, it wasn't Mariella he was fucking on his desk, but the gray-eyed blond temptress in the black S.S. uniform, Alise.

He was wearing the same kind of black uniform, though highly decorated with medals. He was taking her in his preferred way, from behind while she leaned across his desk. Sometimes he would slap her until she was sore, or bang her head against his metal desktop, once leaving her with a bloody lip. She kept coming back for more, determined to have a supernormal child for the Reich. Kranzler himself liked the idea, and looked forward to each of their trysts, dazzled by her beauty, her willingness, and her tolerance for pain. He knew it was only because her paranormal touch enhanced the experience for him, but he enjoyed it.

Today, he didn't have much time to spare, so he was trying to finish fast.

"Dr. Wichtmann wants to breed your cousin with the Italian girl who sees the future," he was telling her.

"Niklaus?" Alise looked back at him, clearly offended. "You want to breed my cousin with a Sicilian peasant?"

"A supernormal." He wiped sweat from his face and kept sliding in and out of her.

"It would be a corruption of our noble German blood! He should be crossed with someone..." She gritted her teeth as he mounted her harder and faster. She was just barely tolerating it. "Vilja and Roza are clearly more Aryan. You could cross him with those two."

"Those two are not showing useful abilities in our tests," he told her. "Mia has a gift. The Party leaderships wants results, supernormal babies. I agree we should cross Niklaus with her."

"Save Niklaus for someone worthy of my family," Alise said. "Breed the American boy with the dirty Sicilian."

He grabbed a handful of her hair and pulled her head back toward him, and she shrieked. "Are you giving me orders?" he asked.

"I'm being insubordinate, sir. I should be punished."

"You should." He covered her mouth and nose with one hand, without warning, making her struggle for air while he came inside her. He didn't release her until he was finished. She lay on his desk, looking up at him.

He loved her, and he hated her for it. He could imagine keeping her prisoner in his own house, making her suffer every kind of pain imaginable. He couldn't get enough of the sweetly evil girl.

"Sebastian and Mia," he said. "I can get Dr. Wichtmann to agree to that."

"Good." She watched him pull his pants on. She dressed herself, now wearing the drab regulation cotton underwear he'd insisted she wear. She smoothed down her skirt, and they walked out the door to go back to work.

# Chapter Thirty-One

Jenny sat in her clear cell and watched the steel door to the outer lab open. Two guards in clear biohazard masks and black body armor entered, followed by two people in hazardous material suits with white crosses inside red circles to show they were medical. These two wheeled a large equipment cart between them. Another pair of guards followed. The four guards had their yellow and black TASER guns drawn, and they all watched Jenny.

One of the medical people in the hazmat suits approached the airlock doors into Jenny's cell and spoke into the console by the outer door. She was a female, middle-aged.

"Jennifer?" the woman asked.

"That's me."

"I'm Dr. Andrea Parker. I'm an OBG, and I'm here strictly to check on your baby."

Jenny didn't say anything. She wasn't sure how to take this situation, but obviously she couldn't trust anyone here.

"We would like to come into your cell and do an ultrasound," the doctor said. "Is that all right with you?"

"Do I have a choice?"

"I don't know why you would turn down prenatal care."

"Because I'm a prisoner here? Because the general is a psychopath? Believe me, I know him from way back," Jenny said.

The doctor looked around the cell where Jenny now lived. "Look, I don't fully know the situation, and I understand you don't want to be here. I also know a bit about your...unusual circumstances. For the sake of your baby, I strongly urge you to let me help you."

"Why would Kranzler care about my baby?" Jenny asked.

"Who?"

"Whatever his name is now. General Ward Kilpatrick. Is he trying to breed more of us again?"

"I...don't know what you're talking about. I was brought in to focus on you. I had to sign multiple confidentiality agreements under threat of God knows what. But your case does interest me."

"Where did you work before this?" Jenny asked.

"Yale University, most recently. And I move around the country, several research hospitals. I specialize in unborn children with severely ill mothers."

Jenny nodded. That sounded promising, but she still wasn't sold. "What did the general tell you? Why did he bring you here?"

"I told you why, Jennifer. To care for your baby. If that doesn't make sense to you, you'll have to discuss it with him. We've brought an ultrasound machine. Don't you want to make sure your pregnancy is progressing well? Don't you want to see your baby, and learn whether you're having a boy or a girl?"

Jenny didn't know what to think. In their last life, Kranzler had been obsessed with breeding those who had a supernatural touch, some kind of Nazi eugenics thing. In this life, maybe he was just curious about her pregnancy with her pox, and probably saw Jenny's baby as a future test subject for himself. She knew that the baby did need care, and she was dying to know whether the baby was well or not.

"Okay," Jenny said. "We'll do it. Just don't try to hurt me, or..."

"Lie back on your bed and don't move," one of the guards instructed. Jenny did as she was told. They would shackle her first thing. In the couple of weeks she'd been here, they'd started letting her wander around her cell, but if anyone came in, she had to submit to being chained down again.

The four guards passed through the outer door to her cell, then the inner door. They approached her cautiously, but she didn't give them any trouble as they cuffed her wrists and ankles. They stood aside as Dr. Parker entered, followed by the other man in the hazmat suit with the medical markings. Apparently he was some kind of technician, because he set up the equipment cart next to Jenny's bed.

"Just relax, Jennifer," the doctor said, smiling slightly behind her clear face shield. "I'll have to lift your hospital gown."

Jenny glanced at the four guards in black armor, all of them male. Dr. Parker followed her gaze, then said, "We need the four of you to look away."

"Sorry, doc," one of the men said, his voice coming from an electronic speaker on the front of his mask. "We have to keep our eyes on her anytime someone is in the cell. Specific orders."

Dr. Parker sighed, then moved to block their view with her own body.

"I'm sorry," she whispered to Jenny as she raised the hem of the gown up to Jenny's breasts, revealing her pale, swollen belly. She squirted some kind of shockingly cold gel onto Jenny's belly, and Jenny hissed a little. "The gel can feel a bit chilly," the doctor warned her, a few seconds too late.

"It does," Jenny said.

"This is the transducer." The doctor held up a plastic wand about the size of a flashlight, but flat and wide at the end. "This will take an ultrasound image of your baby, which we'll see here." She gestured toward a small monitor.

Jenny's heart raced, and the beeping heart monitor announced it to everyone. She was finally going to see her baby. For a moment, she almost forgot about being a prisoner.

The doctor pressed the transducer against Jenny's belly and moved it back and forth. Jenny watched, first excited, then frustrated as meaningless gray and black blobs filled the monitor, appearing and disappearing.

"I don't see anything," Jenny said.

"One second." The doctor moved the transducer again, then gestured at roundish blobs on the monitor. "You see? There's the head, the curve of the back..."

Jenny blinked. It was like an optical illusion—one moment, it was just shifting blots. The next, it was obviously a baby, the head curled inward toward the chest, legs tucked up toward the belly.

"Oh!" Jenny said. She bit down and forced herself not to cry, knowing her captors were watching. It was almost impossible, because the grainy image was ripping her heart open. Then it turned over, swimming like a little fish, and Jenny gasped again.

"Looks like she's awake," the doctor said.

"She? It's a girl?"

"That's right."

"Does she look...is she...healthy?"

"Head to body ratio is good, spine developing correctly...and there, can you see that?" The doctor pointed to a pulsing shape near the center of the baby-blob. "She's got a strong heartbeat."

"That's her heart?" Jenny asked. She heard her voice breaking and cursed herself. She had to keep up a tough shell and prevent Ward from seeing her feelings. The more love and concern she showed for her unborn child, the more control he would think he had over her. Better if everyone thought she was a monster.

"She looks good," the doctor said. "She's on the small end of the scale, but so are you."

Jenny fought the urge to tell the doctor everything—how she needed a C-section for the delivery, and she needed Seth standing right beside her. She told herself there would be time for that. If she started begging for things now, then Ward would have immediate leverage.

"When is this thing going to be out of me, anyway?" Jenny asked. "I'm sick of carrying it around already."

The doctor's eyes widened. "This thing? You mean the baby girl?"

"Whatever. I never wanted to get pregnant in the first place." Jenny scowled. "Now I'm stuck with this stupid baby. I hate it already. Can you do a quick abortion while you're here?"

The doctor gave her a look of loathing. "It's far too late! You only have eighteen weeks left. Expect to deliver at the end of May."

"That's going to take forever. Hey, can I get any painkillers out of this? Morphine, maybe? My feet and back are starting to hurt." Jenny winked. "Anything with opiates would be awesome."

The doctor just shook her head. "You need to keep yourself healthy. It's not the baby's fault that you didn't want her. You have to give her a fair start in life."

"Oh, sure. Just tell the general that I need to go for a long jog in the woods every day. And tell him to let me out of this place while you're at it. And bring me some fucking cigarettes and a bottle of vodka. Not the cheap stuff, either."

"You can't have any of that," the doctor said, backing away. "I don't know how you got here, Jennifer, but I'm starting to think that keeping you locked up might be the best thing for the baby. Let's go."

The technician wheeled the cart as he and the doctor left. When they were outside the airlock, the four guards unlocked Jenny's cuffs and backed out, one by one, their stun guns pointed at her.

Everything was wrong, Jenny thought. Seth should have been here, and they should have been at a normal doctor's office. She'd demanded to see him every day, and had been denied, but now she really needed him. She lay on her bed and clutched a pillow.

They were at the same base as last time, with the same general in charge, but now they were caged and monitored with modern technology. It would be hard to escape.

Only one thing was better: Ashleigh was dead, and so there was no love-charmer, no version of Alise here to play tricks on her. If anyone played mind games this time, it would be Jenny.

* * *

Juliana stood in the lab, looking down at the man with the torture scars strapped to the hospital gurney.

"Are you sure it's okay?" she asked Alise, the only other person in the lab. Kranzler and the scientists would be watching from the dark windows above, but Jenny wasn't thinking about them at all. She could only think of Alise, beautiful Alise, and doing whatever would please her.

"Everything's fine." Alise smiled and, happily, breathed out another cloud of pink spores, which felt delicious on Juliana's arms and neck. Alise had greeted Juliana with a dose of it that morning and walked her to the lab, and Juliana had been craving more. She wished she could touch Alise—she could only imagine what it would be like in the girl's arms, her touch full of warmth and love.

"You should send him to Sebastian when I'm done," Juliana said, dazed. "Sebastian can heal him."

"I'll take care of it." Alise winked. "Go ahead. It'll be good, I promise. I love you, Juliana. I wouldn't make you do anything wicked."

"I love you, too, Alise," Juliana confessed. Then she reached out her hands and placed them on the man on the table—who was, as Alise had pointed out, a convicted criminal who had hurt people.

The man howled as dark blisters and sores ruptured all over his body, radiating out from where her hands touched his bare shoulders. The man went into convulsions, gagging out pink foamy saliva while his tongue swelled and bled.

In less than a minute, it was all over, the man lying still and leaking dark blood from dozens of lesions, his head misshapen.

"You have to get Sebastian now," Juliana whispered to Alise. "Like you promised."

"I told you, I'll take care of everything," Alise said. "Come on, let's get out of the way. I have some catalogs if you feel like shopping!" Alise blew another cloud of pink spores at her, and Juliana shivered in delight.

"Anything you want to do is fine with me." Juliana beamed at her while they left the lab. She was already forgetting all about the dead man on the table behind them.

The next morning, an hour before sunrise, Juliana woke in her bed shaking and drenched in freezing sweat. Alise's spell had worn off, and she understood that she'd killed a man in cold blood. Alise had thoroughly enchanted her with her dangerous power, the one that made people mindlessly obedient to her.

Juliana sobbed as the full impact of what she'd done slammed into her. She'd spent her life avoiding everyone as much as possible, trying to keep the demon plague trapped inside her while it was eager to flow out and infect others. She'd never killed anyone when it wasn't self-defense...except for her mother at birth. Now she'd taken another innocent life, and she could never undo it. The idea that the scientists would have brought Sebastian in after her was a lie—they wanted to study the dead man to understand her powers, and healing him immediately would have made the entire test pointless.

Juliana clutched her pillow tight. She looked across the dim room at Mia, sleeping soundly. How could she ever face her friend again? How could she ever face anyone again? Juliana felt she deserved to die for what she'd done.

She'd wanted to leave before Alise had ensorceled her—now she would insist on it. She promised herself she would never fall under

Alise's spell again.

# Chapter Thirty-Two

A guard appeared at the narrow window in the steel door to Seth's cell. "You have a visitor," the man's voice said over the intercom. "She's eager to see you."

Seth stood up and started for the door, but the guard ordered him to sit back down. Seth returned to the edge of his bed. It had been a long, slow day, broken only by the arrival of breakfast (toast and canned pineapple) and lunch (toast and beans). The guards slid his food trays through a very narrow panel at the bottom of the door, shoving it deep inside his cell with something like a broomstick. Seth always had to catch his tray before it hit the wall and spilled all over his floor.

The days were otherwise extremely long and slow—he kept refusing to cooperate with the secretive government agency that had captured them, and in return he had nothing to read, no television, nothing to do except sit in his cell and wait for nothing to happen. His only diversion was looking through all of his new past-life memories, learning about times he'd lived in nineteenth-century London, in the Italian Renaissance, the Middle Ages. He'd often been cast as a kind of sorcerer or witch doctor. He'd also spent a number of lives as a nearly invincible warrior, leading armies into conquest, quickly recovering from countless arrow and sword wounds, which his men naturally saw as a sign of divine favor, spurring them on to fight harder.

Seth and Jenny had both resolved to never to be used as weapons again.

Now, he waited anxiously as the door slowly opened, hoping that they'd sent Jenny to see him for some reason. He was disappointed when Mariella entered instead, and the guard slammed the door behind her.

"Seth!" Mariella ran toward him, and he stood and awkwardly accepted her hug as she pressed herself against him.

"Have you seen Jenny?" Seth asked.

"No...they wouldn't let me see her." She looked up at him. "But I've been doing their tests, and they're happy enough that I could ask for one privilege. I told them I wanted to see you."

"You did?"

"Of course. I needed to see you....I needed a friend. And you always make feel so safe." She looked up at him and brushed her fingers through his hair. "Aren't you happy to see me?"

"I'm glad you're okay. I just wish I knew what they were doing with Jenny."

"I'm sure Jenny's fine."

"How can you know that?"

"We're fine, aren't we?" Mariella smiled and touched his cheek. "They haven't hurt us, so I don't think they'd hurt her, either. If they wanted us dead, they wouldn't have bothered bringing us all this way."

"And I wish I knew how the baby was doing," Seth said. He'd worried constantly about Jenny losing this one, just as she'd lost all of them in past lives. He knew it was useless to hope, but he hoped more than anything else for a better outcome this time. He needed the baby to live—he could not imagine what life would be like if they lost it.

"You're under a lot of strain," Mariella said softly, tracing her finger down his cheek to the corner of his lip. "So am I. That's why I begged them to let me see you. I need you, Seth." She rose up on her toes and tried to kiss him, but Seth dodged it.

"What are you doing?" he asked, stepping back from her until his legs bumped against his bed. She moved closer, cornering him.

"I think you know." Mariella wrapped her hands behind his neck and kissed him along the cheek. "Play along, they're watching," she whispered. Her fingers drifted down along his muscular stomach, brushing the front of his orange prisoner jumpsuit.

"What are you doing?" he asked.

"Pretend to cooperate," Mariella whispered. "It's our best chance to find a way out."

"I won't even think about working with them until I'm with Jenny again." Seth looked up at the black dome in the ceiling. "Tell them that."

"Cooperating is the smart choice," Mariella told him, not bothering to whisper now. "If you don't work with them, you'll never get out of here."

"I wouldn't bet on it," Seth said. "Tell them I have to see Jenny, or I'll make sure everyone suffers. Especially Ward."

Mariella pulled back from him, looking angry.

"You're making the wrong choice," she told him.

"How can you be so sure you're making the right one?" Seth asked.

"Just remember I tried to help you." Mariella glanced at the black camera dome as she left. "I did my part. I can't be responsible for what happens to you if you don't listen to me."

"I'll remember," Seth said. "I'll remember you turned on us the first chance you got."

She had a hurt look in her eyes as she knocked on the door for the guards to let her out.

"You don't understand anything, Seth," she said.

"I understand enough," he replied. When she was out the door, he let out the breath he'd been holding.

He was glad Mariella had left so quickly, because her visit had stirred up too much of what had happened in the past and the confused feelings he still had for her. Mariella would be remembering those things, too, if she'd recovered her past-life memories like Seth.

* * *

Niklaus knocked as he pushed open the door to Sebastian's room. The young S.S. officer with the cold gray eyes looked without comment on the issue of *Amazing Stories* that Sebastian was re-reading for the tenth time. No more American pulp fiction could be brought to the base, under the irritating new guidelines that allowed only "fine German culture," such as films of Adolf Hitler addressing huge crowds, which Sebastian hadn't learned enough German to understand. Sebastian could so far only understand some common, simple words and phrases.

"Pack your bag," Niklaus said in German. "You're moving rooms."

"Why?"

"Orders," Niklaus replied. "Move now."

"Where am I going?" Sebastian asked, standing up.

"Other room."

"That's very helpful, thank you." Sebastian packed his clothes and meager belongings into the suitcase he'd bought with Barrett's money in Charleston. It matched Juliana's, because she'd picked them out.

Niklaus took him past the double doors to the female dormitory hall, then unlocked a third pair of double doors. Sebastian had never seen them open before.

"What's in there?" Sebastian asked.

"Other room," Niklaus said again.

The mysterious third hallway had fewer rooms, just three doors on each side. Niklaus took him into the first door, into a room much larger than Sebastian's previous dorm room. It was also carpeted, furnished with a fireplace, a dining table, a sofa and ottoman, and hung with paintings. Candles burned in sconces along the wall, and soft chamber music played on a phonograph. It was, Sebastian, could not deny, a much nicer room.

The bed was queen-sized and hung with curtains. Mia and Alise sat on the bed, holding hands and smiling at him.

"Sebastian!" Alise hopped to her feet, and Mia followed, still grasping her hand. "Do you like it? I decorated it myself."

"It's nice," Sebastian said. "Why am I here?"

"Because you've been so good," Alise said. "Everyone is pleased with what you've shown them in the lab. I know I'm impressed! They say you have real power in your hands." She giggled, looking him over.

"I'm glad they're glad," Sebastian said. "But I still don't understand."

"Then let me explain." Alise held onto Mia with one hand, and with the other, she took Sebastian's hand. "You see, when you're good, you get rewarded. You've both been *very* good, going along with all these pesky tests without complaining. So you both deserve a little fun."

Sebastian's body filled with a hot, tingling glow. Mia filled his mind, her smoldering dark hair, her sea-green eyes, every curve of her body perfect. He could only think of his aching need to touch her, so strong that his toes actually curled inside his socks.

"Don't you each see something you want?" Alise pulled them closer together, then circled them, counterclockwise, wrapping their arms around each other as their eyes shared a hungry gaze. "Could you ever want anyone more than you want each other?" she whispered.

Sebastian and Mia pulled closer together, until they could feel each other's bodies through their clothes. Alise touched the backs of their heads and pressed them together until they kissed.

"Love each other," Alise whispered.

## Chapter Thirty-Three

"Eight of diamonds," Mariella said.

She sat at a table in one of the big concrete laboratories, next to a divider wall. A small hole in the wall allowed her to hold hands with the person on the other side. At the moment, that was a nineteen-year-old African-American girl. Like most of the subjects ASTRIA trucked in for this kind of testing, she was an Army soldier recently out of basic training. Mariella couldn't see her, but she knew the girl was sitting in front of a deck of cards, slowly turning them over one at a time. Mariella had to predict the next card before the girl turned it.

A few men and women in white coats watched her from across the room, while Ward watched from the window above.

"Correct," a lab assistant said, and she couldn't help smiling a little. Numbers and letters were difficult to see in her visions of the future, but she always saw things more clearly the nearer they were in time. Over weeks of testing, she'd shown a ninety-one percent success rate at seeing the cards, if the other subject was female, and an eighty-seven percent success rate if she was holding hands with a male soldier instead. Interestingly, and embarrassingly, her rate of accurate predictions dropped to seventy-four percent when she was physically attracted to the soldier in question, as revealed by all her intimate heart, breathing, and brainwave data, which everyone in the room could see on the monitors.

"Ten of clubs," she said.

"Correct."

"Jack of spades."

"Correct."

"Three of hearts."

"Correct..."

When the day's tests were finally done, Mariella was met outside the lab by a pair of guards in body armor. Instead of escorting her back to her own residential area, though, they took her up to the administrative level and right to Ward's office. He didn't rise, only stared at her with his feral green eyes as she walked in.

"Did you want to see me, General Kilpatrick?" she asked Ward.

"How did it go with Seth?" he asked, though he certainly knew.

"Not good. It's going to take more time."

"You were supposed to win him over," Ward said.

"In one try?" she asked.

"He's young and stupid. You assured me it would not be a problem."

"General Kilpatrick, sir, it's nothing to seduce a man...but taking his heart requires time. His girlfriend is pregnant. His feelings can't be changed in a day."

"In this line of work, we only care about results," Ward told her. "We don't care how you get them. Try harder."

"I will, sir."

Mariella left, feeling frustrated. She understood why Seth wouldn't want to cooperate with Ward, but it was their only real choice for now. They weren't going to get anywhere if they stayed caged up in the cellblock. Why couldn't he see it? Why couldn't he at least pretend to play along? Stubborn, stupid boy.

She told herself that her real frustration didn't come from the part of her that hoped to touch him again, the part of her that wanted to put her own feelings ahead of Jenny's. She didn't want to acknowledge any of those feelings, but they kept troubling her anyway.

* * *

Mia couldn't stop kissing Sebastian, and kissing wasn't going to be enough to satisfy her. She grabbed at his shirt and tried to push it up, then grew frustrated and ripped it open instead, little buttons raining down on the carpet at her feet. Her hands went to his bare chest and down his stomach. His skin was radiant, like gold...the entire world seemed washed in a golden fog, and all she could think about was the hungry desire that threatened to consume her if she didn't get even closer to him, feeling his healing touch all over his skin.

His warm hands slid up the backs of her thighs, raising her dress. He lifted it up to her waist, and she eagerly held up her arms so he could take it all the way off. She reached her arms behind herself and unlatched the heavy brass hook on her bra, which was stiff and starched and concealed half her torso.

"Enjoy each other," Alise said, her voice like a distant echo that barely registered in Mia's brain. Mia had entirely forgotten that Alise and Niklaus were still there. Mia paid them no attention as they looked at each other and laughed, and she didn't think of them again after they left and closed the door. Her need for Sebastian filled her body and mind.

She giggled as he threw on her the bed and then lay down beside her. She lost all sense of time as they kissed, her hands exploring the taut muscles of his body while his fingers moved up her stomach, pulled her loosened bra aside, and touched her hard, swollen nipples.

Her hands found their way to the front of his trousers and pulled until they broke open.  She reached inside, taking his hard length in her hand.

He made a kind of growling sound and rolled her on her back, and she hurried to take off her underwear.  When he lay between her legs, she put him inside of her.

*Every* part of him felt good, radiating his healing power.  She felt like a miniature sun had flared to life between her hips, scorching her from the inside.

She whispered again and again that she loved him, she loved him, she loved him...

# Chapter Thirty-Four

Tommy looked over the two rows of eight soldiers each, more of the kids just out of basic training, standing ramrod-straight in their fatigues, their faces blank. Their last order had been to stand at attention, and then the officers and scientists had all left the room, sealing them in with Tommy.

"So, what are you guys afraid of?" Tommy asked. None of them replied, and he smirked. "Going to war? Getting your arm or your head blown off, maybe? What about your families back home? Your parents? Do you worry about horrible things happening to them? Nobody's talking."

"They won't reply unless ordered to," Ward said over the speaker. He watched from the window above, not bothering to dim the lights to make the window look black and empty.

"That's no fun," Tommy said. "Let's liven things up. Ready?"

"Go ahead, Tommy," Ward instructed.

Tommy took a deep breath, remembering what he'd done in Charleston the night he'd caused the riot. His power had been charged up by contact with his opposite, Ashleigh, but she'd been dead for quite awhile now. He didn't exactly miss her, though he'd learned a lot from her.

The fear wouldn't be as strong today, without Ashleigh around, but he only had sixteen people to panic this time, not hundreds or thousands. He'd had an extra-large breakfast to prepare for this, and he knew he'd be starving again afterward.

Tommy summoned the fear, a chaotic blood-red energy that teemed with incoherent voices, whispers and screams that brought flickers of his childhood and his abuse at the hands of Mr. Tanner. He imagined himself charging up like a battery, until the fear was like a thrashing hurricane inside him.

He exhaled, and a storm of bloody droplets blew out of him, raining down on the soldiers and absorbing into their skin. They flinched but remained at attention. He smiled and crossed his arms, waiting.

It didn't take long. First a couple of them began to shudder, and then one screamed, and then hell broke loose. The soldiers scattered, some of them hiding under tables and chairs, some tucking themselves into corners, three of them falling to the floor and curling up right in the center of the lab. They were crying, howling, shrieking, swatting and kicking at invisible attackers that existed only in their minds, babbling mindlessly at scenes of unknown horror visible only to them.

Tommy looked up at the window and grinned. In a few seconds, he'd turned the lab into the rec room at a state mental hospital, soldiers howling and hiding, a couple of them fighting each other. In the window, Ward beamed, while the officer who'd brought in the young soldiers was livid to see how quickly Tommy had scattered them.

"I'd say the enemy ranks are broken, sir," Tommy said to him. "Who's up for a couple of beers?"

The other officer stalked away, while Ward nodded and gave Tommy a thumbs-up.

After the test, a guard escorted Tommy back to his dorm area, standard procedure for all paranormals.

Tommy hadn't told anyone, but each time he used his power in the lab, it kicked up the sick, disoriented feeling that this entire place evoked in him, sometimes making him see ghosts or hallucinations. He locked himself in his room and opened a can of Warsteiner. He guzzled the warm beer, hoping it might settle his stomach.

He heard the creaking sound of his door opening behind him. He turned to see Ashleigh there, dressed in a long black skirt and jacket, with a black tie and a crisp white shirt. His room had shifted to a drab olive color, too. It was his recurring dream, the bizarre one where he wore a swastika and answered to the name *Niklaus*. The hallucinations were back. Fortunately, he held a beer in the dream, too, though the can had a much plainer label and was the kind that had to be punctured with a bottle opener. He took a drink as Ashleigh's gray eyes looked him over. Her name was *Alise*, but she had Ashleigh's eyes, Ashleigh's golden hair, Ashleigh's large breasts...

Alise closed the door as she entered the room.

"What do you want me to do now?" Niklaus asked.

"Must I only come to talk about work and give you instructions?" She stood very close to him. She took the beer from his hand and drank, her eyes never leaving his. "Can I not simply visit my own beloved cousin?"

"Your visits usually involve giving many instructions." He took the beer back from her. "It's been that way since we were kids."

Alise laughed. She draped her hands loosely on his shoulders, gazing up at him. "You've always been there for me."

"Whether I wanted to be or not," he said, and she laughed again. Niklaus, because of his own power, was somehow immune to Alise's enchanting touch. She'd learned this early in life, and always worked to control him in other ways. He found her intimidating. He had other, even more shameful feelings about his older cousin, which he tried to keep secret, but which she occasionally seemed to encourage. Even now, she was caressing his cheek and looking up at him, with something almost like vulnerability in her eyes.

"I would be alone in the world without you," Alise whispered. She rose up on her toes and kissed him, soft and slow, on the lips. She had pecked him there once or twice in his life, playfully, just enough to fuel his own guilty adolescent fantasies. This was different. Her mouth lingered on his and her hand pressed against his heart, hidden beneath his black uniform.

The kiss summoned every kind of feeling—desire, revulsion, self-loathing. He couldn't imagine what his family would think if they knew. He also couldn't resist from grabbing her and pulling her close.

"We must stop," he whispered, breaking their kiss.

"Why?" She looked up at him innocently. "Have you never imagined this, Niklaus? When we swam at the pond on my father's estate, did you never once look at me? Or the time you watched me in the bath...did you think I didn't know?"

"That was long ago."

"Not so long." She kissed him again, then took off her black jacket. "We shouldn't fight our feelings any longer, Niklaus. Life is far too short not to indulge ourselves." She unbuttoned her long skirt and slid it to the ground. She wore scarlet panties underneath, more suitable to a prostitute than a young German noblewoman.

"We can't." His voice was hoarse.

"We can do anything we like. Don't tell me you want me to stop." She opened his pants and brought him out, massaging him as he grew long and stiff in her fingers. She giggled. "Oh, Niklaus, it's so much bigger than last time I peeked at it."

"Stop," he whispered, torn by his desire for the forbidden.

"No." She pushed him until he sat down on the bed, then sank to her knees on the floor. She brushed the head of his cock with her lips, then sucked him lightly, teasing him.

"Please." He squirmed on the bed. "We can't..."

"We must." She stood up, wearing no underwear at all now, her triangle of dark golden curls only inches from his face. He licked his lips as she loosened her tie and tugged it to one side, then slowly unbuttoned her shirt, revealing her full breasts, held up by a matching scarlet brassiere. The idea that she had dressed this way before coming to see him, her mind already made up, only increased his appetite for her.

"You can touch it." Alise took his hand and lay it between her legs. He touched her in awe, then tried to put a finger inside her, but she was far too dry. She moved his fingertip higher and stroked it back and forth. "Here. This way."

He kept rubbing her, and he felt like he was watching from a distance, unable to believe his darkest fantasy was unfolding around him. She pushed his finger back and forth until she was trembling and damp, then she slapped his hand aside and slung a leg over him, straddling his lap.

"We should be careful," he whispered.

"Careful is for the old."

Niklaus thought he might die of pleasure when she took him in her hand again, then slipped him inside her. She grunted as she worked her way down his length, rocking her hips back and forth, which nearly drove him out of his mind.

"Our family...you don't want to get...pregnant..." he gasped.

She shoved him back on the bed, pinning his hands above his head. "Why not? It would be pure noble blood, pure German blood, with both our powers..." She ground herself against his pelvic bone while her face flushed and her eyes closed. "...would be a super-Aryan...a god...a new *Fuehrer* for the future Reich..." She rode him faster, gritting her teeth, and she shouted at him to hurry up and finish.

# Chapter Thirty-Five

Jenny woke to see activity outside the clear wall of her cell. Men moved furniture and cardboard boxes into the big concrete laboratory outside, while others watched Jenny with their TASER weapons drawn, even though she was trapped in her cell with both airlock doors sealed.

She kept her face blank—a stoic approach was the best way to deal with the seer, she thought, whether his name happened to be Helmut Kranzler or Ward Kilpatrick. She refused to complain or act upset by anything he did, because then she was giving him power over her. Her bathroom nook had clear walls like the rest of her cell, giving her no privacy. She'd first avoided showering altogether, then broken down and done a quick few minutes each week. Now she forced herself to do it every night, after most of the staff had gone to bed, and act like she didn't care about the cameras or the dark observation windows above. Let them stare at her big pregnant ass if they wanted. She wanted them to know that nothing they could do would bother her.

Jenny heaved herself out of bed, which was becoming more of an effort every day, now that she was six months into her pregnancy. She eased her weight onto her feet. The baby awoke with her, swimming and kicking inside her. Jenny winced each time she felt the tiny girl kick—not out of pain, but out of fear that the baby would somehow kick loose the pox and get herself killed. The amniotic membrane protected the baby before birth—Jenny knew because, at times, she herself had been born wrapped in a caul, and those mothers had not died from giving birth to her.

"I hope we didn't disturb you, Jennifer," Ward said. His smile was predatory as he emerged from where he'd been skulking, somewhere behind her bed and out of her line of sight.

She noticed that her breakfast tray had not yet been delivered, which meant no coffee. She needed a cup, but wasn't going to ask for one.

"You've been disturbing me since we met," Jenny replied.

"Aren't you curious what we're building here? It's quite a little project."

"I'm sure I'll find out eventually," Jenny said. "Then I'll get bored with it. So let's just stretch out the mystery for now."

"You should know, Jenny, that you're the last to resist," he said.

"What are you talking about?"

"Everyone else has seen the wisdom of cooperating with us. Tommy, Esmeralda, Mariella...even Seth."

"Yay for Seth," Jenny said. She assumed Ward was lying.

"You don't believe me? He did it for *her*, Jennifer. For pretty little Mariella. They've grown very close these last couple of months."

Jenny tried to show him nothing. She didn't want to think about Mariella's prediction, that she and Seth would ultimately be together, how Seth was destined to be the love of Mariella's life, that the sex would be amazing, and all that bullshit Mariella had chattered freely about before realizing Jenny and Seth were together. Now Jenny was isolated from everyone, while Seth and the girl were off doing God knew what together...according to *Ward*, Jenny reminded herself. Jenny would have to lie here alone, feeling her and Seth's doomed daughter splashing inside her womb, until the inevitable happened.

Maybe it was destiny. Maybe Jenny needed to be sealed off from the world, unable to hurt anyone. Maybe she didn't deserve a happy life, or love. She was a monster, and would always be a monster, and not even death could save her from it. She came back, and back, and back.

"Does anything look familiar yet?" Ward asked, walking out to where the furniture had been arranged. It looked like they'd built a small bedroom right in front of her cell...*her* bedroom, she realized. Her own bed, with her own patchwork childhood blanket. Her own bookshelf, her posters on temporary walls made of cork. Her own laundry scattered right on the floor, as if they wanted it identical to the day she'd left it. She realized that it had been at least a year and a half since then, and she was suddenly sick with worry about her father. She'd had no way of getting news from him at all. Clearly, Ward or his people had been to her house.

"We thought you'd feel more at home this way," Ward said.

"Did you see my father?" Jenny asked.

"Oh, yes. Pathetic little man. He probably survived our visit, but I can't say I followed up to check." Ward smiled at her through the thick, clear wall. "Now, our special treat, just for you..."

Two men set up a very tall, very wide projection screen at the far end of Jenny's reconstructed bedroom. All the lights in the lab dimmed. Images appeared on the giant screen, pictures of Jenny's victims, kids from school, old people from church...their faces contorted, twisted, ripped apart by deadly infection.

"This is what you are, Jenny," Ward said. "You are a killer. You'll never change that. Your nature is to bring death to others. It's your responsibility, your obligation, that you use it to kill the *right* people, and not the innocent..."

Jenny pressed her lips together and said nothing, but she couldn't stop her flesh from turning bleach-white. Inside, she was in turmoil, sick and angry, full of hate for Ward and for herself.

A picture of her mother appeared, the one that had hung on her wall all her life, and she almost cried out in pain. She had killed her mother. She would kill her baby.

"No mercy. That's what I respect about you, Jennifer," Ward said, as more pictures of the infected from Fallen Oak took their turns appearing on the screen. "You'll kill anyone who gets in your way. And there's a place for that, there's a use for that, don't you understand? That's all I'm trying to show you. Just accept what you are and why you need to work with us. Stop fighting, Jenny. We should all be on the same team."

Jenny looked from Ward to the grisly images of those she'd killed.

"I don't do teams, Kranzler," she said. "I've been on too many."

She expected him to ignore the word Kranzler like he always did, but this time he pounced on it.

"Kranzler, Kranzler," he said. "It's interesting, Jenny, that you call me Kranzler. I called a friend in Moscow who has access to a certain deep archive of captured Nazi documents. He found a few details about this place. There was a Nazi general—a *Gruppenführer*, was the S.S. term—in charge of this base when it was originally built. Can you guess his name?"

"Do I have to?" Jenny asked.

"Helmut Kranzler. The name you keep calling me."

"What else came up in these files?"

"First, explain yourself. Why call me that name?"

Jenny shrugged. "You already know. You were Kranzler. You brought us all here before, believing we were some kind of highly evolved humans. It was a Nazi eugenics program."

"A Nazi?" Ward snorted. "You're calling me a Nazi?"

"Exactly. And here we are again, doing it all again."

"How did it end last time?"

"The only way it could have." Jenny gave him a thin smile. "Perhaps those old files will tell you. They should. You wrote them yourself."

Ward looked her over, but he fell silent, and she knew he couldn't figure out how to proceed. "Enjoy your entertainment," he finally said as he walked away.

The lights in the lab turned all the way out, leaving her in darkness except for the glowing images on the screen. Ashleigh's parents, Neesha Bailey, Mayor Winder and Cassie. Screams sounded over the intercom, startling her. They went on and on, like some kind of sound effects CD for a haunted house, accompanying the scenes of agonizing death that kept playing in front of her.

She sat down and closed her eyes, but it was impossible to scrub away the pictures, or to block out the shrill screams. Ward wasn't going to break her down this way, she told herself. He didn't know even a fraction of what she'd done—the plagues she'd inflicted on Athens and other ancient cities, the horrors she'd performed for evil monarchs in the age of the Black Death...

Strangely, the one to which her mind kept straying was only a single man, lashed to a hospital gurney, whom she'd killed in cold blood because the love-charmer had told her to. It was hard to believe that she'd once been enthralled to Ashleigh, worshiping her as she'd seen so many sycophants do in so many lives...though the charmer's name hadn't been Ashleigh then, it had been Alise.

\* \* \*

Juliana had been up all morning, practicing for the moment when Alise would walk through her door. Her roommate Mia was gone, had been gone all night without warning. Juliana didn't know whether Mia had escaped or something terrible had happened to her. Alise would be the person to ask, but if Mia had run away, Juliana wasn't going to be the one to point it out. Juliana would want her friend to have plenty of time before anyone starting searching for her.

Alise finally entered, all smiles as usual, as if she hadn't just forced Juliana to murder a man the day before.

"Good morning!" Alise said, her gray eyes full of cheer. "I thought we could go to breakfast together. And good news! *Gruppenführer* Kranzler says he wants me to spend the day with you. Lots of tests for you to do!"

"No more people," Juliana said. "No more animals, either. I'm not killing anyone else."

"Juliana." Alise tsked her tongue. "We've already talked about this. Let's not start over. Here, I know just what you'll need to feel better." She took a deep breath.

"No! Don't you ever use your power against me. You're not going to trick me again, Alise."

"It's not a trick," Alise said. "It's something to make you happy, a sign of my deep love for you...and, I hope, the love you feel for me, too..."

"It's false love. That's your power."

"How can love be false if it feels true?" Alise began to blow out the pink dandelion-petal drops of power that would fill Juliana with love and affection for her.

"Stop it!" Juliana backed away from her, but Alise only blew out a thicker cloud, moving closer with a wicked smile.

"You love me!" Alise insisted.

Juliana fought back the only way she could. She took a deep breath, then exhaled the demon plague, as she'd been practicing.

She'd reasoned that if Alise could send her power across through the air, then she might be able to do the same.

The plague blew out of her like a swarm of tiny black flies, dark spores that spread out as they traveled, swelling up to fill the room. They engulfed the pink spores Alise had blown out, successfully blocking them as she'd intended, but they traveled on, landing like dark cinders on Alise's face, neck, and hands.

Alise screamed and staggered back as tiny lesions stippled her flesh, oozing black and blood. She slammed the door as she ran out of the room, and she screamed all the way down the hall.

Juliana panicked—she hadn't meant to unleash so much, and she was lucky she hadn't killed Alise. The cloud of spores spun in the room around her. She wondered if she could take them back in when she was done, so they wouldn't accidentally harm anyone. She took a deep breath, and the entire cloud flowed back inside of her, like thousands of tiny flies returning to nest in the cells of her body.

Alise returned in less than a minute with a gang of six armed S.S. guards, all of them wearing gloves, their faces hidden behind bug-eyed gas masks. They seized Juliana, bound her hands in front of her, and gagged her before hauling her out of her room.

As they carried her down the hall, and then through a locked door and down two flights of steps, Alise stalked behind them, shouting at Juliana in English to make sure she understood. Alise's face was pockmarked with little dark boils where the demon plague had touched her.

"Do you know what you've done?" Alise screamed. "Do you know who I am? Who my father is? Do you know how often I've stood in the crowd, helping to fill everyone with the proper love of the Fuehrer while he spoke? Do you know how the Party has grown since my father sent me to Berlin? Do you know about the private gatherings I had, inviting Party officials to breed with the finest stock from the League of German Girls? They all know who I am. I am everything here, and you are nothing!"

The guards laid Juliana on the floor of a concrete cell with a narrow cot. She didn't struggle, and they removed her bonds before backing away and slamming the thick wooden door. Alise's hideously infected face looked in at her through the small, barred window set into the door.

"You will never come near me again," Alise said. "Consider this your maternity ward. Congratulations, whore, you're pregnant." She slammed the panel outside the window, leaving Juliana in darkness.

Juliana worked the gag out of her mouth and ran to the closed window.

"What?" she shouted. "What did you say?"

She heard the distant sound of Alise cackling as she departed down the hall.

# Chapter Thirty-Six

Esmeralda remained silent as the guards led her back to her concrete cell and closed the door. She'd gained a few small privileges through her cooperation, such as a larger cell with a refrigerator, a television set and books to read, but she was still a prisoner.

They had her studying more and more bodies, most of them from the Middle East or Afghanistan. Some were members of violent factions in their own countries, while others seemed to be cases of mistaken identity or bad information. All of them had lived lives full of misery, poverty, and violence, amid bombs and gunfire. Experiencing so many brutal lives rattled Esmeralda, wearing her down day after day.

She was truly beginning to believe Ashleigh had been right about something: they reincarnated, often in groups, drawn to each other life after life, bound by love and hate. She'd continued having flashes of another life since arriving here, and she was beginning to accept that it must have happened, they must have all been here before. If that weren't true, then she was losing her mind.

Esmeralda sat on her bed with her legs folded and concentrated. If she had been here before, she was going to learn all she could about it. She was determined to escape, but so far, she didn't have any idea how it would be possible. From the past, she could at least learn about the layout of the complex, though things might have changed considerably. The place had clearly been reconstructed since then. She might also learn why they'd been drawn back into the same situation again, and how to stop it for good.

\* \* \*

"On your feet, you're moving," Alise announced as she walked into Evelina's room. The room had two beds, but no one was assigned to bunk with the Slavic girl who claimed to speak with the spirits of the dead.

"Where?" Evelina asked as she put on her shoes.

"Downstairs." Alise smirked. She was wearing an unusually heavy amount of makeup today, as if covering up acne.

"Again? What did I do this time? Why am I being punished?"

"You can probably think of a reason," Alise said.

Evelina gaped and shook her head. "No, I've done everything Kranzler and Wichtmann have wanted..."

"You're not being punished," Niklaus said, in a rare display of his power of speech. His voice was surprisingly soft. "Party officials are coming to tour the facility soon."

"What does that have to do with me?" Evelina asked.

"Nobody wants to try and explain why there's a racially inferior Slav mixed in with our program," Alise said. "We're supposed to be at the high end of eugenics, the front edge of human evolution. Which means no Slavs."

"This isn't fair!"

"If my cousin hadn't opened his clumsy mouth, you wouldn't be so upset," Alise said. "Now, come along with us. We have other things to do today."

Niklaus and Alise escorted her down two long flights of steps and through a thick door Niklaus had to open with a key and lock again behind them. He unlocked another corridor lined with dim concrete cells visible through narrow barred windows in the doors. Through one of these, Evelina glimpsed Juliana, the American girl with the plague touch. She wondered why they'd moved her down here. Alise scowled when she saw Juliana's window panel open, and she slammed and latched it.

"Here's your new room." Alise smiled as Niklaus pulled open the heavy door to one of the raw concrete cells.

"If they didn't want Bosnians, why did they bring me here at all?" Evelina asked. "I didn't want to come. Why couldn't they just leave me alone?"

"Priorities change," Alise said. "All we can do is follow orders. That's how a civilized society works. In you go, or I'll have my cousin throw you in there and fill your head with dreadful nightmares." She never stopped smiling.

Evelina looked to Niklaus, whose light gray eyes were fixed on her. For some reason, he gave her a small, sad-looking smile, which she found creepier than any violent threat. He closed the cell door behind her, but kept gazing at her through the barred window.

"I'm sorry," he whispered. "Do you need anything?"

"Don't ask her if she *needs* anything, Niklaus!" Alise snorted. "You're not the concierge. Let's go."

His eyes lingered on her a moment longer before Alise called him away. Evelina sat on the cot, trembling, and listened to them walk away. None of it made sense. She'd done nothing wrong.

"What happened?" an echoing voice asked behind her. Evelina jumped and turned, but no one was there. She whispered a prayer in a low voice. "Can you hear me?" the voice asked.

"What are you?" Evelina whispered.

"Juliana. In the next cell."

Evelina approached the ventilation grate low on the wall. "How long have you been here?"

"They just put me here. I don't think they're going to let me out."

"Because of the visitors coming to tour the base?" Evelina asked.

"No, I don't know about that. You know I have this...diseased touch. I learned how to breathe it out through the air. And I...sort of accidentally spat it into Alise's face. Covered her with disease, with dripping sores...it was awful."

"Is that why she wore such heavy makeup today?" Evelina asked. "She looked like a clown."

Juliana laughed through the vent, and then Evelina laughed with her, and she felt a little better.

# Chapter Thirty-Seven

Ward found himself in the small morgue near the underground facility's clinic. It was three in the morning, but he hadn't been able to sleep, so he'd gotten up and paced through the silent, dim hallways, letting his feet take him where they would.

He thought most of the project was moving ahead fairly well. He was lucky to have Mariella so cheerfully on his side, though he remained cautious about trusting her. He still believed she would gain Seth's affection in time. Not only was she attractive, and European enough to seem exotic to Seth, but she was wealthy, her family worth even more than the Barretts. Rich people could smell it on each other, he thought. Jenny Morton had grown up in a shack in the woods. Ward believed that breaking the bond between Seth and Jenny was key to breaking their resistance. If Jenny felt isolated and alone, it would be easier to reprogram her mind as he needed. Already, Seth was starting to give in and cooperate with them in the lab.

Esmeralda was cooperating, but making no secret of her unhappiness at being here. She'd stay in the cellblock for now, until Ward sorted out a better means of controlling her. He was sure that would involve Tommy, who still seemed sincere in his loyalty, but Ward wanted to stage things just right.

Trying to focus on work couldn't distract his mind from the real reason he was awake and wandering—Kranzler. He'd become convinced that the dead Nazi officer was haunting him. Everywhere, but especially when he was alone, he could feel the ghost of Kranzler hovering close to him. He'd even had flashes of Kranzler's memories. Maybe that meant Kranzler was trying to possess him, take control of his former base, but Ward wasn't quite ready to call in the priests for an exorcism. Esmeralda could speak with the dead. Maybe he could present the situation to her, in a very limited fashion, and she could find out some things for him. He didn't have Kranzler's corpse handy, but she might sense the presence of the ghost, Ward thought.

He shivered, wondering why the hell he was down in the morgue. Most of the bodies here were for testing Esmeralda, people who'd been killed in war zones. Interrogating people after they were dead could prove useful, Ward thought, if only he could convince the intelligence bastards to send him the bodies of higher-level operators.

He heard Kranzler's voice, speaking in English, which was unusual. Kranzler usually spoke in German, but somehow Ward had no trouble understanding German when he was caught up in one of Ward's memories.

"Get out of here," Ward ordered the ghost. "Go away! In God's name!"

The voice of Kranzler only grew louder, and Ward found himself in another of the dead man's memories. He was accompanied by the gray-eyed girl called Alise, who'd been quite prominent in the other memories, and another man, tall and dark-eyed, dressed in a finely tailored suit that probably cost a year of Kranzler's pay.

The other man's name was Barrett, and he'd come with the visiting group of high Party officials from Berlin, an event for which Kranzler had been nervously preparing for weeks. The officials had brought a handful of foreign dignitaries, mostly wealthy and aristocratic types from Austria, France, or England, all of them bound by a common interest in eugenics. Barrett seemed extremely comfortable among such people—he wasn't the loutish self-made American that Kranzler might have expected.

Kranzler, Barrett, and Alise had broken away from the main event in the wooden-paneled officers' dining room, where Alise had given a talk about the National Socialist vision for improving humanity and breeding desirable traits, with a lofty vision for breeding supernormal

Aryans, the most evolved humans of all, as the future leaders and warriors of the Reich. Kranzler had followed this up with a shorter talk about the base's need for additional funding, and now their guests enjoyed wine and cigars. The sound of a Wagner record echoed through the underground corridors.

When Barrett had made his request, Kranzler had asked him to step outside the room, worried about how best to refuse this clearly well-connected guest without arousing conflict. He'd motioned for Alise to follow. Barrett had asked whether there was a morgue, and then insisted they go there.

"What I am about to show you is confidential," Barrett said. "It is for you only, Herr Kranzler."

"Alise is our human breeding specialist," Kranzler told him.

Barrett looked over the pretty German girl. "I can see why."

"I would like very much to stay, if you don't mind, sir." Alise touched Barrett's hand, and a powerful smile filled his face. His eyes seemed to grow even darker as he regarded her.

"Nothing could please me more," Barrett told her, and she laughed and leaned against him, as if utterly charmed by his presence. Kranzler knew the opposite was true, that she was the one casting her magic over him. An extremely useful girl, Alise.

"What does the morgue have to do with our breeding project?" Alise asked. "If you don't mind a simple country girl asking a simple question, Herr Barrett."

"Mr. Barrett has made a very specific request," Kranzler told her. "He wishes that we breed him with Juliana."

"I see..." Alise thought it over in a flash—Kranzler could see her mind working, looking at all the angles. They didn't want to displease, but there were obvious complications. Juliana was already pregnant with Sebastian's baby, for one. For another, Kranzler didn't like the idea of anyone interfering with their research, and he was sure Dr. Wichtmann would agree. "Sir, I hope you understand, but we are only crossing those with extreme supernormal traits, signs of evolutionary advance. We have scoured the world and found only a few. This is the main purpose of our entire project."

"I understand completely," Barrett said. "That's why we're here." He walked along the refrigerated cabinet, opening one steel door after another and sliding out the cadavers. He touched each body for a long moment before moving on to the next. "Have you heard of *vodou*,

General Kranzler? It's a form of sorcery brought from Africa by slaves. It flourishes in the West Indies and in parts of the American South."

Kranzler shook his head, wondering what Barrett was rambling about.

"A sorcerer, or *bokor*, can have the power to trap a dead man's soul in his body, and thereby reanimate the flesh. The *bokor* is the master of those he brings back to life." Barrett turned at the end of the morgue and walked back toward them, past the dozen bodies he'd left out on their rolling trays. "The dead that he commands are called *zonbi*." Barrett raised his hand, and every cadaver he'd touched sat up on their trays as if alive.

Kranzler jumped, and Alise took his hand, looking pale.

"The *zonbi* are slaves to the *bokor*," Barrett continued. The undead bodies twisted and rolled off their trays, some of them falling to the floor before gaining their feet. They shambled and lurched in a loose mob behind Barrett as he continued approaching Kranzler and Alise, letting out an occasional moan or a noise like a quiet sob. "I even traveled to Haiti to learn more, but the priests and sorcerers refused to speak to a white man about such things."

Barrett stopped in front of them, while the gang of *zonbi* trailed behind him, their dead eyes blank, mouths gaping, cold limbs moving stiffly.

"I was born with the power of *bokor*, the power to make *zonbi*," Barrett said. "Like Juliana and Sebastian, it transfers through touch. You understand now my long interest in human genetics and evolution, trying to understand my own power scientifically. My long support of the Human Evolution Congress."

Ward nodded. He was doing the same thing with this project, testing other humans with supernormal abilities as a way to understand his own. He watched the approaching *zonbi* mob warily, but they finally fell into a ragged line behind Barrett.

"Herr Barrett," Alise said, "You are clearly gifted with a large, impressive power. I'm sure we would love to test and experiment, to find out more..."

"I am not here as a lab rat," Barrett said. "I only want Juliana."

"There are more complications with that girl specifically," Kranzler told him. "No one can touch her without dying, except for Sebastian...as the man who recruited them for us, you must know this."

"She can touch me," Barrett said. "We've already discovered that."

"Truly?" Alise seemed particularly interested now. "A second person resistant to her plague? She never told us."

"You must let me see her," Barrett insisted.

Alise looked to Kranzler, curiosity in her gray eyes.

"Perhaps we could arrange a meeting, but there must be security precautions," Kranzler said. "And we guarantee nothing. Don't you agree, Alise?"

"Of course we can guarantee nothing," Alise said. "We cannot force people to feel attraction for each other. For best results, both should be at least somewhat willing. None of us can control the desires we feel." She looked Barrett in the eyes for a long moment. "Can we?"

"She's willing," Barrett said. "Even more than she knows. Just leave me alone with her."

Kranzler looked at Alise for her opinion.

"I don't see why not," Alise said.

"We'll keep guards outside the room," Kranzler said. "The girl is dangerous."

"She's no danger to me." Barrett smiled. "Thank you, Herr Kranzler."

"I'm very glad we could accommodate," Kranzler told him. "We only ask that you not give the girl any serious physical harm—she is a valuable test subject."

"I do not intend to give her pain," Barrett said.

"Do you intend to give her pleasure instead, sir?" Alise touched his hand, and he laughed.

"We should rejoin the party," Kranzler said. "Eugen Fischer from the Kaiser Wilhelm Institute is here, and I'm eager to hear his opinion on our approach to racial progress. Even the Fuehrer listens to him on matters of eugenics."

* * *

Ward stood alone in the morgue again, the strains of *Die Walküre* still fading in his ears. The ghost of Kranzler was gone again, for now, but he couldn't help imagining the steel doors around him opening, the trays quietly sliding out, the dead rising from their slumber...

He hurried out, leaving the lights on behind him.

# Chapter Thirty-Eight

Jenny tossed and turned, trying to sleep while terrified screams blasted at full volume into her cell. For days, they'd kept the volume of the screams maxed out, on and on without a break, while all Jenny could see were the huge glowing images of people she had killed. The light from the screen illuminated only the furniture from her old room.

She was sick and shivering, sweaty and unable to eat. The baby felt agitated inside her, day and night, probably because of the screaming and the lack of sleep.

She was desperate to see Seth, desperate to escape this place, desperate for just a few minutes of silence....She'd been studying her situation carefully, and she didn't see how she could escape, especially when she couldn't use the pox without harming the baby. She could easily get herself jolted or shot dead by a guard. If she was going to try anything, it would have to be after the baby was born.

Jenny lay on her side and pressed the thin hospital-style pillow down over her ear, trying to shut out the recorded screams.

* * *

Guards in gas masks came for Juliana in her cell, all of them faceless and anonymous behind their big glass eyes. They gagged her and fitted a leather noose around her throat, and then another one at each wrist. The leather loops were affixed to the ends of long poles so the guards could move her head and arms from a distance, as though she were a marionette puppet.

Strangely, they didn't take her to the lab, but up a level to the residential halls near her old room. They carried her through a locked pair of double doors, into a corridor she'd never seen, and into a room that was neither a prison cell nor a dormitory room. It was lavish, like a suite at a grand hotel, with deeply cushioned furniture, art on the walls, candles, a rug so thick her feet sank into it. Juliana looked more than a little out of place here. Since they'd moved her down to the cell, her only clothes were prison wear—a drab gray dress with no buttons, zippers or ties, no underwear at all, and only thin, cheap slippers that hardly insulated her feet from the cold concrete floor.

"Whose room is this?" she asked, but none of the guards offered an answer. They departed, locking her inside. She wondered if this had to do with her being pregnant. Nobody had spoken to her about it since—there had only been guards, shoveling her food under her door twice a day. Evelina was her only real contact with other people, and they kept their conversations through the vents short and whispered, uncertain whether the guards could hear them.

Juliana stood in the middle of the room, crossed her arms, and waited. She summoned the plague inside her, preparing to lash out if attacked.

In time, the door opened again, and she gaped as Jonathan Barrett entered the room, grinning at her, his dark eyes already drawing her in. She froze where she was, wrapping her arms more tightly against herself, not sure why he was here or what he wanted.

"Juliana," he said. "You're even more beautiful than last time I saw you. How is that possible?"

Juliana doubted it. Her long hair was stringy and greasy, because the guards hadn't hosed her down in a few days, which was the closest she got to a bath. Her breasts hung loose and floppy inside her shapeless dress, and her belly was starting get larger, though her pregnancy wasn't obvious yet.

Juliana looked past him to the gas-masked guards, trying to figure out what was happening. Barrett gave them a nod and they closed the door, locking the two of them inside together.

"Mr. Barrett," Juliana said. "You have to get us out of here. They won't let us leave, we're prisoners. I haven't seen Sebastian in weeks. I don't even know if he's still here...or still alive..." She bit her lip and tried to not to sob. She forced herself to look calm. "You'll take us back home, won't you?"

"Sh." Barrett took her hands, and his touch filled with her a throbbing, electric energy. She was surprised her hair didn't stand up on her head. While Sebastian's touch was warm and gentle, like afternoon sunlight, Barrett's touch felt like needles of lightning. She gasped a little, still not used to touching anyone at all. "I came for you," he whispered.

Juliana trembled, trying not to succumb to the confused whirl of feelings he brought up inside her. She couldn't understand why she reacted so strongly to a man she knew so little.

"To free me?" she whispered.

"I've thought of you every night since you left," Barrett said, his dark eyes burning into her. "The last glimpse I had of you, standing on the deck of the boat, so bright in the sun, your hair blown by the ocean wind..." He stroked her hair, then his fingers caressed the back of her head. She found herself gaping up at him, not sure whether to squirm away or give in to the urge to wrap her arms around him, bury her face in his neck and draw out all the comfort he had to offer.

"Something happens when we touch." Barrett's voice was soft, but full of strength. Full of power. "Like an electric bolt. Like the moment before a storm, when the power gathers in the air. Tell me you can't feel it." His finger traced down her cheek to her trembling lips, and she could only look up into his magnetic dark eyes. Everything else faded away. There was only his face, his fingertip soft on her mouth.

She closed her eyes and sighed, feeling the world slide beneath her feet. His hands went to her sides to draw her closer to him, and she didn't fight the kiss she knew was coming. His lips touched her, and she felt another shock. The tip of her tongue reached into his mouth, and her hands gripped onto his head, holding him there, as if she wanted to kiss him forever. Something vast and dark stirred inside her, woken by his touch.

The long kiss ended, and they looked at each other, holding each other and breathing. The room felt incredibly hot, as though everything in sight would burst into flames. She could feel him thick and hard against her stomach. He was bigger down there than Sebastian, and it seemed threatening and dangerous, like it would cause the most exquisite kind of suffering.

He kissed her again, on her lips, her cheek, and her neck, as if he meant to consume her entirely. He hoisted her up in his hands and kissed her breasts through the thin dress. His lips closed on her nipple through the fabric, and it turned hard as a pebble as his mouth moved on her. His tongue brushed against her breast and she clutched his dark hair in her hands. His hands tightened on her hips.

He carried her to the sprawling bed, which had a massive headboard and footboard made of dark mahogany, inlaid with red tortoise shell and sculpted bronze, something that belonged in a luxurious mansion. She had no strength to resist as he lay her across the bed's silken coverlet. All the reasons she should refuse him passed through the back of her mind like a procession of ghosts...voiceless, powerless ghosts.

Then they were gone, lost in the surge of her uncontrollable feeling as his mouth moved down along her stomach, kissing her. If her stomach was slightly larger and rounder than he might have expected, he certainly didn't say anything.

His hands slid down her thighs, and then he was kissing her hip, her legs, the warm inner reaches of her thigh, and she suddenly wished the cheap, thin cotton of her dress wasn't in the way.

As though reading her mind, he lifted the dress up over her knees, then above her hips. His lips kissed the bare flesh of her stomach, then moved down between her legs. She heard herself moan as his mouth touched her throbbing clitoris, followed by a flick of his tongue. Her thighs squeezed against both sides of his head, trapping him there while he licked and sucked. Juliana screamed as her body quaked, and she grabbed onto his hair with both hands, pressing her face harder against his.

He kept licking her as he slid a finger into her, immediately finding *just* the right place to touch, as if they had an intelligence of their own. She cried out again as wave after wave of pleasure rushed through her body, her hips jumping up and down on the bed, far out of her control. She gripped the silk coverlet in both hands as her head tilted back, her teeth clenched together, and explosions rocked her body, shaking her to her core.

This was followed instantly by a heavy cloud of guilt. He continued working at her with his beautiful mouth and brilliant fingers, and she knew he was going to make it happen again.

"Stop," she told him, but it was barely a whisper. With an effort, she put more force into it. "Stop. Stop!" She sat up and pushed away until her back was flush against the tall headboard. "We can't do this."

"Why not?" He caressed her bare leg, and it felt both terribly good and terribly wrong. "We're meant for each other. We both know it. You make me larger and more powerful than I've ever been. Nothing in the world could stop us if we were together."

"We can't be together, Mr. Barrett."

"My tongue was just inside you. I think you can call me by my first name." He gave her a smile that weakened her defenses, but she held firm and didn't smile back. "There's no reason we can't be together," he said as his smile faded.

"There are lots of reasons. For one, you already have a wife and a son."

"Both of whom would be much happier living apart from me," he said. "I could get them a nice townhouse in Charleston. Or somewhere farther away. Savannah. New Orleans."

"You would send your own son away?" She folded her legs under her, away from his hands, and pulled her dress down over her knees.

"I would do anything to be with you, Juliana. We were meant for each other. We can't let a small thing like timing get in the way. The future we could have together..." He shook his head. "You give me so many dreams. So many *visions* of what I could do. The world will bow to us. If only I could make you see our fate, the way I see it." He leaned closer, as if he meant to kiss her again, but she moved away and stood up beside the bed.

"You have to take us out of here," she told him. "Sebastian and I both."

"Don't tell me you still love that clueless little boy," Barrett sneered. "He's not like us. You and I have demons inside us, the same kind of demons, eager to be together. That's why we can touch."

"I can touch him, too," Juliana said.

"What can he do for you?" Barrett stood and glared down at her. She felt cornered. "I can give you everything, Juliana. More than you ever dreamed of. We can become what we're meant to be. You would be a queen by my side. What can he offer?"

"I love him," Juliana whispered.

"What did you say?" He leaned toward her, scowling. "Say it again."

"I love him!" Juliana snapped. "I love him. And I'm having his baby. We have to be together, Mr. Barrett...Jonathan...and we need your help to get us out of here. Please understand."

"You're having his baby?" Barrett looked her over, confused. Then he looked angry, his jaw clenching repeatedly inside his cheek. He took a breath. "That's not a problem, Juliana. I still want to be with you. The child...I'll care for the child as if it were my own. I promise."

"Your own? Like the son you just casually offered to abandon?"

"That's not what I meant!"

"But it's the truth. I saw how your family lives in fear of you. Why would I ever want that life for myself?" She crossed her arms. She felt powerless in his shadow, knowing he was immune to her demon plague. In fact, he seemed to thrive on it. Attacking him could actually make him more powerful...he clearly had something like her and Sebastian, a touch that made him "supernormal," but he hadn't said what it was.

"Juliana, I am talking about an entirely new beginning," he said. "A new life for both of us."

"Tell me you will take Sebastian and me out of here," Juliana said. "If you love me, you will at least do that much."

"If I love you? You don't believe me? You are the only reason I came here."

"Then help us."

"Why?" Fury swelled in his eyes. "Help you, so you can leave me for him? You would leave me cold, wouldn't you? That's what you're telling me."

She took a deep breath. "If you still wish it...you can have your way. Just once, and only after you take us home, if you still want me then, if that is your price."

"My price? You offer yourself as prostitute? One night in exchange for passage across the ocean. I don't want you as *payment*. I want you to stay with me. I want all of you."

"I can't give you that," she whispered.

He snarled and punched an ornate mirror on the wall, shattering it and bloodying his fist. He stalked to the door and pounded on it.

"Where are you going?" Juliana asked.

"Home," he said. "You'd rather stay with him? Then you can stay here with him, have your child together, enjoy your life."

"You have to take us!" Juliana ran toward him, grabbing his arm. Blood from his hand dripped onto her dress. "You can't leave us. It's your fault we're here!"

"Tell me you don't feel the same way that I do." He leaned in, looking into her eyes. "I know you do. Tell me you'll leave him. Tell me you love me."

Juliana gaped at him, feeling crazed. The guards opened the door and immediately drew their long-nosed Luger pistols when they saw blood, all of them pointing at Juliana. Their gas masks stared at her, as expressionless as insects.

"So you choose him," Barrett said. "You'll regret it."

He stepped out of the room, and the guards locked her inside, alone, her dress dotted with his blood.

# Chapter Thirty-Nine

After yet another strenuous day of testing, in which Mariella had to predict what images the test subjects would see when they looked at a screen in an enclosed booth, she lay awake in bed. It was late, and the underground facility was silent except for the endless coughing and rattling of the ventilation system. She twisted and turned. Her hands found her way to her stomach, momentarily shocked to find it flat and firm instead of round and full of baby. Her past and present memories were starting to collide in a way that left her confused and sometimes scared.

She had continued cooperating with Ward, and he seemed pleased with her performance in the lab. She told herself that she wasn't *really* working with him, that she was just going along, gathering information until the day they could escape. As the weeks passed, though, she began to question her own motives. Maybe she was just taking the safe road, while Jenny and Seth bravely resisted.

Ward was less pleased with Mariella's failure to win Seth over. She'd visited him several times, but he refused to cooperate. Mariella didn't see why he couldn't just pretend. She teased him while telling herself that she wouldn't actually sleep with him if given the chance, even though she knew just how good his healing touch made her body feel, how she still tingled hours after the lovemaking itself was over. She would resist the cravings of her body and her heart, even if he changed his mind and decided to pretend to cooperate as she did. She would keep her feelings to herself.

Mariella rolled over in bed, aching to touch Seth again and hating herself for it.

* * *

"Wake up, kids," Alise said as she flipped on the lamp and approached the four-poster bed. Her cousin Niklaus followed a step behind her, as usual, like an obedient attack dog waited for orders.

"Hi, Alise!" Mia sat up, smiling sleepily. Alise came almost every morning to walk them to breakfast, and Mia was happy she did. Sometimes, early in the morning, she would feel the dark shape of something large looming at the back of her mind, like an upsetting memory she'd forgotten. Then Alise would arrive, and she'd feel so much better, happy and thoughtless, lusty for another round with her handsome lover, Sebastian, and his enchanted touch that made her feel better all over. The world always felt right again after she saw Alise.

"Wake up, Sebastian." Alise shook his shoulder, and his eyes drifted open. His lips curled into a delighted smile at the sight of Alise leaning over him. "Pack your bags. Mia's moving upstairs, and you're moving back to your room."

"Huh? Why?" Sebastian sat up, his hair sticking in every direction, looking confused and hurt. "Wait, what?"

"You're moving back. Play time is over, boy," Alise said.

"What do you mean?"

"I mean we don't need you anymore," Alise said. "You've made your contribution, and now you're done. Oh, don't look so hurt. You've had a fun couple of months with her."

"I don't understand." Sebastian looked back and forth between them.

"Niklaus will help you get back to your room, if you need it," Alise said sweetly. "Won't you, Niklaus?"

Niklaus glared at Sebastian and motioned for him to hurry up.

"Why does Sebastian have to go?" Mia pouted. "I like sleeping with him."

"I know, but boy time is over," Alise said. She watched silently as Sebastian gathered his things and followed Niklaus out the door.

"When do I get to come back?" Sebastian asked.

"We'll see." Alise waved her hand, and Niklaus closed the door after him.

Alise seized Mia's hands, making her feel instantly happy. Mia kissed Alise's hand.

"Mia!" Alise spoke in an excited stage whisper. "I have the best news. Your latest lab work shows that you're pregnant!"

"What?" Mia asked. She felt dizzy, not so elated anymore.

"You're going to have a baby. We've successfully bred you with Sebastian. Your baby will be the offspring of two supernormals! That's what the project is really all about!"

"It is?" Mia rubbed her head. "I'm pregnant?"

"You're so lucky," Alise said. "I've been trying for months, but it hasn't worked out so far. I just learned about something else I might try, though. Anyway, why do we have to keep talking about me? Let's get going. The maternity rooms are one level up, and I know just which one I want you to have. I decorated it myself! There's a little crib that looks like a sleigh, little bears in *Reichsheer* cavalry uniforms...very cute!" Alise took her by the arm and led her out the door.

Mia trembled. "I'm going to have a baby?"

Alise squeezed her hand, flooding her with a fresh wave of happy, loving feelings. "Don't worry, Mia. I'll be right here with you, every step of the way. If we're lucky, I'll be having one, too!"

Mia smiled, fully doped on Alise's love. Alise was right, of course. Mia didn't need to worry, not when she had such a good friend here to help her...

Alise led the way to the maternity beds upstairs, where Mia would live for the rest of her time at the underground base.

# Chapter Forty

"We have a situation," Ward said as Tommy walked into his office. "It's on the delicate side, but I think we've learned to trust each other these past few months, haven't we?"

"Yes, sir," Tommy said. He had no idea why he'd been called in. He wondered whether ASTRIA might be ready to send him on some kind of mission—it felt like he'd been testing and training forever, and he was going stir crazy inside the base.

"I had to follow a very difficult order," Ward told him. "One of the most difficult of my career. You see, the top brass have decided that paranormals are a threat on par with terrorists, a lone individual capable of doing widespread damage or otherwise breaking national security. Those who are not with us are considered 'against us.'" Ward watched him closely.

"I understand. But I've been working with you, sir."

"And that's what makes you so valuable. You're willing to do the right thing, to put the bigger cause ahead of yourself. Not everyone's willing to do that."

"Is this about Jenny, sir? Or Seth?"

"I'm afraid it's about Esmeralda."

"She's not a threat to anyone!" Tommy said. "Her power isn't dangerous, like Jenny's. Or mine."

"That's not exactly the case," Ward told him. "Imagine if she got her hands on the body of a high-level politician, military leader, or intelligence operative."

"That's not very likely," Tommy said. "All she does is put funeral makeup on dead people in Los Angeles. She's not working in Washington, D.C. or anything."

"If we can determine her power, then so can foreign governments, including those unfriendly to our country. So can criminal and terrorist groups. Any of them might kidnap her and use her for their own ends."

"You make it sound like she's in danger."

"Exactly right. ASTRIA is not the only organization searching the world for paranormals. There are enemies of the United States doing the same. After the Fallen Oak incident, the Pentagon does not want any of them running wild, anywhere. ASTRIA's role is to identify, recruit...or neutralize."

"Neutralize?" Tommy felt panicked. "Esmeralda? You're not going to hurt her, are you? Or..." Tommy couldn't bring himself to say *kill her*. He felt the beginnings of rage inside him. If these people had killed Esmeralda, he was never going to work with them. He would take out as many as he could before they killed him.

"No, no. I have clearance to do that, you understand, but like you, I couldn't see how Esmeralda was a bad or dangerous person. So I took the only other option available: capture her, since she refused to come willingly."

"You're going to kidnap her?"

"We have taken her into custody," Ward told him. "And she's been transferred here."

"Here?" Tommy felt a confused mixture of outrage and excitement. "She's right here at the base?"

"Confined in a cell, unfortunately," Ward said. "I wish she had agreed to come when we asked her, but she didn't leave us any choice. We are taking good care of her, though, and she has shown some willingness to cooperate with tests. There's potential there, but we need to bring it out."

"Let me talk to her," Tommy said. "I'll explain what you're really doing here."

Ward paused for a minute, as if thinking this over carefully. "Do you believe she will listen to you? We don't want to upset her."

"She'll listen," Tommy said. "Maybe not right away, but if I can keep visiting her, keep talking to her...She's not stupid. She'll come around." Tommy had no idea whether she would ever agree to work with them, but he was dying to see her again.

"It might help her along, seeing a familiar face," Ward mused. "Having someone she trusts to comfort her."

"I'll take care of it, sir."

"That's what I like to hear." Ward turned his attention to his computer screen. "Dismissed."

Tommy walked back toward his room, but he slowed as he passed the double doors to the third corridor, where he'd seen the conjugal rooms in his flashes of his previous life. It felt strange to think of himself as an S.S. officer, a Nazi...under Ashleigh's control, yet again. He was beginning to wonder how many lifetimes he'd spent being manipulated by her, even while immune to her actual power.

He pushed on the doors, and felt mildly surprised when one of them opened. He walked into the third corridor, wondering if all the luxurious furnishings were still here, the old phonographs waiting to play German chamber music.

He opened the door to the first room. It was empty, stripped down to the bare concrete, with a huddle of cardboard boxes and trash bags in one corner, all the beauty long since carted away by either the Nazis or the Soviets who came after them.

Tommy crossed the room, his sneakers echoing like heavy boots against the floor. He found the little hole in the wall, which had generally gone unnoticed, lost between the curlicues of a fancy mirror frame. He closed one eye and looked through it, but there was only darkness on the other side.

He had stood there, he remembered, in the narrow hidden passage that ran along this side of the hall, enabling researchers to observe the conjugal rooms without being noticed. He had stood and watched through the little lens in the wall, and now felt embarrassed at the memory.

* * *

Niklaus walked up the narrow, dim hidden passage, long after supper when the base was quiet and nobody was likely to be looking for him. He stopped at one of the tiny, glowing circles in the wall, closed an eye, and looked through.

The room was empty, of course, the bed curtains tied back, the furniture dusted. Only a single small lamp provided illumination. It had slipped his mind that they'd already moved Sebastian and Mia out of the room. He'd come here out of habit, along with a dim hope that maybe some other couple had been moved onto the hall.

He'd watched Sebastian and Mia several times over the weeks. At first, it had only been out of curiosity and boredom, a late-night search for entertainment. Watching their bare bodies grind against each other had been far more exhilarating than he'd expected. They fucked with a raw abandon, thanks to Alise's enchantment. On subsequent nights, now and then, Niklaus found himself sneaking back for another look, and once he'd gone so far as to unzip and pleasure himself while he watched, never mind the scientists who might walk in on him at any moment.

They were gone now, and he would not get to see Mia squirm in pleasure again, unless they decided to breed her again in another year. Maybe that would be with Niklaus. He'd asked Alise to arrange it for him, but she'd stalled, and now Mia was pregnant by the American instead.

Niklaus started to turn back, feeling disappointed, until he heard a gasp farther down the hidden passage. He followed it to the last room on the short hall. The walls near the hidden lenses were perforated with pinpoint holes, allowing sound to pass through to observers. He heard the sound again—a high-pitched squeal, then a gasping sound.

Grinning, he wondered who had been paired up now. Tonight's visit might not be a complete waste, after all.

He closed an eye and peered through the lens.

This room was the nicest of them all, everything trimmed in marble and traces of polished gold. The bed was the largest he'd ever seen, its frame and high poster columns carved from ebony. On the bed, he saw the visiting American banker, Jonathan Barrett, stripped naked and furiously mounting a girl Niklaus couldn't clearly see, but she was blond. He assumed it was a nurse or typing pool girl the visitor must have picked up. Whoever it was, she shuddered, screamed, snorted, and writhed, shaking and lost in pleasured agony as he took her faster and faster, to the sound of a Wagner overture on the phonograph.

Niklaus wanted to laugh at the girl's grunting and howling. The guy was really reaming her hard. He'd never known a woman could make sounds like that.

Then she turned her head, and he recognized that the squirming girl with her knees locked around Barrett's hips was his own cousin Alise.

His smile vanished, and he felt his heart shrivel and turn cold. He felt it like a fist in his gut. He'd been with Alise several times now, even though each time, when he finished, he told himself he would never do it again. The part of him that stewed in guilt and shame kept losing out to the part that still lusted for her—he'd never been able to turn her down when she came to his door.

It stung to see her with another man, especially lying back spreading herself wide for him, when she'd always insisted that she be on top with Niklaus, never letting him truly take her. Now she gave herself freely to this foreigner, making sounds like he'd never heard. With him, she had always just panted a little, then panted a little faster near the end. With Barrett, she thrashed and cried out like a wild animal.

He saw, too, that Barrett was substantially thicker and longer then he was, filling Alise far more fully than Niklaus ever could. His cousin seemed enthralled, in a state of ecstasy, looking up at Barrett with droopy lids. She'd certainly never given Niklaus a look like that...a look of surrender.

He quivered where he stood, opening and closing his fists. He had an urge to charge in there, scream at his cousin, and maybe put his Luger to Barrett's head and shower his brains all over the wall. *No,* Niklaus thought. *I won't start with his head.*

Before he could do anything, the door to the conjugal room opened. *Gruppenführer* Kranzler was there, arms crossed, eyes looking coldly at Alise and the foreign man. Niklaus froze where he was, wondering how Kranzler would react to seeing Barrett on top of his best aide.

Kranzler just watched for a minute, while Alise and Barrett continued on, faster and louder, wrapped in their own world.

"It's a useless effort," Kranzler finally said, startling the two on the bed. "She's as barren as a rock in the desert. Trust me."

Barrett paused, sweating and catching his breath. He looked from Kranzler to Alise. "Doesn't feel useless to me," he finally said.

Kranzler glared at Alise for another long moment, and Niklaus recognized the expression. Jealousy. So she'd been fucking Kranzler, too. Niklaus wanted to punch his fist through the wall.

Finally, Kranzler snarled, "You may continue entertaining our guest, Alise." He slammed the door as he left. Barrett looked down at Alise.

"Keep going. I'll show that ugly bastard who's barren," Alise hissed.

Barrett started up again, and Alise soon clenched her eyes and screamed in pleasure again as his oversized cock slid in and out of her.

Niklaus felt a shining, glittering hate for his cousin Alise, recognizing that she had no real love for him at all. She was only using him. She wanted to get pregnant, and she didn't seem too picky who the father might be.

He stalked away down the hidden passage, the sound of Alise's high-pitched cries following after him, mocking him.

Instead of bursting in on them, he paced up and down the male residential corridor. He should be relieved, he told himself. He should never have thought of Alise that way in the first place, never fantasized about her, never given in...She had brought out the worst in him, as she always did.

Someone else had been on his mind, in every way Alise's opposite, small, quiet, looking as fragile as Niklaus often felt on the inside. Evelina, the Slavic girl who could speak to the dead.

The next day, he went down to the cellblock to visit her. He'd been fascinated by her since the day he and Alise had moved her down, maybe because she seemed so innocent and harmless next to Alise. He had strange feelings toward Evelina, and attraction was the smallest part of it. He felt the need to protect her, and to make life a little easier for her.

He had resisted his feelings while he and Alise were intimate together, but now that he understood Alise didn't truly care for him, he grew emboldened enough to go and speak to Evelina.

He knocked on the closed panel in her door, then waited a moment, working up his nerve, before he opened the panel and looked at her through the barred window.

She sat on her bed, looking back at him and waiting.

"Hello," he said.

She raised an eyebrow, but didn't reply.

"How are you?" he asked.

She glanced around at her concrete cell. "How should I answer that?"

"I don't know."

She watched him expectantly, her eyes dark and vibrant.

"I brought you...there was Bavarian chocolate on our last supply train," Niklaus said. "Not much, but S.S. men all got some. I saved a little. Would you like it?" He held up a square of chocolate wrapped in tin foil, offering it through the bars.

"Why are you giving me that?" She remained on her bunk.

"Come on. Take it."

"Is that an order?" She slowly stood and walked toward him, her eyes full of suspicion. She unwrapped it, revealing the rich chocolate, and her eyes widened. "Is it poisoned?"

"Why would I poison it?"

"To kill me?"

"I wouldn't do that."

"Am I supposed to trust you?" Evelina asked.

Niklaus sighed and thought about it. "If you were going to die...wouldn't it be better to die by chocolate poisoning instead of a firing squad?"

"This is true." She looked at the chocolate but made no move to eat it. "Why would you give me this?"

"I just...feel I should help you," Niklaus admitted. "Is there anything else I can do?"

"Yes. Unlock the door and let me go home."

"I can't. I'm sorry. I wish I could."

"You can't? You're standing outside my door. You're even wearing an S.S. uniform. I think you could get me out of here if you tried."

"They would kill me," Niklaus said.

"Maybe you'll get lucky and they'll use chocolate." Evelina gave him a thin smile.

"Are you going to taste it or not?"

"What's the hurry? I have days and days to pass." She placed it on the wobbly bookshelf that held her clothes, which now consisted only of the cheap, plain gray dresses and slippers the Nazis had issued her.

"Saving it for later." He nodded. "That's smart."

Evelina shrugged.

"Can I bring you anything else?"

"Besides a key to my door?" Evelina glanced around her cell. "I have nothing to do here. Can you bring me something to read?"

"What would you like?"

"Novels, newspapers, magazines, it doesn't matter! Just anything to keep my mind busy."

"I can do that." He smiled at her, but she didn't return it.

"And more chocolate," she added. "If it isn't poisoned."

# Chapter Forty-One

Seth stood over the young man on the table. He was Hispanic, around Seth's age, a veteran of the Iraq War. His name was Frederico, and his left leg was missing from the knee down. Seth couldn't stop himself from thinking of the day he'd met Jenny. Everett Lawson had run over Jenny's dog with his red truck that had the stupid flame decals on the sides. Seth had stopped to heal the dog, and in the process grown back the dog's leg, which had been missing for months or years. That was how Jenny had discovered Seth's power, and how Seth had really discovered Jenny. He smiled for a moment at the memory.

"Can you do it?" General Kilpatrick asked from the window above, looking down on Seth, Frederico, and the researchers and guards within the big concrete lab.

"I can do it, but I won't be up for golf afterward," Seth said. He'd resisted all of Mariella's attempts to flip him and make him cooperate with Ward, laced with not-very-subtle hints that Seth might be welcomed into Mariella's bed if he did. Today, though, Ward had played a dirty trick on him.

ASTRIA had brought in a pool of severely wounded war veterans, amputees and others with injuries that couldn't be fixed by medical science. One of Ward's assistants, a thuggish-looking guy named Buchanan, had brought a digital tablet down to Seth's cell and held it up to the window, showing him all the wounded who'd been brought with the promise of a new, experimental kind of medicine that could fully heal them. The veterans, mostly young men and women his age, were waiting anxiously, their faces showing faint glimmers of hope under masks of grim resignation.

Seth knew he'd feel guilty if he sent them away without helping, so he'd agree to call a truce with Ward long enough to heal them. It had been a difficult decision for Seth, because he knew that his cooperation was exactly what Ward wanted, but he decided that he couldn't turn down the chance to help these people. He still wore an orange jumpsuit, and he would still be returned to his cell afterward. It had been interesting to finally leave the cell, though, and see how much the base had changed since last time around. More computers, fewer swastikas, white tile instead of concrete. Some of the guards wore specially designed biohazard armor, complete with air filters and oxygen bottles, to protect them against those with a paranormal touch.

Now, Frederico looked up at Seth from the stretcher, looking confused.

"Nobody explained what you're going to do. It's not another surgery?" Frederico asked. "I don't see any equipment."

"I can't really explain it myself," Seth told him. "Everybody ready?" Without waiting for an answer, he took a deep breath and lay both hands on the young man's leg stump. He closed his eyes and pushed the healing energy into him to speed things along.

Seth felt it draining out of him, weakening him. He opened his eyes to see Frederico gaping at the sight of his leg. Long, thin tentacles grew out from his knee. Two of them stiffened like wires, forming the framework of his tibia and fibula, finally meeting to form a sketchy framework, the little bones of Frederico's new ankle. Others lashed around the bone, forming muscle and tendon.

Frederico crossed himself and whispered a rapid "Our Father" in Spanish.

Seth grew weaker and weaker as the bones and muscles thickened and the new foot formed itself from thin air. It wasn't exactly thin air, Seth knew. All the fat on Seth's body was already gone, leaving fine details of his own veins and muscles visible under his skin. His muscle tissue was starting to burn away, too, but he held on and kept healing.

Less than a minute later, the young man's new leg was complete, and Seth collapsed onto the tiled floor. Two guards hurried over to lift him up.

"How?" Frederico spoke in an awed whisper, wiggling his toes. The new leg didn't match the other one perfectly, because the new skin was baby-soft and hairless. Frederico stared at it, his eyes huge. "How is this possible? You didn't do anything! Are you touched by God?" Frederico gaped at Seth.

"Urggh, food," Seth mumbled, half-unconscious. "Take me to food."

The guards and a lab tech helped him into a wheelchair. Seth's head nodded forward as they rolled away. He heard Frederico's voice, shouting his thanks again and again, somewhere behind him like a distant echo.

* * *

"I want to see Juliana," Sebastian insisted. "Take me to her, right now!"

He stood in the hallway of the male dormitory, arms crossed, blocking Niklaus in his room as Niklaus was trying to get out.

"Move aside," Niklaus said. "Or do you want me to move you?"

Sebastian just stared at him, his eyes burning. It had been two days since Alise separated him from Mia, and she hadn't touched him since. The spell of her power had finally worn off, leaving him furious and worried sick about Juliana, whom he'd hadn't seen in weeks. He'd been like a drug addict, thinking of nothing but his next dose. Looking back, he could see how Alise had manipulated him, doing her best to make him forget about Juliana, reassuring him that she was doing well whenever he remembered to ask, then dosing him hard so that his mind was full of empty bliss for hours.

Now he was awake. He was himself again, and he needed to find Juliana. He felt sick for the way he'd spent his time, the power that Alise wielded over him. Her ability had turned out to be far more dangerous than Sebastian had ever expected.

"Juliana," Sebastian said. "Now, Niklaus."

Niklaus stepped closer, until he was only inches from Sebastian. "Last warning."

Sebastian didn't move. "Now," he said again.

Niklaus punched him in the face, sending him staggering back into the hall, drops of blood falling from his nose. Sebastian quickly healed and recovered, and he lunged at Niklaus, hitting him in the stomach. He knew better than to punch anyone in the face, or anywhere there was bare skin, because Sebastian's fist was accompanied by a burst of healing energy that sort of made his punch pointless.

Niklaus doubled over with Sebastian's fist in his solar plexus, but then lunged forward, slamming Sebastian against the far wall of the corridor. Sebastian tried to bring his elbow down on Niklaus' head, but Niklaus twisted free and then began pummeling him. With each impact, Sebastian felt his courage wane and fear grow inside him. He fought back as best as he could, hitting Niklaus in the chest and stomach and sending him staggering back for a moment, then Niklaus came back with an uppercut to his jaw, filling Sebastian's head with exploding stars.

Niklaus shoved him against the wall and clutched his throat, filling him with fear. Niklaus leaned in close again, his gray eyes burning, his teeth bared in a smile.

For a moment, Sebastian saw through the human mask of Niklaus to the monster behind it, a thing the size of a great mountain, made of rock and bone, a thousand horns on its massive dinosaur-skull head, dark fire burning deep inside its bony eye sockets. It made an ear-shattering inhuman screech, loud enough to tear worlds apart. *The fear-giver*.

Then he was trembling and useless, staring into Niklaus' eyes.

"You made a mistake," Niklaus whispered. "Let's get you into a cell downstairs."

Niklaus punched him again, then dragged him out of the hall, shouting for more guards.

Sebastian spent hours shivering alone in a dim concrete cell, terrified by every sound that echoed through the cellblock, paranoid that they were going to punish Juliana for his actions. Frightened that she might already be dead, and nobody had told him.

Niklaus' spell gradually wore off, but he was still trembling when the panel outside his barred window opened. It was Alise, her usually bubbly smile gone, her face hard and cold and slathered in makeup.

"Here he is," Alise said, to someone he couldn't see. "Why did you have to mess it all up, Sebastian? Everything was going so well for you."

"I just wanted to see Juliana."

"That's too bad. Now you'll never get to see anyone, not for a long time. A shame, with your children on the way."

"I don't have any children."

"Oh, no one's told you?" Now Alise's smile was back. "Juliana is pregnant with your child. So is Mia. The first two babies of our supernormal breeding project, true Aryans of the future."

"What breeding project?"

"You'll never see either of the children, of course," Alise said. "They belong to the Reich. They will be raised and educated properly. One day, they might command armies. You'll never know. You'll be down here, wishing you had never caused us any trouble."

Sebastian walked to the barred window, anger burning away the cobwebs of fear Niklaus had left in him. "They're both pregnant?"

"One day, my child will command both of yours," Alise said. "I intend to have a son, and raise him to lead the Reich."

"You're pregnant, too?"

Alise scowled at him. "You have a visitor. Someone who wants to say good-bye." She stepped aside, and another face took the place of hers. Jonathan Barrett, of Fallen Oak, South Carolina. Sebastian immediately wanted to spit in his face.

"What are you doing here?" Sebastian asked. "Coming to see how you've destroyed our lives?"

"Are we not having a happy day today?" Barrett asked, grinning.

"You'd better get us out of here, Barrett. This place is a prison run by crazy people."

"You got exactly what I promised," Barrett said. "Scientific testing of your abilities. I heard you were doing well here until recently, Sebastian."

"You're a liar," Sebastian said. "I'm warning you, Barrett. You get us out of here now, or I'll make you pay for it."

"And how are you going to do that? You look so cozy there in your cell."

"I may not know how, but it will happen," Sebastian said. "I never forget. If you leave us here, I will come back and I will destroy everything you care about. Your ridiculous idea of a legacy. Whatever you create, I will ruin. I'll burn your house right to the ground. I'll burn your *name* right out of history. Nothing you do will last, and everyone will forget you ever lived."

Barrett chuckled and shook his head. "Sad. Truly sad, threats made from a cage."

"Mr. Barrett," Alise said, "We'd better get going. You don't want to miss your train."

Barrett nodded. "Nice visiting with you, Sebastian."

"This is your last chance, Barrett. Get Juliana and me out of here now."

Barrett smirked and walked down the hall with Alise.

"I mean it, Barrett!" Sebastian shouted after him. He banged his fist on the door. "I won't forget. Even when I'm dead, I won't forget."

Barrett laughed without looking. "Destroy me from beyond the grave? You're amusing, Sebastian."

They walked out of his sight. Sebastian slammed his head against the door, furious with himself for ever getting tricked by such a man. His hatred for Barrett seethed all the way into his bones, right down into his soul.

# Chapter Forty-Two

Tommy's heart raced as he approached the narrow armorglass window looking into Esmeralda's cell. She looked up at him from her bunk, her eyes widening slightly in recognition, but otherwise her face remained blank.

"Let me in," he told the two guards that accompanied him.

"We don't take orders from you," one replied, while swiping the access card the opened the door's electromagnetic lock.

Tommy didn't have time to fight, so he nudged past the guard and pulled the door open. The guards waited outside as he stepped into the cell. Esmeralda looked him over quietly. She wore an orange jumpsuit so that everybody at the facility would know she was a prisoner.

"Hello," he said. It seemed a little weak, since he hadn't seen her in months, but he wasn't sure what else to say.

"You finally decided to come see me." Esmeralda spoke softly, looking at the concrete floor and avoiding his eyes. "That took long enough."

"What do you mean? I thought you just got here."

"I've been here for weeks. Or months. I don't know, it's hard to keep track anymore."

"General Kilpatrick didn't tell me that."

"Who could have guessed he was dishonest?" She looked up at him, and her eyes were full of hate, startling him. "Lucky you, you agreed to do what he wanted. If you'd said no, you'd be locked up here like me."

"The general says it's because of national security. They don't want any paranormal types like us running loose."

"Oh, no, can't have people running loose," Esmeralda said.

"I just think we have a chance to use our powers for greater good, like General Kilpatrick says. We should take the chance."

"Who decides what is good and what is evil?" she asked. "The guy who kidnapped me? Or is it you who decides? Or is it me?"

"Just...the people in charge. The experts." Tommy didn't really know how to answer her question.

Esmeralda sighed. "You always believe what people tell you, Tommy. You're like a fucking clueless, needy child. If you don't have Ashleigh to lead you around, you find somebody else. You never look at anything with your own eyes or measure them with your own mind. You never make your own choices."

"You're still giving me the same shit after all this time?"

"You're still doing the same shit, so you don't leave me much choice."

"I came down here because I was worried about you. They told me you were here, and I insisted on seeing you. I didn't know you hated me so much, or I wouldn't have bothered."

"I don't hate you, Tommy," she said. "I just can't be what you need. And you can't be what I need."

"Don't you care about me at all?"

"Do you love me, Tommy?"

The question surprised him. "Of course."

"Don't say 'of course,' like it's obvious. Help me get out of here and away from these people. Help me get back home."

"I can't do that," he said.

"You're not caged up. They like you here, they let you wander around, you're so happy to work with them. You're in a better position to get me out of here than I am. Can't you talk to them?"

"They won't listen to me."

"So you won't help me."

"I just don't think I can get you out. I'll try. Is there anything else I can do, though? To make things easier for you?"

Esmeralda lay back on her bunk and stared at the ceiling. "If you're not going to help me, you can leave me alone."

He stared at her for a long moment. "Esmeralda, I'm sorry. I said I'll do what I can."

She didn't answer him or look back at him again. After a minute, he left the cell, feeling sick and hurt all the way through. Esmeralda had no love left for him, and maybe he deserved it.

* * *

"I found these for you," Niklaus said. He slid a pair of fashion magazines through the bars of Evelina's cell, and she took them eagerly.

"No books today?" she asked.

"Sorry. Maybe next week." He smiled as she flipped through the magazines.

"Thank you, Niklaus. These will help." She looked up and returned his smile. His heart kicked up its beat. He'd been visiting her a few times a week, and she was gradually warming up to him. "When are they moving me out of here? Have you talked to Alise yet?"

"She said...not yet. I don't know what's taking so long." Alise had originally told Niklaus that Evelina was only being moved down temporarily, while the Party officials and a few trusted foreigners toured the base. That delegation had come and gone weeks ago, but Evelina was still here. He'd asked Alise about it, and she'd told him there was too much "racial impurity" in the program as it was.

"I hope they hurry. Maybe you can help." Evelina smiled again. She looked beautiful to him, dark hair, eyes that were large, soft, and brown, making him think of a wild young deer. It pained him that there was always a wall between them, both literally and otherwise. She was a captive, he was one of her jailors. How could she ever fall in love with him in those circumstances? He didn't deserve such a girl, in any case, after his incestuous trysts with his cousin that left him feeling permanently disgusted with himself.

"I am doing all I can for you, I promise," Niklaus said quietly. "I will watch out for you."

"Thank you, Niklaus." She hesitated, holding her breath, then reached her hand to the bars. Niklaus touched her fingers, for the first time, and it filled him with a simple, warm happiness. Her eyes widened and she pulled back—he'd almost forgotten about the fear in his touch.

"I should go," he said. "They told me Alise was looking for me."

Evelina frowned and backed away. "You had better go, then."

"I'll come back soon. I promise."

She nodded and quietly watched him walk away.

Upstairs, Niklaus ran into Alise as he emerged into the dormitory area.

"There you are!" She grabbed the sleeve of his uniform and turned him right back into the stairwell. "We're running late."

"Late for what?"

"This way." She walked back down the way he'd come, toward the cellblock below. He followed her.

"What's happening?" he asked.

"Kranzler is cleaning out the program," Alise said. "Roza and Vilja never demonstrated enough abilities to impress the scientists. They know too much for us to let them go, so I convinced Kranzler to move them over to kitchen staff instead."

"I won't be breeding with either of them?" Niklaus asked.

"Not as part of the program." Alise's voice had a cold, flat tone. She'd apparently given up on her attempts at pregnancy. She'd stopped visiting Niklaus at night, which was a relief. A dead look had crept into her eyes and now seemed permanently fixed. The heavy makeup she now wore made her appear even more corpse-like.

"But not everyone can be trusted," Alise told him as Niklaus unlocked the door to the cellblock. They walked past the guard station, where Niklaus nodded at the two S.S. men on duty, their gas masks on the desk before them, ready to be grabbed at a moment's notice. Alise leaned over and whispered in one man's ear, her fingers touching his face, and he smiled and handed over a key.

"I think I understand," Niklaus said as the entered the corridor of cells. He approached the door to Juliana's cell. The American girl with the deadly plague had spooked everyone since her arrival.

Alise continued on past it, towards Evelina's cell.

"Juliana is back here," Niklaus told her.

"Juliana is pregnant with a doubly supernormal baby," Alise said. "As everyone keeps reminding me. Come here, Niklaus." She inserted the key she'd gotten from the guard into the door to Evelina's cell.

"What are you doing?" Niklaus asked. "She's done nothing wrong."

"She was born the wrong race. There's probably even Muslim in her, look how dark she is. Open the door, Niklaus."

His heart pounding, Niklaus pulled the door open. Evelina stood up, holding one of the fashion magazines in her hand. She smiled when she saw Niklaus and Alise.

"Am I moving back to my room?" Evelina asked. "Thank you, Alise."

"Execute her," Alise said to Niklaus.

Evelina's eyes widened in fear, and she stopped walking toward them.

"You can't mean that," Niklaus said.

"Shoot her!" Alise ordered.

"No," Niklaus said, his voice shaking.

"What did you say?" Alise's eyes narrowed into angry slits. "Niklaus?"

"I can't. I...she's a woman."

"Niklaus?" Evelina whispered, shaking now, wrapping her arms around herself as if cold. "Please..."

"For God's sake! We don't have time for this." Alise rolled her eyes and took the Luger pistol from his belt. She fired three times, missing Evelina once and then hitting her in the stomach and the chest. Evelina screamed, and Alise fired again, blowing away the upper left corner of Evelina's head. A gout of blood splashed across the wall behind her, and she fell to the floor, her eyes seeming to plead silently with Niklaus as she died.

Niklaus felt like he was drowning. It had happened too fast for him to stop it, and now it was done.

"Look at her brains all over the sink!" Alise cackled.

Niklaus ran into the room, dropping to his knees next to Evelina's body. Horror filled him, and then agony, as it sank in that she was gone. He cradled her bleeding head in her body. A look of hurt and betrayal was etched into her lifeless face. He'd said he would watch out for her. He'd lied.

"Gross, you're getting her all over you," Alise said. "Let's go tell someone to clean up this mess."

As she turned away, Niklaus reached for his holster and found it empty. Alise still held his gun. If he'd had it, he would have shot her right in the back.

Instead, he knelt in the cell, clutching Evelina's body, and he began to sob, mumbling curses down on himself and his wicked cousin.

# Chapter Forty-Three

"They tell me you're ready to deal." Ward grinned as he approached the clear wall to Jenny's cell. Behind him, the projection screen had gone mercifully blank, and the recorded screams had been silenced.

"I don't think I have any choice." Jenny spoke in a quiet, defeated tone. She was less than a month from giving birth, and she'd found no way to ever escape without using the pox. "It's time to stop thinking about myself and do what's right for the baby."

"And that is?" Ward folded his arms, still grinning.

"I'll do whatever you want, if you guarantee the baby's safety."

"Not a problem."

"I just have a couple of conditions."

Ward smirked. "And those are?"

"First, the birth has to be done in a very specific way. I can explain the details to Dr. Parker, but it has to be done right, or the baby will die."

"As long as Dr. Parker agrees, and nothing violates our security."

"Second...I need the baby to stay here with me. Live here with me, if this is where I'm going to live."

"I'm not so sure about that, Jenny." Ward's face hardened, his smile gone.

"She's my own baby."

"And we have to think about her health and safety, don't we? You could be deadly to her. Like you were to your own mother."

Jenny wanted to snarl at him, but she kept herself looking calm. *Nothing for me, everything for the baby*, she reminded herself. "But I can't just give her up."

"I'll tell you what, Jennifer. You behave yourself, follow orders, and don't cause trouble, we might set up a spot for her right here outside your cell. You won't be able to touch her—we can't have her dying, can we?—but you'll be able to watch."

Jenny nodded. Her baby did need protection from her. The thought broke what remained of her heart.

"Is that all?" Ward asked, and she nodded again. "Good. We'll plan to start your tests after you give birth. You won't have that baby to hide behind much longer, Jennifer." He glanced at her huge belly. "You're making the right choice here."

Jenny frowned, and soon he walked away, leaving her alone with her thoughts and the growing baby kicking and turning inside her, eager to be born.

* * *

Juliana stood in the laboratory looking down at the young man on the stretcher, bound by straps and gagged, straining helplessly to pull free, looking up at her with fear in his eyes. She couldn't move from where she stood. A leather collar and cuffs bound her neck and wrists, each mounted on the end of a long pole, and three guards in gas masks stood behind her as puppeteers, controlling her movements.

"No!" Juliana shouted, and the middle guard jabbed his pole into the back of her neck, making her stumble forward. The other two pushed and turned their poles until Juliana's hands landed on the man's bare chest. He convulsed, dark lesions opening all over his abdomen. "Stop it!" Juliana screamed, but they ignored her as always.

They'd been forcing her to continue the tests against her will for weeks. She wished they would just shoot her, but they were far too interested in the baby growing inside her. It had a been a very hard pregnancy, being pushed around by guards, examined by doctors in gas masks, never seeing Sebastian or anyone else who cared about her. She tried to keep her sadness buried deep inside where no one could see it.

She felt deathly ill as she watched the blisters and sores spread out across the man's body, rupturing him open. He coughed up a mixture of stomach acid and blood, and some other sticky black fluid drooled from his nostrils.

In less than two minutes, he was dead, half his flesh eaten away, his bones swollen out of shape.

Juliana swayed on her feet, feeling dizzy. A deep cramp seized her insides, and she thought she would vomit everywhere. The cramp turned more painful, tight enough to choke off her breathing, and then it released. Her thighs felt hot and damp. She looked down to see a small wet spot on the front of her gray dress. It grew larger as the wet heat spread down her legs, and drops fell from under to her dress to land on the concrete floor between her ratty prison slippers. The drops were bright red.

"The baby," Juliana whispered. Her legs crumpled under her, but the guards held her up with their poles. "Please help the baby."

The steel door opened, and three medical staff in gas masks ran into the room. With the guards' help, they loaded her onto a stretcher, strapped her down, and removed the leather straps from her wrists and neck.

She felt increasingly dizzy as they rolled her down the wide corridor between the labs. They brought her to the clinic area in the northwest quadrant of the base, and into a surgery room.

Juliana felt her stomach heave, and then a tremendous pressure built inside her. A rush of blood and water spilled out from her, fanning out across the bed, and then something else, a solid mass.

The nurses cut away her dress. Juliana watched as they reached between her legs and pulled it out of her. Her baby, a girl.

The baby was curled up, dripping gore, and not moving. Her skin had a gray pallor.

"Is she all right?" Juliana whispered. "Is she..."

Nobody spoke to her. They deposited the cold, unmoving baby into a steel pan, then dumped the placenta on top. They sealed it with a lid and carried it away, and she never saw it again.

A pained wail emerged from deep inside of her, through her clenched teeth, startling the guards, nurses, and doctors around her. She'd lost the baby, and it was gone forever.

Every imaginable kind of pain overwhelmed her, and then she blacked out under the bright lights.

# Chapter Forty-Four

Jenny lay in the hospital bed in her cube with her hands cuffed to the bed rails, with the entire lower half of her body missing, as far as she could feel. The epidural had kicked in, and she felt a little panicked, knowing she wouldn't be much good if she had to run or fight. A nurse in a hazardous material suit rigged up a green surgical curtain to shield most of her lower body from her sight.

"Don't bother," Jenny whispered. "Whatever you're gonna do, I've seen worse."

They put up the curtain anyway, ignoring her. Jenny looked out through the clear wall. Ward stood just outside, smoking a cigar, accompanied by several researchers.

"Seth," Jenny whispered to Dr. Parker. "He's supposed to be here...I told you."

"I'm sorry," Dr. Parker said, her voice fuzzy and mechanical through the tiny speaker on her hazmat suit. "They decided it was too much of a security risk."

Jenny looked at Ward again. "Seth needs to be here."

"I'm sure Dr. Parker can manage just fine without him," Ward replied, blowing smoke.

"We had a deal," Jenny said.

"To be honest, Seth isn't that interested in you anymore," Ward told her. "He's been shacked up with your pal Mariella for a few months now. They've been having a good old time together." He winked.

Jenny didn't believe him. She pushed back any memories of Sebastian and Mia's relationship in their last life. She was already surrounded by enemies at this most vulnerable moment in her entire life. She had plenty to worry about without letting Ward get under her skin.

Nobody spoke much while they made their preparations. Jenny could feel the thick tension weighing down the room. The doctor and the two nurses were clearly afraid of coming into contact with her flesh and blood, even in their hazmat suits. The two guards flanking the airlock door kept their hands on their stunners, as if Jenny were going to lash out while her womb was cut open in the middle of a cesarean delivery.

The room became very quiet.

"Jenny, we're making the first incision," Dr. Parker said.

"Okay," Jenny whispered. Everything in the world fell away except her absolute terror at what was about to happen. She looked toward the wall of her cube again, some part of her half-expecting to see Seth, but there was only Ward and his hateful sneer, flanked by guards, scientists, and a nurse watching the row of monitors.

Jenny watched the women working on her, barely able to see their faces behind their biohazard masks, clear shields that reflected the bright lights above. She couldn't help thinking of alien abduction stories from the History Channel, people waking up under bright lights to find strange extraterrestrials performing unknown operations on them. That experience, hallucinated or not, was probably about as emotionally cold and inhuman as this surgery.

She had no way of seeing what the doctor was doing beyond the screen, and she didn't dare speak or ask questions that could distract them. The medical staff didn't speak to her at all. Jenny might as well have been a farm animal getting a veterinary visit. A cow, maybe, because her body felt so swollen and heavy.

She waited and waited, listening to the electronic beeps echoing her pounding heart.

"Uh-oh," the doctor whispered.

"Uh-oh? What's uh-oh?" Jenny asked, imagining the scalpel

stabbing the little baby through the foot, or the arm, or the head.

"Please be quiet," the nurse closest to Jenny said, scowling at her.

"Clamp," Dr. Parker said, ignoring Jenny altogether.

Jenny heard her heart beep even faster. She was sweating, barely able to think, her head swirling with nightmares and the memories of countless bloody miscarriages and heart-ripping stillbirths.

An eternity seemed to pass, then another, then another.

"Breech," Dr. Parker said quietly.

Jenny didn't dare ask another question of the semi-hostile medical staff, but she remembered that a breech meant the baby was positioned backwards, and it was considered not good. Her sweat felt like ice, and her heart beat even faster.

She had no idea what was happening beyond the green sheet of plastic. She could distantly feel movement and pressure, but couldn't tell what any of it meant, and the doctor and nurses weren't talking.

After another thousand eternities, Dr. Parker stepped back, holding what Jenny first saw as a strange, dark sea creature, wet and dripping in the doctor's gloves. It took a moment to resolve into the shape of a baby. A gray, unmoving baby.

She felt a grieved sob building inside her chest. It had happened again, just like all the other times, despite their precautions and the help of modern science. Seth should have been there. If Seth were there, he could have helped. Maybe he could still help.

"Seth!" Jenny shouted. "Get Seth! Now!"

"Afraid not." Ward chuckled over his cigar.

Jenny shot him a look of pure hate. She was going to kill him, she realized. She would hunt him down in every incarnation, killing him again and again, maybe for all of eternity. She would never forgive, never stop wanting to punish him.

The doctor massaged the baby, and as if by magic, the baby's gray skin gradually grew pink and warm. The baby's mouth opened, and she let out a powerful scream. *Hello, world.*

Jenny gasped, then whispered, "Hi, baby girl." Tears filled up her eyes. Her arms tried to reach for the tiny girl, but of course Jenny's wrists were still handcuffed.

*I can never touch her*, Jenny reminded herself. *Never.* The word "never" seemed painfully cold and heavy enough to crush her. *Never.*

Jenny gaped as they clamped and cut the cord and cleaned the baby, then weighed and measured her. The baby was tiny, as Jenny must have been when she was born, her eyes clenched shut as she howled and cried. Jenny winced as they stuck her foot for a blood sample.

"It's okay, baby," Jenny said. "You're okay."

Hearing Jenny speak up, the baby stopped crying for a moment and opened her tiny, crystal-blue newborn eyes. She looked in Jenny's direction, and Jenny's heart both melted and fell to pieces. This was her, the little one who'd been stirring in her stomach for so many months. A complete little person with little ears and feet.

"You'll be okay," Jenny said again, hoping that was true. She looked around to see if anyone else felt the same awe she did, but the medical staff seemed in a hurry to finish up and get out. The doctor was already stitching her up.

"Name?" asked the nurse who stood by the monitors outside her cube, who now held a digital tablet.

"Name?" Jenny asked, confused.

"The child's name," the nurse said, impatient. "For the records."

"Oh." Jenny's mind was a blank. This was the kind of thing she should have spent months thinking about and talking over with Seth. Instead, she'd spent her entire pregnancy worrying whether the baby would live, and whether Jenny and the baby would ever escape this place, and whether she would ever see Seth again.

"What will you call her?" Ward asked. "I'm curious myself."

Jenny scowled at him. "Miriam," she said. It had been her mother's name.

"Last name?" the nurse asked. "Morton?"

Jenny thought about it. "Barrett."

"Middle name?"

She was at a loss. "Use Morton, I guess." Jenny watched them lay the baby in an incubator, which looked like a scaled-down version of Jenny's own cubic cell. "Can I...see her?" Jenny asked the nurse.

"You can't get too close," Dr. Parker said. "We don't know whether she has any immunity to your touch. From what you've told us, it's doubtful. Do you understand what that means?"

"How can we find out?" Jenny asked. "I don't want to test it by touching her..."

"I'll see how your blood samples interact, and we'll go from there." Dr. Parker nodded at the nurse, who wheeled the incubator toward the airlock door. The tiny baby, now named Miriam, squalled and reached a little hand back toward her mother.

"Where are you taking her?" Jenny asked, trying to sit up, even though the doctor was still stitching her. "Don't take her away!"

"It's for her own safety," Dr. Parker said. "You should know that better than anyone."

"But so soon?"

"They're very vulnerable to disease at this stage. Their immune system hasn't developed."

Jenny nodded—she might hate everyone around her, but she knew Dr. Parker was right about that. "You'll be okay," Jenny said, feeling her throat close up. She said it again and again, as if repeating it would make it true, while the nurse wheeled the incubator away to the steel door set in the concrete wall of the laboratory. Jenny could hear the baby cry all the way out the door.

"When do I see her again?" Jenny asked.

"We'll see," Dr. Parker replied, not looking at her.

"Can they please bring her back? Just for a minute?" Jenny asked, but the doctor only shook her head. Jenny pulled at her restraints again. The lower half of her body was still numb and had just been through surgery, and everyone around her wore biohazard gear. She didn't have a chance of fighting her way out.

Any remaining strength vanished from Jenny's body. Her head flopped back on the bed, and she closed her eyes and let herself cry and cry, ignoring the final flurry of activity around her, ignoring whatever taunting words Ward said over the intercom. Eventually, everyone was finally gone, all the surgical equipment removed from her cell, and the lights were mercifully dimmed. Jenny lay in the dark, sobbing and aching and already missing the baby with all her soul, until the combination of painkillers and exhaustion finally overwhelmed her and dragged her down into darkness. She felt like she was drowning.

* * *

Juliana gradually awoke to the dim, fuzzy world around her. She felt a light, constant breeze, and then slowly realized she was moving.

She was strapped the gurney, her dress still soaked in blood. She'd only been out for a few minutes. The Nazi doctors had been extremely stingy with the pain medicine.

Now she rolled down a familiar concrete corridor, attended by two nurses, who wore surgical masks, caps, and gloves, and two S.S. officers in gas masks who were more concerned about flirting with the young blond nurses than watching the small, blood-soaked form of Juliana. She was firmly strapped to the gurney, and they clearly believed she was unconscious and badly weakened. They were only half right. Juliana quickly closed her eyes again and remained limp on the gurney.

They rolled on past Juliana's cell, toward the end of the corridor. They must have been taking her to the showers, Juliana reasoned, to wash off all the blood and gore before depositing her back in the cell for the night.

She heard the squeal of the bathroom door opening, felt the bump as they crossed the threshold to the shower room, which was just another concrete-slab room with a few nozzles in one wall.

Juliana summoned up the demon plague within her, growing boils, cysts, and bloody pustules all over her body. With years of practice in her carnival act, she'd developed great control over how and where the plague appeared on her skin. She made sure that every inch of herself looked as repulsive and malignant as possible, raw swollen skin leaking diseased fluids—except for her face, which she kept pristine.

She heard the four people around her make disgusted sounds. The nurses begged the S.S. men to unstrap Juliana and lay on her on the floor for them, but the men snorted and refused, though they wore thick leather gloves. They made the nurses agree to drink with them later, and then they loosened Juliana's straps.

Juliana's eyes opened. The guards stood at the head of the gurney, on either side of her, while the nurses were at her feet. She'd had months to study the gas masks, to imagine the fastest way to grab the strap and loosen it from their necks.

One of the guards saw her eyes open, and he pointed and shouted. Now Juliana let the ugliest, most repugnant combination of dripping boils, festering sores, and leprous ulcers erupt all over her face. A nurse screamed, and everyone made sounds of disgust. While her face distracted them for a few seconds, she reached up with both hands, ripped loose their straps, and touched her plague-filled fingertips to their throats. She imagined a dense, angry cloud of tiny black flies chewing through their skin.

Blood dripped out from their loosened masks, splattered Juliana's fingers. One guard collapsed, and the other pulled away from her, only to stagger back into a concrete wall and slide down, leaving a streak of dark blood above him.

The nurses screamed and ran. Juliana's first instinct was to let them go, but then she realized they would only go alert all the guards. She wouldn't have enough time to escape.

She filled her lungs with the dank air of the prison showers and breathed out a long stream of dark spores toward the nurse's retreating backs. They made it to the doorway before the plague caught up with them, eating through their hair and scalp and bone. The both stumbled and fell to the floor, their heads bursting open like rotten pumpkins, leaving puddles of infected bones and brains.

Juliana eased her way off the gurney and landed unsteadily on her feet. Her balance was poor, and her body already felt strained to the breaking point...but there was something else rising inside her, dark, ancient, and cold. Something eager for righteous killing. Something that delighted in death.

She knelt by the guards, ignoring the gore that dripped from their bug-eyed masks. One of them had a thick ring of keys, which he'd probably borrowed from the cellblock guards at the desk outside the corridor so they could put Juliana back into her cell. She took the keys, along with the two Luger pistols from the dead guards' holsters.

Juliana stepped her bare feet over the decaying spill from the nurses' ruptured heads. She stalked up the corridor, opening the door panels to look into each cell. Most were empty. She felt renewed anger when she saw the fading red stains on Evelina's floor and wall. The girl had been gentle and quiet, her voice through the vent providing Juliana's only companionship for weeks of pregnancy. They had simply decided that her race was now too much of an inconvenience, and so they'd killed her. Juliana hoped she would see Alise on the way out, so she could leave her pretty face contorted, swollen, and lifeless.

Sebastian was the only other prisoner remaining on the hall. He took in a sharp breath when she opened his door, wearing her blood-soaked gray dress. He ran to embrace her, and the plague sores on her skin faded slowly.

"Juliana! What happened? Are you hurt?" Sebastian asked.

"The baby's gone," Juliana said. Her voice was flat, without a spark of emotion. All that remained inside her was a cold, endless darkness. "Our baby. Now we're leaving. You take these, I don't need them." She held out the two pistols.

"Our baby?" Sebastian held her tight, his voice full of grief. She felt nothing. "Oh, God, no...Alise only told me a few weeks ago."

"There are at least two guards at the desk outside," Juliana said. "If they're wearing their gas masks, you shoot them. If not, I'll kill them. It'll be quieter."

"We're leaving right now?"

"Anyone who gets in our way dies."

He gave her a look of shock, tinged with a little fear. She stepped out of his cell and began walking up the corridor towards the heavy door at the end, keys in her hand.

Sebastian caught up with her. "We...should get Mia out. She's pregnant, too."

"With your baby." Juliana's voice remained flat and cold.

"Yes...but...only because of Alise, I promise! She can cast a spell on you—"

"I've been under her spell before," Juliana told him. "I killed a man, and I was sad about it. Tonight, I'll kill a lot of them, and I won't care. It's funny how things turn."

"Okay...but listen, honestly, I had no desire to be with her, as soon as Alise stopped doping me I got into a fight with Niklaus about seeing you, that's how I ended up down here."

"At least we were on the same floor."

"I'm really, really sorry. You don't know how terrible I feel, how much I wish—"

"Stop talking." Juliana inserted the key into the door and pushed it open.

The two guards at the desk turned with sly smiles on their faces, expecting to see the nurses and their fellow S.S. men. They stood and shouted when he saw the prisoners in gray clothes—Juliana's hands and dress dripping blood, Sebastian pointing two pistols at them.

One guard reached for his gas mask on the desk in front of him, while the other reached for the pistol at his belt. Both of them were too slow. Juliana exhaled another writhing swarm of plague spores into their faces, eating away their flesh. Their eyelids, noses, and lips rotted away, and dark hives erupted on their eyeballs and facial tendons. They howled in agony, but they died quickly and toppled over behind the desk.

Juliana unlocked the door to the outer corridor, then ran to unlock the stairwell door.

"I didn't know you could do that," Sebastian whispered as they ran up the concrete stairs, their footfalls echoing up and down the stairwell.

"Alise taught me," Juliana said. "Sometimes being under her spell has its benefits, am I right, Sebastian?"

Sebastian opened his mouth to answer, then left it hanging open, as if he'd realized there was no good reply.

The door to the dormitory level opened, and Juliana recognized the doctor who'd examined her during the miscarriage, along with the head of research Dr. Wichtmann, and a pair of younger biologists who worked in the labs.

"Juliana!" Dr. Wichtmann gasped, looking her over. "You should...you should be resting! We were coming to check on your condition."

"He has a gun!" One of the biologists pointed at Sebastian.

"In all honesty, I have two," Sebastian replied, raising both of them.

"*Herr Doktor*," Juliana said to Wichtmann, "Allow me to return the kindness you've shown me as your guest."

She seized his hand and opened her jaws, unleashing death and pain on all of them. They fell to the concrete, their limbs twisting and jerking, their bodies writhing like bugs in poison. Wichtmann himself rolled down the stairs, leaving dark splashes of his decaying, plague-infested flesh and blood behind him like footprints. His balding head cracked against the concrete landing.

"She's one floor up." Sebastian ran up the next flight. Juliana glanced over the dying, bleeding, groaning men, then followed him.

The door to the maternity level opened onto a spacious area with the guard station at the far side from the stairwell, next to the door to the maternity rooms. The three guards leaped to their feet the moment they saw the blood-spattered prisoners emerge.

Juliana breathed another cloud of plague spores at them, which thinned and spread out as it drifted across the room. They had plenty of time to draw their weapons, so Sebastian charged at them and opened fire with both pistols, waving the guns back and forth to try and hit all three of them.

One S.S. guard caught a bullet to the chest, and another was shot in the arm while reaching for his pistol, then in the leg. The third guard, apparently smarter than his co-workers, had ducked behind the desk, gas mask in hand. Scattered plague spores landed on the wounded guard's face and neck, conjuring bloody lesions, as he dropped out of sight behind the desk.

Sebastian and Juliana continued running toward the desk, then ducked and squatted in front of it.

"This is your last chance!" Seth shouted in German. "Come out or die!" He winked at Juliana, then stood and pointed his pistols over the desk. Nothing happened, so he jumped up on the desk and walked across it.

Bullets fired up at him, and one caught him through the leg. Sebastian toppled to the desk, pulling the triggers on both his pistols, but they were empty.

Juliana stood in time to see Seth growl and leap on the Nazi guard in the gas mask, who waved a smoking pistol of his own. Juliana ducked as he fired it wildly. She crawled around the desk, and found Seth had pinned the Nazi with his legs and stripped off his gas mask, and was now beating the guard's head with the butt of an empty pistol, drawing blood from his nose and jaw.

Juliana touched the guard's head, killing him fast. She looked toward the guard who'd only been wounded, but he was curled up in convulsions. She killed him, too. Seth dropped his empty gun and took two more pistols from the dead S.S. guards.

"Everyone must have heard that," Sebastian said. "It's probably still echoing in Kranzler's office. They're all coming for us."

"Then let's prepare to kill all of them." Juliana opened the door to the maternity hall. They found Mia in one of the spacious bedrooms, sprawled on a quilted bedspread on a queen-sized bed, next to an empty bassinet with a teddy bear dressed like a German soldier. Her stomach had grown much larger. Her eyelids barely lifted as she saw them, and she gave a drowsy smile.

"My friends," Mia said in a drugged voice, half-heartedly waving one hand without raising it from the bed. "I love you both so much."

"We're leaving," Juliana said. "Get moving."

"Leaving? No...Why?"

"We have to escape," Sebastian said. "Can you get up?"

"Hmm, yeah." Mia's eyes closed. She was deep in Alise-induced ecstasy.

"We have to go now!" Juliana took her by the shoulders. Mia's dress had shifted, leaving one shoulder bare, and Juliana accidentally burned her with her touch. Blisters welled up on Mia's shoulder and neck, and she hissed and pulled away. She sat up, rubbing the infected area and scowling at Juliana, as if the pain had woken her. Then a flash of recognition crossed her eyes.

"Juliana!" Mia looked from her to Sebastian, then touched her swollen stomach. "Oh, God. What have I done? Oh, God, Juliana, I'm sorry...I...." She started to weep, covering her eyes. "I'm an awful person."

A shrill, clanging alarm echoed through the entire base at a deafening volume.

"They're coming for us," Juliana said. "We have to go. They could be here any second." The barracks and armory were in the southeast quadrant of the base, while the cellblock and dormitories were on the southwest quadrant, not far away.

Mia nodded and pushed herself to her feet, ignoring Sebastian's offered hand. "I'm ready."

They hurried out along the corridor, Juliana and Sebastian side by side, Mia protected behind them.

"They could already be waiting for us outside that door," Juliana said.

"Let's go out shooting, then," Seth said.

"Wait, I can look." Mia grabbed Sebastian's arm and closed her eyes. "Not yet, there won't be anyone out there. But a lot of them are coming, we're going to have trouble."

Juliana opened the door and led the way out.

"The stairs to the exit are just one level up," Sebastian said, angling toward the stairwell.

"But there are probably more guards on that exit than any other," Juliana said. "In case we try to escape. I think we should cut across to the administrative area and use that exit. It'll be less protected against us escaping."

"But the stairs are right there!" Sebastian argued.

"No, I think she is being smart," Mia said. "They would expect us to try and leave the same way we entered."

"I'm going up the stairs!" Sebastian insisted, tucking one pistol in the back of his pants. He grabbed Mia's hand, startling her.

"You'll die up there," she said quickly.

"Just checking." He let go of her hand. "So we go right through the center of the base, through the labs, towards the offices and apartments of the people in charge. Is that actually our plan?"

"Yes." Juliana began to run. He hurried just behind her, trying to catch up.

Mia took Sebastian hand's as they ran.

"What are you doing?" he asked.

"Keeping us alive." Mia gripped him tighter as they approached the door to the central corridor. "Two guards coming through there in a second! Juliana, watch out!" She ducked, pulling Sebastian to the floor with her.

Juliana turned against the wall by the door, tucking herself out of sight as the door opened and two S.S. guards bolted through it, their pistols drawn. Juliana stepped out behind them and exhaled a cloud of her plague, and it ate into the backs of their heads.

On the floor, Sebastian raised his pistols in case he needed to shoot them anyway, but the two S.S. men crashed to the floor with the back halves of their skulls eaten away.

Sebastian stood, and Mia stood behind him and embraced him. She lifted his shirt and pressed her hands against his stomach.

"Stop cuddling!" Juliana shouted.

"I'm healing," Mia said. "Some of your...whatever that was hit me. How did you do that?"

"I just imagine that I'd like to see everyone in the room dead," Juliana replied. She looked closer and saw the small, dark sores fading from Mia's hands and arms.

She turned and ran through the door, momentarily indifferent to whether they followed her or not, feeling a flash of hate for both of them. Even though Alise had entranced them, Juliana couldn't help how she felt.

At the moment, all she wanted to do was kill. She ran up the central corridor of the base, hoping to see Kranzler or Alise, the plague boiling and blistering all over her.

"There is a guard station ahead!" Mia warned, clasping hands with Sebastian as they ran, trying to catch up with Juliana. "Juliana, be careful!"

Juliana realized she'd miscalculated. She was accustomed to moving one level below where they were, and she'd expected to reach the wide corridor between the big concrete laboratory rooms. Instead, on this level, they were approaching the observation deck from which Kranzler and Wichtmann had watched the experiments.

She stopped and turned. With the alarm clanging and echoing, there was no point in whispering. "Mia, how many of them? Where?"

Mia closed her eyes and explained the layout of the guard station next to the large double doors to the observation deck, and predicted where each guard would be sitting. "I keep seeing us getting killed here," Mia added.

They spoke quickly to work out their attack. Juliana went first, blowing out the thickest, darkest cloud she could muster, taking out the guards who hadn't put on their gas masks. She fell flat on the floor and rolled aside, making herself as small and difficult a target as possible. The cold darkness inside, the thing driving her forward despite her pain and exhaustion, seemed to know all about fighting, as if she carried the experience of many battles inside her.

Two of the guards had already strapped on their masks, so Sebastian had to shoot them. He rounded the corner after Juliana, knowing exactly where to point his pistols, killing the guards before they had time to see him and register that he was there. Mia followed, touching Sebastian's neck.

"We're safe for a minute," Mia announced. "Then the guards from the barracks are going to come up behind us, with gas masks and machine guns."

"Then we're going to charge through these doors onto the observation deck," Juliana told her.

Mia squeezed Sebastian's hand again. "Nobody there is wearing gas masks."

"Good." Juliana smiled, then approached the double doors and flung them open.

The observation deck was in a panic, people shouting questions at each other, talking on phones, trying to find out what was happening. Heads turned at the sight of Juliana in her bloody dress—scientists, typing pool ladies, and a cluster of S.S. officers at the center of the room. Frightened whispers spread as it became clear that the guards outside had been defeated.

Juliana spotted Kranzler standing behind his desk, smoking a cigar and glaring at her, flanked by more S.S. officers.

"What do you want?" Kranzler growled, not appearing

particularly shocked that she'd managed to escape the cellblock.

"I want to go home," Juliana said. "But you'll come after me if I leave. Won't you?"

"You're free to leave," Kranzler told her. "No one will stop you. I'll give the order."

"I don't believe you."

"It's the truth." Kranzler sat down at a desk in front of a pile of paperwork. "Go ahead."

Juliana looked at the frightened faces in the room. The S.S. men had their hands on their pistols, waiting for Kranzler's order.

She walked deeper into the room, watching people shuffle back from her on either side, bumping against the windows overlooking the labs. Kranzler's Nazi officers stood where they were, watching her closely.

Juliana was badly tempted to look back over her shoulder and see what Sebastian and Mia might be doing, but she didn't want to spoil the impression that she was alone.

"Why did you do this, Kranzler?" Juliana asked. "All of this?"

"You must know by now." Kranzler indulged in his cigar, smiled as he exhaled. "To identify surpernormal humans, those far ahead on the evolutionary curve. To study them. To breed them. To improve the human race."

"Is that what you're trying to do?" Juliana slowed her approach, expecting the S.S. officer to start firing at any moment. "And what did you learn about me?"

"The same as the others who have true powers," Kranzler said. "Sebastian, Mia...It transfers through touch. It is not biological or chemical in nature. It defies all known physics." He looked her over. "You and I might have more in common than you know. We should be on the same side. We should work together for the advancement of the human race. The Reich will raise up humanity, purify our race of all impurities, and push us forward into the future. You could be a powerful tool in the Fuehrer's arsenal, Juliana. The other supernormals are amusing, sometimes useful. But you...yes, you are like a goddess of death. Your power shows great potential."

Juliana stopped in place, chewing her lips, as if considering it. "Do you mean this? Even though I've killed some of your guards?"

"Your remarkable ability to kill is precisely what I admire. You would be lavishly rewarded. No more prison cells or dormitories for you. Your value is far beyond that."

"I do have a question, *Gruppenführer*," she said. "Alise used her power on me, though she cannot touch me." Juliana wished Alise were in the room, but there was no sign of her or Niklaus. "She was able to form strange pink spores and blow them through the air. Do you think I could do that? Would you know?"

"That's exactly what I believe." He stood, approaching her now, a broad-shouldered man who towered over her, with a swastika on his black sleeve. "With time...with help and training from me...you could be far more powerful. You could destroy armies. Let me guide you. Let me be your teacher. I have a great knowledge about it, drawn from my own personal experience." He stared at her carefully. "As I said, we are more similar than you think. Like you, I have a supernormal touch."

Juliana watched him raise his hand and open it. She decided it wasn't worth the risk of waiting to find out what it might be, if he was telling the truth. If he did have a supernatural power, she would deny him the chance to use it against her.

She exhaled the dense plague she'd been building up inside her. After using it so often, she was developing better control over the airborne plague. She imagined one of the endless flocks of blackbirds she'd seen as she traveled the South with the carnival, a river of cawing black shapes that flowed from horizon to horizon. The first time she'd seen one, she'd stood mesmerized as countless thousands of them crossed the sky. The flock had taken almost an hour to pass.

She directed her plague like the river of blackbirds, swirling around the heads of Kranzler and the other officers, attacking their eyes first. They drew their pistols automatically, screaming in pain, and a few fired blindly in her direction.

The Nazi officers howled and covered their red, rotting faces with swollen, ulcerous hands. The plague flowed thicker around them, streams of it burrowing bloody tunnels into their faces and chest. Kranzler and the other officers fell dead, their faces eaten open all the way to their throats.

Juliana looked around at all the remaining people in the room while the plague spores floated in a swirling cloud above Kranzler's festering corpse. They stared back at her.

Juliana exhaled again, and the cloud of spores expanded rapidly, beyond her control now. The airborne plague filled the room, and dozens of people collapsed to the floor, coughing up blood. Their scalps and skin sloughed off as they clawed over each other, desperate to escape through one door or the other, shrieking and groaning.

She finally looked back. Sebastian was proceeding cautiously into the room, a pistol in each hand, but nobody was interested in challenging him now. Mia clung close to his back, hands under his shirt again, using his touch to protect her from the cloud of plague eating away at the slowly dying crowd of Nazis.

Those closest to Juliana were already dead, while those farthest away, by the windows, were slowly sinking to the floor, moaning as their flesh crumbled, crackled, and peeled from their bones. The demon plague had spared no one.

"More guards will be here soon!" Mia shouted. "Gas masks, machine guns..."

Sebastian closed the doors through which they'd entered and latched a security bar in place.

"That won't hold them long."

"Let's find their exit," Juliana said. She turned and led the way again, through the double doors. To her left was the clinic and pharmacy area for the base. To her right, the suite of offices from which Kranzler and his cohorts had ruled the base, and she went that way.

They passed the offices and reached an intersection of corridors.

"If it's laid out like our section, the exit should be somewhere..." Sebastian pointed to their left.

"You're right," Mia said, still holding onto him. "But the guards are waiting for trouble, and they have machine guns. We don't make it out alive, that's what I see."

"We can't go back!" Sebastian said.

"No, they're coming from that direction, too. We'll die fast," Mia agreed.

"Where can we go and survive? Hide in the offices? Can we try that?"

Mia concentrated. "You'll die. We have to move from here!"

They ran down a side corridor, towards the network of supply and maintenance tunnels. Sebastian kept pointing to different doors, asking Mariella what she saw.

"Where do we go?" he kept asking. "That storage room? That maintenance closet?"

"That...yes! We live longer if we go in there." Mia smiled, pointing to the door marked MAINTENANCE.

"Are you kidding?" Juliana asked.

Sebastian pulled on the door. "It's locked!"

"Here!" Juliana threw him the keyring she'd lifted from the guard. "Maybe one will work."

"Which one?" Sebastian started testing them, one key after another.

"It ends up being that one." Mia picked out a key, and Sebastian skipped to it.

"Yes! Thanks!" He opened the door, and cool, dank air whirled out. "It's a...cave."

"The S.S. are going to gun us down in about ten seconds!" Mia told them, letting go of Sebastian and running into the open door. "Unless we go this way now!"

"I'm convinced," Sebastian said, following Juliana into the door and closing it behind them.

They moved into a rocky cave space where the air was stale and thick. It was dimly lit by scattered electrical bulbs, and it echoed with the familiar rattling sound they'd heard every night from the ventilation panels in their rooms, only a hundred times louder. They faced a piece of machinery as big as a small house, with wide ventilation ducts running horizontally over their heads, feeding fresh air all over the administrative quadrant. The lower levels beneath the offices, she knew, were the residence and recreation areas for the officers, the scientists, the medical staff, and the administrative personnel.

A single enormous vertical duct extended from the top of the machine and vanished into the rock ceiling overhead. It would reach all the way to the surface, sucking in air from above. Juliana now fully understood why they would need such an elaborate ventilation— the air in this cave area tasted like death, with no plants anywhere to refresh it.

Sebastian opened the access panel to the machine, which was the size of a small door, and he stepped inside. Juliana leaned in for a look.

He stood in a steel-walled cavity the size of Juliana's room down in the cellblock. A constant blast of fresh, cold air hammered down from the giant shaft to the world above, creating a windstorm that blew Sebastian's hair back and forth across his face. A coal-powered furnace heated the air, its exhaust whisked away by a narrow duct— even in spring, the mountain air in Germany was chilly. An array of large fans all around him sucked the heated fresh air away along a tangle of aluminum ducts to feed the rooms inside the base.

"Look!" he shouted to be heard over the clanging machinery and whooshing air. He jumped up, reaching into the wide vertical duct, and then he hung there, swinging in midair, one hand out of sight. He waved with the other. "Rungs." He dropped to the floor, his nose crinkling. "Smells like somebody cleans this duct with some nasty chemicals, too. Don't breathe too deep in there."

"Do the rungs go all the way up?" Juliana asked.

"It looks like it. Will we live if we go this way?" Sebastian asked, taking Mia's hand so she could look into his future. Juliana couldn't help resenting it.

"Maybe...it's all confused, I can't see..." Mia's forehead crinkled.

"What if we stay right here?"

"They'll hunt us down."

"'Confused' sounds better to me than getting hunted down. Ladies should go first." Sebastian held out a hand to Juliana.

"Pregnant ladies go first." Juliana folded her arms over her bloodstained dress. She watched Sebastian boost Mia up into the duct.

"I can't!" Mia swayed in his arms, unbalanced as she held onto the metal rung in the wall.

"You're doing fine." Sebastian smiled up at her, and she smiled back, soothed by him. Juliana could have killed them both.

Mia reached up for the next rung, and the next, and he lifted her until he could place her feet on the bottom rung.

"There." Sebastian reached for Juliana. "Now it's your turn."

"You go first," Juliana told him. She could hear the sound of approaching boots.

"I can't. Then you won't be able to reach," he said.

"I'm a better jumper than you think," she told him. "I need to be last in case someone climbs up after us. And you need to be with Mia so you can play your looking-into-the-future game."

"It's helped us a lot," Sebastian said. "We'd be dead without it."

"We'll be dead right now if you don't get up there and out of my way. Climb fast."

"If you really think—"

"Go!"

Sebastian jumped up and grabbed the rung with one hand. He began climbing hand over hand, pulling himself up toward the giant steel fan and the night sky above.

Juliana looked at the armored steel plate mounted on one side of the shaft. It could swing down and around to seal off the vertical air duct in case of chemical attack. She would just barely be able to jump up and grab the lever that set it in motion.

"I'm not coming," Juliana said. "They'll just hunt us down, and they'll keep doing horrible things to more people, won't they? I have to put an end to it."

"You can't stay here!" Sebastian said.

"We won't make it if I don't take the guards out while I can," Juliana said. "We had our chance, Sebastian. We lost it. Just make sure Mia and her baby get out alive. That's what matters."

"Juliana, please don't do this," Mia begged.

"You should hurry," Juliana said. "Look into the future if you don't believe me." She backed up for a running start, then jumped and pulled the lever. The armored plate swung down from the side of the duct on a hinge, then back up the other way to seal it. She heard Sebastian shout her name a final time, and Mia pleaded with her to stop. She never saw them again.

Juliana turned to face the sound of approaching boots and shouting German voices. With the vertical intake duct sealed, the array of powerful ventilation fans created a vacuum as they sucked the air out of the cavity where she stood. It felt as if the fans were trying to pull the hair from her head and the skin from her face.

The maintenance door opened, and an S.S. guard in a gas mask looked in, spotted her, and dodged aside. A column of them entered, all in gas masks and carrying machine guns.

Juliana summoned up the demon plague a final time, drawing on the last of her energy. As she breathed out, she imagined her entire body unraveling, all the way down to her heart and bones, every bit of flesh translated into deadly spores.

She breathed out a dense, dark cloud, feeling the mass of her body beginning to dissolve, as though she were hollowing herself out. The ventilation fans sucked the spores away, channeling them throughout the base.

The guards raised their machine guns, and she spread out her arms.

"Go ahead," she told them, breathing out another dense clouds, feeling her bones weaken.

Four of them opened fire, hammering her with round after round. She staggered back, light as a ballerina, as the bullets tore her apart.

Then she floated, watching her ruined body fall to the floor like an old costume worn to rags. With her body dead, her mind followed the streams of plague flowing through the air vents, spinning through underground rooms and hallways, her consciousness suddenly formless and whirling free like a dust storm.

She had no control of the swarming spores. She could only watch distantly as they flowed through hallways and apartments, killing Nazi officers and nurses alike, then spreading through the complex, killing off the kitchen staff as well as the guards, scores of people falling dead. Even the guards in gas masks were not safe, because her final cloud of spores, filled with all her anger and hate for her captors, was so virulent and aggressive that it ate right through their greyish-green wool uniforms and burrowed deep into their flesh. If there were any innocent souls among those in the underground base, God would have to pick them out from the plague-ridden mass of bodies Himself, if God cared about such things.

She watched them die and die, all of them at once, every plague spore providing her a vantage point, as if she were thousands of different places at the same moment, looking out from thousands of viewpoints. She felt like a sandstorm, sweeping through the bodies of everyone, leaving no one behind.

In time, she drifted back to gaze at her own bullet-shattered corpse, with no more emotion for it than a cast-off piece of clothing on the floor. She'd already begun to see that her life as Juliana was only the most recent chapter in a story that stretched back a hundred thousand years, all of her lives as a human being. She recalled that she was an outsider on this plane, in this world, not a human soul at all. If human beings had an afterlife, that was not for her to experience. She could only wait for the opportunity to be born again. Until then, she was isolated. Between lives, her kind could only communicate through formless feelings and sensations. True communication and contact required a human shape.

She was dead, beyond pain, beyond suffering, beyond desire,

beyond hope.  In the native formless condition of her soul, she could only watch, wait, and listen.

# Chapter Forty-Five

It was three in the morning when Tommy opened the door to Esmeralda's concrete cell. He left the lights off, though the camera in her ceiling probably had a night mode. He shook her by the shoulder. "Wake up. We're going."

"What?" Esmeralda sat up, rubbing her eyes. "Who...what are we doing?"

"I'm helping you escape," he whispered. "Like you wanted. We have to go now. I brought you these." He dropped a folded set of surgical scrubs onto her bed. "You don't want to be wearing the orange jumpsuit."

Esmeralda looked at the thin blue shirt and pants.

"We have to go now. You know they're watching," Tommy urged.

She nodded and got out of bed. He relished a moment of seeing her in the simple cotton bra and panties they'd issued her, the delicious curves of her warm, brown body...her long, glossy black hair, her deep, dark eyes. He'd missed her badly. He'd made a few more visits at Ward's instruction, explaining why she needed to agree to work with ASTRIA. He knew her life would be in danger if she didn't start acting happy to cooperate. The flickers of past-life memory he'd experienced since arriving Germany made that clear. When Ward, or Kranzler, was done with you, your life became disposable.

"I'm ready," she whispered.

"They'll be coming for us." Tommy led the way out into the cellblock corridor. He'd spent more than a week working out his plan, such as it was. He'd blasted a guard full of fear and taken his access card, then gone down to the cellblock and terrified the guards there, breaking their minds.

"We should get Jenny," Esmeralda whispered as they hurried along the corridor.

"I thought of that," Tommy said. "Look."

Mariella and Seth emerged from Seth's cell. Like Esmeralda, Seth had changed from his jumpsuit into surgical scrubs. Mariella had come down with Tommy, and she'd freed Seth from his cell with an access card taken from one of the cellblock guards.

Seth looked suspiciously at all three of them—Tommy, who'd always been his enemy in their past encounters; Esmeralda, who Seth had seen possessed by Ashleigh's soul; and Mariella, who had been cooperating with Ward for months.

"If this is a trap, you're all dead," Seth told them. "I mean it."

"It's not a trap, Seth. The guards could be here any second." Mariella took Seth's arm, and her expression turned to one of horror. "They'll be here in a minute, a response team with biohazard masks and automatic rifles. We have to run!" She pulled Seth behind her as she ran north along the wide corridor.

"Who is she?" Esmeralda whispered to Tommy as they started running.

"Mariella," Tommy said. "She can see the future."

Tommy had taken a huge risk asking Mariella to help him break Esmeralda free. Mariella saw Tommy as someone loyal to Ward, and he was supposed to see her the same way. He'd only approached her with the idea because he remembered that she had decided to escape in their last life. Tommy no longer cared what happened to himself— he was determined to help Esmeralda. So he'd taken the risk, suggesting they could free Jenny and Seth at the same time. He had gambled that Mariella wanted to help her friends.

It was paying off—once they freed Jenny, the five of them would be far more difficult for the guards to stop than Tommy and

Esmeralda would have been on their own.

They passed the guards who'd been on duty at the cellblock desk, one of them now trying to hide behind a fake potted plant, the other waving his TASER and screaming at shadows on the ceiling.

From his previous life, Tommy knew every inch of the facility, the side corridors and maintenance tunnels. Anything might have changed since then, doors and hallways could have been sealed, but between Tommy's memories and Mariella's ability to see the future by keeping her hand on Seth's arm, they found the safest course through to the lab corridor, avoiding the guards ahead and the heavily armed team pursuing them from behind.

Mariella predicted that two guards had been stationed in the lab corridor, dressed in biohazard armor but armed only with TASER guns, unlike the response team coming up behind them, who were armed with machine guns. They'd been ordered to stand in front of the door to Jenny's lab.

"I'll go first," Seth said when they reached the door. The small guard station by the lab corridor was unmanned. Ward was clearly relying on digital surveillance to replace some of the roaming guard patrols and numerous small guard stations of the Nazi days. This also meant that someone was watching, telling the armed response team exactly where to find them.

Seth closed his eyes for a moment, and his skin slowly took on an unearthly white glow, making him look almost angelic. Even his hair gleamed like gold. He must have been summoning up his power, turning it up the way Tommy could turn up the fear if he really wanted to blast someone's mind apart.

"Tommy, you have to help me," Seth whispered. "Whatever they do to you, I'll fix. Ready?"

Tommy nodded, and Seth charged through the door, shouting at the top of his lungs, Tommy running alongside him. Tommy was ready to lash out, breathe out fear as he'd done in Charleston, but he held it in for now. It wouldn't do much good against the two guards' biohazard armor, he thought.

As Seth and Tommy approached, the guards shouted at them to freeze and raised their yellow stun guns. Seth pulled ahead, guarding Tommy, and he took an electrified barb in the chest. It trailed wire back to the guard's stun gun, like a sharp little harpoon.

Seth crashed to his knees, his spine snapping back and forth like a whip, foam spilling from his mouth. He flopped over onto the tiled floor and lay there like a fish choking on the air.

Tommy zigged and zagged toward the guards, making it more difficult for the second guard to get a good shot at him. While he did, the first guard pulled a long, steel flashlight from his belt, ready to bash Tommy.

Neither guard expected Seth to leap up from the floor, ripping the stun gun from the first guard's hands. Seth threw himself directly at the second guard, not bothering to weave and duck like Tommy, and he caught the second TASER barb in his stomach. He tumbled again to the floor.

Tommy dodged behind Seth and attacked the first guard, grabbing for the blunt flashlight in his hand. He held it up while the guard tried to force it down on Tommy's head. With his other hand, Tommy grabbed for the straps of the guard's masked helmet, but the guard's other arm rose to block him.

While Seth writhed on the floor, the second guard came after Tommy, cracking his steel flashlight down on Tommy's head and back. Tommy held onto the first guard with the fixation of a rabid dog.

The blows stopped coming, and he heard the sound of girls screaming. Through the blood leaking down into one eye, he saw that Mariella and Esmeralda had attacked the second guard, Esmeralda trying to wrestle the steel flashlight from his hand, Mariella ripping at his mask. When she pulled it off his head, Tommy grabbed the man's face and filled him with fear.

The guard crawled away, sobbing and screaming about "Mr. O'Grady's dog." The girls turned their attention to the first guard, still wrestling with Tommy. Mariella stripped his helmet off, while Esmeralda pulled his steel flashlight free and cracked him across the head. The guard sank to the floor, unconscious.

The girls helped Seth to his feet. His blue eyes were dazed, and he smelled like burnt hair.

"We have to keep moving," Mariella said. "The real guards are coming."

Tommy swiped his stolen access card through the slot next to the steel door to Jenny's lab, but the little indicator light stayed red.

"This card doesn't access her lab," he told the others.

"Tommy, look at you!" Esmeralda touched his face. "You're

bleeding."

"Maybe this guy can open it." Seth took the ID card from the unconscious guard and swiped it through the notch in the reader. The light flicked from red to green, and he hauled open the heavy door and ran inside.

Jenny was locked inside a clear-walled cell with its own ventilation system. The lights were dim for the night, and the only sound was Jenny's heart monitor. Seth ran to the clear cube and saw her asleep on a hospital bed inside. He pounded on the wall beside her.

She awoke slowly, and Seth wondered whether she was heavily medicated. She blinked at him while he spoke.

"Jenny, we're getting out of here," Seth said. "But we have to hurry."

"Why's Tommy here?" Jenny asked.

"He's helping me escape," Esmeralda said. "All of us, together."

"The guards are on the way," Mariella added. "We don't have much time."

"We have to get the baby." Jenny hurried to the airlock door of her cell, and Seth ran to meet her.

"You had the baby?" Seth asked. "The baby is..."

"Alive, Seth," Jenny said. Her eyes glistened. "She made it. She's alive."

"A girl. And she's alive." Seth slowly smiled at Jenny.

"They're keeping her at the clinic," Mariella said, pointing northwest. "I've been listening."

"There's nowhere to swipe the access card," Seth said, studying the door's control panel, which had a small numbered keypad. "It's a combination lock."

"I've been watching them do it every day," Jenny told him. "It changes every week, but right now I'm pretty sure it's 335598."

Seth keyed in the code and pulled open the outer door. He ran into the airlock and opened the inner door, and Jenny jumped on him, wrapping her arms around his shoulders and holding him tight.

"Seth, it's been so awful without you," she whispered. "Horrible."

"I missed you so much," he said. "But the baby's really okay?"

"A healthy little girl." Jenny smiled through her tears and kissed him.

"We *really* have to get going now," Mariella said, touching Seth's arm.

"Stay where you are!" a voice commanded over the intercom. This time, it sounded like Ward. "Guards are on the way."

The five of them hurried out the door. Mariella again watched the ever-shifting future and picked out the safest route through the base.

They made it to the short corridor in front of the clinic's closed double doors.

"We're done!" Mariella shook her head. "The clinic is full of staff, and the armed guards are almost here..." Everyone could hear the sound of boots echoing on tile. "I don't see what we can do."

"Tommy, can you panic the medical staff?" Seth asked. "Send them out here to block the guards?"

"Maybe." Tommy cast a worried look behind them.

"Let's go!" Jenny opened the door and led the way in, Seth at her side, followed by Tommy, Esmeralda, and Mariella.

The medical staff were already in a panic, the doctors and lab techs running out to the front desk area, where the nurses at the desk were on their feet and shouting. It looked like everyone had just been warned that the escaped prisoners were on the way.

Several of them screamed at the sight of the five paranormals charging into the clinic. All eyes went to Jenny, but it was Tommy who attacked, unleashing a plume of dark red droplets from his mouth, which settled over the medical staff like a mist of blood.

"Where is my baby?" Jenny screamed at the terrified nurses, letting the pox blister her face. "Where?"

"Down that hall..." A nurse pointed to a door, her finger shaking. "Last exam room, very last on your left."

"There are bombs all over this base!" Mariella shouted. "You have five minutes to get outside the walls, or you're all dead! Run that way!" She pointed to the open doors through which they'd entered, and the fear-infected medical staff ran out screaming, a dozen people or more. Esmeralda slammed the doors behind them.

"That won't block them for long," Jenny said, looking anxiously toward the door that led to her baby.

"Do you see all of them wearing gas masks?" Tommy asked Mariella.

"More than half of them, rows of them," Mariella said. "There are some extra guards near the back who aren't wearing any...maybe they didn't have time to suit up or they joined at the last minute...but..."

"That's good enough," Tommy said, approaching the doors. "You'll want to barricade these doors after I leave."

"You'll get killed." Esmeralda touched his face. "You can't do that."

"I just want you to get out safe," he told her. He pressed the gold Indian-head coin into her hand, the one they'd traded back and forth all their life. "I'll see you again. You know this isn't the end. Maybe I won't be such an asshole next time around."

"I doubt that." Esmeralda smiled, but her eyes gleamed with tears. She kissed him, then held the coin against her heart.

"I love you, Esmeralda," he said.

"I love you, too," she whispered back, and he couldn't help smiling. At least he would die with those words in his ears.

Tommy steeled himself, then hurried out through one of the doors, closing it again behind him. He hoped they would take his advice about blocking the clinic from the inside. If his attack worked, the entire base would soon become chaotic and dangerous.

The response team already filled the corridor, but they were a little disorganized as they parted for the crazed doctors and nurses to pass through them. Tommy wished he'd had the foresight to dress himself in medical scrubs, too, instead of a t-shirt and jeans. It would have helped him blend with the escaping mob.

Instead, the guards in their biohazard masks shouted and raised their machine guns at him.

Tommy breathed deep and exhaled, pushing out the fear from deep inside of him, giving them both barrels, everything he had. He poured all his energy into it. There was no point in holding anything back now—he doubted he had more than a few seconds to live.

The mist of fear flooded the corridor, so dense and dark that the light in the hallway turned deep red, painting everyone and everything the color of fresh blood.

"General Kilpatrick's orders!" Tommy shouted. "Everyone in a biohazard mask is the enemy! Shoot on sight!"

His shouting brought the attention of all the masked guards, who turned their guns on him. The support guards at the back, armed but without biohazard masks, shouting in fear and opened fire on the rows of guards ahead of them. The body armor and helmets shielded their torsos and heads, but the bullets sliced through their arms and legs. The masked guards began to fall, taken from the rear by surprise, flurries of machine-gun rounds hammering their backs hard enough to crack their ribs through their armor.

Most of the remaining masked guards dropped and swiveled, returning fire and escalating the battle. A couple of them near the front remained focused on Tommy, raising their guns at him.

"Do your worst," Tommy challenged. He exhaled a last thick mist of red, and then the bullets tore through his arms, stomach, chest, throat, and face, cutting him apart. They kept firing even as the fear-giver rose and looked down on his bullet-riddled body, just a useless slab of meat now.

His life as Thomas White was ended, and he felt satisfied that he'd done his best to pay his debt to the dead-speaker, atoning for his failure to protect her in their last life. He struggled to remain focused on the dimming world of the living, determined to see her get out alive, though he now watched from beyond the grave, unable to give her any more help.

* * *

"What are you doing here?" Alise demanded, slamming open the door. Niklaus sat on his bed, drinking cheap Polish vodka and smoking cigarettes. Though the alarm had been clanging for a few minutes now, he remained where he was, in his undershirt and black uniform trousers, boots propped up on the bed's flimsy footboard. "Are you deaf?"

"No," he replied. He swigged vodka and smiled, offering no other explanation for his inaction.

"The supernormals are escaping!" Alise shouted. "We're finding guards dead of Juliana's plague. I checked Mia's room, and it looks like she went with them. They cannot be allowed to escape, Niklaus!"

"Maybe someone will stop them." He shrugged.

"We need your help! Get up!" She smacked his leg.

"I'm going, I'm going..." Niklaus reluctantly stood and took his time pulling on his belt, his jacket, checking that his pistol was fully loaded. He smirked at himself in the mirror as he put on his cap. It struck him as absurd, the black uniform, the silver skulls and lightning bolts, the twisted red cross on his arm. He thumped the swastika. "What is this thing, anyway? Does anyone know? Besides a big target that says, 'Shoot me in the arm, snipers!'"

"We don't have time for your drunken babbling." Alise took his arm and steered him out into the hallway. "Take care of this, and I'll give you a nice reward. Don't you miss me in your bed?"

Niklaus pulled his arm free of her grasp. "We should hurry."

"You're right." Alise began to run, and Niklaus watched her from behind, long golden hair sweeping her slender back in her black S.S. jacket. He thought of how callously she'd killed Evelina, and he forced himself to do the thing he'd been wanting to do for weeks.

Niklaus drew the Luger and aimed it at her back. If she looked him in the eyes, he knew he wouldn't be able to pull the trigger. It had to be from behind.

He fired a shot into the center of her spine, and she fell and screamed, her legs twisting limply beneath her. He trudged toward her, in no hurry at all. Everyone else would be distracted by the alarms and the escaped prisoners. There was nobody else here on their dormitory level.

She turned her head to look up at him, and her gray eyes, the ones that matched his, were full of pain.

"Why?" she whispered. She lay on her stomach on the floor, paralyzed from the waist down, a pool of blood growing around her.

"You killed her." Niklaus sat on the floor beside Alise and leaned against the wall. He kept the pistol pointed at his cousin.

"Who? Who did you love more than me?"

"I loved Evelina."

"A Slav? You shot me over a..." She coughed, drooling foamy pink saliva. "...over a dirty goddamned Bosniak?"

"I told you I didn't want to shoot her."

"You could have..." Alise coughed up thicker blood. "You could have told me. I would have let you keep her. Because I love you, Niklaus. Remember I loved you, and you killed me. Remember it...my only love..." She coughed again, and her cheek rested flat on the floor, her eyes staring into nothingness.

Niklaus stared at her body. Maybe he'd been wrong to do it. With her dying words, she had given him only love, despite his betrayal. He wished she'd been hateful and angry, as he would have expected. He wished he felt triumphant, at least, for finally working up the courage to avenge Evelina. Instead, Alise's death now struck him like a knife to the heart. Her final outpouring of affection was the worst thing she could have done to him. He knew it would stay with him for the rest of his life.

He looked at her dead body and wept. Her death had not brought Evelina back, nor did it bring him any peace. His cousin had been his guide through life, his trusted friend, his lover. He was alone now, forever.

Niklaus put the pistol into his own mouth. He couldn't face his family again, after having a sinful relationship with his cousin and then murdering her. He wished with all of his being that he could bring her back to life and be with her again. Life without her would only be agony and guilt.

He pulled the trigger.

# Chapter Forty-Six

Little Miriam lay in her incubator in the last room on the hall, just as the nurse had told Jenny. Jenny was the first into the room, but she held herself back, forcing herself to wrap her arms tight around herself and make herself small, as she'd done when she was a younger girl whose main concern in life was staying invisible at school. Those teenage days already seemed ancient to her, after all the strange turns of her life since then.

Outside the clinic, screaming and scattered gunfire sounded all over the base. It sounded like Tommy's final attack had been successful, driving a number of people crazy with fear. Unfortunately, those people carried automatic rifles. The baby squirmed and cried in her incubator, and Jenny resisted every instinct that told her to pick up the tiny girl and comfort her.

"You're okay," Jenny whispered. "You're safe now. Your parents are here."

"There she is." Seth spoke quietly as he entered the room. He didn't hesitate as he went to pick her up and hold her close. Bathed in his soothing, healing touch, the baby stopped crying, and even closed her eyes and rested her head against him.

"You're going to be a good father," Jenny said, her voice almost breaking. She knew that she would always have to be a distant mother, avoiding any contact with her own daughter.

As if feeling her distress, Mariella carefully wrapped her arms around Jenny and hugged her close, risking infection and death to comfort her. Jenny leaned her head on Mariella's shoulder, keeping away from the bare flesh of her neck, and she cried.

"You'll need some of these." Esmeralda had opened cabinets in the room and found one stocked with standard baby supplies. She grabbed bottles of premixed formula and a stack of diapers, and she handed Seth a cloth sling, still sealed in the original plastic. "Be sure to support her head."

"I can't believe it," Seth said as Esmeralda helped strap the baby sling around him and secure the baby inside it. The baby snuggled against his chest again, eyes closed. "She's actually asleep. It's all gunfire and horror-house out there, and she's just taking a nap."

"You're good for her," Jenny said. "Your touch."

"How do we get out of here?" Esmeralda asked.

"They'll have all four exits covered." Jenny pulled away from Mariella and wiped her eyes. "Maybe we should find the vent shaft for this section. The vent got you both out of here last time, didn't it?"

"It got us up there," Seth agreed. He was still staring at his little daughter, brushing her soft cheek with his fingertip. "I just hope this guy's access card opens the maintenance doors."

"Just remember to come with us this time, Jenny," Mariella said. "Do you promise?"

"Of course." Jenny managed a small smile, looking at the sleeping baby through her tears. "I'll never leave her."

# Chapter Forty-Seven

Mia climbed the slippery metal rungs inside the vertical tunnel, struggling upward against the air blasting down from the huge intake fan above. The wind was so loud that she and Sebastian couldn't possibly hear each other unless they shouted, which could draw the guards. Mia didn't feel like talking, anyway. They'd heard the gunfire echoing from below, and she had felt Juliana's death like a ripping sensation deep in her heart.

Juliana's last wish was that Mia and her baby escape the base alive. Her friend had died to protect her, despite her betrayal with Sebastian, for the sake of the little baby. If Mia survived, she and her baby would owe their lives to Juliana.

They stopped climbing when Sebastian, above her, reached the top of the vent. She held on tight, trying not to think about the long, hard drop below if she slipped from the small rungs.

She watched him inspect the giant fan that was in his way, underneath a mesh screen that kept out falling debris. They needed to stop the fan and move the screen aside before they could leave. High-speed wind pounded her face, and she had to scrunch her eyes to watch him inspect the machinery.

Sebastian found the bundle of wires feeding electricity into the fan, grabbed it, closed it eyes, and pulled as hard as he could. An explosion of sparks hit him, scorching his face and hands. The hair at the back of his head caught on fire, and he smothered it with his bare hand.

Mia tried not to cry out in pain as stray sparks landing on her, burning her arm in three places.

"Sorry," Sebastian whispered, and she could hear him because the fan was quietly slowing to a halt.

The screen beyond it was secured in place by a ring of large screws, and they had no screwdriver. Seth tried the keys on the ring taken from the prison guard until he found a key tooth he could wedge inside the heads of the screws. Turning the screws this way was slow and difficult, and sliced up his fingers until the key was dripping blood, but he managed to gradually remove each one. Mia winced each time he cut himself.

A light flashed over the top of the vent, fully illuminating it in the night. With the alarms ringing, the guards in the watchtowers were swooping the spotlights looking for trouble.

Sebastian climbed up the narrow gap between two fan blades, and one of them scraped open a wide swatch of flesh along his hip.

"Careful," he whispered down to Mia, his teeth clenched tight with the pain. "The blades are sharp."

She climbed a little higher, waiting while he heaved the metal mesh to one side like a manhole cover and poked his head into the open air above. Mia smiled. She hadn't seen the stars in months.

He pulled the screen back into place and ducked as another spotlight hit the vent shaft.

"Now!" Sebastian whispered when it was gone. He pushed the mesh aside and climbed out. Mia threaded her way between the blades, imagining them springing back to life, cutting her in half. She was five months pregnant, and her enlarged stomach took a horrible scraping from one of the blades as she squeezed past it. Sebastian took her hand and helped her out onto the narrow circular ledge surrounding the intake fan. He touched her bleeding stomach to heal her, and she couldn't help smiling at the soothing warmth.

"No rungs out here," he whispered. "About a five-foot drop. I'll catch you. The spotlight's coming back already." Sebastian dropped to the ground below.

When he was ready, Mia pushed herself off the edge, landing in his arms. She looked up at him, feeling for a moment the deep affection that had existed between them under Alise's spell. She was having his child.

Whatever she felt in that moment, she felt it alone. He stood her on her feet, already looking for their next move.

"The warehouse," he said, pointing to the long brick building against the western wall of the base. A pair of S.S. guards flanked the door. "There's a road that forks off toward it. I think there must be a side gate there. Probably safer than trying to go out the front."

"If there's a gate, there will be more guards," Mia whispered.

"You stay here," Sebastian said. A slanted corrugated tin panel stood over the intake vent, blocking rain and snow from above, but also creating a pocket of shadow, further darkened by the coal smoke from the ventilation system's furnace exhaust. She thought might be able to hide from the spotlights if she kept herself small enough. "I'll deal with the guards first and signal you when it's safe," Seth told her.

"Are you sure?" she whispered, but he was already running, avoiding the spotlights. She heard a distant clink of metal against concrete, and both guards at the warehouse turned their heads towards it, away from Sebastian's approach in the shadows. She heard it again, and a third time, and the guards raised their pistols in that direction.

Mia realized what was happening—Sebastian had pocketed the screws he'd taken from the vent screen, and now he was flinging them, one at a time, to create a distraction for the guards as he approached them in the darkness.

Sebastian crept up to the warehouse and jumped on the closest guard, stabbing him in the throat with a key grasped between his middle fingers. The other guard turned to see his comrade staggering toward him, blood gushing through the hands at his throat. Sebastian was pushing him forward, using him as a shield while the other guard began shooting. Sebastian shot back, using the pistol from the stabbed guard's holster. The guard fell to the ground. He'd taken them out, but now every spotlight rushed toward the sound of gunfire and found Sebastian.

Sebastian crouched low and shoved open the warehouse door, ducking aside as bullets rang out at him. He fired back as he crawled inside.

Mia shivered as she listened to shouting and gunshots inside the warehouse, unable to see anything within. She did see a number of guards on foot, running toward the warehouse with guns drawn. Sebastian was trapped, and she didn't know what she could do about it.

Then Sebastian raced out of the warehouse door, blood-spattered and cackling like he'd lost his mind, leaking from a bullet wound in his side and another that had torn a chunk from his leg. He held a machine gun now, and he blasted a spray at the guards converging on the warehouse, momentarily scattering them.

He didn't come back for her, but ran hard toward the front gate, as if trying to attract everyone's attention. The spotlights followed, and he turned and opened fire at them. He hit one, and it flashed and burst into flame.

The scattered S.S. men regrouped and chased after him, while more armed guards ran at him from the gate. They shot him up and down from two sides, the bullets chewing him up, and he shot back until he toppled over. The guards surrounded him and kept shooting.

Mia shuddered. She knew Sebastian could heal fast, but no one could survive what the guards were doing to him, blasting his head and torso with dozens of bullets at close range. He was gone, just like Juliana. Mia was alone, except for the small baby still growing inside her.

She only saw one option—go to the warehouse and see if she could make it all the way outside. If he'd cleared the way for her, leaving no guards behind, she might have a chance while all the Nazi guards were still distracted, laughing as they kicked his mutilated corpse.

Mia ran as fast as she could, her footsteps as loud as thunder in her ears. She expected bullets to cut her down at any moment, but she managed to make it inside the dim warehouse.

She caught her breath as she explored it, stepping over the gunshot bodies of dead guards. She found the enormous, armored steel cargo door, and she trembled as she found the button that activated its system of chains and pulleys. It began to rise, loud and clanking. She didn't hesitate. The moment she saw a slice of the night outside, she dropped to her hands and knees and crawled under the rising door, her stomach dragging the concrete floor.

Outside, she found herself on a loading dock. She stood up, ran to the edge, and jumped to the pavement below.

Mia ran into the woods, out of range of the spotlights. She kept running for a long time.

* * *

The loud, clanking ventilation machinery looked like it hadn't been upgraded in the intervening decades, though it now sat inside a narrow concrete room instead of raw cave rock. Mariella opened the access panel and found rows of electrical heating coils had replaced the old coal-burning furnace, warming the air before the array of fans pumped it through ducts to the underground rooms.

Mariella looked up the wide vertical shaft from which fresh, cool air pounded down from the giant fan above. The big vertical duct was now thick with water stains and mildew. No Nazi janitor had been ruthlessly scrubbing it with cleaning chemicals this time around. Unfortunately, this meant the rungs built inside were also slimy, and looked even more slippery than last time.

"I'll go first," Mariella said, leaning her head out to speak to Seth, Jenny, and Esmeralda. She'd gotten them this far safely, using Seth or Esmeralda to help her watch the future. "You're the one carrying a baby this time, Seth."

"I wish they had one of these back in the day," Seth said, opening a small tool cabinet against one wall. From the array of hand tools suspended by magnetic strips, he picked the two largest screwdrivers and a pair of wire cutters and handed them to Mariella. "Good luck. Watch out for sparks."

"I could have used that warning *last* time, thanks," Mariella told him.

They climbed the slippery rungs as fast as they dared, Mariella first, then Seth with the baby in her sling and her head resting against his chest, then Jenny and Esmeralda.

Equipped with the right tools, Mariella opened the top of the vent much faster than Seth had done in their past life. There were spotlights again, so she waited until one had passed before looking out.

The yard was in chaos. It looked as though everyone in the base was flooding out through all four exits, probably thanks to the terrified medical staff running and screaming about bombs. Guards were everywhere, too, but they didn't look very organized. Some of them ran around howling and firing their guns at random, shooting real bullets at whatever nightmarish illusions filled their minds. Some of the other guards fired back. Everyone else was in a panic, trying to get from the low pillbox buildings to the front or side gate without getting shot. Tommy had done his job well.

Mariella waited for another spotlight to pass, then helped Seth climb out. The baby stirred at the sound of gunfire and screaming, but Seth touched her face and soothed her.

Jenny and Esmeralda were the first to jump to the ground. Seth went next, his arms around the baby, landing in a squatting position with a painful wince on his face. Jenny and Esmeralda grabbed him from both sides, keeping him steady so he didn't topple over. Mariella joined them on the ground.

"I'm not going with you," Mariella whispered. "I'm going back inside."

"You can't do that!" Jenny told her. "Why would you?"

"They have so much information on us," she said. "We have to destroy Ward's records, or it will be too easy for someone else to pick up the pieces and track us down. He's a control freak. I wouldn't be surprised if all the data is right here on site, in the file server room. I don't think even his superiors know what he's really doing here."

"Ward will still be looking for us," Seth said.

"Maybe. You're going to encounter him again tonight," Mariella said. "The future's too uncertain, I can't see how it will turn out. But maybe you'll defeat him. Maybe he won't live."

"You definitely won't live if you go back now," Seth said.

"I might," she said. "You go on without me. I'll catch up if I can."

"This is crazy," Jenny said. "You know you have to come with us."

"No," Mariella said. "Jenny, you won't remember, but I survived last time. I eventually got home to Sicily. The Nazis never came for me again, even though my family took their money—I guess they got busy with other things. I spent years waiting, but nothing happened. I had my baby, Jenny. I got to raise her and watch her grow up, and she gave me six grandchildren. I watched them grow up, too. I lived to be more than seventy years old." She smiled. "I named her after you, you know. Juliana."

"You survived?" Jenny whispered. "I assumed we all died that night."

"I made it out, with my little girl, and I had a long life," Mariella said. "You died to give me that, and I'm going to do my best to give you the same. I owe you."

"Please don't," Jenny said, clearly fighting back her feelings. "I don't have many friends."

Mariella hugged Jenny tight, then kissed her on the cheek, though it covered her own face with painful sores.

"I love you," Mariella whispered, and Jenny let out a sob, then bit her lips to keep the rest inside.

Mariella said good-bye to Seth, and to the drowsy baby Miriam, and to Esmeralda, and told them to run. After the spotlight passed again, the three of them ran past the crowd that was gathering outside the warehouse, where the base's employees were demanding to be let out the gate. Jenny and the others continued toward the motor pool area, where they planned to steal a truck.

Mariella ran the opposite way, toward the helicopter pad. One of the privileges of cooperating with Ward was that she'd been allowed to spend time outdoors each night, though no one was permitted out during the day for security reasons. She'd noticed the helicopter pad and the shed beside it. She hoped the shed held what she needed.

She ran across the concrete pad, keeping her head low to avoid stray bullets from the crazed guards running around the yard. She reached the shed, but the door was padlocked. She kicked the door, frustrated.

"Identify yourself!" a voice shouted. A guard in the standard black, insignia-free uniform stood only yards away, leveling an automatic rifle at her. "What are you?" he screamed, dancing around but keeping the gun aimed right at her.

From his demeanor, Mariella guessed that he was under the spell of Tommy's fear. She remembered hearing Tommy shout orders to the guards he'd frightened. With their minds clouded by fear, they'd eagerly done what they'd been told.

"Orders from General Kilpatrick!" Mariella shouted, as Tommy had done. "We have to destroy the base before it falls into enemy hands!"

The guard gaped at her, then nodded, as if this somehow made sense to him amid the confusion and gunfire.

"Open this door!" she shouted at him. The guard raised his

machine gun, and she winced as he blasted at the door and padlock. There might have been helicopter fuel inside the shed, which made shooting it up a fairly unwise decision. It worked, though, and Mariella kicked in the door.

She ran inside, looking past the small selection of tools for light helicopter repair. She was disappointed in what she found. She'd reasoned that, since the base was remote, there might be spare fuel on hand for the helicopters that came and went. She'd hoped for some kind of portable tank in which she could carry a few gallons, but there was nothing like that. There was only a single enormous tank, mostly embedded in the ground, with a giant hose on a spool, all of it much too large-scale for her purposes. She looked around desperately for any kind of container, but there was only a bucket with no lid.

She shook her head and glanced outside the shed to see whether it was safe to leave. She saw her crazed guard standing at attention, protecting her, heedless of the stray bullets that hurtled back and forth across the yard. It gave her an idea.

Mariella took the end of the hose and walked to the door with it, and the huge spool creaked forward behind her. She told the guard to come inside.

"I'm taking this," she said, nodding at the heavy nozzle and hose in her hands. "You stay here. When I yell, I want you to turn on the pump."

"Yes, sir," the guard said.

"But not until then. I'll yell 'Now!' Do you understand?"

"Yes, sir!" The guard saluted her. He must have been an actual soldier at some point before joining the mercenary outfit that provided the base's guards. Hale Security, Mariella had heard someone call it.

Mariella took the hose and ran across the yard, crouched as low as she could. A spotlight crossed her, but at this point she was just one more patch of crazy in the middle of a riot.

She reached the vent intake from which they'd all emerged, which was almost as tall as she was. She jammed the nozzle of the fuel hose into her belt, then took a running start and jumped, grabbing onto the lip of it, then scrambling her feet up the side, praying the guy didn't throw the switch too soon, or that he didn't get distracted or shot before she called to him.

She lay next to the large fan that she'd disabled, took the nozzle from under her belt, and dropped it into the vertical duct. She kept feeding the hose in as fast as she could, but it was heavy, and so was the spool turning at the far end. When she had a several meters of hose dangling inside the duct, she screamed "Now! Now, now now!"

The hose instantly fattened as it filled with helicopter fuel. Mariella climbed her way down between the fan blades, then wrapped her arms and legs around the thick hose and slid down it like a fireman's pole, traveling down several stories in less than a minute, friction burning her hands and peeling away the skin. She grimaced through the pain, hoping that her weight was helping to unwind the hose from the spool.

She landed hard on her ass inside the metal cavity from which the array of fans sucked fresh air away into different rooms inside the base. She climbed out of the access panel, which they'd left open, pulling the heavy, full hose with her. She peeked out the maintenance door, then dragged the hose into the hall with her, sweating and straining with the effort.

She walked along the hallway in the direction of the northeast quadrant, where the administrative offices and private apartments were. When the hose would go no further, she opened the nozzle all the way.

It jumped out of her hands like an enormous live snake, snapping back and forth among the walls and ceiling as it gushed out fuel, filling the hallway with an acrid petroleum odor. The fuel flooded the narrow back corridor, rising high enough to glug away through low vents near the floor, spreading through the ducts of the facility's air system.

Mariella, dripping with fuel, cautiously made her way out to the front of the clinic and looked over the bleeding bodies left from the firefight Tommy had set off among the guards. She took a heavy automatic rifle from one of the bodies, thinking she might need it.

With no one to touch, she couldn't see into future, but it sounded like most of the facility had evacuated. Occasionally, she heard incoherent shouting and screaming, as if she were deep inside some amusement-park haunted house. The voices drew closer and closer.

Her heart pounding, she reached the administrative quadrant and made her way to the lowest level. Here, the fuel poured out from the air vents and had already pooled ankle-deep on the floor, since it could drain no lower.

She approached the file server room, where the door was sealed airtight, protecting the racks of servers inside from the rising flood of fuel. Mariella intended to change that.

She tried the security guard's access card a few times, but the lock didn't open. She backed up, raised the automatic rifle at the door, and squeezed the trigger. The gun kicked her hard as she fired, and its nose lifted up and up, making her shoot higher and higher. She released the trigger, pointed the gun at the foot of the door, then held it down again, letting the gun strafe the door as it rose under its power.

When she'd emptied the ammunition, Mariella ran to the wreckage of the door and used the gun as a club to bash it all the way open. She stepped into a freezing-cold room lined with quietly humming hardware. The fuel flooded in with her.

She pulled and pushed the servers free, knocking them over into the rising fuel. She heard boots sloshing their way toward her, along with shouting voices.

Mariella turned to see three guards approaching her with automatic rifles like the one she'd taken.

"Raise your hands! Stay where you are!" one guard shouted. Not one thing had gone right for her so far, so it wasn't a terrible surprise that she'd just lost her slender chance of escaping and setting the fire from outside.

Mariella raised her arms, with a cigarette lighter concealed in her left hand. Her mother had always told her that smoking would kill her.

"Go on and shoot me, then," Mariella said, and she flicked the lighter. Her fuel-soaked fingers ignited, and the fire quickly engulfed her and filled the room. She screamed, and the guards mercifully shot her dead before the flames swept out to consume them all.

# Chapter Forty-Eight

Jenny, Seth, and Esmeralda started towards the fenced motor pool by the front gate, intending to steal transportation, but the trucks there came to life, including an apparently empty armored personnel carrier, and charged toward the front gate, the drivers callously running over anyone who got in the way.

"That's not going to work," Jenny said, watching all the available vehicle charge toward the gate, which opened for them. The panicked crowd poured out on either side of the trucks, everyone desperate to leave before the rumored bombs exploded.

"Looks like we're walking," Seth said. He rearranged his shirt, pulling the baby sling inside. The tiny girl cooed against his skin, her eyes closed.

"That kid can sleep through anything." Esmeralda shook her head.

They joined the general exodus of people through the open front gate, Jenny in her hospital gown, Seth and Esmeralda in their stolen scrubs. Nobody paid attention to them, despite the baby bulging from under Seth's shirt. If any of them did recognize Jenny, they were wise enough to keep their mouths shut. Everyone seemed focused on saving their own necks. Jenny definitely liked it that way. Maybe they wouldn't need to hurt anyone else tonight.

They jogged down along the steep road with everyone else, and Jenny felt a weight lift from her. They were free, they were alive, the baby was safe.

Then screams sounded from ahead. Pedestrians raced to clear the road as the trucks came back, led by the personnel carriers, which swerved hard toward Jenny, Seth, and Esmeralda and slammed to a halt in front of them. Armored men in biohazard masks poured out of the vehicles, armed with assault rifles. One of them ignited a flamethrower, while two aimed grenade launchers them.

"We got enough firepower to turn you all into grease and smoke," Ward said. He led the men, dressed in full biohazard armor like the rest, grinning inside his face shield. Jenny recognized his two assistants Buchanan and Avery, who flanked him, carrying assault rifles. "Don't try a thing. Especially you, Jenny," Ward instructed.

Jenny felt frozen. The men were all sealed up, protected from her by technology designed specifically to shield them from her power. She looked at Seth, frightened, her mind moving fast, searching the memories of hundreds of lives for anything that might help her.

She remembered what Dr. Heather Reynard of the CDC had found, what Alise and even Kranzler himself had told her. The pox was not biological or chemical. It defied any known laws of physics. It was supernatural, made of the spiritual dark matter of her undying soul.

Who had ever said that gas masks, armor, or the latest biohazard-resistant plastics were any protection against the supernatural? Maybe there was a chance she could summon something aggressive enough to chew right through. Maybe her own beliefs had placed artificial limits on her powers.

"Everybody on your knees," Ward instructed. Jenny knelt slowly, placing her hands behind her head. Seth and Esmeralda wisely knelt behind her.

She closed her eyes and imagined the pox, which she'd always seen as a swarm of tiny black flies infesting her body, crawling through her stomach and veins, waiting to strike at any living thing. She imagined the flies dividing themselves into smaller flies, which divided themselves again, becoming a much larger swarm of much smaller pox.

She took it as far as she could imagine, seeing them become

microscopically small, then smaller than an atom, able to pass through any kind of matter at all. The pox had a strange charge to it, a speed and energy she'd never felt before.

Jenny opened her eyes, locked her gaze on Ward's mask, and breathed out a black plume that felt like ultra-fine silk as it flowed from her mouth. The river of liquid black punched through the center of Ward's armor, straight into his heart, then swarmed out along his limbs and up his face, turning momentarily into a teeming black mass with Ward's features.

Her consciousness was in the pox, just as it had been when she'd died last time. She coursed through him, ripping his flesh to threads and rotting his bones. Ward's body sagged to the ground, his liquified remains flowing out through the gaping hole in his chest armor, his mask brimming with dark fluid where his head had been.

Ward's two assistants raised their assault rifles toward Jenny, and she reached the swarm of pox out in each direction, burrowing through their masks and into their skulls, instantly transforming their faces into unrecognizable clumps of ulcerated tumors.

Most of the Hale Security men, seeing that their armor was no protection, broke and ran to save their own lives. A couple of them remained and tried to shoot her, and Jenny ripped through them, leaving them with decayed remnants of flesh clinging to their bones. She had an incredibly precise control over the pox, as though every spore in the swarm responded directly to her mind, something she'd never felt before.

She realized her entire mind had transferred over to the swarm. Her body had fallen to the ground, vacant of any soul, and Seth had run over. He was trying to heal her with his touch, while Esmeralda was repeatedly calling her name.

In her strange state, in the gray area between life and death, she perceived something that, clearly, none of the others saw. From Ward's body, a great, dark mass boiled upwards like the smoke from a burning city, blotting out the stars above. Within the gigantic shape, she saw wriggling, squirming movement, like hundreds of tentacles covered in large, unblinking eyes, each tentacle tipped with a long, sharp beak for prying and digging. Her ancient enemy, the seer, most recently incarnated as Kranzler and then as Ward.

The seer moved sluggishly, still disoriented from his recent sudden death. If she moved quickly, she thought, she might be able to finish her attack.

She poured her amorphous swarm-shape into him, chewing into him in thousands of places at once, ripping apart the fabric of the exotic dark matter from which he had formed, destroying one of the last fragments of the primordial chaos. She ripped him limb by limb by limb, scattering chunks of him all across the sky, like some ancient god carved to pieces and hurled into the depths above to form a constellation. The torn fragments of him were so dark to her that the night sky beyond it was a bright gloom by contrast.

She ate into the core of him, concentrating herself into a denser swarm and surrounding what remained of him. She felt the turbulence of his pain and surprise, and a final pulse of anger so intense it seemed to burn the sky from horizon to horizon.

Then he was gone, countless little threads of dissolving energy scattered as far as she could see. She had destroyed him down to the root. The seer would not be back for them, in this lifetime or any other.

She gathered herself together and turned her attention back to Seth and Esmeralda, still kneeling over Jenny's fallen form, Seth still trying to revive her with his power. They were safe now—the baby was safe. Ward was dead, his project erupting in flames behind them. She watched the dark, hot smoke pour from the ventilation shafts inside the walls. The mountain rumbled as the entire yard collapsed, fire and embers shooting out through the vents, as if the endurance of the structure below had somehow been connected to the seer's soul. Or maybe the burning helicopter fuel had simply weakened some essential structure, leading to the collapse of the underground base, leaving only a smoking, rubble-filled crater behind. She would never know. She only knew that Seth and her baby were safe.

She considered it best to leave her body where it lay. The doctors had determined that the baby, Miriam, had no immunity to the pox at all. None. As long as Jenny lived, she would be the greatest threat to her daughter's young life. Stepping aside, not returning to her body, staying dead...that was the only way to keep the baby safe from her.

With all of their kind currently dead, except for Seth and Esmeralda, the girl would not need the protection of her mother's deadly powers...only protection from them. Jenny's death would be the ultimate act of self-sacrifice for the good of her child.

She pulled herself up and back, letting the world of the living grow dim and distant, as it did when she was between incarnations. She would rest, and she would wait.

There was one problem—it felt like a single, hair-thin thread, but stronger than steel or diamond, holding her to the earthly plane. Miriam, her little girl. She could hear Miriam crying. A part of her refused to leave the baby.

She let herself be drawn back toward the living for a moment. She looked into the baby's face, currently gazing in awe at Seth's chin. She looked at her own pale, lifeless body.

An insight arose in her, the result of a few lifetimes of struggling to hurt no one, as well as her intense desire to return to the only child she'd ever had in any of her lives.

Before, when moving into a developing human body still in the womb, she had spread her swarm-like soul through every cell in the body. She began to wonder now whether that was necessary. Perhaps she concentrate herself into a very small shape, hidden deep inside the core of her body until she needed the pox. It would leave her dangerously vulnerable to being attacked by others...but it would also free her to touch other living things without harming them, her deepest wish for several lifetimes now.

The plague-bringer focused herself, drawing herself inward until she was a tiny, extremely dense mass of energy. She floated down toward the unconscious body below, and she landed on Jenny Morton's heart like a black snowflake. With a thought, she made her heart start beating again.

Jenny opened her eyes and took in a delicious breath of cool mountain air. She smiled up at Seth and the baby, feeling more at peace than she'd ever been.

# Chapter Forty-Nine

In June of 1934, Jonathan Seth Barrett sat in his office in his Fallen Oak house, surrounded by the heads of of great beasts he'd killed, the African lion, the American buffalo. He stared at the telegram on his desk. Much had changed in the past year, not least the final death of Prohibition, which was why he now drank bourbon inside of Appalachian white lightning or whichever bottles of questionable, no-label rum happened to get smuggled up from the Bahamas.

Outside, the sun was white-hot, hot enough to broil shrimp on the roof. The high, narrow windows of his office were open, bringing the searing light into his study. His new electric fans churned the air but didn't do much in the way of actually cooling the house. Only a stiff, cool breeze and a little cloud cover would accomplish that.

He struck a match printed with the name of one of his favorite speakeasies in Charleston—not a speakeasy anymore, he reminded himself, just a plain old nightclub. The world was changing, and he felt like all the adventure was draining out of it. He lit a cigar, tossing the match into the rhinoceros-foot ashtray he'd bought on his trip to Egypt years ago.

The telegram from Berlin didn't say much, only vaguely stating that the project and all involved with it had been terminated, with a hint that further inquiries were not welcome. Many of Barrett's long-time correspondents in the eugenics community were dropping contact as they drew behind the dark veil of Nazi secrecy. He didn't give a holy damn. For all the money he'd donated, none of those scientists had figured out a single thing useful to him. Barrett had concluded that the eugenics folks really had no idea what the hell they were talking about.

He poured himself another tall glass of bourbon. He could read between the lines. He hadn't needed the telegram, anyway. He'd felt it in the spring, like an earthquake shaking him from the other side of the world. Juliana was dead. The telegram, in its small way, was only a confirmation of what he knew deep inside.

He knew it because he'd begun to feel hopeless. Knowing she was in the world had expanded him, making him larger than he was, freeing him to dream bigger than he ever had before. He'd left her there out of anger, because she'd chosen the other one, the pretty blue-eyed boy with the healing touch. Her rejection had hurt him far more than he'd let on. He'd been certain that she shared his feelings, that they were truly meant for each other.

He'd assumed they would cross paths again, that fate would bring them together, but he'd been terribly, absolutely wrong. She was gone, and the world felt like a much smaller place without her.

From then on, Barrett would age much faster, and he would shrink into a bitter, hollow man with a heart like broken rock. His ambition retreated. He would settle into being a manager of his past investments, abandoning his run at becoming a global titan.

He wandered out onto his sprawling back porch, looking up at the high brick wall of the necropolis he'd built for his family, a monumental place to bury himself and his descendants. He would rot and die here, watching his wife retreat into opiate addiction until the day he buried her, watching his son cringe and tremble, never emerging from his shadow.

His son would manage to marry, though, and have another son of his own, named Jonathan Seth Barrett III, as Barrett would insist. In that direction, at least, lay some hope for his legacy.

# Chapter Fifty

JONATHAN SETH BARRETT XVI, read the inscription on the monument. Seth's great-grandfather, the egomaniac he knew more recently by the name Alexander, had planned for at least sixteen generations to be named after him, one more than the Ptolemy dynasty that had ruled over the final centuries of ancient Egypt's decline.

Seth pulled the goggles down over his eyes, fitted the sharp end of the chisel into the letter *J*, and swung the hammer. The chisel bit the stone, rendering the letter illegible. He only had to chisel out every single letter of his name from the hard, dark granite, and he only had to do that sixteen times. It was a hot, humid summer afternoon in Fallen Oak, the sunlight bleach-white all around him, and he was already sweating.

He struck out the next letter, and the next. It sometimes took a few swings of the hammer to fully scratch out a single letter.

His great-grandfather had built this necropolis in his backyard out of an obsession with legacy. It was an obsession that had led him, five thousand years earlier, to order the construction of the first large pyramid in Egypt to serve as his tomb, when he had ruled as the pharaoh Djoser and used his undead minions to conquer the Sinai Peninsula and mine its minerals.

Seth finished chiseling out the name from the sixteenth row of monuments, then moved up a row to chisel out JONATHAN SETH BARRETT XV. It was going to be a long day.

The dead-raiser had transformed the Barrett family into a pharaoh-style death cult, using threats to make them uphold the memory of their malignant ancestor. He had terrified his son and grandson—Seth's grandfather and father, respectively—by demonstrating his power to raise the dead, then threatening to haunt them from beyond the grave if his wishes were not obeyed.

Wish number one: the firstborn son of each generation had to be named after him. Seth was the fourth, and he was going to be the last. If Seth ever had a son, he would name him anything but "Jonathan Seth."

Seth chiseled out row after row of names, his muscles starting to ache and his shirt plastered to him with sweat. He didn't know what he would say if the police came to investigate the hours of banging and chiseling, but he wasn't entirely sure whether Fallen Oak even had a police department anymore. The little downtown was overgrown already, the town square thick with weeds and wildflowers. Between the still-unexplained disappearance and rumored death of so many people, and the closing of Mayor Winder's timber plant, the town was drying up fast.

He smirked as he remembered Barrett's grandiose plans for his model town, proudly explaining the importance of Fallen Oak's position on the local roadways and the rail and telegraph lines, clueless that the interstates, telephone, and eventually the internet would make every advantage obsolete. It was sad to see the empty shells that remained, but he'd fulfilled his promise to Barrett. The man's vast, dark Charleston-style mansion was reduced to a charred stump. His most recent incarnation, Alexander, had been killed by Seth's power. Seth himself had pretty well ruined the Barrett name in town, to the point that they'd tried to lynch him along with Jenny. Seth himself would eventually inherit Barrett's entire fortune.

Today, he struck the final blows, punishing the dead-raiser in a way that would matter to him, erasing his name from history, the same method used by ancient priests to destroy the ghost of a horrible king.

Seth reached his own name, smiling as he chiseled it away. He paused to touch his brother's name. CARTER MAYFIELD BARRETT. He left that one in place.

He moved back a row and chiseled away his father's name, and his mother's for good measure. There was no reason for them to be buried here in Fallen Oak, he thought. They should be buried in Florida, where they'd lived happily with their boat and their sunlight and rum.

He chiseled out his grandfather's name, feeling satisfied. He knew that his grandfather had suffered from mental problems, from severe paranoia, especially late in life, obsessed with the idea that Barrett's ghost was hounding him. He'd even built a very modest house on the grounds, far from the main house, and lived there much of his life. It had fallen into disrepair since his death.

Finally, Seth faced the large central monolith towering above the others, the burial place of the first Jonathan Seth Barrett. He placed the chisel in the center of the dead man's name.

"I win," he whispered, and then he swung the hammer.

# Chapter Fifty-One

Esmeralda Medina Rios stood on the white beach at the western edge of the world, squinting into the glaring sun as it crept toward the Pacific Ocean.

She was home, almost. She hadn't yet gone to see her mother or told anyone she was back home in Los Angeles. For the second time, she would have to put together the broken pieces of her life. No matter how quietly she tried to live, her kind kept seeking her out. She hoped to see none of them again.

In her hand, she held a gold coin dated 1908. It was engraved with an Indian chief's head, the word "Liberty" on the front, and a bald eagle on the back. She had kept it all her life as a reminder of the strange, haunting boy she'd met in Oklahoma as a small girl.

Tommy was gone now, but she knew without a doubt that he loved her, and he waited for her somewhere. They would meet again, and there would be time to try again. Not in this lifetime, though. In this life, she would have to find her way alone. Esmeralda was used to that.

Esmeralda raised the gold coin and flung it far out over the waves. It glinted as it tumbled into water and vanished like a miniature setting sun, and the splash was too distant for her to hear.

"Good-bye," she whispered. "Until next time."

Her heart was heavy as she turned away from the ocean and the vast space of the sky, toward the busy city and crowded roads. With each step, she felt herself grow lighter, free of the burdens that had weighed her down, free of the enemies she'd never wanted. Her life was her own now, to create as she liked.

She was, at last, truly free, and the day was filled with light.

# Chapter Fifty-Two

The hilly woods behind the Morton house in Fallen Oak were soaked in cool, green sunlight falling from the lush summer canopy overhead. Jenny walked the overgrown path with the baby cradled in her arms. Tiny Miriam gazed around at trees and boulders with huge, fascinated eyes.

Rocky loped along the trail beside Jenny, swishing his big blue-mottled tail. In her absence, Rocky had overcome his skittish ways to become the sort of dog who lay snoring under the kitchen table most of the day. He'd been excited to see her, jumping up to lick her hands and face. He certainly didn't live in fear of people anymore.

The baby started crying, for the thousandth time that day, as Jenny pushed through thick, mossy growth and into a tiny meadow. She gazed at the cairn of stones that marked her mother's grave. Small, bright wildflowers sprouted through the rocks.

"Hi, momma," Jenny said. The baby cried louder. Jenny sat on a low, heavy oak limb and touched the baby's face, whispering to her, and the baby settled. It was strange to Jenny, touching someone in a way that comforted instead of killed.

"I thought you'd want to see her," Jenny said. "I named her after you. She's so pretty, isn't she? I think she looks like you." Jenny bit her lip, listening to a red-winged blackbird singing in the tree above her. It was a sound that always made her think of long, blissfully slow summer afternoons.

"I don't know if you can hear me," Jenny said to her mother, "But I think maybe you can. If things as wicked as me live on and on, life after life, after all the evil things I've done...I think people must live on, too, somewhere. I don't know if you come back here or not, getting born again. Maybe you do. If I keep going after death, then you must, too.

"I wanted to say I'm sorry for ending your life like I did. You could have had a good, long life if it wasn't for me. I'm sorry." Jenny didn't bother hiding her tears. There was no one to see her. "I also want you to know that you're the last. I know how to keep it inside now. I don't have to hurt anybody else."

Above her, another blackbird sang, joining the first.

"Your record collection's gone," Jenny said. "All my stuff's gone, too, my pictures of you. Ward took them all, and that whole base collapsed from the fire, so it's all burned and buried. Mariella really wrecked the place." Jenny shook her head. "It was good to have a friend for a while, a real friend who understood me. I wish you could have met her. I wish I could have met you."

Jenny sat for a while, listening to the birds sing and feeling the baby doze in her arms.

"I don't know what we'll do now," Jenny said. "I'd be happy to just stay here awhile. The town's gotten spooky with everybody gone, but I always liked ghost towns. I want to get a good camera and take pictures of everything falling apart, flowers growing up through the cracks in the streets. I think it's pretty. Sad, but pretty, too."

Jenny stood up, startling the blackbirds into flight. Hundreds of them launched from the trees around her, as if they'd all been hiding, listening quietly.

"Bye, Momma," Jenny whispered. The flapping birds startled the baby awake, and she began crying.

"It's okay," Jenny told her, holding her close as she walked back up the trail. "Everything's gonna be okay now."

\* \* \*

"Oh, let me see that baby!" June squealed. She set her Miller

Lite, snug in its vintage Jimmy Buffett beer cozy, on the picnic table and reached out her arms. Jenny handed little Miriam over to her. "Ain't you just the most precious thing?" June asked the baby.

Jenny joined her dad, who was turning the ears of corn roasting on the grill, next to the ribs he'd been smoking all day.

"Yard looks good," Jenny said. Since June had moved in, she and Jenny's father had tamed part of the back yard, moving her father's junked old appliances and pinball machines closer to the shed and concealing them behind white lattice screens. The cleared area had the picnic table, lawn chairs, and grill, plus shrubbery and flower beds by the house, wind chimes by the back door, a chipped stone birdbath under the shade of an old maple.

"Probably shoulda had it this way when you were little," her dad said.

"I liked the dangerous rusty object theme, too."

"Bet they didn't have this over there in France." He brushed a homemade mustard concoction onto the ribs. "Carolina sauce."

"They sure didn't. And don't even ask about grits and cornbread."

He laughed and looked at her. Jenny put an arm around him, and he automatically stiffened up, still not used to the idea of her touching anyone. Then he relaxed and hugged her around the neck, kissing her head.

"You sure you're going to be okay?" he asked in a low voice. "Ain't nobody out there looking for you?"

"They already sealed and buried the original Homeland Security investigation," Jenny said. "The people who captured us this time are...well, we dealt with them. My friend Mariella said she thought the general wasn't telling his superiors what he was really doing, they thought he was just doing some card-reading experiments or something. She would know best, she pretended to work with him for months." Jenny paused, thinking about her lost friend, then shook her head. "I looked up ASTRIA on the net. They were just a joke Cold War agency, looking for UFOs and Russian psychic spies. I don't think anyone knew what Ward was really doing out there. And now it's all destroyed." Jenny shrugged. "We could get by for a long time with nobody bothering us, maybe. It's not like we're on the FBI's Most Wanted list or anything."

"If you think you're okay." Her dad didn't sound entirely

convinced, but he'd always worried too much.

"Running and hiding didn't help," Jenny said. "We tried that already. Might as well be where we want to be."

"Well, you're both welcome to stay here as long as you want," he said. "I don't guess Seth's house is an option, since there ain't nothing left but a brick or two, and it's federally condemned and all."

"We'd have to bring a tent," Jenny said.

"Found them!" Seth walked out of the house with plastic cups, which he sat out on the table and filled with iced tea. Jenny took a cup. It was frigid and sweet, just what she needed after her walk in the woods.

"When are you going to have another one?" June asked Seth, while smiling at the baby in her lap. "How many you gonna have? Four? Five?"

"Um," Seth said. "So, those ribs look great, huh?"

They ate outside at the table, leaving little Miriam in her car seat, where she seemed happiest. They ate the smoky ribs and corn, cole slaw, cornbread, green beans cooked with fatback. Jenny truly felt at home.

Later, Seth and Jenny walked out to the driveway to watch the sunset burn down through the trees. Seth held little Miriam against his shoulder, humming to her.

"You think we ever get to go where they go?" Jenny asked, watching the light fade. "After we die, I mean?"

"Where everyone goes, you mean? All the normal people?"

"Yeah. We can find each other between lives, just floating around out there in empty space, but where does everyone else go? Somewhere different? Do you think we'll ever get to move on? Like in some future lifetime, after you die, you're not just waiting and watching between lives, but there's someone there to meet you...or a door to someplace else where we've never been..."

"I guess we'll see," Seth said. "I don't want to go anytime soon."

"Me, neither." Jenny kissed the Miriam's cheek, which only seemed to annoy the baby.

"Do you think she's like us?" Seth asked. "Will she have some strange power she can use to terrorize us when she's a toddler?"

"I hope not, for her sake," Jenny said. "I hope there's nothing supernatural about her at all."

She looked up at Seth, his kind blue eyes, his strong arms holding their small child.  She felt so much love for them she thought she might burst.  She was grateful that she got to be with him until the end of time.

She rose up and kissed him softly on the lips.

"I love you," Jenny said. "Forever."

**The End**

# From the Author

Instead of a regular "About the Author" page, I just wanted to leave a note for you, the reader. Your support successfully convinced me to continue Jenny's story beyond the first book. I really enjoyed writing this fourth book, reconnecting with the characters, and bringing the storyline around full circle, even including Ashleigh and Alexander again, though in a different form.

If you've enjoyed this series, I hope that you will help tell others about it or add a review of *Jenny Pox* or *Jenny Plague-Bringer* to your favorite ebook store. Books live and die on the word of mouth of readers, and I think there are many more people out there who would enjoy the story but haven't heard of it yet.

I invite you to connect with me online for updates, giveaways, and new books, and here are some links for that (I spend a ridiculous amount of time goofing off on Twitter):

www.jlbryanbooks.com
@jlbryanbooks on Twitter
J. L. Bryan's Books on Facebook

My newer series, Songs of Magic, are all-ages books, really inspired by the birth of my son, and by the need to write something my young nephews and niece would finally be allowed to read! They are lighter, funnier books, and I hope you'll try them. The first one is usually either free or ninety-nine cents:

### The Songs of Magic series
*Fairy Metal Thunder*
*Fairy Blues*
*Fairystruck*
*Fairyland*

I have another project in mind for 2013 that I think will appeal to the readers who enjoyed *Jenny Pox*—it has elements of horror, paranormal, romance, and historical fiction, as well as teenage characters. It's a story I first wrote several years ago, but I'll be writing a new version of it from scratch. I can tell you that the name of the novel will be *Megido*, and it will take place in a remote town in a particularly hellish part of the Texas desert.

That's all the news for now! Thanks for reading!

-J.L. Bryan
October 13, 2012

Made in the USA
Middletown, DE
05 July 2023

34605565R00239